THE FLAMES OF PASSION . . .

With one powerful movement he tore the sheet from her and involuntarily gasped at the sight of her, more lovely than he could ever have imagined.

Lyonene saw his face, and fear replaced her anger, for she saw the face of the Black Lyon, the face that had forced grown men to their knees in surrender. She would not have believed he could have had such a terrible look—and now it turned toward her.

Instinctively, she attempted to cover herself when he tore the sheet away . . .

Avon Books by
Jude Deveraux

THE BLACK LYON
THE ENCHANTED LAND

JUDE DEVERAUX

The Black Lyon

AVON BOOKS
An Imprint of HarperCollinsPublishers

This is a work of fiction. Names, characters, places, and incidents are products of the author's imagination or are used fictitiously and are not to be construed as real. Any resemblance to actual events, locales, organizations, or persons, living or dead, is entirely coincidental.

AVON BOOKS
An Imprint of HarperCollins*Publishers*
10 East 53rd Street
New York, New York 10022-5299

Copyright © 1980 by Jude Gilliam White
ISBN: 978-0-06-072721-5
ISBN-10: 0-06-072721-7
www.avonbooks.com

First Avon Books special printing: April 2004
First Avon Books paperback printing: October 1980

Avon Trademark Reg. U.S. Pat. Off. and in Other Countries, Marca Registrada, Hecho en U.S.A.
HarperCollins® is a registered trademark of HarperCollins Publishers

Printed in the U.S.A.

10 9 8 7 6 5 4 3 2 1

To Pamela Strickler, my editor,
because she believed in me.

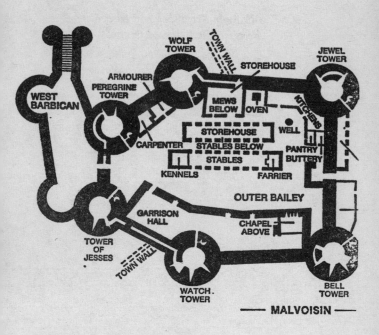

WEST BARBICAN

ARMOURER

PEREGRINE TOWER

WOLF TOWER

TOWN WALL

STOREHOUSE

JEWEL TOWER

MEWS BELOW

OVEN

KITCHENS

WELL

CARPENTER

STOREHOUSE

STABLES BELOW

STABLES

PANTRY BUTTERY

KENNELS

FARRIER

OUTER BAILEY

GARRISON HALL

TOWER OF JESSES

TOWN WALL

CHAPEL ABOVE

WATCH TOWER

BELL TOWER

— MALVOISIN —

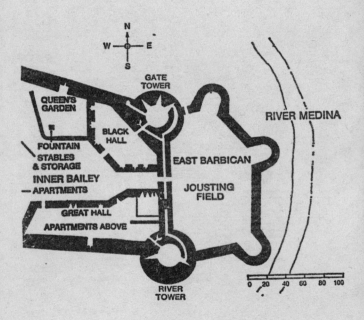

Chapter One

Lyonene could hear Lucy's heavy step on the stone stairs and snuggled deeper beneath the thick coverlet. The January winds whistled outside the old donjon, threads of cold air cutting under the wooden shutters, but her bed was warm and she planned to put off leaving it as long as possible.

"Lady Lyonene." Lucy pulled the bed-curtains back. She was an old woman now and far too fat. She'd been with Lyonene since the girl's birth and was much like a mother to her. "The lady your mother bids you dress in your gold tunic with the green surcoat and mantle."

Lyonene, who had turned toward the light only reluctantly, now looked with interest at Lucy. "The green mantle and surcoat?"

"There is a guest, an important guest, and you are to wear your finest clothes for the introductions."

Lyonene threw back the bedclothes and put a small foot on the rush-covered oak floor. The shutters were closed tightly against the cold winter, and the only light came from the small fireplace and the tallow candle on the tall iron stand by the bed. The soft glow highlighted the full curves of her slim young body. Lucy helped her mistress into the thin linen shift and then the woolen tunic, the tightness of which emphasized her womanly body. The sideless surcoat hid nothing.

"Know you this guest? He is friend to my father?"

"Oh no, my lady." Lucy fastened the thin leather belt about Lyonene's slim waist. "He is an earl, a man your father has not met, and he is a young man."

Lyonene stopped and stared at her maid. "He is handsome? He is a handsome young earl, fair, and rides a white stallion?" Lyonene teased the old woman.

"You shall see soon enough. Now get your comb so I may remove some of the tangles from your hair."

Lyonene obeyed and then asked, "Tell me more of him. What color are his eyes? His hair?"

"Black. As black as the Devil's eyes."

Both women looked up to see Gressy and Meg entering the small chamber with armfuls of clean linen for the bed. Gressy, the older girl, spoke. "It is an earl come, and not just any of the king's earls, but the great Black Lion himself."

"And black he is, too," Meg added.

"His eyes and hair are black as Satan's. Even his horse is all black."

Lyonene looked at them in horror. She had heard stories of the Black Lion since she was but a girl—stories of strength and courage. But each story was misted with a sense of evil, that mayhaps his strength was ill-gotten. "You are sure it is the Black Lion and no other?" Her voice was quiet.

"No other man could have such a look. I vow he gave me gooseflesh just to be near him." Gressy gave her mistress an intense look.

Lucy stepped forward. "Cease your foolish prattle! You'll scare the poor girl. Now get on with your work. I must go below to the Lady Melite." She gave Lyonene's hair a final combing and settled the transparent circle of silk in place with a thin gold fillet. "Now be still and do not muss yourself." She paused at the door, pointing a warning finger at Meg and Gressy. "And no more of this gossip. If black hair made us part of the Devil, there'd be a lot of us dreading the Day of Glory." She sniffed and patted the little bit of gray hair that showed at her temple between the barbette, a piece of linen that totally concealed her neck and chin, and the cascading veil that extended to her shoulders. Lucy imagined that her own locks were still the soot-black of her youth.

When the door was closed, Lyonene sank to the stone windowseat. "Tell me of him," she whispered.

"He is a large man . . ."

"Strong . . ." Meg interrupted, but then, at Gressy's quelling look, she went obediently to her side of Lyonene's bed to catch the billowing sheet.

"Aye," Gressy continued, looking back at Lyonene and

feeling confident in her audience. Lyonene would be the mistress of her own castle someday, but for now there was one area where Gressy was superior, and that was in her knowledge of men. "He's the Black Lion and named for his Devil's blackness and for having the fierceness of a lion. It is said he can unseat twenty men at a tourney and that in Wales, in the wars there, he could hack a man or his horse in half with one blow."

Lyonene felt her face drain of color, and this encouraged Gressy to elaborate on half-heard tales.

"It is said his first wife tried to kill herself to escape him."

Lyonene gasped and involuntarily crossed herself. Suicide was a mortal sin.

"And the seven men—seven devils—he has near him . . ." Meg inserted, too excited to fear Gressy.

"Aye," Gressy said, her voice conspiratorial. "He travels with seven men, great huge men, black-haired all, but none so black as the Lion on his black horse."

"He has come here and I am to meet him?" Lyonene could not keep the fear from her voice.

"Aye. Your father and mother are below now with him. No one denies the Black Lion a request, however small." She straightened. "Come, Meg, we must go to prepare a room for this Devil's knight." She left the room, the wide-eyed Meg trailing behind with the dirty laundry. Gressy was smugly pleased that she had caught the undivided attention of the two girls, for she considered them both girls, although neither was more than two years younger than she.

Outside the heavy door, Meg found her voice. "Is it true, Gressy, that this man is a spawn of the Devil?"

The older woman put her face close to Meg's. "They say he never smiles, has never laughed. It is also said that the woman who makes him laugh will become his bride."

Meg leaned against the damp stone wall. Gressy's face was dim in the dark hallway. She felt her heart thud with a sinister terror. The Devil's bride! That was a horrible thought.

Lady Melite, Lyonene's mother, had also heard stories of the Black Lion, and she dressed carefully, scolding herself for her trembling fingers. She already wished he had not come. There had been too much turmoil lately, and now a troublesome earl to care for! She fastened the undecorated belt around the voluminous surcoat, so different from her daughter's. She pulled the top fabric out and over the belt, completely hiding it. She fastened a dark green mantle about her shoulders with two intricately wrought gold brooches, connected across her collarbone with a short chain.

"What with Sir Tompkin coming on the morrow, and the house servants to organize . . ." She stopped her mumbling and then laughed. I am getting to be too much like William, dreading an event before it happens, she thought. He is a man, no more. We will offer what we have, and he must be content. She straightened the long linen veil that covered the back of her head and hair and fell past her shoulders. She prided herself on having a still-beautiful throat and did not wear the covering barbette. Leveling her shoulders, she went below to greet her guest.

William, Lyonene's father, was fascinated by the Earl of Malvoisin. The tales he had heard about this man were also exaggerated, but with a man's point of view in mind. He looked now at Ranulf's right arm, the muscles outlined clearly by the perfectly tailored chain mail. It was said that the Black Lion could, while riding at full gallop on that black horse of his, cut a four-inch oak post in twain. William hoped he could persuade the earl to demonstrate this impossible feat. The baron could not help staring at the earl's chain mail. It was silvered. William thought with amusement how difficult it was for him to provide each of his twelve knights with even a mediocre grade of chain mail, and here this man had a hauberk just for tournaments. Even his men were splendidly dressed in mail that had been painted either green or black—Malvoisin's colors.

"Ah, here is my wife, the Lady Melite. This is Ranulf de Warbrooke, Third Earl of Malvoisin."

Ranulf lifted his eyebrows slightly in surprise at William's introduction. "It is an honor, my lady, and I hope my uninvited presence will cause you no more hardship than is necessary." He bowed to her.

William often accused Melite of making judgments too quickly, and so she had stopped volunteering her opinion to him, often waiting weeks or months for him to reach

4

the same conclusions that she had drawn in but moments. Now that quick judgment did not fail her—instantly, she knew this man Ranulf de Warbrooke.

"You are most welcome, sir, and it is we who are honored . . . no . . . pleased by your presence here, and all will see to your comfort." Her voice had changed in midsentence from formality to genuine warmth, for she liked this young man.

Ranulf was startled by her warmth. Usually mothers with daughters were greedy for him, for his money and title, or else afraid of him on account of his reputation. He sensed neither of these in this elegant little woman.

"Come, sit by me by the fire and tell me of the news. We so seldom get visitors here at Lorancourt." She held up her arm and Ranulf took it and led her to two chairs by the roaring fire.

"But I understood that you have had many visitors lately."

She waved her free hand in dismissal. "They come to see Lyonene, to appraise our property and eat our food. They come to show their pretty forms to one another on the lists. No one has time to talk to an old woman hungry for news. But sit for a while and let me hear all."

William stood behind them feeling as if a bird's breath could fell him. Melite, usually the most sensible of women, had taken the arm of the most fierce knight in England and had led him to a corner as if he were a gossiping old woman. And whatever had she said about their coming to see Lyonene and to appraise our property? This was too intimate a statement to make to a stranger. He must speak to her.

"Describe this new thing, a button, to me," Melite was saying.

"It is a little ornament on a shaft sewn to the clothing, and lately the women have cut a hole on one side of the garment and inserted the button through it, making a fastening."

"I see. Then we would not have to sew on the sleeves of the tunic any longer."

William sank on a bench by the fire. The Black Lion, the greatest warrior in all of England, perhaps in all of Christendom, and his wife talked to him of women's fashions!

5

Melite turned to her husband and smiled sweetly. "Would you send Lucy to fetch Lyonene? I desire our guest to meet with our daughter."

"Oh, 'tis a handsome man, this Black Lion!" Lucy gushed to Lyonene. "His hair curls about his neck just as my boy's did once." Lucy, though proud of her son, who was now a monk in the Benedictine Order, was sad at times about him, too. "He is tall and strong, and your mother has him eating from out her hand. Great warrior he may be, but I would take an oath he is a gentle man."

"What of his black hair and eyes? Were you not frightened?"

"For truth, I was, but your mother knew his character from the first moment, and it is she I trust." She tilted her head and looked questioningly at Lyonene. "You would do well to choose such a man for a husband."

"Husband! Lucy, you have heard the stories of his character!"

"Aye, stories. I know not one whiff of truth in them."

"He is an earl, and an earl does not marry a baron's daughter. I do not know how you could have such a thought. Know you his reason for coming to Lorancourt?"

"I did . . . happen to hear a bit of conversation."

Lyonene tried not to smile.

"He has a brother who is squire to Sir Tompkin, and as that knight is soon to come, the earl wishes to visit a day or so with his brother."

"Well, I am glad this Black Lion is not above love for his own kin. You say my mother talks easily with him and he is handsome?"

"Most terribly handsome, but if you dawdle longer he will be an old man before you see him."

Lyonene descended the stone steps slowly, touching the worn walls as they spiraled to the lighted hall below. She found her hand trembling and tried to still it. The stories of this man rang in her head as everyone's opinions whirled together. She reached the bottom step, paused, and then smoothed her skirts and her hair, taking a deep breath to still the fluttering of her heart. From her vantage point on the dark stairs, she could view the scene in the Great Hall. The enormous fireplace roared with several logs blazing in it. At a small distance from the fire were two chairs, one occupied by the petite form of her mother, the other revealing only a mailed arm, the silver gleaming dully in the firelight.

She succeeded in calming herself and looked toward the other end of the hall, to the other fireplace, which also was blazing. On low benches or squatted on the floor rushes were seven men, all in mail, all with tabards bearing the Black Lion's coat of arms. Their voices were quiet and she heard one of them laugh. They did not seem to be the devilmen that Gressy spoke of. They looked rather tired, and Lyonene felt a desire to go to them to see that they were given what food and drink they needed. If the Black Guard were tame, mayhaps the Black Lion would be also. She stepped into the light.

"Lyonene, my daughter, is come."

Lyonene kept her face lowered. She must control her urge to stare and remember her manners. Her mother spoke to this man as if they had known one another for many years. She was aware that the Black Guard had come to their feet and that now the Black Lion also stood before her. Her nervousness increased.

Ranulf had not felt so at ease in a long time. Only Eleanora, the queen, had ever made him feel so comfortable as this woman had. Even after having seen Melite and knowing that she had once been a beautiful woman, he was startled by Lyonene's extraordinary beauty. Her head was lowered and he could not see her face, but her thick, curling hair tumbled down her back past her waist. It was tawny, a dark blond with thousands of dancing lights caught by the fire. Her figure was amply revealed by the tight tunic, and it made his mouth dry. A tiny waist, curving hips, a soft, inviting bosom. He could not remember ever having been so affected by a pretty woman.

Lyonene raised timid eyes to Ranulf de Warbrooke, not sure what she expected but fearing the worst. He was dark, with eyes as black as coals and sable curls of hair that seemed to be ever unruly. The top of her head did not reach his shoulder.

But the expression in his eyes was what intrigued her. Like her mother, she could judge a person's character quickly. The Earl of Malvoisin's eyes reminded her of a dog she had seen once. The dog had been caught in a

trap, his leg nearly cut in half, and the pain had made
him almost mad. It had taken a long time for Lyonene
to soothe the animal and gain its trust so that she could
release the iron jaws of the trap, and all the while the dog
had looked at her with just such an expression of wari-
ness, pain and near-dead hope as did the man who stood
before her now.

"I am most pleased you could come to Lorancourt, my
lord, and pray forgive me for my tardiness in welcoming
you."

Ranulf extended a hand to her and she put her small
hand into his warm, large one. His touch could not have
affected her more if he'd put a lighted brand to her fingertips. She almost gasped at the sensation but was glad
she had not, fearful of giving offense. Gone was any
knowledge of anyone else in the room. She became a dis-
embodied hand, all feelings and thoughts transferred to
the fingertips of that one small area. She stared stupidly
at the two hands, one small and fair, the other large, bat-
tlehardened and coated in short dark hairs.

He spoke again and she seemed to feel his voice
through the tips of her fingers. "A beautiful woman need
not ask forgiveness. A smile will be enough." His voice
had lost some of its smoothness; there was a hesitation in
it. He put his other hand beneath her chin and lifted her
face so he could look at her.

She looked again at him, seeing a strong face, a jaw
well-cut, slightly arched brows over the black eyes, a
straight nose, the nostrils somewhat flared. Her gaze fell
on his lips, which were well-shaped but held too rigid.
Lucy had been correct; he was a handsome man. She
smiled, timidly at first and then with more warmth. She
looked behind the lips that did not smile and saw a . . .
yes, a sweetness there, the same gentleness that her
mother had seen. Of a sudden, she had an urge to laugh,
so great was her relief at her findings. She moved against
the fingers that held her chin. Never had a man's touch
made her feel so alive.

Abruptly, Ranulf dropped his hand from her chin and
relinquished the hand he held. "I must see to the Frisian,"
he mumbled and made his way to the door, the Black
Guard following suit.

"Well!" William collapsed in the cushioned chair before

the fire. "If a man were to live a thousand more years, he would not understand the mind of a woman. My wife treats the king's champion as a gossiping washerwoman, then my daughter fair faints at the mere sight of him, and then she laughs in his face. If my lands are not forfeit in two weeks, I will not know why."

"William," Melite began, but she knew she could not explain her own actions, much less those of her daughter. "He seems well content. Come, Lyonene, there are duties to see to."

Lyonene was anxious to leave the room, for she did not like to think her reactions to the man were so obvious. But it was true that she could not have felt more strongly if the slate roof of the donjon had rolled back and lightning had struck her.

Lyonene dreaded being alone with her mother for she knew there would be questions that she could not answer.

As if knowing her thoughts, Melite said, "No, there will be no questions. I ask only that you be kind to our guest, not because he is a great warrior or the king's earl, but because he deserves our kindness."

Mutely, Lyonene nodded.

"Now, go see to those two silly maids of yours and see that our Black Lion has a fitting den." She smiled and smoothed her daughter's lovely hair.

Lyonene climbed the remaining stairs to the third floor's private sleeping chambers. There were six chambers, one for her parents, one of her own and four for guests. She was alone on the floor, the servants busy below in the kitchens. She could take her time in choosing a chamber for Lord Ranulf.

It was an hour later when she felt that the room was ready and went to her own chamber. Lucy had left some bread and cheese and a mug of milk on the mantelpiece. As Lyonene sipped the warm liquid, she adjusted the louvered slats in the wooden shutters so she could look across the bailey. As she watched, one man left the group of the Black Guard and made his way to the gate of the bailey wall; he carried a long stick at his side and a bag strapped to his waist and pushed to his back.

Without thinking what she was doing, Lyonene threw off her green mantle and surcoat and pulled on another surcoat—a woolen one—over the gold tunic. She withdrew from a chest her warmest cloak, a heavy gray wool with a deep hood, completely lined in white rabbit's fur. Clutching the cloak tightly, she made her way down the stairs to the Great Hall, telling herself that she only wished for some fresher air. She took with her a large flagon of wine that had been set to warm on the mantel. She was amazed at how easy it was to pass unobserved across the open bailey yard and out the gate. The watch guards cared not who left the castle, only who entered.

Ranulf sat on the cold, hard ground, his back against a tree, heedless of the piercing wind. His thoughts were absorbed with a lovely, green-eyed girl. Ah, Warbrooke, he chided himself, she is not for your dalliance. She is a girl, an innocent intended for marriage, marriage to a young man near her own age, her own rank. But still he could not relinquish the vision of her. He closed his eyes and leaned his head against the rough bark, the remembrance overwhelming him, a tangible thing: emerald eyes under high, arched brows, a small nose, and her mouth—lips full and soft, tempting. Her hair intrigued him as he thought of it spread about her, covering her shoulders and lying across her breasts, the color unusual, a tawny gold.

Mon Dieu! What ailed him so that he sat here dreaming of a bit of a girl when there was work to be done? He had seen pretty girls afore now—aye, many girls—but there was a difference, somehow, with this one. When he had touched her chin, he had thought he might disgrace himself by kissing her before her parents and his men. What would have been their reaction had he buried his hand in this unknown girl's hair and . . .

"I have brought you wine." Lyonene's soft voice shattered his thoughts.

He stared at her, unsmiling, studying her, not aware of the offered refreshment.

"It is cold and some time before dinner and . . ." She looked away from his intense stare, shy of a sudden, regretting her impulsive action.

He took the warm mug and sipped the delicious sweet wine, the smooth liquid trickling down his throat, his eyes never leaving hers. "You will share it with me?"

"Aye," she said, smiling at him, her fingers lightly grazing his as she took the cup. A drop of wine rested on the rim and she touched the spot with her lips, amazed at her boldness. She returned the mug and took a linen packet from under her mantle, unwrapping it to show bread and cheese.

Her smile at him was brilliant, and he found he could only watch her, her eyes sparkling like the finest jewels, her cheeks pinked by the cold air. The hood hid most of her lovely hair, but the white fur framed her face and contrasted beautifully with the thick, long lashes.

Neither of them seemed to need words, and both sat quietly enjoying the wine and food. A sudden gust of wind blew the dead leaves of the forest about them.

Lyonene covered one eye with her hand as a sudden sharp object struck it. "My eye!" she cried, tears blinding her, the pain increasing each moment.

"I will look." Warm hands held her face; strong, gentle fingers forced her to uncover the eye.

"It is a rock, a boulder," she sobbed.

"Nay, I do not think so. Look up at me and I will find it. Open your eye, slowly."

His voice was soft and soothing, and in spite of the pain, she made herself open her eye, her trust in him complete, sure in the knowledge that he would remove the pain.

"There! See, it was but a speck of dirt, truly smaller than a boulder."

She blinked several times to remove the sting. From the moment he had touched her she had known that he would take away the pain. She was now very aware of his hands on the side of her face, the dark eyes that stared into hers, eyes bordered by short, thick lashes. The irises were truly black—yet, at this close distance, she could see that they had tiny gold flecks in them.

"You are well now? Your eye no longer pains you?"

She did not answer immediately, and as he began to draw his hand away she held it for a moment to her cheek. "Nay, the pain is gone. Thank you."

He moved his hand and looked away and Lyonene was afraid she had offended him. She felt as if a stranger were gradually overtaking her body, for she could not believe her forwardness of this morn. She tried to make conversation. "I wonder—however do you stay so warm when I am so cold, and it is I with the fur mantle?"

Ranulf looked startled. "We will return to the castle to the fire." At the look of disappointment on Lyonene's face, his heart leaped. She did not want to leave his company any more than he hers. "Come then and I will show you a sport to make you warm."

They stood and she watched as Ranulf took the long stick and bent it to fasten a long string of silk to either end.

"Have you seen this ere now?"

She shook her head.

"It is a Welsh bow, and it is called by some, because of its length, a longbow."

"It does not look to be a bow at all." She gave him a skeptical look. "How can one fire an arrow from a mere stick?"

"You have not seen it used and already you decry it?"

She sniffed and put her chin into the air. "You must allow my father to show you the workings of a good crossbow."

Ranulf raised one eyebrow at her. "Find you a target that is as far as your father's best archer can shoot."

Lyonene pointed to a white-barked tree not far away. She watched as Ranulf pulled the six-foot longbow string to his ear, an arrow with black and green feathers held lightly between his fingers. The muscles on his arms stood out. The arrow was released with a sharp twang of silk. Lyonene gasped as she saw it land more than twice the distance of the tree she had chosen.

Ranulf merely looked at her, one quick glance that made her remember her boast of crossbows. Then, before she could recover from her surprise, he began to insert arrows, drawn from the leather bag at his waist, and fire them with a dazzling rapidity. In less than a minute, he had fired ten arrows, never once missing the tree.

She stared up at him. "I have never seen the like." She lifted her skirts and ran toward the distant tree. She struggled to pull an arrow from the tree and was startled when Ranulf appeared beside her and easily removed the arrow she could not. She had not heard him approach.

She turned to him, laughing. "I think there is little that my father can teach you."

Ranulf said not a word, but his expression showed that he agreed with her.

"You must show this Welsh longbow to him. He will train his men to use it."

"Nay, I do not think so. Even my own men refuse to use it. They think it an unchivalrous weapon and have a fear that it will somehow reduce them to foot soldiers."

"I see that you do not have such a fear yourself." Her eyes twinkled and laughter threatened to escape as he raised one eyebrow at her. "Think I could learn to shoot this long stick?"

"You may try." Ranulf demonstrated the proper handling of the new weapon.

Lyonene took it in all confidence but found she could not bend the bow more than an inch or two. She looked in exasperation to Ranulf.

Quickly, he stood behind her, his great arms about her, and pulled the strong bow back. As Ranulf bent to sight the arrow, he was aware of the fragrance of her—roses and smoke—and of her cool cheek so near his. He could feel every luscious curve of her against him, her buttocks pressed against his groin. He ached to turn her to him, longed to feel her softness near him, to kiss her moist lips, parted slightly now in concentration. He tried to give directions to her concerning the bow but found that his voice betrayed his desire since her ear was so close to his lips; he could almost taste the flesh of her earlobe between his teeth. She released the arrow.

"I hit it!"

She turned in his arms, and he held her, lightly, not even daring to breathe for fear he'd crush her in his surging desire.

Lyonene felt her heart would burst, it was beating so hard. His arms were about her, his hands on her back, and she could feel the warmth of him through her heavy woolen surcoat. She looked from his eyes to his lips, and she hoped he would kiss her, yes, she wanted him to kiss her, and her heart beat faster as unconsciously she swayed toward him, her soft breasts touching his chest. She felt his sharp intake of breath. His face was so close that she could feel his breath, so warm and soft. How would it feel to kiss a man?

His arms dropped away.

"Dinner will be served and my mother will expect me." She searched for something calming to say. She smiled up at him. "Thank you for the archer's lesson, and now, Lion, we needs must return to the castle, for my father's temper would make even a lion tremble when his viands are late."

At his look of puzzlement at her name for him, she continued. "It is strange, is it not, that we are both named for lions? My father vows that on the day of my birth I gave him such a look of contempt that he named me for a lioness, but my mother says he thought of the name Lyonene because of the color of my hair."

Ranulf lightly touched a strand of her tawny hair. "I could not think you could give anyone a look of contempt."

She laughed. "You do not know me, for I am possessed by a terrible temper."

"Then the name well suits you, as I fear mine does also. At least you are not cursed with an ugly blackness such as mine."

"Bah! It is only the jongleurs who demand all men be fair with eyes of blue. You would make other men seem colorless." She turned quickly. "See the tree at the edge of the wood? I will race you." She gathered her skirts and mantle edge over her arm and ran.

Ranulf stood quietly and watched the lovely sight of firm, shapely calves and little feet running so inexpertly across the forest's floor. When she was halfway to the tree, he caught up with her in a few easy strides.

Lyonene looked over her shoulder to see him easily gaining on her. She remembered a trick she had used as a child to win races against the boys of Lorancourt. When Ranulf was nearly beside her, she sidestepped into his path, throwing him off balance as he swerved to keep from hitting her, and thus she gained a few seconds' time.

She heard Ranulf's snort behind her and laughed in satisfaction at her successful trick. Then the breath was near taken from her as he threw a strong arm around her waist, lifting her from the ground, still running, not even hesitating when he took on the added burden of her weight.

When Lyonene recovered from her surprise, she began laughing, and by the time they reached the tree she was near helpless. He sat her down and she leaned against the tree, tears rolling down her cheeks, blurring her vision. "I won," she gasped.

"Won! You did not even race with honor. You cheated."

She wiped her tears and saw to her joy that Ranulf was smiling and that his features had softened. He looked like a boy. "My head reached the tree first, before any of you arrived, so I won the race." She could hardly keep the laughter inside her.

Ranulf pulled one of the curls that lay wildly about her cheeks, her hood having fallen away. "You would never make a knight. Your lies would dishonor your liege lord."

Lyonene opened her mouth in mock horror. "And you, Lion, would be worse as a woman with your picking up of whatever great objects lie in your path."

"Great objects!" His hands encircled Lyonene's waist and lifted her, her head high in the air, her hands on his shoulders. "You weigh less than my armor."

Suddenly she was serious. Looking down at him as he smiled up at her, she smiled back. "Whatever my trick, it is rewarded by seeing a lion smile."

Gently, Ranulf lowered her. He, too, was serious now, and his desire for her returned. He could not touch her without the blood in his veins fair boiling. "Go to the hall; I will follow. You mother will not like her lioness spending the morning alone with a man."

Without a word she left him, running to the castle, up the worn stone steps and into her room. Only then did she stop, flinging herself on the feather mattress of her bed.

Melite had seen both Ranulf and her daughter enter the forest a while before. If it had been any other man, she would have sent a servant to bid Lyonene return, but she knew her daughter was safe with Ranulf. She never questioned her knowledge of this man, trusting only in her feelings and her senses. She smiled to herself—she was going to work hard to bring about a marriage between her daughter and the Earl of Malvoisin. She truly wished he were not an earl; then she would have a surer chance of bringing about her desire. Aye, desire. She laughed aloud, then looked to see if anyone had noticed. Desire is exactly what she planned. There was nothing surer than two young bodies close to one another. If William knew what she planned, he would be furious. He did not like men near his daughter, no matter what he said of marriage, but Melite planned to help nature by encouraging the flowering of this delicate young bud of love.

Lyonene watched Ranulf from her shuttered window as he returned from the forest. She knelt and poked at the fire with an iron rod. The image of his smiling face appeared to her in the midst of the blaze. She didn't seem able to see anything but him; she could hear his voice, feel his hands about her waist. She sat heavily on a bench by the fire and dropped her head into her hands. Everything was whirling together. She had never felt so strange in all her life.

"Lyonene!" Lucy's heavy form waddled into the room. "What are you about, girl, when your mother has so many guests below? And a fire in the room during the day! Have you a wee fairy in your head?"

"No, Lucy, I am just happy. 'Tis naught awry at all. I am very hungry. Could we not go below?"

Chapter Two

Ranulf felt confused. For a long time now he had been near content. There had always been women and they had freely given of their bodies, but too often he had sensed that he had been only a conquest to them, that they boasted of having been in the Black Lion's bed. Ranulf had never fooled himself as to his status in King Edward's court. Of the eleven earls, only two were young and unmarried: his friend Dacre de la Saunay and himself. He knew that many women would sell their souls to become a countess. Yet for all their flirting, all their protestations of love for him, none had offered him laughter.

He remembered Lyonene's clear eyes, sparkling in the cold, and her reddened cheeks. Most of all he thought of her laughter. For a few minutes he had forgotten himself, forgotten the responsibility of being an earl, forgotten the past. Yes, most important, for a short time he had not been haunted by Isabel—Isabel, whose sneering remarks had so unmanned the young boy who had loved her. Ranulf looked up at the gray, overcast sky. He was no longer that young boy, but today the years between might never have been.

"You sit here alone while there is a feast awaiting? I vow I have never known such hunger; it is long since we ate last."

Ranulf looked up to see Corbet, one of his Black Guard, standing over him. "I fear I have neglected my men. Is all well with you?" He rose to stand beside the knight, measuring an inch or two taller than Corbet. Were someone to observe them separately and together, they would say that Corbet was a strong and handsome knight but that his lord put him into shadow, so commanding was his appearance.

"This is not Malvoisin, but neither is it a tent on cold

Welsh soil. The Lady Melite is kind and the daughter would make any man warm to look upon her, even 'twere it a blizzard."

Ranulf turned on him. "Do not speak of her so." Angrily, he left his vassal and strode ahead to the castle.

Corbet watched Ranulf's broad back and then smiled. If ever a man needed a wife, it was his lord. Unlike most of the other men, Ranulf was not content with several women; in truth, he seemed to avoid women altogether, using them only when necessary, although they plagued him much at court. Corbet was proud to be part of the elite Black Guard, and although Ranulf kept a distance from his men, they knew more about him than he would have supposed. They all saw the gentle man that lay under the fierce exterior. Corbet stopped his musings and followed his lord to the great stone donjon. For himself, he dearly wished the lovely Lady Lyonene would return to Malvoisin with them; a beauty such as hers would be a joy to look upon each day. He envied Ranulf.

As Ranulf entered the door, he saw he was to sit by Lyonene and felt as giddy as a young boy. A servant poured scented water over his hands from a dragon-headed aquamanile, and another boy gave him a clean linen towel. The priest blessed the meal, and they all sat. They watched silently as a boy cut a long, thick piece of bread and set it on the white tablecloth before Lyonene and Ranulf. The trencher was to be shared by every two diners. Each person had his own cup, and the honored guests' and family cups were silver, encrusted with uncut jewels.

The first courses, the heavy meats, began to arrive: stag, boar's head, pork, mutton.

"Your men are well-mannered. I like it that they do not make eating noises. My father's men are not so considerate." She nodded to the left lower table.

They both watched as the men grabbed huge pieces of meat, stuffing them into their mouths, not waiting to use their knives for cutting.

"I have a name for each of them. Would you like to hear them?"

Ranulf nodded.

"The two on the end are Hen and Rooster. Can you guess which is which? The next is Cat. See the way he moves his hands and eyes? Next is Bear. Once, when I cut my leg as a girl, there were tears in his eyes. Then Pigeon; his head moves so. And the last is Hawk. He is my favorite."

Ranulf studied this man who was Lyonene's favorite. "Why do you care for him?"

"He is kind. He thinks well, he can sing, and he is quite good to look at, do you not think?"

Ranulf stared at her. "I would not know when a man is such as you say, good to look at." His voice was stiff.

She studied his black eyes, the thick curling hair, which he left uncovered. "I should think you would know."

Ranulf, to his consternation, could feel the blood rushing to his face. Confused, he looked at his men and saw that they had paused in their eating to stare at him. He turned back to Lyonene, who smiled up at him mischievously. He returned her smile slightly. "You are an imp. What man is going to follow a knight who blushes?"

Lyonene's laugh rang out, a pretty sound which was infectious. She put both hands on his arm and touched her forehead to his shoulder.

Ranulf tried to ignore the fascinated stares of his men. No one else in the hall seemed to think Lyonene's laughter anything out of the ordinary. With relief he saw the next course arrive—capons, pigeons, pies of small birds.

Lyonene took a spoon and lifted half a fat capon covered in mustard sauce, placing it on the trencher before them. Never had she felt so at ease with a man before, yet there was a sense of excitement through her, as the few times she had touched him had shown her.

"I am sorry. I did not mean to laugh so. My father says I laugh at aught, and I fear he is right. You are not angry with me? I will give you the best part of the chicken."

"I am not angry." He smiled in earnest now. "And if I get any of the chicken, it will be better than the meat, for you ate all of it, sparing none for me."

"Not so!" she cried, and then laughed again but covered her mouth. "You tease, Lion!" she whispered.

"Yes, Lioness." He leaned close to her and wanted greatly to kiss those full, soft lips that had a smear of mustard on the corner. The tip of her tongue licked it away, and he felt cheated. He wondered if it were the wine, for he could swear the room was as hot as a tent in summer.

There were several people who watched the Earl of Malvoisin and Lady Lyonene. The Black Guard had never seen their lord act this way with anyone. The only person who made him smile was Queen Eleanora and sometimes Geoffrey or Dacre. Yet this young girl had transformed him into a knight's page.

Melite sat next to Lyonene; she had arranged the seating herself. She did not wish her guest to feel he should divide his attention between the two women. At each laugh from her daughter, her resolutions set more firmly.

Father Hewitt, the castle priest, also looked on. Although many marriages were made for property, the church frowned upon that and encouraged marriages between people who cared for one another. He smiled now as he watched Lyonene with this great warrior knight. When he had seen the man with his seven Black Guards early this morn, they had seemed a formidable group and he had dreaded their presence, but Lyonene had so tamed the Black Lion that, when her head was turned, he looked upon her with the lovesick expression of a young squire gazing at his chosen lady.

"There are no swans at this meal, but Cook has promised one two days hence," Lyonene said.

"I cannot stay for two days."

"Oh!" Lyonene's face and voice could not hide her disappointment. "I did not think. Mayhaps you find Lorancourt a poor place?"

"Nay. My steward sends word that I must return. There are cases to judge and my neighbors send mares for Tighe."

"Tighe is your great black horse? I would think any mare would be afraid of him."

"Tighe is a kitten, but you are right—he is used to no female, mare or woman."

"I know little about you." Her face went white and her arched brows lifted. "Do you not have a wife?"

Ranulf studied her. "Nay, I have no wife. Nor sister, nor mother."

Color returned to Lyonene's face. It could make no difference to her, of course, but she was glad he had no wife.

The meal was over, and now several of the men seemed to look about for a place to sleep. Lyonene sighed and knew her mother would have many chores for her in the castle. She had never minded them before, had even at times enjoyed them. Most certainly, she had never felt this way about a man before. She did not want to leave him, but wanted very much to stay with him.

"Now I must attend to Tighe's needs." Ranulf hesitated. "Would you like to see for yourself how gentle he is?"

"Aye." Lyonene looked away. She was too eager. "I must come separately. My mother will need my help."

Ranulf nodded.

Lyonene could not understand her mother. Everything she did, Melite corrected, so that only a little time had elapsed before Melite told her daughter to leave, saying that she was too clumsy this day. Lyonene did not see that she was any different from any other day, but she hurried to the stable before her mother changed her thinking.

Ranulf stroked Tighe's thick mane and wondered at himself for jumping at every sound and looking constantly toward the stall door. His breath caught in his throat at the sight of Lyonene, her lips wide in a smile of triumph, her green eyes brilliant from a run through the cold air.

"I must return soon," she whispered; they were like conspirators.

Ranulf whistled low and Tighe turned a finely shaped head to him. Cautiously, Lyonene approached and the beautiful black horse nuzzled her shoulder. Her laugh trickled out as she stroked the lovely head.

"You were right, he is sweet. It is just his size and his blackness that scared me." She looked startled and stared at Ranulf, so near her. "Like you." Before he could answer, she went on, "Why must he be so big?"

"Strength. A man's armor gets heavier every year, and he needs a horse that can carry the weight and not tire easily. It is said that someday a knight will have a horse just for carrying him into battle; the horse will be too big to ride at other times."

Lyonene rubbed the Frisian's nose. "I do not believe

any horse could be larger than Tighe, and certainly not more beautiful."

From the far end of the stable, they heard two men begin to speak. Lyonene looked up in panic. "It is my father. He will not like my being here without Lucy. I must hide."

War had taught Ranulf to be resourceful and to think quickly. Now he grabbed a russet cloak from a peg at the back of the stall and threw it across Lyonene's shoulders, covering her hair with the hood. He moved her so her back was to the door and stood facing her. As she looked up at him with a slight smile and such complete trust, his arms went around her and his lips touched hers, gently at first.

William was forgotten, and neither heard his footsteps or knew when he looked into the stall. He saw Ranulf kissing a serf girl, for only the serfs wore russet, and he left, chuckling to himself. He liked to know his guests were well entertained.

At the first touch of Ranulf's lips, Lyonene thought all her senses had flown. She felt only his lips, his body next to hers, and she had never experienced anything that made her feel like this. She slanted her head to the side and put her arms around his neck, pulling him closer and closer to her. His arms tightened and she felt his strong, hard body pressed to her, every inch of her hungering for more of him.

His lips parted and she followed his example, moving her lips under his. She clung to him, meeting his demanding, searching mouth. Her heart beat wildly, thundering in her ears. She would never let go; she never wanted this moment to end.

Ranulf pushed her from him, his body aching at the sight of her closed eyes and moist, parted lips. "Go." His voice was harsh.

She nodded and silently left the stall, her legs weak and trembling from the force of her emotion.

Melite watched her daughter enter the Great Hall. She studied the green eyes that stared vacantly about her. "Lyonene! I need you."

Lyonene was glad to be recalled to the world. Her head spun with too many emotions and thoughts for her to be left alone.

"There are baths to be prepared for our guests, and you must help." Each of the Black Guard was of noble birth and must be treated accordingly.

Lyonene looked up in surprise. Her father did not allow her to help bathe the guests. "I do not know what to do."

"You must see that Meg and Gressy do as they are told and that there are soap and herbs for the water, that there are clean towels for each man. Of course you know what to do."

One of the private chambers in the top of the donjon had been chosen for the bathing. Hot water was carried from the kitchen below and the great iron tub filled and refilled. Lyonene was very tired when, hours later, she saw Ranulf enter the bathing chamber. She knew her mother had left him, their most important guest, until last so that he would not need to rush, and that Lady Melite would reserve the honor of her help in bathing for Ranulf. She was so confused by this day, confused by this man who had entered her life on a great black horse and in these brief hours had taken over every emotion and thought she had.

Meg came to Lyonene and gave her a sly look. "You are to tell Lady Melite that Sir William needs her and she must come straight away."

"I cannot . . . You must tell her, Meg."

Meg looked at the chamber door in horror. "He is in there; I would be afeared."

Lyonene narrowed her eyes at the girl and sent her scurrying. She knocked timidly on the door, opened it only a crack and began relaying her father's message.

"Lyonene, are you daft! Come in and close the door, the heat will escape. Now tell me the message."

Careful to avoid Ranulf's eyes, eyes that she could feel burning into her back, she gave her message.

Melite hastily pulled her mantle across her shoulders. "I beg your pardon, my lord, but I must see to my husband. My daughter will help you with your bath, but I warn you, you must have patience, for she is inept at the task. Now, Lyonene, do but remember your last experience and be careful not to get your surcoat and mantle wet. I will return in a moment, but hurry now, for the water grows cold."

Alone, Lyonene could not turn to look at him. His voice came to her, and the sadness in it changed her mood.

"I need no help; you do not need to stay."

She turned to smile at him and found herself staring wide-eyed as he sat in the steaming tub. His shoulders were wide, his chest thick and the great muscles on his arms clearly defined. The firelight gleamed on the smooth, damp skin, bronzed by the sun. His entire chest was covered in a thick fur of curling black hair. She could not help laughing. "You look to be the Black Lion all over." She hurriedly looked away, appalled at her boldness.

Ranulf returned her smile, and they were at ease with one another again. "Your mother was right. The water grows cold, and my patience grows thin." He held out a bar of soap. "Come, wash my back."

As she stepped forward, she remembered her mother's warning. She removed her mantle from her shoulders and then the sideless surcoat and the leather belt beneath. From a little leather pouch she took gold scissors and snipped the tight sleeves of her tunic, putting them with her other clothes. "Now I will not get wet."

Ranulf watched her undress and was glad for the debilitating heat of the water. Dressed only in the gold tunic, which fitted her like a second skin, none of her lovely body was hidden. Her breasts rose with each breath, and he remembered too well the feel of them against his chest.

Silently, she took the soap from Ranulf's hand and lathered it. She was hesitant about bathing him, not sure of where she should begin or exactly what she should do. She shrugged and thought she should bathe him as she did herself. All hesitancy fled as she touched the warm, smooth skin of his back. The thick muscles bunched beneath the glistening surface, creating hills and valleys, waves of smooth planes. Her hands delighted in the undulations, causing a not unpleasant tightening along the sinews at the back of her neck.

She followed the contours of the wide shoulders to his arms, her hands generously soaping the hair on his forearm. His fingers were long and beautifully shaped, the nails smooth and well cared for. There was an especial pleasure in the feel of her own sensitive fingertips against that hard palm, the callousing reminding her of the strength of the enormous man who sat docilely under her exploring hands.

His chest was of iron, the granite of it relieved only by the covering of bronzed flesh and the thick mat of curling black hair. She lathered the sable mat vigorously, watching it twine around her fingers, her hands small and light against the dark mass.

His neck was indicative of all the reserved, restrained power of the knight, the muscles lengthened and tightened from years of strenuous training. Her fingers traced the steel tendon that ran down the back of his neck to his spine. She pressed on it with a great deal of strength, but Ranulf seemed not to notice. She smiled and looked, for the first time, at his face.

He stared at her with the strangest expression on his face. For some reason, she felt the blood stain her cheeks. She did not know where she erred. Her mother had bid her bathe their guest, and she did but obey. She knew she enjoyed the task; was that showing on her face?

"I think I displease you. My mother has ever meant to train me in this bathing. Mayhaps I am too slow?"

"Nay." His voice was hardly more than a whisper—harsh, ragged. "If you wish to cease . . ."

"But I have not finished." She tried to conceal her blushes. "Close your eyes," she ordered, no longer able to bear his scrutiny.

She could continue in peace, now, to look at him, still and quiet, trusting her, waiting patiently for her gentle washing. She ran light fingers over the handsome face, feeling the thin scar along his cheek, not able to resist the sculptured curves of his lips. Her own lips seemed to burn, even her teeth to tingle as her body remembered his kiss. His lashes moved, as if he were about to open his eyes, so she quickly ran a soapy finger over each eyelid. She did not want him to see her, for she feared her thoughts would show on her face. She must remember that this man was a king's earl. When he left in a few days, she wanted no memories that would shame her.

She splashed warm water on his face to rinse it and then soaped his hair, a great thick down of black locks that curled and twisted in an unruly way. She rubbed his scalp hard.

"You must tell me if I hurt you."

His grunt made her laugh, for he left no doubt as to his thoughts on her ability to hurt him. She poured a bucket of water over his head to rinse him.

She moved to the end of the tub and motioned for a leg to come out, and she ignored his muffled protest. She was delighted to find that his legs also were covered in short, dark hair.

With the last leg done, she looked up at him, seeing an expression of contentment on his face, the muscles relaxed, his wet hair clinging closely to his head. She could not help but laugh, and he looked at her in surprise.

"My father, my maids and your men walk about you on their toes, as if they fear you, yet I do not think you look so fearful at this moment. The Black Lion looks more like a drowned puppy."

Ranulf glared at her, but one corner of his mouth twitched in amusement. "I cannot see how such a lovely lady as your mother was cursed with such a mannerless daughter. Now stop your fun of me and fetch that rinse water."

He stood up from the tub with his back to her, and she paused to look at his nude body, glistening with water, the firelight playing on the droplets that shadowed and highlighted the bronzed muscles.

Ranulf cast a glance over his shoulder, questioning her long pause. In spite of her good intentions, she had soaked the entire front of the figure-molding tunic, leaving little to his imagination. He turned away quickly. "Lyonene, that water grows cold!"

She did not seem to notice the unneeded sharpness in his tone, but quickly stood on the stool and poured water over his magnificent body. She turned away as he took one of the towels warming before the fire and did not look again until he stood before her clad in a brief loincloth.

He smiled at her, teasingly. "I vow I have not been bathed so since my mother bore me. Are you sure you have not done this many times?"

"Nay, only once." The memory made her smile as she tried to control her laughter. "That time ended in such misfortune," she said, putting her hand over her mouth, "that my father never again allowed me near when my mother helped with the bathing."

Ranulf sat down on a stool near the fire. He tried to keep his mind from her transparent dress, her eyes sparkling in amusement. He was acutely aware that they were alone in the quiet little room. He knew he should dress and go to his men, but he could not. He could not yet cover his skin where she had touched him.

"I would hear this story."

"It was in this very room when I was but ten and two."

"A great time ago, I am sure."

She ignored his sarcasm with dignity. "An old knight came to visit my father, and I thought him to be a silly man who often asked me to sit upon his knee." She did not see Ranulf's frown. "He wore a beret with a great red feather that curled about the top of his head and moved when he talked, which he did continuously.

"I often came in here to play and escape him. One morn I brought my new tiercel with me and also my puppy. We played for awhile, but then Lucy called me to help her at some task, I left my hawk and puppy behind. When I returned, my mother was here helping the old man to bathe. I did not see my animals, but thought my mother had shooed them from the room.

"Below stairs, Gressy and the cook began a terrible battle and my mother left the room, telling me to finish the bath."

"Just as today," Ranulf added.

She looked at his near-nude body, the power and strength of it obvious, leashed for this moment only, and thought there was little resemblance between the two men.

"Everything happened at once. I walked to the fire for a moment and the old knight jumped from the tub and started to pull on his braies. He made a lunge for me, the tie string broke, the breeches fell to his ankles and he tripped on them, landing face down on the rushes. My hawk screamed and my puppy ran from the shadows, making a leap for the red-feathered hat that lay on a stool."

Lyonene was encouraged by Ranulf's smile, the light in his eyes.

27

"What happened then? I hope you ran for your mother."

"Nay. I could not, for I fear I began to laugh. The door burst open with my father yelling that I was not to be left alone with any man, but then he stopped, for there was the old knight lying face down in a pool of water, the tiercel flying round and round his head and my puppy perched on his skinny behind, tail wagging and a broken red feather dangling from his mouth."

Ranulf began to laugh, an almost forgotten occurrence. "I can just see him!"

"He kept screaming that he was attacked by demons, hundreds of demons."

They both laughed together at the conjured picture. "I am sure your laughter did not help the poor man's temper. I hope your father made you apologize."

"Nay, he did not," she laughed. "He said naught to me, but carried me to my room."

"Carried you!" Ranulf wiped a tear from his eye.

"Aye," Lyonene gasped, dissolving again. "I was laughing so hard I fell to the floor; I could not walk."

Melite quietly opened the door. She was greeted by a wet Lyonene and a nearly nude Ranulf crying with laughter. Lyonene looked up to see her mother smiling at them. "I was telling the story of the old knight with the great red feather."

Melite came closer, laughter twitching the corners of her mouth. "My daughter knows not the whole story. After her father carried her to her room," she continued, looking in mock reproach at Lyonene, "the old knight refused to stay a moment longer at Lorancourt, so William and I solemnly helped him pack his bags and saddle his horse, but we dared neither look at the other nor mention the happening in this room. Just as the man mounted his horse, the tie to his hose broke and it fell about his ankle. William and I, it is shame to say, fell together in laughter as helpless as Lyonene's. The man rode off screaming at us that he was going to London to sue us. We never heard from him again."

Melite's added story brought new peals of laughter, and the three of them laughed until their sides ached.

It was Melite who reminded them that it was time for supper and that their guest needed to dress.

Clothed again in perfectly tailored hose, a tunic and tabard, Ranulf prepared to leave the room. Melite went ahead of him to find servants, and Ranulf had a few seconds alone with Lyonene. "I have never enjoyed a bath so much as this one. I do not think I have ever laughed so. Thank you." He looked at her lovely face, eyes bright from laughter, and he imagined her at Malvoisin and liked the idea very much.

Supper was a light meal, soups and stews, twice baked bread, fruit preserved in honey and spices and cheeses. The jongleur that William had hired finally arrived and the meal was quiet as they listened to the man's long tales of ancient knights, Robin Hood and King Arthur's court. Impromptu, he composed a song about Lyonene's beauty. He sang it with gusto, for usually barons' daughters were not so pretty, yet custom demanded a song of praise of the marriageable young women.

Ranulf remembered the jongleur's songs about Isabel, the songs that had great influence on a boy of only ten and six years. He looked at Lyonene as she smiled at the jongleur. In a pique of jealousy, he thought of taking the lute from the singer and singing to Lyonene himself, but he knew there would be time for such things. Yes, he was beginning to feel there would be time for such things. The smile that she flashed up at him warmed him and he returned it.

The meal was ended and the tables stacked against the wall. It was dark outside, and the castle grew colder. Ranulf was reluctant for the day to end for he feared to wake and find it had been only a dream.

Lyonene had no such fears, for she looked forward to the morrow as another day such as this. She bade her parents and her guests a good sleep and went up the winding stairs to her room. It was while she was before her door arguing with Lucy that Ranulf approached his chamber.

"May I assist in any matter?"

Lyonene gave him a look of desperation. "Lucy's sister in the village is ill, but Lucy fears to leave me alone for even one night. I promise her I shall not come to harm surrounded by so many guards."

Ranulf took the old woman's plump hand and kissed it.

"Will it put you at your ease if I swear on oath to protect the lady with my life?"

Lucy sniffed, but Ranulf's treatment of her had more effect than she would admit—that the king's earl should kiss her hand! "And who, pray tell, will protect my lady from handsome young gentlemen such as yourself?"

"Lucy!" Lyonene gasped.

Ranulf bowed low before the rotund little woman. "I have heard that Lady Lyonene keeps fierce dogs and a great hawk in her room that attack any intruders like a pack of demons."

Lucy could not keep from laughing for she knew the story well. "The two of you are a pair—nary a serious bone in your body. I'm off then and . . ." She threw up her hands. "I hope I do not live to regret this."

Lyonene and Ranulf watched as she waddled down the stairs, mumbling to herself. Awkward together in the ensuing silence, they were quiet.

"I hope you will like your chamber and that everything pleases you."

Ranulf ran a finger along her jaw. "I am well pleased by Lorancourt and everything in it." He knew he could not stand so close to her in the darkened hall and not pull her into his arms. "Good night," he said abruptly and left her.

Lyonene went to her own chamber and began to undress. It was a good feeling of freedom to be alone without Lucy. She stood in her chemise before the fire. So much had happened this day. She remembered their laughter over the race, and the story she told, his blush, and then she remembered his kiss and the feel of his skin as she bathed him. She moved away from the fire, for she had grown very warm.

He had said he could not stay for two days more, and she dreaded his leaving.

She climbed into the high feather bed, pulling the thick woolen comforter about her. Exhausted, she soon fell asleep.

Ranulf paced the small chamber for a while, his soft leather shoes silent on the thick rushes. It had been ten and five years since the boy he once was had lain in a girl's parents' chamber and dreamed of a happy life.

Since then he had changed, convincing himself that what he had once sought was not possible. There were few happy marriages, and he had no longer considered the possibility of such a future. King Edward pressed him to marry a Castilian princess, very rich and very ugly. He had almost resigned himself to the fate of such a marriage. But now there was Lyonene.

He must consider. Was it love he felt for her or just the sin of lust? He dismissed this. Lust he had felt often, but never had he considered marriage to the woman.

For a moment a picture formed of Lyonene sitting before the great fire in Malvoisin, a fat, healthy baby on a carpet at her feet. The lights played with her hair, and as he entered the hall, she would rise and greet him. He brushed the picture away with his hand.

He sat heavily on the edge of the bed. He had learned the ways of war and had often been afraid before a battle, but never had he felt such fear as now. Could he once again turn his life, his heart, over to a young girl? Could he overcome it again if Lyonene betrayed him as Isabel had?

Silently, he opened his door and just as silently made his way into Lyonene's chamber. She lay on her back, her face turned toward him, her hair spread in a great waterfall about her. One hand was hidden beneath the covers, the other, palm upward by her face.

He touched her hair, lifting a healthy strand from where it fell down the side of the mattress, letting a curl wind about his wrist. Her lashes were little wings on her cheeks, her mouth slightly puckered, tempting him.

"What if I put my small heart in your hands, my love?" he whispered. "Will you care for it or shun it?" He played with the hair, rubbing the fine silky stuff between his fingertips. "If you are but kind to me, I will love you more than any woman has ever been loved, but . . ." His face darkened and had Lyonene awakened, she would have seen the countenance that had earned Ranulf the name Black Lion. "If you play me false, if you but play a game, you will know a hell on earth such as there has never been before."

His features relaxed, and gently he touched her fingertips. She sighed in her sleep and her eyelids fluttered. He held his breath that she would waken. She turned over to the other side, exposing one bare shoulder. Ranulf stood and softly kissed the satin skin and pulled the covers closer about her. "Ere long I will warm you and you'll have no need of cloth covers. Remember, little one, it will be your choice of heaven or hell."

He left the room to seek his own chamber.

Chapter Three

Lyonene slept later the next morning since Lucy was not there to call her. The sound of horses, of metal striking metal, woke her. She opened the shutter a bit to see below. Her father had made a list, a long field dug out and filled again with fine, soft sand. Here she now saw the Black Guard in full armor, the iron hauberk and chausses showing black in the early morning sun. Never had she seen her father's men train so enthusiastically or so hard as Ranulf's men. Two men wrestled with one another, two slashed at each other with broad swords. Another jumped onto his horse again and again using no hands, bearing the weight of the iron-link armor easily. Her heart pounded as she saw her Lion ride toward a thick post set in the ground and cut it in half with one blow.

She smiled in satisfaction and closed the shutters. When she was nearly dressed in an ivory wool tunic and a loose scarlet wool surcoat, she heard a trumpet that heralded the arrival of more guests. Her heart fell because she knew more guests would mean more work and less time spent in pleasure.

She heard the voices as she neared the Great Hall. Her father introduced her to two men, Sir Tompkin and Sir Hugh, one tall, one short, both stocky, square-shaped men. Melite bade Lyonene show Sir Tompkin to a guest chamber.

All the way up the stairs, the man talked of his daughters—of their beauty, their charm, their marriage prospects. Lyonene hardly listened, so distraught was she from having her day ruined.

"Warbrooke!" the man snapped. "See that my mail is cleaned, and do not neglect your duties now that that brother of yours is come."

Lyonene's head came up abruptly at the name Warbrooke, her Lion's name. She guessed the blond boy she saw was brother to Ranulf. As he left the chamber, Lyonene made excuses to follow him.

"You are brother to the Black Lion?" She caught him in the dark hallway. He was very different from his brother—fair, with laughing blue eyes and a gaze that roamed roguishly over her body.

"And now what has my brother done to cause interest from so lovely a lady?"

Lyonene blushed; her feelings were too obvious to everyone.

Geoffrey smiled at the pink-cheeked girl. Ranulf had done well for himself this time he decided; usually he found his brother's taste in women appalling. Some of the hags he knew at court! They were enough to turn a man's stomach. "I take it you are Lady Lyonene? Sir Tompkin has been fuming about you for days. It seems too many would-be suitors to his hideous daughters speak overmuch of your beauty. I can see now their reasons for rapture."

Lyonene smiled at him. "You are well taught in the manners of courtly love. And you are not at all like your brother, although your smile is somewhat the same."

Geoffrey's face lost all expression. "Smile? And what know you of my brother's smile?"

"Why, that he has a pleasant smile and that his laughter is a good sound, although almost overly loud."

The young squire stared at her for so long a while that she frowned at his intensity.

"I seem to have said something wrong. I meant no criticism of your brother when I said his laughter was too loud, but the walls almost shook. My maids wondered greatly at the sound."

Geoffrey recovered himself. "Ranulf waits below and . . ."

"Oh no, he is on the lists with his men."

He gave her a wide grin and she looked away. "Come with me to the lists then that I may greet this laughing brother of mine. In truth I believe you mix him with another. He has black hair and . . ."

"Oh, yes. And black eyes, and his horse is most gentle."

Geoffrey drew his brows together and shook his head. "That Ranulf would allow someone else to touch that precious horse of his is beyond understanding. I can see this information will pale beside what is obviously of a much greater concern to you, but my name is Geoffrey de Warbrooke, lowly squire to Sir Tompkin."

She looked up at him. "You are not at all like Lion. There he is!" She hurried forward.

Geoffrey stared after her, bewildered. Ranulf had always hated being called the Black Lion; in truth, he had always hated any reference to his blackness, for a reason unknown to Geoffrey. He had heard the stories of his brother and seen the way he was feared by the common folk. Only at court, among his peers, was he treated without fear. This girl, a mere baron's daughter, had called Ranulf Lion.

"I can see I am most unneeded here," Geoffrey said as he stood by his brother, who stared down into Lyonene's eyes.

Ranulf turned in surprise. "Geoffrey!" He grabbed the much smaller boy and hugged him, kissing each cheek and then a hard kiss on the mouth. "I did not know you came. Where is that odious old man you follow about? Do not tell me you have been knighted and come to join my Black Guard?"

"You know there is another year before my knighting, and I am too lazy to join such a guard as yours. I will not sweat myself to your high stench each day. I do not know how this lovely lady abides you. I had not heard of this passion of yours. You have kept the secret well."

Lyonene turned to watch one of the Black Guard throw a long lance at a far target. She avoided the stares of both men. "I must return to the donjon. I will see you at dinner?" She gave Ranulf a fleeting glance.

He took her small hand and caressed it before holding it to his lips. Neither of them was aware of the people who watched. She lifted her skirts and began to run to the old stone tower. Only at the wooden steps that led to the second floor did she remember to walk correctly.

"What think you of Lady Lyonene?" Ranulf tried to control the excitement in his voice.

Geoffrey was not fooled; he knew his brother too well. "I have heard she has the temper and quarrelsome nature of a magpie and . . ." Geoffrey laughed aloud when his brother turned to him a face so distorted with rage as to be hardly recognizable. "Do not murder me, brother, please. I do but jest."

Ranulf relaxed and looked away sheepishly. "I admit she has had an effect on me. But tell me true what you think of her."

"I hear she has made you laugh." He watched his older brother's slow smile, amazed.

"I do not understand myself, but the girl has bewitched me. Is she not the most beautiful woman alive, for all she is but a child?"

"Come sit by me, brother, and tell me of this girl. You have known her long?"

Ranulf leaned back against the wall behind the stone bench and ran his hand over his eyes, through his sweat-dampened hair. "I came here to see you, and but met my Lioness yestermorn. I do not know what has overtaken me. From the first moment I saw those green eyes I have seen naught else. I did not sleep much last night, and now I fear I will kill myself, for I cannot keep my mind about my work. What is wrong with me?"

It took Geoffrey a while to answer, so stunned was he. "I think, my brother, you have fallen in love with the girl."

"Love!" Ranulf sneered and then relaxed again. "I have thought of this but cannot credit it. She is a child. My daughter, Leah, would have been near as old as she."

"Well, you could always make her your mistress and when you tire of her, give her to one of your men for wife."

Ranulf turned a scowling face to his brother, but Geoffrey only laughed. "Then you must marry the girl. I can see she is eager for you, although I do not understand why. I am sure you will make a poor husband."

"I cannot marry her." His voice was barely audible.

"Ranulf, you must forget Isabel! Many men have unhappy first marriages. You were but a boy, and she several years older than you. You cannot live always in the past. This girl adores you, so marry her before another takes her. Of course she is but a baron's daughter. Mayhaps the great Earl of Malvoisin will not lower himself to . . . You understand my words? If you do not take her, another will. What think you of the idea of another holding her, kissing her . . . Ranulf! Unhand me!"

Geoffrey picked himself up from the dirt at Ranulf's feet. "I go now to clean Sir Tompkin's mail. You will think on my words?" He left his silent brother alone.

"Lyonene! I have repeated my question four times. Where is your mind?"

"I am sorry, Father. What did you ask of me?"

"It does not matter now. What is wrong with you this day?"

"I think," Melite said, looking at her husband over her sewing, "that the problem with our daughter stands outside on the lists."

William frowned. "Sir Tompkin?" His voice was incredulous.

There was disgust in Lyonene's voice. "Hmph! Sir Tompkin indeed! That fat old man!"

"I'll not have such disrespect in my house, girl."

"William, it is the Earl of Malvoisin who causes Lyonene so much trouble," Melite whispered.

"Ranulf de Warbrooke!" He looked at Lyonene's bowed head. "You moon for the king's earl?"

Lyonene stood before the fire, stretching with a cat-like grace. "Is he not handsome? Is he not the kindest, gentlest man? And does not his hair curl most splendidly?"

William's eyes widened to the fullest possible and his mouth fell open as he looked to his wife, who sat with a satisfied grin on her face.

"Lyonene," Melite said quietly, "go and comb your hair. Have Lucy build you a fire and stay in your room until dinner."

Lyonene did not question her mother's highly unusual request, but just obeyed.

"Now, wife, I pray you to tell me what happens in my

own castle. My daughter is moonstruck for the Black Lion? She cannot expect aught to come of such a dream. She would be as likely to marry an earl as I would to marry the king's daughter."

"You have yet to ask him."

"Ask him! Are you daft to think I would do such? He will laugh in my face. It is well enough to tell my friends an earl has visited me, but that I aspired to an earl for a son! Nay, I'll not hear such laughter!"

"William, have you not also seen that our earl 'moons,' as you say, for our daughter?" When he did not answer, she smiled. "Go and look to the lists. You will see the truth in my words."

Unbelieving, William walked to the shuttered windows, pulling one of the louvers down so he could see out. Ranulf sat on a bench, his head back against the wall, staring into space. As William watch... a few of the Black Guard turned puzzled stares to their master.

William returned to the fire and sat down heavily.

"I do not know that he will accept our daughter in marriage, but we may ask. Was there not an old story that the Earl of Malvoisin was once married to a baron's daughter, a woman he loved?"

William's face lit. "It is so! When he was a lad, he caused great scandal by marrying the girl. King Henry was said to be greatly angered. There was a child born but five months after the marriage. When the woman and the child died but a few years after the marriage, it is said he near went insane with grief, that his pain was so great that he has never laughed since." He whirled to face his wife.

"Go on. And what of the rest of the gossip?"

"That whoever makes him laugh will be . . ."

"His bride, I believe the silly saying goes. I am sure it began as a jest, but, for whatever reason, Lord Ranulf is not a happy man." She smiled sweetly at her husband and knew he remembered Ranulf's laughter of the day before. "Shall I send a page to fetch our guest? I do not believe we should prolong our lovers' agony. I do not wish my grandchild born only five months after the wedding."

They sat in silence until Ranulf sat before them in his

training costume, tight hose with a short tunic and tabard that barely reached midthigh. He kept looking about the shadows of the Great Hall and then toward the yawning black stairwell.

"My Lord Ranulf," William began. He could not see what his women saw in the massive form of the man before him to cause so much love to be directed toward him. He could not control his shudder as he remembered the strength he had seen the man demonstrate this morn. He loved his daughter and hoped he did not make an error. "My daughter, Lyonene, is . . . unmarried and of a marriageable age. She has near driven me mad for a year, for she has turned down dozens of men who have desired her for wife." It was difficult to continue, for Ranulf's brows had drawn together in a black look.

Melite decided to help her husband. "What William means to say is that we have reason to believe Lyonene would accept you, and therefore we offer you our daughter in marriage."

William continued. "I can offer a dowry of two and a half knights' fees. Lyonene is also my heir and upon our death stands to inherit all of Lorancourt."

Ranulf tried to calm his racing heart. He cared naught for the dowry, but he must, for William's sake, appear to consider it. The Warbrooke estates contained twelve castles, one of which was Malvoisin. The other eleven all at least equaled Lorancourt. A castle was supported by so many knights' fees, ranging from five to over a hundred. Ranulf did not know how many hundreds of knights' fees he owned.

Melite seemed to know his thoughts. She put a hand over his large one, which rested on his knee. "I believe I am right that you have grown to care for my daughter. My interest is in her welfare, not talk of knights' fees and inheritances. Do my eyes and senses tell me true?"

"Aye. She is the prize. Not any dowry could equal her."

William missed the messages that Melite and Ranulf passed to one another. "Then it is agreed?" He was astounded.

"On a condition. It must be put to Lyonene as a request. I will not have her forced into a marriage." His

39

eyes narrowed with memory. "She must agree freely. There is no other man, no previous betrothal?"

William waved his hand. "None, and, if my wife is to be believed, the girl will agree readily enough. You will be wanting guests of the court?"

Ranulf considered for a moment. "Nay, I can ask no one, for Edward and Eleanora would come and bring all their retainers, near three hundred people, and few of the other earls travel with less people." He watched William's stare of horror—to feed and lodge so many people! Ranulf continued, "It is cold, too cold for a tourney now, so if it does not offend you, your lovely wife or my Lady Lyonene, the marriage will be simple and I will leave with my bride soon after for Malvoisin."

William's feeling of relief was almost tangible. "Aye. It will be as you wish. Now, for the day. The banns must be posted for three Sundays. This is Saturday. If you were to sign a betrothal agreement today, we can plan the wedding for three weeks hence. Does that suit you, my lord?"

"Aye, of course." He rose to leave. "Then I leave on the morrow, for there are many preparations to make, and I will return in three weeks' time." His eyes gleamed as he looked at Melite's smiling face. Impulsively, he placed his great hands on her shoulders and kissed her cheek.

She took his arm and walked with him to the stairs. "It is near time for dinner. I have sent a message to your men; mayhaps you would like to change your clothing."

Quietly, Ranulf went up the worn steps to his room. As he slowly washed and changed into a dark-blue velvet tunic and tabard, he chuckled to himself. What would his Black Guard think if they knew their leader was as nervous as a green boy, all because of an emerald-eyed lioness?

Lyonene stared through the open shutter, needing the blast of cold air to revive her. Her back was to her father, and his news had nearly felled her. Lord Ranulf had agreed to marry her! She could not help a rebellious feeling over the fact that the marriage had been arranged without her knowledge. She thought of her cousin

Anna. A page had come and said her father wanted her below stairs. Moments later she had found herself married to a man she'd never seen before.

Lyonene took a deep breath of air and thought that, all in all, she was blessed with a good father. Of course it had been Ranulf who had stipulated that she must agree freely to the marriage. She closed her eyes and leaned forward, the air biting her cheeks. To spend all the days of her life such as the last one! To have him kiss her at any time she desired.

"Daughter, will you give the man your answer?"

"Aye, father, I will marry him," she said quietly.

William shook his head and silently left the room. He could not grasp the idea that his daughter was to become a countess. He did not see Ranulf until he walked into him.

"She did not agree," the dark knight stated flatly.

"Nay," William answered, "she has agreed." He looked at Ranulf with something akin to horror—the Black Lion was to be his son-in-law. Was not the son supposed to be afraid of the father? "Go to her. I am sure she would care to see you." Then he shrugged and went down the stairs.

Lyonene did not leave the open window when she heard the door reopen. "Lucy, come here and see this glorious day." She whirled at Ranulf's deep voice.

"And what makes this cold, drear day so glorious?" He was very serious.

She felt shy of a sudden, for, after all, he was a stranger to her. Ranulf walked to the carved oak chest that stood against one wall. He lifted her ivory comb and studied the figures on it. "You have spoken to your father and agreed to the . . . bargain?"

"Aye," she answered quietly, "but is not a marriage more than just a bargain?" She began to smile. "At least this marriage, for I fear you do not bargain to gain, since you chose a poor baron's daughter to wife. Would you not want a rich wife with green estates and . . . "

"Knocked knees, mayhaps?"

Her eyes sparkled. "And how do you know my knees do not knock?"

He did not smile, but the corners of his eyes showed merriment. "That is true, I do not know, so I shall find out. I do not propose to marry a woman with ugly legs."

She stepped backward from him. "Do not come near me. I will call out."

"And who will dare to stop the great Black Lion? I shall toss all the men out the window and then I shall still have my way with you." He leered at her, and she tried to cover her giggles as they escaped her.

He threw an arm about her waist and then sat on the bed with her in his lap. She uselessly tried to pull away from him, but her laughter made her even weaker. Ranulf made half-hearted attempts to lift her skirt. He held both her hands in one of his.

"Now, this ankle is not too crooked."

"It is not crooked at all!"

"If it is not, then it will not mate with the other, which is most definitely bent."

"What is this?" Lucy demanded, appearing from nowhere. "I knew I should not leave this girl alone. You unhand my girl and leave this room at once! I will have no such play while I am near."

"Lucy, we are to be married."

The old woman may have missed one blink, but otherwise gave no other sign that she heard. "Well, until you are married, you are in my keeping. Now you, young man, unhand her ankle and leave this room. You are not allowed alone with my girl until after the wedding."

Ranulf set Lyonene from his lap and bent to kiss her.

"No more of that! You have a life together. There be no sense in tiring of one another early."

Obediently, he started to leave.

Lyonene's laugh stopped him. "What of your threats now, Lion? Will you not carry them out?" She nodded her head to the open window.

Ranulf looked at Lucy, who ran to close the shutters. He grimaced. "I am not so strong as that. Mayhaps I should fetch my Black Guard." He paused and frowned. "And the Frisian, and . . . "

Lyonene's laughter followed him as he closed the door behind him.

"Is he not wonderful, Lucy? Is he not the kindest, gentlest . . . "

"Yes, yes." Lucy was impatient and hardly listened to Lyonene's prattle as she straightened the room.

"And does he not have the most perfect body?"

Lucy dropped the clothing she carried. "Lady Lyonene. You forget yourself! Your lady mother and I have taught you the manners of a lady, not those of . . . of the joy women."

Lyonene looked at her in wide-eyed innocence. "Whatever could you mean, Lucy? I did but refer to his knightly form. You could not mean other than that."

Lucy stared at her young mistress, realizing she had been trapped again. Happily the bell rang to announce dinner, and they went below.

Lyonene wondered how many years it would take before her heart did not jump at the sight of Ranulf. He stood with his back to her, talking to the much shorter Sir Tompkin. He seemed to sense her presence, for he turned and held his hand out to her. He did not release her as Sir Tompkin frowned and went to table.

"I am afraid the man is most angry, for he has tried for years to marry one of his wretched daughters to me."

They sat together at the high table, the bread trencher shared between them. "Sir William says the betrothal can be signed after dinner. You are sure you wish to spend your life with me? To place your welfare in my hands?"

"I am most sure. It is you who should beware." She ate a piece of salt-cured ham.

Ranulf frowned. "And what hidden danger awaits me?"

"Why me, of course. You know little of me but that I have straight ankles. You know naught of my character."

"I am not convinced about the ankles, but tell me your flaws of character."

"I have a terrible temper, my mother says I am very vain . . . "

"With good reason."

"And I am too often not a lady and say what first comes to my head."

"Those are grievous faults."

"Do not laugh at me, Ranulf de Warbrooke! I see you also have faults."

He could not contain the smile that spread over his face. "I am called the Spawn of the Devil and you dare to think I have faults?"

She waved her hand in dismissal. "I am sure the name stands you in good stead during war, but what others call you is not your fault."

"And what do you believe is poor in my character?"

"Excessive pride, truly an arrogance. There are others, but that is the greatest flaw."

His kissed her cheek hastily and then remembered where he was and straightened. "Pride is the least of my faults." His face hardened and he became very serious. "You are mine, and I will allow you not so much as to glance at another man. Remember that well."

She gave him a radiant smile. "That is an easy request, for in all my ten and seven years I have never desired a man for husband until I met you. I do not think I shall see another man I fancy soon."

"You are but ten and seven years? You are younger than I had thought."

She laughed aloud. "I make long avowals of my fidelity and you exclaim over my age. Will you not say some such thing as you are near double my age? It is true you seem very old. I am sure you will not last the winter."

"You are an impertinent wench! Do you not know the Black Lion eats three girls such as you each day afore dinner?"

Oblivious to the staring people around them, she put a finger on his lower lip. "I do not find that a horrible way to die at all," she said gently.

He stared at her a moment and then bit her finger, a little too hard, until she drew back in pain. "Do you not know it is the man who is to pursue the woman? Behave yourself and eat your dinner. Even now I shall never be respected by my own men again, for they have seen me led by a chit of a girl for near two days."

Happily, she gave her attention to her food and the songs of the jongleur. She had not even been aware that he had been singing.

The meal was cleared and the tables dismounted and stacked against the walls. Father Hewitt brought ink and quills and the betrothal papers to a small table set before the fire. Sir William signed them hastily, but Ranulf paused. The old priest put his hand on the man's strong arm. "You are not sure, my lord?"

"I but remembered another time so much like this one." He signed his name, a hard, black flourish.

"Now, it is customary for rings and kisses. Lady Lyonene, you have a ring I believe?"

She held out her hand for Ranulf's and with trembling fingers placed a gold ring on the third finger of his left hand—the arm nearest his heart, the finger that contained a vein leading directly to his heart.

"I do not have . . . " Ranulf began, but then his face lighted and he put his hand into the fitchet opening of his tabard and unbuckled a leather pouch from his belt. He emptied the contents on the table—a few coins, several jewels including an enormous ruby, three iron keys and a bit of wool, ragged and worn. He took the wool and unwound it to reveal a ring—gold, with clasped hands on the back to represent unity and a sun and moon to signify the lifetime bond of marriage. There were three emeralds across the top.

"It was my mother's ring. She bid me always carry it."

"You cannot give it me, for then you will at times be without it."

He took her hand and slid the ring into place. "I will wrap you in a bit of wool and carry you and the ring. Now go and find your mother, for I have sorely neglected my men, my horse and my brother."

"You are to kiss me." Her voice was almost hurt that he had forgotten.

He bent and kissed her cheek, but her arms went around his neck to hold him close. For a brief moment he crushed her to him. "Go," he whispered, "before I shame myself and my king before your family." He pulled her arms away. "Notice I do not include you in the shamed ones, for I vow you are a shameless hussy."

She giggled at him. "Go to your horse then, and I will do my work and not give you another thought."

Melite followed her daughter up the stairs. "Someday

I shall pay for this," she muttered. To see her daughter so happy was a joy to her, but she wondered where she had gone wrong that she had reared such a forward girl. "It is William's fault," she answered herself. "If he had named his daughter Joan as I wished, she would not be like this. No Joan ever threw her arms around a man not her husband and begged him for a kiss, at least not before her parents. But a girl named for a lioness!" She smiled. It was indeed fortunate that Lyonene was to marry a man like Ranulf and not a weakling like Giles, the young boy who lived on the neighboring estate and had since childhood vowed he'd someday marry Lyonene.

"Mother! Whatever are you saying? I believe you are talking to yourself!"

"You may be impertinent with Lord Ranulf, but you may not do so with me."

Lyonene laughed and then sobered. "I am sorry, Mother. It is only that he has called me just so this day. Is he not a wondrous man?"

Melite sighed, for she saw several hours ahead of hearing of Lord Ranulf's charms.

They spent the afternoon in the great bedchamber of William and Melite, which also acted as a solar. Lyonene could not concentrate on her sewing. She constantly held the ring to the light to catch the sparkle of the emeralds and too often ran to the window to look toward the lists.

"Lyonene," Melite said casually, "this year's apple crop was especially good. Go to the kitchen and have Cook give you a few."

"I am not hungry."

"Nay, but I thought mayhaps that black horse of Lord Ranulf's would be."

Lyonene jumped from her chair and ran to her mother to give her a quick hug and kiss her cheek. She had almost reached the door when a thought came to her and she looked back. "Someday, I shall ask you what message my father sent that was so urgent that I was left alone to bathe my Lord Ranulf."

There was only a flicker across Melite's face, but it was enough to answer her daughter. Laughing, Lyonene went to the kitchen.

The stables were warm and sweet-smelling as she carried a small basket of apples toward the enormous horse in the end stall.

She stroked his head and opened the door. The horse daintily ate the apples from her hand as she ran her hands over the powerful neck.

"Lyonene! What do you do? You should not be in Tighe's stall. It is dangerous!" Geoffrey called to her.

She smiled at him over the low wooden wall. "He is as gentle as his master." She rubbed the velvet nose, then took an iron comb from the wall and began to comb the long, profuse mane.

Geoffrey stood before the gate, an expression of awe on his face. "The horse is a stallion and not at all gentle. I have never seen him behave so with anyone besides Ranulf. Did you not know he nipped your father's stable master?"

"The man, I am sure, deserved the punishment. See how sweet he is?" She stooped before one of Tighe's legs and stroked the long hair that grew from knee to the floor. "I have never seen a horse with hair like this. Of course Tighe is very vain; a horse so beautiful would have to be."

"Lyonene, I have never seen a girl such as you. My brother is most fortunate."

She stood and fed Tighe more apples. "Something I do not understand is why he is not married. I know he was married before, but that was long ago. How the women of King Edward's court have let such a gentle, kind man escape is beyond me."

"Oh, but they have tried. But always there is something in their eyes and manner that shows too well, and that is their greed."

Lyonene felt the blood rush to her cheeks and looked away. "But I, too, am greedy for him."

Geoffrey laughed. "The women of the court are greedy for his wealth as much as for him. It is this that is easy to see. They appraise his clothes, the sable lining of his mantle, the jewels on his hem, even the accounts of his estates."

"Estates? But there is only Malvoisin, an island south of England."

"Malvoisin is only one of many. There is . . ."

"Do not tell me! I do not like to think of my Ranulf as one of the king's earls. It frightens me more than a little. I almost wish he were a farmer like my father; then he would stay at home and play with our children."

"What is this I hear of children?" Ranulf came toward them. "I have yet to touch the girl and already she believes herself to be a mother."

Geoffrey looked from one to the other. "I will go and talk to Maularde."

Ranulf chuckled as his brother left.

"What is so amusing?"

"Maularde rarely talks to anyone." He turned back to her, the stall gate separating them. "I think you marry me for my horse." He watched her comb the long mane. "When we are at Malvoisin I will find a suitable mare and mayhaps Tighe can produce a daughter for you." The big stallion hit Ranulf's shoulder with his head. "See, even the idea pleases him. Now, come out here to me. I will have to sell him if you spoil him more."

He put his hands on her shoulders and stared at her intensely. "I wish to remember you well, for I leave in the morn."

"You cannot! Not so soon." She swayed toward him. "Could you not stay until the banns are read, until the marriage? Then we may leave together for my new home."

"I cannot. I have told my steward I will be there, but I could not stay near you for so long. I will return on the day of the marriage and you will be mine. Now you must return to your mother."

She backed away from him. "You ever send me to my mother. I would stay with you."

"You cannot stay with me until you are my wife—I could not bear it. Now go or I will carry you."

She grinned at him wickedly and did not move an inch.

He unceremoniously tossed her over his shoulder, a most unladylike position. She screamed for him to release her, which he did before they reached the stable door.

"I am sure I am the most abused bride in all of England and sure the only one who was not kissed properly at her betrothal."

"You do not know . . . I cannot kiss you every moment and naught else. I leave early on the morrow. If you meet me then, I will kiss you before I go. Now do not tempt me further."

She walked slowly back to the old stone donjon and up the wooden stairs.

At supper the betrothal was announced and a cheer given. The Black Guard stood and lifted their cups to her, and each man said a sentence to Lyonene's beauty and charm.

"They are pleasant men," Lyonene said, laughing. She did not notice Ranulf's whitened knuckles or the deep scowl on his face.

After the meal, Lyonene played her psaltery, a harp-like instrument, and sang. Her voice was clear and pretty and she looked only at Ranulf as she sang the old love songs.

He kissed her hand as he bade her good sleep, and they parted for the night, both very aware of the one thin wall separating them. Ranulf was glad Lucy had returned from the village so he would not be tempted to enter her room as he'd done the night before.

For a brief instant, before he slept, questions came to his brain, questions as to the wisdom of marriage with this unknown girl. It was true that she looked at him as no other woman ever had, but did she also look at other men so? Was she a better mummer than the women at court, to make him believe she cared for him and not the wealth of Malvoisin? He dismissed the thoughts, but they were to haunt him later.

Lyonene stretched luxuriously—a tawny cat. She felt that something good was to happen today, an excitement she could not name. Then, eyes fully open, she sprang nude from the bed, careful not to wake Lucy, and hastily dressed. Lion would leave this morn and she must see him.

In the Great Hall below in the dim light she saw that her father's men yet slept soundly, but the Black Guard were not present. Silently, she made her way to the door and toward the stables. The sun did not even show pink yet, it was so early.

She stood at the stable door, her eyes focusing in the dark building.

"My Lioness awakes early." His voice was low, his breath soft as he sent shivers of pleasure through her body.

She whirled and sent him a brilliant smile. "And so does my Lion, it seems."

"Careful with those smiles, Lioness, or I may find a den for us." He rolled his eyes in meaning.

She covered her mouth over the giggles that trilled out. It was then that she saw Geoffrey standing so close. Over his shoulder was a horse's bridle. "You go also?"

Geoffrey was very aware of the scowl that grew on his brother's face, but it scared him not. This new jealousy of Ranulf's deserved some teasing.

Lyonene looked into the blue eyes of her brother-in-law. He was more handsome at close range, with lashes that shadowed his cheeks. She watched with interest as he lifted her limp hand and kissed the back of it. His eyes sparkled into hers. "I may kiss you before we leave?"

As he took her slim shoulders in his hands, his eyes met Ranulf's, teasing his older brother. His lips met Lyonene's briefly, and they were pleasant and sweet. With a smile, he left her to finish with his horse. Lyonene turned to watch him mount. "Well, my brother," he said, "why do you tarry? Kiss Lady Lyonene and let us be off." He motioned his horse out the stable door, leaving Lyonene and Ranulf alone.

Her heart and breath had changed at the mere thought of kissing her Lion again. She turned to him, her face as serious as his. A big hand buried itself in her hair, and he roughly pulled her to him, his chest steel against her woman's softness. His lips met hers in an urgency that she eagerly met. Her arms twined themselves about his strong body, pulling him closer to her. She could feel his thighs against her, and she instinctively moved her hips against his.

He almost threw her from him, and she leaned against the stable wall, her breast heaving, her lips parted and exceedingly soft.

"You expect too much of me. It is well that I leave."

His voice was harsh and low. "See that your mother keeps you safe."

"You will not forget me?"

"Never, my Lioness. I will think of naught else."

"Nor I." Tears choked her words.

He kissed away each tear that formed on her lashes and then he was gone. Lyonene did not know how long she stood there, and even though the sun was shining when she entered the stone castle, for her all thought of sun was gone.

Chapter Four

Melite saw the lost expression on her daughter's face when Lyonene came into the Great Hall. She knew her son-in-law had gone, and now the long three weeks' wait stretched before them. Melite sighed. To her daughter it would be an eternity, but to herself there didn't seem to be enough time for all that had to be done.

First of all, there were clothes to be made. Although there was not a big enough dowry for Lyonene to make a difference to an earl, Melite planned to dress her daughter as befitted a countess. She set out to look for William, for only he had the key to the storeroom that held most of the portable wealth of Lorancourt.

William complained somewhat, but he finally agreed with his wife that Lyonene must be clothed properly. Jewels and furs, satins, silks, velvets and fine wools were brought from the dark, cool room. Lyonene gasped at the beauty of the stuffs, afraid to cut them and chance ruining the materials.

For three weeks, Gressy, Meg, Lucy, Melite and Lyonene sewed. They outlined tiny lions with green silk thread along the border of one tunic, filled the space with lamb's wool and covered it to make padded animals. Each lion was bordered with tiny seed pearls.

Her wedding gown was given special attention. It was a tunic of saffron samite silk, very tight, and its sleeves were fastened with a row of tiny buttons from wrist to elbow. The sideless surcoat of tawny velvet was cut away drastically to reveal the generous curves of Lyonene's breasts and hips. The wedding mantle was of green brocade from Sicily. Pale-green phoenix with tails ready to burst into flame were woven onto a darker green background, and the entire cloak and hood were lined in rabbit fur that had been dyed a third shade of green.

Lyonene wished fervently that she had gotten her betrothed's measurements for a tabard to make as a wedding gift, but she finally settled on two gold cups. She did not notice her father's white face as he arranged for a goldsmith to come to Lorancourt to hammer two of his four precious gold plates into stemmed, jewel-encrusted goblets. To Lyonene, it was reassuring to hear the man and his apprentice hammering for hours each day as they formed the gold sheets around iron balls to make the shape of the cups. She knew that as the cups took shape, the time came closer for her wedding day.

Each night she fell into bed exhausted, as Melite had planned, but always there was the sweet vision of Ranulf before she slept. There were things she began to remember that had not bothered her when they were together. She thought often of his earldom, of the court of King Edward, where Ranulf would be a frequent visitor. She began to question his reasons for marrying her, and as the day approached she found herself jumping at every little noise and crying often. Gressy's added stories of the horrors of the Black Lion did not help her growing anxiety.

Geoffrey grimaced. If his besotted brother asked once more if Lady Lyonene were not beautiful, he would use his estoc and calmly slip the blade between the man's ribs. They had ridden hard to reach London in one night, and Geoffrey looked forward to a soft bed, with maybe a barmaid to keep him warm.

Ranulf did not like London with its open sewer trenches along the streets and all the scavenging pigs that roamed about eating the slops. The streets were narrow, and no air reached the riders between the three- and four-story buildings. The inn where they had spent the night was only fairly clean.

He rode along the street of the goldsmiths until he found the sign he wanted. Only three of the Black Guard had accompanied him, the other four tending to Geoffrey, who refused to leave his bed and his plump barmaid so early in the morning.

Alone, Ranulf entered the cramped little shop. A small, dark man came forward.

"I would purchase a gift, a bride gift, and I would have your finest work."

"All my work is my finest. What is your desire?"

Both men stared at one another, both unsmiling but understanding the other.

"I would have a belt, a very special belt. It is to be of your purest gold and your finest wire. There are to be lions—a lion and his lioness, and there are to be scenes in the manner of lions hunting together, at the kill . . ." Ranulf stopped, feeling embarrassment before this solemn little man.

"I understand. Now what of colors?"

"The male lion is to be enameled in the blackest of black and in the gold eye is to be a black pearl. The lioness . . . " Ranulf closed his eyes for a second in delicious memory. "The lioness is to be the true tawny gold of a lioness, and the eye is to be set with an emerald." Ranulf paused, remembering Lyonene's emerald eyes. "It is to be links, each link containing a scene, and no longer than my finger to the first joint, no wider than my thumb. Can you do such delicate work?"

"If I am paid enough gold, I can do anything."

Ranulf stiffened. "There will be gold aplenty."

"What size is the lady? How many links?"

Ranulf was puzzled. He held up his hands, forming a circle. "I can span her waist with my hands."

The jeweler made some mental notes. "Ten and five lengths. Now the clasp. Of what is it to be made?"

Ranulf considered for a moment. "A black pearl and an emerald." They talked for a few moments of price and set a date to have the completed piece. He returned to the inn satisfied. Geoffrey had spent the day in a more leisurely fashion and was now ready to leave. The two brothers prepared to leave. Geoffrey parted from his brother to return to his duties as squire to Sir Tompkin.

It took two long, grueling days to reach Malvoisin, and Ranulf again marveled at the even, gray stone walls as they towered before him. He and his men made their way through the west barbican into the outer bailey amid cheers and hallos from the many castlefolk. They dismounted as they entered the maze wall that protected the private inner bailey. His steward, chief falconer, master cook and head stableman lived with their families in the apartments in the quiet inner bailey.

The Black Guard went to their own abode while Ranulf made his way to Black Hall.

For the entire time he was at Malvoisin it rained, and although he judged many cases in the hundred court, too often the people could not venture out in the deep mud.

The rain kept him inside the stone walls of Black Hall. A few times he had joined his men, but they had their own women and were content. He was anxious, and the constant pounding of the rain made him more so.

He sat before the fire, another cup of strong wine in his hand. The house was silent, for it was late and the servants abed. He tried to remember the two days he had spent at Lorancourt but could not grasp a clear picture. Too long he had had no reason for laughter, too many years he had been haunted by the words of a dying woman.

A flash of lightning lit the room briefly. It had been raining that night, too. She, the woman who was called his wife, had come home late, the little three-year-old Leah, her daughter, trying hard to keep pace with her mother.

He had been married to her for three years and had never once bedded her. At first he had been awed by her, green young boy that he was and she years older. She'd laughed and said Ranulf might love her when he was worthy of her, when he had become the strongest knight in all of England.

Men thought he trained now, but in those days he had rarely slept or eaten, so determined was he to please his wife. He had not protested when he knew a child was to be born, and later the little girl had been a joy to him, a balm against his evil, adulterous wife.

By the time he realized she slept with other men—many other men—he was too attached to Leah to think of sending the child's mother away.

Ranulf stood and walked closer to the fire, his head on his hands against the stone mantel. He had not thought she hated him enough to kill the little girl he'd grown to love.

When they'd returned home on that wet night, there had been a triumphant look on Isabel's face as she'd watched Ranulf lift the shivering child. He never left Leah's side during the three days that the fever consumed her. It was only after her death that he had heard of his wife's illness, that she too lay on her deathbed.

Her horrible dying words came to him. "I am glad she is dead, because I am dying also and I would take all from you that I could. I loved a man once, Leah's father, but he was poor and my father would not have him. You were there with all your riches and all your men, and you took away the one I loved. Do you think I could ever bear your black ugliness, that any woman could? No, Ranulf de Warbrooke, no woman will ever love aught about you but your fine furs and gold cups. Go now and get a priest and never let me need to look on your devil's blackness again."

He crumbled the silver cup he held, jewels flying about the room, blood-red wine covering his hand. He should not have betrothed himself again! There were too many likenesses between this marriage and the other—a father eager to have an earl for a son, a girl . . . He sat down again.

No, there were no similarities between Isabel and Lyonene. But what of this young girl? She had seemed to feel the same for him as he for her, yet he had never felt so for another. For what he knew, she could have treated many men before him with the same eagerness, the same desire.

The storm grew worse and his temper with it. It seemed that his every memory of his betrothed pointed to some falseness, some deceit.

Hodder found his master asleep in the solar the next morn, and when he was awakened, the blackness of his mood matched his coloring. The thin valet watched his lord grow steadily worse in temper each day, eating little, drinking over much, remaining unwashed, unshaven.

The rain continued, wetting everything, seeping into crevices and dulling moods. It was with joy that Corbet greeted the sun on the day they were to leave for Lorancourt. The seven men were ready and waiting in the courtyard for their master, but he did not come.

Hugo Fitz Waren, oldest of the Black Guard, sought him out.

"My lord, the sun is high. We must make haste to reach Lorancourt for the marriage."

"I do not go. I will send Sir William wagons of gold to repay him, but I do not marry again."

Hugo sat on a stool at Ranulf's feet and tried to control his gasp at the sight of his master. "So the great Black Lion fears a girl half his age and less than half his size? And what will you send the girl to compensate her for the loss of the husband she loves?"

"Do you not know the Earl of Malvoisin is too rich to ever be loved?"

"He is not too rich to wallow in his own pity. You may look at me so, but I do not fear you. I know of this other wife of yours."

"Do not speak of her to me."

"Until I am forcibly silenced, I will speak. You cannot blame all women for the faults of one."

"They are alike, these wives of mine."

"They are somewhat akin, I agree, both being baron's daughters. You are a man of honor and have not seen the girl for some time. When you see her again you will forget your fears." Hugo leaned closer and saw his master was no little drunk.

"Hodder! Throw some clothes on your master. We go to Lorancourt and return with a wife. Be sure his wedding garments are packed."

It was a tired, confused Ranulf who rode north to Lorancourt. His head ached and his stomach burned, but it was all better than thinking and hearing the voices that haunted him.

Chapter Five

Lyonene looked at the rays of the early sun as they slanted across the rush-covered floor. She had been ready for what seemed to be hours now. Her betrothed and the men from Malvoisin had arrived yester eve, and there were many baths to ready before they were presentable for the wedding. She had not seen Ranulf.

Meg rushed into the little room. "You look lovely, my lady."

Lyonene smiled at her, feeling as if her stomach might leave her at any moment. "What is that you carry?"

The girl gasped. "It is from his lordship, the great black one, your . . ."

"Let me see. It is for me, is it not?"

"Oh, yes, and lovely it is, too."

Both Melite and Lyonene gave her a harsh look for opening a gift meant for another. Meg handed the box to her young mistress carefully, with reverence.

It was long and thin and covered with sheets of ivory on all sides and top and bottom. Each flat area, six in all, was covered with scenes of courtly love, a man and woman together. "It is lovely," Lyonene gasped.

"No! Open it; the true gift is inside."

Astonished that there could be more than the beautiful box, Lyonene lifted the lid on its silver hinges. The lion belt gleamed and the emeralds sparkled. Melite took the box as her daughter studied the tiny lions and lionesses. "I have never seen such as this," she whispered. She held it to the light, feeling the thin gold wire, the smooth pearls and enamels. "Is it not lovely?"

Melite smiled at her daughter, glad to see such happiness. "It is indeed lovely. Now fasten it or we shall miss your wedding."

Lovingly, Lyonene put the belt about her waist and

let it fall just to the top of her hips. She caressed it and felt she could not take her eyes from it. "Did you send my husband my cups?"

"Aye, my lady."

The hand that William took as he led his daughter down the stairs was trembling. He helped her onto the pretty little mare. She was to ride sidesaddle for the auspicious occasion; the rest of her family and important castle retainers followed on foot. William led the horse the short distance to the castle chapel. The day was cold and clear, and the ceremony would be held outside the church door, marriage as yet considered a legal matter and not completely a holy one.

Lyonene smiled to see the two brothers side by side. They both wore the Malvoisin black and green. The younger brother was in green with a trim of black and a mantle lining of white fur; the older brother wore black with a thin green braid about the edges of his tabard, his mantle lined in the rich black sable. Her father helped her dismount.

The look Ranulf gave her almost frightened her. He was not at all as she remembered. He seemed to frown at her and not be glad to see her. There were circles under his eyes.

Father Hewitt asked who gave the woman in marriage and who took her. Her father relinquished her arm and she took Ranulf's, but he did not look at her. She wanted some reassurance that he was the same man she'd betrothed.

The priest's questions were answered and the doors to the church thrown open. She released her pent-up breath and pulled on Ranulf's arm until he looked down at her. He looked tired, but he was her Lion. She smiled up at him. "You ever forget when you are to kiss me," she whispered.

He gave her a faint smile and bent slightly toward her.

"It is too late now, for now Father Hewitt must bless our marriage."

As they knelt before the altar for the wedding mass, she was more aware of some change in her husband, a change not caused by mere lack of sleep. The long ceremony ended, and they were once again in the early morning sunlight.

Ranulf lifted Lyonene into the broad saddle of the Frisian and mounted behind her, his arms encircling her to hold the reins, while the wedding guests threw sundry grains at them and called, "Plenty! Plenty!"

"Ride with me now, away from here, to Malvoisin." His breath was soft in her ear.

She turned in his arms. "I ever beg you to kiss me and you refuse, yet now you wish to carry me off and neglect our guests."

The reins were dropped as he pulled Lyonene to him, crushing her against him. It was not a sweet kiss, but one from the longing, the doubt he still held.

She leaned against him, her arms yet about his neck.

"Go with me now," he urged.

"I cannot. I could not think only of myself."

"Do but think of me then."

She looked into his eyes and saw the pain there. "On the morrow all my days will be yours, but this one belongs to my parents. Come, there will be dancing and we have cooked for days."

"And will there be many men guests?"

"Of a surety, but women also. Ranulf, what is wrong? Has some misfortune befallen you? You do not smile at me."

"Do you not know the Black Lion never smiles?"

She could not help the shudder that passed through her. It was as if another man occupied the form of the man she had learned to care for. "Let us go now. I do not care for the others. Let us ride now to your island."

"Nay." His voice was cold. "You have chosen the others, so let it be. It is not for me to ever deny a wife."

She leaned back against him and felt him stiffen, and she was frightened by his action as much as by his words.

The old donjon of Lorancourt was decorated with serge bunting, the black and green of Malvoisin, and a great feast had been prepared. There was a large white swan, baked and dressed and then reassembled so that it looked almost alive, every feather repositioned perfectly. There was a roast boar stuffed with rabbits that were stuffed with partridges. Pies of every type covered the white tablecloths.

There were many who raised their cups and drank to the health of the young couple.

"Ranulf, you look tired. Are you so unhappy at this marriage?"

His eyes showed no humor. "I have yet to see what I have married."

She blinked to control the tears that came to her eyes. "The belt is most beautiful. I thank you for it."

He barely nodded to her and drank deeply of his wine.

Lyonene sat quietly, unaware of the noise or the many people around her. Where was the man she remembered, the laughing man who had teased her and held her? "Can you not tell me how I have displeased you so?"

He softened toward her somewhat and touched her cheek with the back of his fingers. "I am a vile-tempered man and 'tis no fault of yours. Mayhaps we could leave this for a while and find some place to be alone."

"No more of that!" a voice called to them. "You will have a lifetime of her, and for the rest of us, we must mourn her loss." It was Sir John de Bano, a near neighbor, a man Lyonene had known all her life.

She smiled up at him.

"Lady Lyonene must show us this blasted Irish game of trucks. William can never remember the rules and neither can I. If Giles had come, he could tell us, but he has not."

"You will come and play the game with us?" she asked Ranulf. "It is a most unusual game and requires great skill."

"Nay, I am not in a mood for games. Go with them since you seem to enjoy their company."

She started to tell Sir John she would not leave her husband when the older man pulled her arm, motioning for her to come.

"Do not fret," the man told her when they were alone. "I was just so at my wedding. Scared me half to death. I knew all my life had ended. I felt Maggie to be a stranger, although I had known her for years. Now come along and show us this cursed game and enjoy yourself! He will recover by himself."

"I hope you are right, but he seems a different person from the one I met."

"And he is. He is a husband now and not a carefree bachelor."

"If that is so, then I should have run away with him and not married him."

Sir John gaped at her. "You are like a daughter to me and I at times thought you were to be one, so I will do a father's duty and tell you not to speak so again but to Father Hewitt. Your words are a sin, and you must repent them."

She lowered her head so he could not see her eyes. "Yes, Sir John."

"Good. Now come along to the trucks table."

Lyonene could not enjoy the game or any of the merriment, for her eyes always strayed to the silent Ranulf, who joined in nothing and only sat and drank. Each time she tried to approach him, she was laughingly whisked away to a far side of the hall. Only Geoffrey talked to Ranulf, for the other guests were very aware of his status as one of the king's eleven earls.

The tables were set for supper and the free-flowing wine, ale, beer, verjuice, must and metheglins added to the already high spirits of the guests.

"You are enjoying yourself?" Ranulf made the question seem like an accusation.

"I will find a way to slip away to the garden. You will meet me there?"

"I could not deprive you of your beloved guests."

"Please, my Ranulf, I do not know the cause for your anger. I pray you to tell me that I may not displease you more."

More words were impossible, for just then the band that played from the balcony surrounding the Great Hall tripled its sound and the room filled with loosely clad dancing girls. The guests roared their approval, and the tables were quickly cleared so the guests could join the dancing.

The dances fit the temperament of the people, now filled with drink and food, for they were rowdy, energetic and romping. Lyonene found herself flung from the arms of one man to another. She was breathless from the fast-paced dances.

"So now you have sold yourself to be a countess." It was Giles, Sir John's son, and by the color of his eyes, he had been drinking heavily.

"Release me, Giles! How dare you come here in this condition!"

He held her wrists and pulled her into a dark window seat set in the six-foot thick stone walls. "You are the one who dares! What does your new husband say of us?"

"Of us?" She was incredulous. "There is naught to say of us. I have known you since we were children, 'tis all."

"What of our talk of marriage?"

"Our talk of marriage was about who we would marry, and when. We did not speak of marriage to each other."

"Did you not know I always meant my wife to be you?"

"Giles! You are hurting me!" He did not loosen his grip. "You have had overmuch to drink. Go home and sleep, but do not say more of these false things to me."

"False! You call my love for you false? What is it you love most about him, his gold or his earldom? Does it please you to be a countess?"

Although it hurt her toe through the soft leather slippers, she kicked his shin with all her might. The surprise made him relinquish his hold enough that she escaped him. She near ran to Ranulf's side.

"Do not say to me you grow tired of the attentions of so many guests who have fallen to your charms."

She turned on him and curled her upper lip in a snarl, then left him. She made her way to the door of the hall and went below to the cold winter garden. The coldness of a dark stone bench felt good, for her temper boiled in her.

Her wedding day! Meant to be a most happy occasion, it had turned into a disaster. A husband who had changed into a scowling stranger, a childhood friend turned to a drunken madman. She wished with all her heart she could ride away and leave them all.

"So, you cannot bear his presence even for one day. You have paid a high price for your silks and velvets."

"Do not come near me, Giles, What you talk of is nonsense. I have never loved you or ever thought to marry you. I marry Ranulf because he is a good and kind man, for no reasons of wealth."

"You say to me the Black Lion is good and kind when all of England knows of his character? Next you will tell me he is a laughing boy who loves you well."

"I tell you naught of my husband." She turned back to the castle, but he caught her wrist. The slap she placed on his cheek made his ears ring. She picked up her skirts and began to run, but his sobs stopped her. Giles had once been her friend and now she could not bear the terrible sounds of his pain. She turned back to him.

"Giles, do not take on so. I did not know of your feelings for me. You have ever been my friend."

He grabbed her arms, his head lightly resting on her shoulder. "I have always loved you, always."

She patted his arm lightly, but pressed him away.

"A most touching scene." They both turned to Ranulf, who stood a few feet from them, and the hate in his voice made her blood freeze.

An ugly laugh came from Giles. "So, you are the husband, the wondrous earl who can buy himself any bride he chooses. You may think you have won her, but she will always be mine. Do my words reach you? She is mine!"

Lyonene did not see Ranulf move, but Giles flew through the air to land with a heavy thud several feet away. He made no more sounds. The look on her husband's face was terrifying, and she could not move.

"They are here." A woman's voice spoke near them. "They could not keep from one another. We have come in time," she said, laughing.

Soon the cold courtyard was filled with laughing women, who surrounded Lyonene.

"She will be yours soon enough, Lord Ranulf."

Only Melite noticed her son-in-law's face. She placed a hand on his arm, but he did not seem to notice, so she followed her daughter.

Lyonene stood as stiffly as a doll while Lucy and her mother removed her wedding garments. Silently she stepped into the six-foot-square bed. Still she did not speak as they pulled the fine linen sheets just across her breasts and placed several feather pillows behind her head. Carefully they arranged her great masses of tawny locks about her head and shoulders.

"She's lovely, my little girl." The tears flowed down

Lucy's plump cheeks. "Oh, my lady, I hate to leave her like a lamb to be slaughtered."

"Hush, Lucy!" Melite commanded. "She is frightened enough as it is. Do not encourage her."

"And well she should be, too, for they say he's a spawn of the Devil's."

Melite drew herself up, her eyes stormy, and pointed her finger toward the door. Sobbing, Lucy left.

"Lyonene! I have told you what happens between a man and a woman. It is an act of love, and there is no need to fear it so."

Lyonene lifted her eyes to her mother's. "I believe he hates me."

"What has happened? What have you done?"

"I do not know; only that he is more than angry. Giles told him some lies and he hates me for them."

"Giles! I thought he might cause problems so I asked Sir John to come without his son. I did not even see him." She looked toward the door. "They come now. Be kind to him and patient; do not let your temper say things. I must go. You are a woman now and must solve your own life." She kissed her daughter's cheek and left.

Melite flattened herself against the stone stairwell as the Black Guard carried their lord up the stairs, his feet higher than his head.

"Now we learn what man we serve! If there is not a babe nine months hence, we go to serve Robert de Vere, who has six sons."

"A lion for his shield and a lioness for his bed. Could a man ask for more?"

As the men entered the room, they quieted, for the sight of Lady Lyonene sitting in the bed, the soft globes of her breasts barely hidden by the sheets, her hair a thick halo about her, made each of them wonder at all the women he had ever seen, for none came near to rivaling Lyonene. Ranulf wondered at their silence, but then he, too, drew in his breath sharply at the sight of her.

When he wore not a stitch, they lifted him and hastily tucked him into bed beside his wife. Corbet doused the candles until there remained only one at the foot of the bed. Sainneville, also of the Black Guard, stopped his fellow knight as he made to extinguish the last candle. He rolled his eyes toward the couple in the great bed. "Were you he, would you wish for a dark room when you rolled back that thin sheet?"

There was silence as each man considered this. They left the room, laughing.

"Ranulf," she began when they were alone. He jumped from the hand she placed on his bare arm.

"Do you reconcile yourself to a rich husband? Do you plan to bear my caress while you hunger for another? Or mayhaps you have known his well over the years."

"Giles is naught to me! Nor has he ever been."

"The boy did not seem to agree with your words. He could not have created his thoughts from air!"

"But he has. We played together as children and often talked of when we'd marry, but I always spoke of a man unknown. It does not seem to have been so with him."

"I understand more fully. The boy loved you, but you denied his love, for you were after richer game. You have had good hunting and have brought to table the Earl of Malvoisin. Shall I tell you of my estates, my knights, the number of gold plates I own?"

"Cease! I am innocent! He is but a boy filled with dreams and has meant naught to me. It is you, I . . ."

"Love?" he sneered. "You can say you love me? Come, let us hear the soft words. Mayhaps they will appease the Lion's wrath and make him sweet and malleable in your little hands again."

She turned an icy green stare toward him. "I do not lie and I cannot say I love you, or will ever love you."

With one powerful movement, he tore the sheet from her and involuntarily gasped at the sight of her, more lovely than he could have ever imagined.

Lyonene saw his face, and fear replaced her anger, for she saw the face of the Black Lion, the face that had forced grown men to their knees in surrender. She would not have believed he could have had such a terrible look, and now it turned toward her.

Instinctively, she attempted to cover herself when he tore the sheet away. One powerful hand cupped her breast, too hard. His mouth came down on hers and bruised her lips. One thigh forced its way between hers, and she fought him with her hands, but his strength was such that he did not seem to notice.

She clawed at the skin on his arms and back and was

satisfied by a grunt from him. She gasped for air as his lips moved to the corner of her mouth. His other leg parted hers, and she screamed at the first sharp stinging pain. The tears came to her eyes as he seemed to fill her until she would burst.

He lay still and she felt the pain subside a bit, but then he began to move again and the pain began anew. A minute passed and he moved slowly, deliberately, and somewhere within her she felt a spark of pleasure. His breath came hard and fast in her ear, and as he began to move quickly, the pain still inhibited her.

She felt him shudder against her and his body grow limp, his weight pressing down on her. Her arms clutched him close to her, their angry words forgotten for the moment.

He rolled from her to the other side of the bed and did not speak or look at her, his manner telling her that his anger was not at all appeased.

She moved to the far side of the bed, the tears silently flowing down her cheeks.

Chapter Six

Ranulf sat before the dying fire, his mantle slipping unnoticed from his bronzed shoulders, oblivious to the cold. He refilled his wine cup and drank deeply, his senses almost numb to the wine's effects. He had not expected the girl to be virgin. His red-rimmed eyes stared at the sputtering blaze. He had not expected many of the happenings of the last few weeks, and he was disgusted with himself now for his own lack of honor, his lack of control.

He drank more of the strong wine as he heard a broken breath from behind him. When he had realized her pureness, he had hesitated, tried to redeem his harshness, but he had done a poor job of it. The fear he had seen in her eyes, and, no less, the hatred of him, had renewed his rage at her.

When the boy had said she was his, that she had married for gold, Ranulf had been consumed with an anger of such violence that he could not see or think. It was good the women had taken his wife away, for he did not like to think what his actions could have been.

His wife! Aye, he was married to her, a bit of a girl, whose green eyes haunted him, followed his thoughts even now. She had proven herself pure in one way, but did she in truth desire that other man—that boy? Were the words he had spoken true or were hers? Time would answer him, a life of time together which stretched blankly, darkly ahead of them.

The weak winter sun lighted the room, making it seem colder, and Ranulf stood and dressed, his eyes careful not to stray to the sleeping girl in the bed.

When he was ready, he stood above her, staring at her tangle of hair, her tear-streaked cheeks. "It is time to wake, for we leave soon," he said quietly and watched as her eyes opened, wide, fearful, and he looked away.

Lyonene moved one leg and winced at the bruises on her body. So, this was the act of love, she thought, the act her mother had said was a joyous union. She had found little joy and much pain in the vile act. Her husband stared through the wooden shutters while she hastily began to dress. She was thankful he did not plan to repeat the act this morn.

She clenched her jaw and braced herself for more of his anger. "I am ready."

He turned to look at her and she was startled, for his face was void of all expression—empty, uncaring. "My men wait below, and we begin the journey soon. Your possessions are prepared for travel?"

She lifted her chin into the air. "Aye, they are." He lightly touched her waist, and she could not help her flinch at his touch. The memory of pain was too fresh, and she was relieved when he did not touch her again.

They walked side by side down the stone stairs, and Ranulf paused before greeting the people who eagerly awaited them. "Gethen Castle shall be your dower castle. It is worth in the neighbor of twelve knights' fees."

She did not understand why that should make her so angry, this offer of a gift of such magnitude, but it did. She could feel the anger in her rising. "I do not wish for your property," she said, eyes flashing and showing her growing rage.

"And I did not wish for . . ." He caught himself. "You will be paid for what you have lost," he said more gently.

Lyonene could but stare at him, anger pulling her scalp tight. Unbidden, curses from her father's men came to her mind. She had lost more than the little blood that splattered the sheets when she had agreed to marry this man. He seemed to think all the world was his for the buying. The rich were not just an accounting of wealth, but a breed apart from ordinary folk, believing their riches gave them control over others, or attributes that others did not have. Her lip curled. "You cannot pay me for what I have lost." She stepped ahead of him, going gratefully into the familiar hall of Lorancourt.

"My brother!" Geoffrey called. "It is good to see you have survived the night." His eyes twinkled but soon lost their shine as he studied the newlyweds, neither touching the other, each solemn and with eyes the hardness and

69

sharpness of splintered glass. So they had quarreled already, and he was sure it was Ranulf's fault.

He took Lyonene's arm and pulled her aside. "All is not well, my little sister?"

She did not answer, and for a moment he lost himself in the crystal-clear depths of those twin pools of green fire. God! But she was a beautiful woman, and for a moment all thought of his brother was lost. He shook his head slightly to clear the fog. "My brother will not be an easy man for husband, for I fear he is haunted by many ghosts."

She gave him a slight smile, but it did not warm her eyes. "I am his wife, so I do not think it of importance as to my happiness or lack of such. I'm sure," she added, giving a sidelong look to Ranulf as he stood talking to her mother, "that I will be well-rewarded for all that I do. Now you must excuse me as I must say good-bye to my mother."

Only then did Geoffrey see any sign of emotion in those eyes.

Lyonene sat astride the little chestnut mare, trying not to think of the tearful farewell or the doubtful future ahead of her. She rode ahead of the guard, beside her silent husband, his thoughts unreadable.

"Your ladyship, may I present the Black Guard?"

Lyonene looked into the smiling eyes of a dark knight, a short, stout man, handsome. Glad for the diversion, she turned in her saddle to look at the seven men.

"Herne, with the reddish beard, Roger, Gilbert, Sainneville, who tends to be a jester, Hugo Fitz Waren and Maularde."

Each knight bowed in the saddle to her; each looked at her pleasantly, and some of her spirit returned. "And your name, sir?"

"Corbet, at your service; no deed too small or insignificant to be performed in the continuing duty of serving his lord's fair lady."

Lyonene could not keep her laughter contained, and Hugo saw Ranulf's back stiffen. "Sainneville may tend toward a jester," she said with a smile, " but you, sir, are a flatterer of the first water."

"Madam, you must believe me. Until I saw the sparkle of those emerald eyes, I was as tongue-tied as my horse, no more words could I speak before a lady. I swear it was the sight of such superior beauty and the sound of your melodious laughter that has freed me from the bondage of my speechlessness." He bowed low. "I am your servant forever."

Astonished, Lyonene turned to the men behind her. "Is he always so?"

They smiled as a group. "Always," they chorused.

"Lord Ranulf," Sainneville called. "You should see to your wife, for it seems Corbet has begun to coat her with his honey and we fear his catching more than flies." There was laughter in his voice.

The laughter ceased when Ranulf turned a scowling countenance to them. Lyonene was immediately aware of the fear her husband instilled in his men, and she turned back to stare ahead.

They paused for dinner, and Ranulf helped her from her horse, his hands tight around her waist. "You are not overtired?"

"Nay." She managed a weak smile. "I am not, but it is good to stop. You also are well? Your eyes . . ." She looked away, shy and also confused at the memory of the previous night.

He did not answer her, but led her to a tree and left her there as he gave orders to his men and the serfs who served them. He returned to her side with a napkin of cold meats, bread and cheese. He opened it and offered her first choice. The air between them was heavy with tension.

"It is far to your island?" she asked at last.

"Aye, it is five days' ride, but we have the use of lodgings each night." His dark eyes stared at her, hard and unreadable.

She reached for another piece of cheese, and her hand touched his and she drew in her breath at the touch. Instantly, she found herself crushed against him, his face near hers, his breath soft, warm. He needed no words to say his thoughts, for his eyes told all. He wanted to believe her, so desperately wanted to believe in her again. The pain was there, a steel spike behind his eyes, an ancient wound, healed over and concealing the poison beneath. She saw his questioning, the silent pleas he gave her, and she answered him in the only way she knew how —by pulling his lips to hers.

The sweet music of the birds joined in the rolling waves of desire that covered her body. The smell of grass mingled with the soft, delicious feel of Ranulf's lips as he moved them against hers, so gently at first, searching, exploring, on a quest for treasure. His arms supported her, his strength in strong contrast to her growing weakness.

She was aware of naught but him, but some instinct made him draw back and look at her as his hand held the back of her head and his thumb caressed her temple. Reluctantly, she opened her eyes, rubbing her head against his palm—how small he made her feel!

"I would like to believe," he whispered, and when she parted her lips to speak, he closed them with one fingertip. "I will know. Words are too easy, given too freely. I fear those little hands of yours hold much that is mine."

She did not know why the simple words caused her to experience such a violent tremor of fear, as if she had been given foreknowledge of some evil to come.

They saw the fire even before they saw the towering walls of the donjon of Bedford Castle. Lyonene was startled at the instant reaction of the men, and she spurred her horse hard to keep up with the thundering black horses ahead of her.

The entire village seemed to be ablaze, and the screams of the serfs and the animals caught in the raging heat tore at her, freezing her momentarily.

"Get to the donjon," Ranulf bellowed at her, his furious face towering above her.

"I can help," she screamed as she saw a child tearing across the courtyard. She started to dismount. Ranulf's steel grip on her arm stopped her. The noise roared and the horrible light shadowed his face into a creature unknown, unearthly, a black devil.

"I have no time for this. Obey me!"

She could but do as he said and turned her nervous horse to the inner bailey, the gates locked in some semblance of protection against the threatening fires.

No one was about except the lone gateman, for all the castlefolk had fled to help fight the fire. She found the stables and paused for a moment, watching the flames leaping, licking above the low stone wall as they sought more fuel, more sacrifice to their gluttony. She turned to the horse to unsaddle it and then to look for a chapel to offer her prayers for the safety of the people.

"I knew he would not allow his precious little jewel so near such destruction," a voice hissed near her.

She whirled around. "Giles! What do you here?" She looked around her nervously. The roar of the fire seemed deafening even in the stable, or mayhaps it was her own fear and panic that threatened to drown her.

"You did not think me so callous a lover that I would concede the battle so easily? Surely you knew me better."

"I do not know you at all. Why have you followed me?"

"That is easy enough to answer." His eyes raked her body as she backed to a wooden stall wall and braced herself there. There was no escape from the boy, once a childhood friend, now a glazed-eyed madman. "I was willing to admit defeat had I been beaten fairly, but how could I compete with the riches of your earl? I placed you second only to the Holy Mother, yet all the while you schemed to betray me."

"Giles, you are wrong." She moved even closer to the wall, as if a door might appear by some magic. The heat increased in the stable, and a horse moved restlessly in fear.

"You do not need to be frightened of me. I do not plan to hurt you. Nay, I have learned a great deal from your ways. I have lost what I so eagerly sought." His eyes went to her breasts, outlined so clearly, heaving in her fright. "But as you sold yourself, so shall I sell what little of me is left. Do you remember this?"

He waved a piece of paper before her face, and she was puzzled.

"It is one of your letters."

"I wrote you no letters."

"Aye, that is true, but Lucy once let it be known that you often wrote stories and such. Remember your Gilbert?"

Lyonene was truly bewildered, for she remembered no Gilbert at Lorancourt. Then the seed of a memory stung her. She stared at the paper and the dirty hand that held it. "You started the fire," she whispered.

"Aye," he said and laughed. "I am glad you see how far I will go to get what I want." He stepped forward and ran a caressing hand down her shoulder. "When I am wealthy, I will buy several women such as you."

"Giles . . ." she began.

"Cease!" He pulled his arm back, and she turned her head in anticipation of the blow. He stepped back and watched her as he caressed the paper in his hand. "I have five of these letters, and it was an easy thing to change Gilbert to Giles. Shall I read to you what a fine letter of love you have written to me?"

She shook her head, knowing now what he held. She had always been a bit of a dreamer as a child and when her indulgent father had allowed his only child to learn to read, she had studied not rhetoric or even the gospels but, instead, a small book of chivalrous stories, secretly purchased for her in London by her mother. Lyonene had read the stories again and again and begged the jongleurs for more stories. Soon she had begun to create her own stories, sometimes writing them and often setting them to music, singing them to her parents on quiet evenings. But there was a time, not long ago, when she had created a lover for herself, a young man, a knight, strong and brave, and she had written letters to this imaginary man. She knew what the letters said, knew what fate Giles held for her in that hand that had already caused so much destruction. He held the end of her thoughts of happiness with her new husband; the delicate thread that held them together could not stand another blow.

"Lyonene, you are easy to read. Does he distrust you so much?"

"You have yet to say what you want from me." Her shoulders sank wearily.

"Gold."

"I have naught but my clothes. He has given me nothing."

"Do not play the fool." He looked outside the stable and saw that the flames no longer lifted above the stone wall. He returned his attention to Lyonene. "I see your husband succeeds in taming the fire more readily than I had thought. Listen to me now. He will be tired when he returns and will sleep heavily. When you are sure he will not wake, toss me a jewel from the pouch on his belt."

"Nay! I cannot."

"This letter is the least I can use for payment if I am

not obeyed. What think you of becoming a widow so soon?"

"You do not know what you say. Do you forget he is the Black Lion?"

"I see you do not forget," he sneered. "I am not as these lordly knights of the kings, as you well know. They are governed by rules that have no hold for me. How think you I came to be inside these castle walls? No one sees a serf. Think you he will notice when a serf walks past him? He will not know until he finds a blade between his ribs."

Lyonene could not speak, the terror climbing along her spine, crawling, creeping, a slimy, many-legged thing.

"Ah! I knew I guessed right. Now I must go. Do as I say and do not betray me."

He left her alone, her breath shallow, her body trembling, but trembling deep inside, as if her very bones shook. What to do, she screamed inside her throbbing head—what to do! She made her way inside the deserted donjon, trying to run but finding herself unable to do so. A dark corner showed a stool, and she sat on it, nearly falling against the cold, plastered wall.

Her first thought was, "What if . . ." If she had gone away with Ranulf after the marriage, if she had not left him at all the day of the wedding, if she had not gone outside . . . Useless, wasteful thoughts. She wished her mother were near her, that she was not so alone with a husband who had fallen on her in violence one night and this day had offered her a truce—one that promised now to be shattered.

Giles was insane, for surely no man could act as he had and have all his mind. She could see it now, see what she had so long ago overlooked. Melite had once said that Lyonene always took the runt of any litter and made it her own, be it pig, dog or, at times, people, and, as everyone laughed, she added that she usually succeeded in making the runt into a peacock.

Giles was proof of her failure. She remembered the first time she had seen him, hiding in a corner, afraid of his own shadow, awed by his two handsome older brothers, awed by the lovely seven-year-old girl named for a lioness and adored by all. Lyonene had hardly looked at the two boys, but instantly sought out the puny, colorless Giles, his thin legs weak from lack of exercise.

Sir John had protested when the two children, the same age but so incredibly different, had clasped hands and walked together outside into the April sunlight. Melite had stopped him, and they watched the children leave.

Lyonene and Giles had spent much time together for the next ten years. She'd once heard Giles's father protest that his son was no use at home anymore, and he'd stand and watch as the little girl would bully and badger the boy until Giles did what she wanted. That was what surprised Sir John the most, that she did not coax and plead as he would have thought. He himself had tried every way possible to get Giles to stay atop a horse, but he could not.

"What do you mean you cannot ride a horse? I can!" the eight-year-old girl had bragged. "Now get on and cease whining!" She had little patience with his excuses, and before Sir John's eyes, the boy blossomed into a healthy lad.

Lyonene tried to focus on the present, to pull away from the memories, once so sweet but now lowered to the filth of the London streets. She could not, of course, have missed seeing some of the little things that had bothered her at the time, but she had not wanted to see them, remember them. There was the kitten that had scratched him. She shuddered and watched as one of the dogs nosed about in the rushes for the lost bones.

More memories came to her: the lacerated flanks of a horse that had thrown Giles, the burned hand of a serf girl who had fallen into the fire when she tripped on Giles's outstretched foot.

She ground the heels of her hands into her eyes. But there was goodness, too, she thought, goodness that outweighed the few bad deeds. There was goodness enough that he was worth saving.

The sound of a horse's hoof on the stones outside made her stir herself to life. She rose slowly, like an old, tired woman, and looked toward the door. One of the Black Guard stood there; she could not remember his name.

"My lady, you are well?" his voice was quiet and deep, and she remembered him as the quiet one who hardly spoke—Maularde.

She nodded to him and somehow managed a sliver of a smile, but she saw he was not relieved or convinced of her peace. "I may help you?" The words struggled from her throat.

"Aye, we need food. Where are the castlewomen?"

She looked about her for the first time, amazed to see the solid walls, that life had gone on in the last hour. "I do not know. I will look to your food." She started to the door with the guardsman following.

The kitchen was away from the main dwellings to help prevent fires. The air was thick with smoke, but Lyonene did not notice, nor did she see the guardsman as he carefully scanned the deserted courtyard. She would have been interested in the way the man noted the lone serf, limping painfully, near the horses. The dark knight watched the man for a long while, thoughtfully, obviously considering some problem.

Lyonene found one of the kitchen girls wrapped about a young boy, and her own problems came back to her vividly. She had an abstracted air as she sent the boy to help with the fire and set the girl to preparing food. Soon baskets were ready to be taken to the hungry men. Maularde had found more of the castle servants and soon a sheep was turning over on the fireplace spit.

She helped Maularde load the wagons, and he did not protest when she climbed beside the driver as the guardsman mounted his horse. Lyonene wanted to occupy herself—anything to delay the time when she would need to make a decision as to Giles's words.

Over half the village was gone, and since the wall had been allowed to decay in places, she saw more flames outside, heading toward the game forest. That was where she heard Ranulf's voice, loud, giving orders that were not meant to be delayed. Lyonene nudged the driver and he directed the horses toward the sound.

"What do you do here?" Ranulf demanded. "Get back to the donjon."

"But what of the injured? Can I not help?" She was horrified at his appearance; only the whites of his eyes were not covered with the black filth.

"Nay, the monks have come."

She saw then the coarse brown robes, the tonsured heads, as the men quietly helped the burned people. She silently nodded at Ranulf and then looked ahead as the driver turned the horses and returned to the inner bailey.

Ranulf paused from his exhausting labors for a moment and stared after her, not sure of his thoughts, but the urgency of the fire gave him little time for else.

Lyonene went back to the kitchen to reassure herself that all there were working. The long day's travel, the emotional upheaval began to tell on her and she limply dragged herself into the stone tower.

"You have thought on my words?" The boy seemed to appear from nowhere.

"Giles, you cannot ask this of me. We were friends once. How can you turn against me so?"

The young man stepped from the shadows, his blue eyes frenzied, penetrating. "It is you who have turned from me. I was naught before you made yourself into some heathen deity and decided my life for me." He stepped close to her, and his expression changed to the one she had known for many years. "Remember you the brown mare, the one that tossed you into the water? Had I not been there . . ."

"Do not remind me of those far-away days." She turned abruptly toward the door, but Giles's hand caught her wrist.

"I know you too well. So now you will call a guard against me? Do not think I am fool enough to have come alone. My capture, my death, will grant you naught but riddance of me. Did you see the men near your husband? Know you which are my men, which will kill him if I am harmed?"

"I do not believe you."

His eyes were feverish, burning. "You are prepared to risk my honesty? Do you know me to be a liar? Lyonene," he murmured, touching a lock of her hair but then frowning when she drew back, "what can a jewel or two mean to such as him? You have seen his clothes are hemmed with jewels."

"Leave me!"

"Aye, I will leave you, but beware all who go near him. The thought of gold will tempt even the most faithful knight." He smiled when he saw she had his meaning, his hint that even one of the Black Guard could have a hand in his treachery. "This night, while he sleeps, I will wait for you beneath the window. If you are not there, then on the morrow he will have the letter or a knife in his stomach." The boy shrugged. "I do not know which yet, but I do not think you want either." Then he was gone.

Lyonene slowly made her way to the largest bed-chamber and began to wash and ready herself for bed. She must trust Ranulf, she must tell him of Giles's plan. She thought of that long-ago day of happiness she had spent with Ranulf, when she had called him her Lion; that man would understand, would believe her. If only Giles had not been drunk and said those things to Ranulf on her wedding night. No, she did not want a repeat of that rage.

As she pulled her green velvet robe from one of the bags that had been hastily thrown into the room, a small pouch fell from the bag. It was Ranulf's, somehow mixed in with her clothes, and she knew too well what jewels it contained.

"No!" she said aloud and pushed it back into the bag. She could not begin her marriage with such lies and deceit. She clutched her hands again and again, their coldness making her skin white, her wedding ring loose. She absently toyed with the gold, felt the two clasped hands worked in the metal.

It was late when she heard the noise in the courtyard, the dogs barking, the sounds of water being poured, splashing. She knew they had returned and were washing the black from their bodies at the well. She sat very still, her heart pounding.

A torch flickered in the hallway and outlined Ranulf's dark form in the doorway, his broad shoulders seeming to droop from tiredness He walked to the fire, holding his hands before it, and she could see his hair was damp. He turned to her so quickly that she cried out, a weak little sound as she saw his hand go to his sword.

"You remain awake?" He was too tired to show an emotion, either glad or otherwise. "It is near dawn. You should have slept."

"I . . . I wished to speak to you."

Ranulf sank to a stool by the fire, his head on his hands. What complaint did she have now, he wondered. He could not even think. All he saw was the burned flesh, the open mouths with their silent cries for water, the bones charred. "Can it not wait till the morrow? I am more than weary."

"Aye, I guess it can." She could not add to his burden;

there was no jewel worth that. She rose and stood by him, touching a damp lock of the black hair gently, timidly, not knowing how he would react.

He took her hand and rubbed it against his jaw, the spiky whiskers near removing the skin from her hand. "I am grateful," he said quietly, and she felt tears coming to her eyes.

As he rose and went to the bed, she knew what she must do—rid herself of Giles. The bond between Ranulf and her was too fragile yet, and a letter saying such things as she had written would shatter that bond too easily.

She heard the ropes creak as Ranulf stepped into bed. "Come to bed," he said in low voice, heavy with sleep.

"Aye, in a moment. I but bank the fire." As she had thought, she heard the heavy, steady rhythm of sleep almost instantly. Quickly, she found the pouch and a smooth, hard stone and walked silently to the shuttered window. She had only to move one slat and drop the jewel below. Her hands shook badly and she prayed she did the right thing. There was a slight noise below as she released the stone and she turned quickly to the sleeping Ranulf, but his breathing never changed.

Still trembling, she removed her robe and climbed into the big bed beside her husband. She lay frozen, rigid, so incredibly aware of the unfamiliar nearness of him. He rolled toward her and one arm moved out and landed heavily across her throat. Gasping, she lifted the weight as best she could, only to find that his hand had begun caressing her. His eyes were still closed, but his hand seemed to search her nude body as if in understanding. Without a word he pulled her beneath him, the weight of him, the remembered pain of the night before frightening her, tightening every muscle in her body.

His thigh forced her legs apart, and she felt hot tears gathering, then the first pains as he thrust himself upon her. At least it was over more quickly this time, but it was still a while before she slept, the hair at her temples wet from many tears.

Ranulf woke first the next morn, as he always did, just before the sun fully rose. Lyonene lay beside him, turned slightly on her side, facing him. His first thought was that 'twere it possible, she looked even younger, even prettier in her sleep. He hadn't had any time with her in their two days of marriage. That boy's words haunted him, words so like his first wife's. He wanted so badly to believe in the girl beside him, that she did not try to deceive him, was not false with him. He did not ask for love. No? What then did he want? It seemed that women either feared him as the Black Lion or desired him for his riches. He remembered his father saying once that his eldest son could no more kill a man than become king's champion in the joust. Ranulf wondered how his father would have reacted to that son, who had trained for the church, as he was today —feared by many, hated by a few, but little loved. A woman had changed all that.

Lyonene stirred in her sleep, bringing him back to the present. He was walking into battle again, unarmed, unclothed. What wounds he received this time he was not sure would heal. He touched her cheek, close to the tiny ear that curled in an intricate, mysterious way. Her eyes flew open instantly and the fear he saw there startled him.

Lyonene saw the soft curve of his lips, the gentle expression in his eyes and knew his thoughts. She was not ready yet for more of the painful lovemaking. She rolled from the bed and quickly donned her robe, kneeling before the fire, nervously jabbing at the coals with the iron poker. What if he called her back to bed? He was her husband and she could refuse him naught.

Ranulf turned on his back and frowned up at the dusty bedhangings. She had a right to fear him; he had used her hurtfully that first night. It was a shame that such should have been her introduction to lovemaking, but he would replace those memories tonight at Aylesbury Castle, when there would be time to show her the art.

He turned on his side, head propped on his hand. He was enjoying her nervous movements, her obvious avoidance of him. On the morrow he would ask her how she felt about the nights after the one he now planned for her.

"You will rise soon?" she asked, her voice a bit shaky.

Ranulf chuckled at some jest she did not share. "Aye, very soon." He watched her push some clothes into a bag and saw her hastily stuff a brown leather pouch back into place. He frowned again at some memory, half-forgotten, that the pouch stirred. He seemed to see a shadowy figure, but could not grasp the whole picture. When Lyonene went to the window, he recalled the wispy memory. But surely it was a dream.

"You said you wished to speak to me last night. May I know your thoughts now?" He tried to keep his voice neutral, far different from what he felt inside. He tried to detach himself as he watched her clenched hands, saw she would not meet his eyes.

"It was naught. I only . . . Ranulf!" She ran to the bed and he pulled her into his arms.

She was shaking, and he held her tightly, wondering at the delicacy of her body, fearful of hurting her. Something had upset her greatly. He lifted her chin and marked that her eyes were dry. "What is it? What troubles you?"

"I . . . I wish you to be careful, to be on guard." A lump closed her throat.

"It is the fire that has made you fearful of my safety?"

"Aye . . . Nay. It is else."

"Then tell me. I will not harm you for a few words."

"It is Giles, he . . ."

"You dare to speak his name to me!" He pushed her from him roughly. "Be you glad I did not kill your little friend. Had I found him to be your lover, to have gone where you now shun me, I would have killed him and you mayhaps also. You should be grateful I have tried to believe your words over his. Now call that maid of yours and dress, for we leave soon."

He hastily threw aside the bedclothes and began to pull on his own clothes. Two days wed and she had caused him more anger than he had ever known—deep anger, going to the core of him, hurting more than his ax wounds, his anger at the Welsh during the years of war or the Saracens on Crusade. This girl came closer to him than aught else ever had. Only Isabel . . . He stopped his thoughts, regretful of any memory of her.

"Here, Lyonene, come here." She stood before him, gathering her courage. "I fear I cannot abide your talk of another man." It cost him some to say even this much. "I am recovered now and you may speak your mind."

If the mere mention of Giles's name caused such rage, how would he react to five letters addressed to another man? Was she so childish as to think he would listen to reason before tearing her to pieces? He might regret his action later, but she would not risk it now.

"There is naught to say," she whispered and turned away.

Ranulf also turned away, for he knew she lied. He left the chamber without a further word to her. In the courtyard, he did not hear Maularde's quiet voice at first. He was using all the control he could muster to believe in her, to try and recapture those first two days together of happiness. How could two people so attuned to one another have become so estranged?

"Lord Ranulf," Maularde's soft voice insisted. "I have news that you need to know."

Ranulf listened intently, incredulouly, to his guardsman, his scowl deepening with each word, each revelation. "I will watch for him," Ranulf concluded.

"And my lady?"

"She is mine and must be my . . . responsibility." Burden, he had almost said.

Chapter Seven

Lyonene watched Lucy climb into the wagon, too old and too fat now to ride a horse, and then turned to her own place beside her husband. Ranulf stared at her a moment, his black eyes intense, searching her face, before lifting her to her horse.

They rode in silence, and several times Lyonene wanted desperately to tell Ranulf of Giles, but each time, the solemness, even the sheer size of him, stopped her.

"We will stop early for dinner. The fire has taken much strength, and there is no rush."

He helped her from her horse, left her a moment to tend to the people in his charge and then returned. "You would walk with me?" He held his arm for her.

Happily, she took it, and he led her into the woods, within sound of the others, but out of sight. "I fear I make a poor husband, as my brother has warned me. Here, let us sit and talk a while."

The cold ground seemed to seep through her, and she shivered.

"You are cold." He spread his mantle and pulled her near him, his arms and cloak surrounding her, his heart beating against her cheek.

"You will be glad to be home again, my lord?" she asked.

Ranulf could not suppress a small frown, so quickly had she gone from "Lion" to "my lord." "Aye, the Welsh clime is too harsh since I have grown used to the softness of my isle."

"Tell me of it."

He described with pleasure the island, the meadows, the woods, the nearness to the sea.

"You live there alone with just your men? No family?"

"My parents died when I was very young." He lifted a

curl of her hair from his leg, rubbing it between his fingers. "It seems we know little of each other and must struggle for words, yet once we had not enough time to say all there was."

Lyonene blinked back tears, for she felt the same way. She turned her face to his and smiled at him slightly. He touched his lips to hers, and she lost herself to his demanding kiss. It was as if he sought to draw the essence of her soul from her with that kiss. Yet her growing passion was replaced by something more, something higher than mere earthly passion. The tears rolled down her cheeks, hot, wrenching tears.

"Tell me." Ranulf drew back from her. "What plagues you so?"

"I will tell you," came a quiet voice from the trees. Giles stepped into view. "Do you not wonder that a bride of three days should cry when her husband kisses her? You will draw sword with me, Lord Ranulf, and we will see who wins this woman."

"You are a boy. I cannot fight with you. My wife has told me of you and I trust her."

Lyonene could see the pain on Ranulf's face as he said these words.

"Then mayhaps these will persuade you of the truth of my words." He tossed a leather pouch at Ranulf's feet.

"Nay!" Lyonene screamed and made a lunge for the letters, but Ranulf had them first.

Slowly, he withdrew one, then the others, his face losing color, expression, emotion. When he had finished, he turned to his wife. Lyonene felt she could have handled rage, violence, any emotion but the look of total bewilderment and agony that flashed across Ranulf's eyes.

"You wrote these letters?" he asked quietly.

"They were not written to Giles, I swear it. They were . . ."

"To another?" He brushed her hand from his arm and looked across to the young man before him. "She is my wife now, for all her past deeds, and I will not kill boys."

"You bastard! You are so good, so pure you cannot dirty your sword with a commoner, but there is one sword you have bloodied when you wielded it against a baron's daughter. Think you she loved you at first sight or mayhaps it was the silver on your mail? We planned all this, did you not guess? Already she has ransacked your goods and tossed me a jewel." He flung the stone at Ranulf's feet.

When Ranulf looked from the ruby to his wife's terrified face, she saw then the rage there, the hatred in his eyes. "Get you from me. I must kill this boy for you. Will you rejoice when he is dead? Will you seek another to replace him soon?"

"Ranulf! You must hear me out. He lies! The letters were written to a man unknown, a girl's dreams. He said he would kill you if I did not give him the jewel."

"I am to believe you think this boy threatened my life? That you stole from me to save me from this child? Nay, woman, I believed you once, but I can no more. Now get you from me." He nodded his head to someone behind her, and one of the guardsmen grasped her arm and pulled her from the clearing. "Ranulf, please!" she cried.

"It is too late for your pleas. Take her from here that she does not see the horror she has wrought."

Lyonene turned then and left, stopping by the horses when she heard the first clank of steel against steel. The battle did not actually take very long, but to Lyonene it seemed hours, and each clash, each sound, made her heart leap in agony.

He stood before her and she looked into those cold, hard eyes. "See you the blood you have spilled this day. A boy who will never grow to be a man because of you."

He swung into the saddle of his horse, leaving his wife to be helped by Hugo Fitz Waren. She could look at none of the men, knowing they all must hate her, and so she was surprised when she felt a hand on her knee, a light touch, quickly gone, but reassuring. She turned to the others of the Black Guard. One by one, the men solemnly nodded to her, telling her they believed her words, for in truth it had been easy to see the boy was not of his right mind.

Only once on that long journey to Aylesbury Castle did Lyonene attempt to speak to her husband, and the black hate she saw there soon made her hold her tongue.

"Your lordship," Pask, the steward of Aylesbury Castle, warmly greeted Ranulf. "We are proud that you honor us again with your presence. The cook has worked for days preparing your meal, and it promises to be a meal worthy of you and your men. Ah, you bring a lady?"

"She is my wife." Ranulf's tone caused the small man's eyebrows to lift. "Put her things in the room across from Edward's; I will take his."

Lyonene was too tired to care where she slept. She was plagued by memories of a childhood friend, now dead, and a husband who hated her. Lucy dropped on the narrow bed.

"This has been an evil day. Sir John's boy always was a bit odd. It was only you who gave of your time to him. I always knew . . ."

"Please, Lucy, could we not speak of it again? I am tired and wish to rest."

"Aye, Lady Lyonene," she said as she helped her young mistress to dress. "Shall I send a tray to you?"

"No, I am not sure I shall ever eat again. I would just like to sleep, to lose myself in sleep."

Lucy tiptoed from the room.

Ranulf paced, ignoring the tray of food that stood before him. He had been a fool to marry again and certainly to marry for any reason but advancement. The Castilian princess would not have caused him problems such as he had now.

Lyonene—emerald-eyed beauty with tawny hair and thick, dark lashes—she was his wife now, and look at the hell he had been through for three days. Maularde had told him of Giles's presence, and he had given her every chance to explain, to be honest with him, and yet she had not. He had tried not to kill the boy, but he had been mad, insane as he attacked. Ranulf rubbed his hand across his eyes as if to erase the memory. He knew too well what it was like to be young and so in love.

Love? What did he know of love now? This girl had led him easily, yet now that she had her marriage to him she had changed. She was no longer eager for him, nor did she seem happy, as she once had at her father's house. All seemed to point to a trick, to the truth in the boy's words.

Too many thoughts overlapped. Frustrated, he removed his clothes and walked to the bed, only to stare at the empty coldness of it, puzzled for a moment. Without dressing, he stepped into the cold hall and pushed open the door to Lyonene's chamber. She did not waken until she felt herself roughly lifted, the bedclothes twisted about her sleepy body.

Ranulf's dark eyes were even darker in the dim light, his face shadowed by a day's growth of his heavy black whiskers. He did not look at her as he silently carried her, and she longed for his glance, for the sound of his voice. He threw her onto the feather mattress of the wide bed. Only then did she notice his nudity, the sight of him riveting her eyes, making her heart beat faster as he looked at her, her leg and hip exposed by the twisted covers.

"Whatever else you are, you are my wife, and you will not rid me from your bed." He straightened the covers and climbed beneath them, pulling her to him.

"Ranulf . . ." she began.

"I do not wish to speak of this day, not now or ever again. The boy is dead now and whether his words be false or no, I will know."

"How will you know? I will tell you . . ."

"Nay, I wish for only one thing from your lips now." His hand caressed her stomach, and he felt her tense and hold herself rigid against him. Mayhaps she thinks of the boy, he thought as he fiercely pulled her to him, causing her to gasp in pain as his hand held her chin and pulled her mouth to his. "You think of him now? You wish you had him near you?"

"Nay, I do not," she gasped, trying to pull away from him. "Please do not hurt me more. I will lie still. It hurts less so."

He dropped his hand and moved away to stare at her thoughtfully. "Last night, after the fire, did I . . . hurt you again?"

She nodded her head.

"Damn, but you try me sorely! I have known you but weeks, yet you have upset my whole life, now as well as the past. This morn I read a letter writ by you, mayhaps to a boy I needs must kill. I have no proof of your innocence; in truth all seems to point to your guilt. The first day I met you, you threw yourself at me with such force I was near blinded, and I have no proof you have not treated other men so. Now I am wed to you for three days and I have been driven to rape you twice and kill a boy for you. Yet here you lie in a tangle of hair and naught else and all I wish to do is make love to you."

Lyonene blinked up at him, torn between wishing he would kiss her and wanting to avoid what she knew the kissing would lead to.

He pulled her close to him, and she buried her face in the thick mat of hair on his chest, rubbing her cheek against the softness. "I do not know of your loyalty yet," he said, "whether you be an innocent or worse than Eve, but I know I desire you more than any other woman I have ever seen. Here, do not pull away. I will hurt you no more. I fear I have used you badly in my clumsy attempts, but I will try to redeem the time we have lost."

He lifted her mouth to meet his and softly, gently, touched her lips, taking a long, slow time before building the pressure on the sensitive flesh. He moved his lips, raking his teeth on her lower lip before drinking of the sweet honey of her mouth.

Lyonene felt herself go liquid at his now gentle touch, at the feel of his skin, the size of him. He rolled her on her back, and she stiffened against the pain she knew came next, regretting the end of the sweet moments of his kisses. But he did not seem to notice her movements and began to trail hot kisses from the corner of her mouth to her ear, tasting her earlobe with the tip of his tongue.

His lips moved down her neck, causing her to arch her neck, to surrender herself to him more fully. One hand moved along her hip, her waist, strong fingers on her ribs; then he touched her breast and she almost protested, so startled was she, but the sensation his hand sent along her body was not to be thwarted. His mouth traveled slowly down her body, igniting exquisite new fires.

She felt herself leaving her body, her reason fleeing, and all that remained was a new, unfulfilled desire, a desire for something unknown. He seemed to have a hundred hands, a thousand lips, all seeking, touching and filling her mind till she was only sensation, nothing else. Frantically, she put her hands into his hair, the thick, soft mass curling about her fingers—her sensitive, vibrating fingertips.

"Lioness, sweet Lioness," he murmured, the deep rich tones adding to her wildness, the tremors of violence that shook her body. He came to her and there was no fear, no pain, only the beginning of the end of a need that consumed and blinded her.

She did not need to follow his example, but the desire that overpowered her took hold and she more than met his passion. At last she cried out as she sank her nails into his back and arched to meet him. Slowly, receding waves shook her and she gradually relaxed and fell back on the white linen sheets. As Ranulf moved to roll from her, she pulled him back, not able to release him yet, exulting in the heaviness of him, the way his dark skin covered her body, damp, smelling strongly of earthy, masculine sweat.

He rubbed his damp face in her neck, playfully, whiskers caressing, and moved to one side of her so he could see her face in the light from the thick candle by the bedside. He smoothed back a damp strand of hair from her temple.

"I pleased you?" she whispered.

He gave her a startled look and seemed amused by her question. "If you but knew . . ." he began and then stopped. "Aye, you pleased me exceedingly well and I fear you have taken all my strength," he added as he saw her eyelids flicker in weariness. She was asleep almost before he finished speaking. In spite of his satiety, his tiredness, he watched her for a moment, curled against him, looking even younger than her few years. His passion was spent, and he remembered the day. He rolled from her and slept, his dreams troubled.

In spite of the passion of the night, the morrow brought no respite from the pain between Ranulf and Lyonene. Giles's death hung over them, as did the boy's accusations. They crossed the ferry onto the Isle of Malvoisin, and for awhile Lyonene's thoughts were overcome by the beauty and massive strength of the enormous castle complex. Black Hall was a stone house, furnished as she had never seen before, with the new tapestries Queen Eleanora had brought from Castile and windows covered with leaded panes of glass. She saw Ranulf's pride in his house, which she would have shared if he had but given her some cause to feel that she was wanted, that he did not always regret his marriage to a baron's daughter.

In her loneliness, for Ranulf was nearly always gone,

she sought to busy herself in the intricate workings of the castle.

"What is this you do while I am gone?" he demanded one evening as he threw his wet tabard to Hodder. "William de Bec says you interfere with the running of my castle."

Her eyes flashed at him.

"All of Malvoisin has been under my steward's care for many years. He is a freeman and I would give him no cause for complaint."

Lyonene straightened her back, meeting the anger in his black eyes. "Excuse my impertinence, my lord, I but wished to be useful. Pray tell what I am to do here each day if I cannot have a hand in ordering what is reputed to be my own home. I am not accustomed to being idle."

His face was cold, the expression ungiving. "Mayhaps William can find some gold for you to count. You have earned that pleasure." His eyes looked meaningfully to the bed where they shared their only moments of happiness.

Lyonene stared at him wildly, suddenly feeling dirty and despicable. She ran from the room, finding the hall blocked by Lucy's massive form. She turned and ran to a small door that led to the tower in the back of Black Hall. The darkness inside the tower was absolute and she unseeingly made her way up the cold stairs. The room at the top was filled with light, blinding her. She touched her cheek and realized then how wet her face was.

"My child," a man's voice said. "Come and sit here." A fat man, tonsured, in monk's garb, put his arm about her shoulders. He led her to a crude wooden chair by a charcoal brazier. "Sit down and drink this." He handed her a pewter flagon of dark wine. "I am Brother Jonathan," he said to Lyonene's silent form. "And you are the lovely Lady Lyonene, Lord Ranulf's bride."

The tears started afresh.

"Come now," he said. "Married not a month and already such a quarrel?"

Lyonene gulped the wine, choking but needing the warmth.

Brother Jonathan patted her arm. "Tell me of it. I am a good listener."

"I cannot," she managed to gasp.

He was quiet a moment and then said quietly, "I have heard that yours was a love match, that you loved one another from your first sight."

Lyonene tried hard to remember those first two days with Ranulf. "Aye," she whispered, staring at the fire, thinking of the time he had held the longbow for her.

"But something has happened since then? Something has caused you to lose sight of your love?"

"Aye, it has."

Brother Jonathan smiled and wondered what slight incident could have caused the break. Probably Ranulf's jealousy, he thought. Ever since his first wife he could not abide anyone touching what was his, be it his horse, his home, his men or, he imagined, his woman. "I have known Lord Ranulf since he was a boy and he has reason to . . . to be somewhat intolerant. Tell me, do you still love him? You cannot have stopped so soon, not if it were a true love."

Lyonene blinked her blurred eyes. "I . . . do not know. He has changed so. When I met him he smiled and laughed with me, now he does but glower and at times he frightens me. I have tried to explain about Giles but he does not listen."

So! Jonathan thought, it was another man, probably someone who dared to look upon Ranulf's wife. He smiled patiently. "Lord Ranulf is not a cruel man, but he sometimes cannot reason about some things. He is a gentle man under his harshness. Did you not once see that?"

"Yes." She began to smile and some of the memory of Ranulf came back more clearly, blocking the time after their wedding night.

"Good, then." The monk smiled. "It is up to you."

"Me? But how may I change him? I can do naught that pleases him."

Jonathan blinked. That is not what he'd heard from the servants' gossip. "You must prove to him that you love him. You must do whatever you can to prove to him that you care for him."

"Aye," Lyonene whispered. "I must show him." She set the empty mug down. "I will prove to him that I am not as he thinks. Somehow I will find a way. Thank you, Brother Jonathan."

She left the room, and the monk sat blinking for a moment before refilling his cup and taking her chair. Ah, the young, such tiny problems they had in the world. He wondered again what had caused Lyonene's distress. Probably a spat over a new dress, or mayhaps not that serious.

Ranulf did not return to Black Hall that night, and Lyonene lay quietly in the big bed, staring upward, unseeing. She felt that it had all been her fault, that her husband hated her for something that she had done. She thought of Brother Jonathan's words and she made a vow that someday she would prove to Ranulf that her love for him was true, that she loved no man but him.

In the morning she went to the south of the isle to see to the welfare of the serfs there. Sir Bradford, one of the youngest garrison knights, joined her for the ride back to the castle.

"I think I feel a touch of spring in the air," he said. "Or mayhaps it is just my hearty wishes that make it feel so."

She laughed. "I, too, grow weary of this cold. On the morrow I shall follow the river and look for signs of early crocus."

They both looked up to see Ranulf thundering down on them, his face black with rage. With one arm he pulled Sir Bradford from his horse and then leaped from the Frisian's back to stand above the boy, hand on sword hilt.

Lyonene jumped from her own horse's back and threw herself between them. "What is this you do?" she demanded. "Why do you draw sword against this boy?"

"That, I think, you can more easily answer than I. Did you think you could meet so that I would not know? I have warned you, but you have ever defied me, and now you have gone too far."

She stood straight before him, refusing to bow to him. "What you say makes no sense. The boy did but ride by me this day and we talked, no more. It is you with your temper that has made it more."

"Ah!" he said with a deathly coldness. "You have given me no reason to doubt you? On our wedding night you meet another boy, one I must later kill. You steal from me to pay your lover and now you start afresh with this boy. Do you wish to see his blood also? Does your greed include his death as well as his seed?"

Anger near blinded her. "You are the only man I have allowed to touch me, and each day I regret that anew. Would that I had gone away with Giles or anyone, better to have taken my own life before I said vows to one of your vile nature."

Ranulf's hand swung and hit her across the mouth, cutting her lip and sending her sprawling. "Then we will undo what we have done. On the morrow I travel to Wales and when I return, do not let me find you here." He mounted his horse and rode away.

Lyonene lay still a while, blood trickling from her torn and bruised mouth. She waved away Sir Bradford, and the boy left her alone. Tears came first, tears of despair and desolation. She had not meant to say what she did, but always her temper made her words uncontrollable. So what now of her noble vows to prove her love? Her husband had ordered her away from him, and there would be no more opportunities to prove aught to him.

"Ranulf," she cried into the grass, feeling the sobs tear through her. On the morrow he left for Wales and it was over between them.

Suddenly she sat up and stared through her tears into the distance. Was she named for a lioness for naught? Had she no more courage than a serf? She would not give up so easily as this.

Her head spun with ideas. If he traveled to Wales, he would not travel alone. There would be women to clean and cook for the men.

She wiped her tears away and began to smile secretly. He would not refuse her again once his anger was gone. She knew that if she had more time, she could make amends for what had passed. She knew she could find some way to prove her love for him.

Confident again, with a purpose in mind, she rode back to Black Hall. There were many things to do before the morrow.

Chapter Eight

The wagons stood ready in the outer bailey, and Lyonene pulled the russet cloak closer about her, the hood hiding her downturned face. It had taken quite a bit of preparation to execute this plan and she wasn't going to ruin it through a chance recognition by someone in the courtyard. Her new maid, Kate, had been willing enough to follow her mistress's plan, although Lyonene had felt her staring once with a strange expression on her face. The girl was to pretend that Lyonene had an illness and that no one was to disturb her except Kate. By the time the deception was discovered, Lyonene might well be in Wales.

She stamped her feet and scratched at the coarse wool of her serf's garb; it was cold in the early morning half-light. Lyonene thought again of what she was doing, wondering at Ranulf's reaction when she revealed herself to him. He had said he did not want to see her again and she dared much in this masquerade. She grimaced at her lack of clothing other than the rough serf's wool. But try as she might, she could find no way to conceal a thick bundle of fur-lined garments in the wagons, for they were checked constantly by several men and the discovery of such a bundle would expose her and ruin her plan.

"You, girl!"

Lyonene looked to see a woman calling her. She ducked her head and fought the quick anger that threatened a rebellion at this coarse woman's commands.

"Do not stand there all day! Come and help me with these barrels!"

Lyonene followed the woman into the inner bailey, her heart pounding, for before her stood the entire Black Guard mounted on their great steeds, and in their midst stood the riderless Frisian. Lyonene looked quickly at the beautiful black horse, the mane full and lush, the thick tail falling all the way to the ground, and the lovely hair that flowed from knee to hoof now moving gently as he lifted one great hoof in impatience to be gone. He was a fitting horse for such a master as the Black Lion.

Lyonene held the little wooden barrels, one under each arm, and began to follow the woman to the outer bailey, when she paused abruptly. Lyonene followed her eyes. Ranulf walked to his horse, and she felt a surge of pride as all eyes in the courtyard flew to him and his men straightened in their saddles, obviously proud of their master.

He swung one great leg across the Frisian's broad back and paused as he stared at one of the windows in the second floor of the Black Hall. Lyonene gasped as she realized it was the window to her little bedchamber.

"May the tortures of hell descend upon that woman!" the woman beside Lyonene hissed between her teeth.

Lyonene looked at her for the first time. She was older, near as old as her mother, but the bones in her face showed that once she had been handsome. In fact, even now her eyes riveted Lyonene's, for they were very unusual—narrow, slanted, almond-shaped and exceptionally beautiful. She narrowed them now as she stared ahead to the object of Ranulf's gaze, and Lyonene was astonished at the malevolence they contained.

"It is said that she does not care for my Ranulf."

A flash of anger tore its way through Lyonene and she controlled it only with great effort. "What mean you by your Ranulf, does he not have a wife?"

"Aye, he has a wife." Her voice was a sneer and she turned to look with interest at Lyonene, but the younger woman looked away. She looked back at Ranulf, and Lyonene clenched her fists as the woman's strange eyes melted into an adoring gaze. "He has a wife, but one who does not care for him as he deserves." She gave a low, throaty laugh. "She is a fool to forsake my Lord Ranulf's lovemaking for that of another."

"What know you of my Lord Ranulf's lovemaking?" Lyonene could not keep the anger from her voice nor help the slight emphasis she placed on the word "my."

The woman lazily looked at her, and Lyonene met her smirking eyes with a smoldering gaze that she did not try to conceal.

"Ah," she drawled. "So my Ranulf has found one to replace me. I have not heard of you; he hides you well. But then as his mistress you must know of his particular skills, and you have me to thank."

Lyonene frowned and was about to ask her meaning when they both became aware of the movement of the horses. She turned startled eyes up to see Ranulf towering above her as he sat atop the Frisian, but Ranulf's eyes were not for her but for the woman standing next to her. Lyonene covered her face with the shadow of the hood before he saw her.

"Maude, it is good to see you this lovely morn. I am glad that you travel with us again."

"Only with you, my lord. I travel only with you, and should there be anything you need I will gladly . . . provide it."

Lyonene stole a glance at Ranulf, and her teeth clenched tighter at the soft, adoring expression he wore as he gazed down at this brazen old woman. He did not care that everyone in the courtyard heard their words and knew well their meaning. She looked away before he should turn and see her, as if he would ever notice her while this fat, slant-eyed woman so obviously offered herself to him.

"Ah, Maude, I miss you much since you went to the village. Have you . . . entertainments planned for this lonely journey?"

"I have boxes of colored silks and whatever else will be needed." Her honey voice was a caress, and Lyonene knew she was going to give herself away if this did not end soon.

"I will look forward then to the evenings." He did not even glance at Lyonene's concealed face before he turned and left them, with the Black Guard following.

Maude, beside her, made a noise and Lyonene looked up to see her mocking eyes. "You are possessed of a strong will." She smiled at Lyonene's still blazing eyes. "Were I in your place I would not have been able to control my anger so well."

Lyonene's chin came up. "I know not of what you speak—this anger."

The low throaty laugh came again. "You need not fret that I will take your place with my lord, for my days are over and I must live only with memory of his sweet ways."

She tossed her head. "I know of no sweet ways."

The laugh came again, only longer, deeper. "So that is the way of it. You do not know his touch yet, you only wish to." She glanced toward the window of the Black Hall and her mouth hardened, her voice flinty. "She shuns him, so I hear—may the Devil rot her—so mayhaps Maude can give you your desire."

"You speak lightly of the Devil rotting a woman you do not know. Mayhaps Lord Ranulf shuns her and it is not as you think."

Maude was staring at her intently. "Then she must be very ugly or ill-tempered so that he cannot bear to touch her. Mayhaps she has the pox."

"She does not!" Lyonene said hotly and then stopped at Maude's piercing stare and looked away.

"You seem to know much of the matter. How are you so sure I do not know my Lord Ranulf's wife? And you seem to harbor much pride, too much pride for a serf."

Lyonene's blood seemed to freeze, for she had come close to giving herself away and she could give no answer.

Maude broke the deafening silence. "Come, we take these barrels to the wagons and begin the journey. There will be enough time to learn your reasons, but more important there will be time to teach you to please my Lord Ranulf so that you may learn all you desire of his sweet ways."

Lyonene bit her tongue to still her retort to the old woman's jibes. She wanted only to get to Wales to meet the queen. What happened on the journey did not concern her.

Lyonene rode uncomfortably on the little donkey behind the four wagons and the Black Guard and Ranulf. She could not see her husband, and several times she had to look away as she caught Maude studying her.

For some reason known only to her, Maude seemed to help Lyonene remain anonymous and thus several awkward situations were avoided. Lyonene was thankful that the Black Guard were not as her father's men, from whose advances a serving girl was never safe. She looked now to the ground where the men sat under several trees. They were polite as Maude served them with food. Lyonene stirred the cauldron over the fire with sharp jabs as Ranulf said something to the woman and Maude's throaty laughter floated across the breeze.

Ranulf had been correct when he had said they would travel fast, and at the end of the day there was little time for anything but a hasty meal. Not accustomed to cooking, Lyonene had trouble helping Maude prepare the meal and was grateful for the woman's patience. She glanced at Ranulf's great black serge tent and felt glad that Maude took his food to him, although she found herself holding her breath until the old woman returned. Maude threw her a taunting look and laughed.

She watched Maude go to a wagon and carefully remove a wooden box.

"Come," she called over her shoulder. Curious, Lyonene followed, although she did not like the way the woman assumed she would go wherever she called.

The cooking fire was hidden from the four tents of the men and Lyonene had wondered why, but she now felt it had been for secrecy's sake. The box was inlaid with hundreds of tiny pieces of mother of pearl and silver that glowed in the reflected firelight. Almost with reverence, Maude lifted the lid and withdrew what seemed to be a garment of softly transparent silk. It was like a man's braies, only longer, with jeweled cuffs at a length that must be the ankle. About the wide waist was also a band of gold and sparkling jewels.

Another garment was brought forth, a gathered strip of silk whose function Lyonene could not guess. A jeweled vest came next, delicate, tiny, transparent. Then there were many veils, soft and alluring; Lyonene had never seen such silk. She knelt, tentatively touching the finery.

"It was my mother's and then mine. Now I have grown too fat to wear it."

"What is it and how could anyone wear such a garment? It would reveal more than it covered."

Maude's laughter escaped. "You are right—that is the purpose of a dancing costume." She watched Lyonene's puzzled eyes. "My mother was a Saracen, brought from the Holy Lands by my father. He fell in love one night while she danced in . . . in a place there. He was a good man and cared naught that my mother had often . . . danced." Her voice was strained.

"He brought her back with him from the Crusade and he was good to her. I was not very old when he died, and overnight my mother turned into an old woman. Although she often danced for my father, after his death she never danced again. But she taught me the dance and gave me the silken clothes." She grinned at Lyonene. "I have not been so faithful as my mother to any of my husbands."

She stood up and bade Lyonene follow her example. A startled gasp escaped from Lyonene's lips as Maude roughly ran her hands over the younger woman's body.

"You will do," Maude stated. "Now remove those garments."

"I will not! I cannot imagine your reasons, but I will not remove my clothing."

Unperturbed, Maude continued. "How else do you expect to wear the clothes if you do not remove your others? It will not fit over them."

"I have no intention of wearing your dancing thing. The silk is nice but I do not intend to put it on."

Maude's voice sneered. "Do you think you are the only young girl brought on this trip to Wales? Have you not seen the other two who cast hungry eyes on Ranulf? They paid much to go on this journey and they did not pay with gold. So, you take my meaning? They know that Lord Ranulf sometimes chooses a young girl to pass the night in his tent on these journeys and they are willing to sell anything to get that privilege, for he is a gentle lover and pleases the women and afterward is very generous with his gold."

She watched as Lyonene looked anxiously in the direction of Ranulf's tent.

"There is no woman there tonight, but tell me of your feelings when one night you hear a woman's low laughter coming from that tent and then her cries of pleasure? Would you then be glad you shunned my mother's dancing silks? Could you be content to sit and listen to Ranulf's sighs as he . . ."

"Cease!"

Maude smiled. "I thought as much. I will teach you the dance. It takes years to become expert, but these English soldiers are not taught to appreciate such a dance. My Lord Ranulf will see you only in the dim candlelight."

Lyonene blanched. To wear that thing, and before a man! It was not thinkable.

Maude read her thoughts. "If you do not go to him, then you will need to listen to the other women's cries. Shall I describe what the last woman on the last journey told me of Lord Ranulf's bed?" She laughed as Lyonene covered her ears. "Then come with me and we will see how well you learn the dance."

With shaking fingers Lyonene began to remove her coarse woolen clothes as she stood before Maude, hidden among the trees. When she stood completely nude, Maude turned her again and again to inspect her, while Lyonene clenched her teeth, resolving with each second to remove herself from the old woman's penetrating gaze.

"Good. Very good. It is hard to believe that once I had a body such as yours. Now we will dress you."

About her hips and between her legs went a jeweled belt, barely covering her. The transparent garment went over her legs, the gold bands tight around her slim ankles. She saw then why the waist was so wide, for it did not reach her waist at all but rested on the belt above her hips, far below her navel. The slim gathered strip of silk went about her breasts, tied behind her back. Lyonene's breath escaped her when Maude tied the fabric very tight, and she gasped when she saw that as a result of the taut fabric, her breasts strained and pushed and curved well above the silk, little of them concealed. The tiny vest only emphasized the curves of her breasts and the deep indentation of her waist, the hips that swelled above the sparkling belt.

Lyonene's embarrassment was brief, for the beautiful clothes gave her a strange feeling of sensuality, and she liked the feel of her long hair as it touched her bare arms and the back of her waist.

"Yes, yes," Maude trilled. "It has its effect on you. That silk is blessed with many nights of pleasure and it holds its memories."

In spite of herself, Lyonene could not erase the feeling of sensuality that the bare skin and silken costume gave her.

Maude brought a strange stringed instrument from behind a tree, and Lyonene listened as she played a foreign tune for a moment. Then, humming, she rose to begin sensuous movements, moving her hips and stomach in a slowly rotating motion. She nodded for Lyonene to follow her actions and was surprised at the ease with which she made the intricate movements.

"Good, yes, good," Maude murmured as she returned to her instrument. Lyonene closed her eyes and moved with the music. She heard little commands from Maude, so put that they seemed to blend with the music: "Bend your knees more. Now, slowly, yes. Now, faster. I want to hear the bells."

Lyonene had been vaguely aware of the tinkling of little bells but now she realized that the sound came from her costume, that the bits of gold that covered the edges of the vest, belt and cuffs were hundreds of bells. The faster she moved, the more they gave out their sparkling little sound. It gave her a special delight to hear their sound, related as it was to her movements. The music became faster and the bells rang louder.

She could almost imagine Ranulf's eyes, dark and inscrutable, as they watched her. She felt a sense of defeat when the music stopped and Maude bade her remove the dancing costume.

"You have done well. Tomorrow I will tell my lord of a new dancing girl, and he will be pleased. But now you need rest, for you will be tired on the morn."

Still carrying the strange feeling of deflation, Lyonene went back to the camp to sleep near Maude under the clear stars. She was exhausted and slept heavily.

In the morning Lyonene's muscles were sore and every movement astride the little donkey hurt. She was glad for the pain, because it kept her from thinking about what she was doing.

Again they paused only a short time for dinner, and Lyonene was very aware of the other two women who constantly hovered about Ranulf. She could hear Corbet's voice as he made caustic remarks about the women and the way they flaunted themselves.

She still marveled at the demeanor of the Black Guard. She had never entered their Great Hall at Malvoisin, but at times she had seen women in the courtyard—quiet, well-dressed women—and knew they lived with the

Black Guard. She wondered at the discipline of such men, so unlike what she had known as a child.

Nightfall brought more practice of the new dance learned from Maude. Lyonene liked the graceful movements and learned quickly. Later, she was tired and sank heavily into the straw mattress.

A slight sound woke her and she looked toward Maude, sleeping soundly near her. On instinct, she looked toward the great black tent and saw Ranulf, standing outside, clad only in a white linen loincloth. She turned on her stomach and feigned sleep when he glanced toward the noise. Her chin propped on her hands, she watched as he sat on a rock not far from her. The moonlight glowed on his bronzed skin, and she saw his shoulders droop, not so much from tiredness but from . . . mayhaps sadness.

She had a sudden urge to go to him, to clasp his head of tousled hair to her breast, to soothe him. He stood up, yawned and stretched, his back muscles standing out under the golden skin. She shivered slightly and pulled the rough blanket closer about her, for the idea of comforting him had fled from her and had been replaced by another, stronger emotion.

They began the journey again before the sun rose, and Lyonene nodded sleepily as she rode the little donkey. At dinner the two women were even bolder in their pursuit of Ranulf. Angrily, Lyonene threw the iron cooking pot back into the wagon. Ranulf's voice halted her. He was still beneath the tree, but she felt his gaze on her. Quickly, her face deeply shadowed by the hood, she turned toward him only for an instant. Maude leaned toward him, talking quietly as her lips near touched his ear. Ranulf made no effort to move away from her and directed his gaze toward Lyonene as she secured the cooking items to the side of the wagon. They were in truth talking of her!

The meal finished, Lyonene tried, subtly, to get Maude to tell her what she and Ranulf had spoken of but had no success. Maude's laughter was infuriating, but Lyonene at least knew that Ranulf did not know his wife journeyed with him disguised as a serf.

They left the main road and traveled to a castle on the third night, and the thought of a roaring fire pleased Lyonene as they neared the stone walls and the donjon towering above.

They had just entered the bailey when a man came running toward them only half-dressed, in braies and a linen shirt that opened to show a hard, smooth chest. He was a handsome man, with blond hair, broad shoulders and slim hips. He ran to Ranulf with open arms and the two of them fell together, hugging and turning about, lifting one another from the ground.

"Ranulf, you grow more ugly every time I see you."

Lyonene opened her mouth to speak, but felt Maude's hand on her arm. It was not easy to remember to be a serf.

"And you, you are as weak as a girl. Weaker than some girls."

They hugged again, kissing one another's cheeks, and started toward the wooden steps leading to the second floor of the donjon, their arms entwined about one another's shoulders.

Lyonene impatiently waited as the Black Guard followed their master, and then she was allowed into the castle. Ranulf had taken a seat before the fire at one end of the hall. The other man stood beside another chair, leisurely dressing in clothes held by a servant.

"What news of Malvoisin? I heard some tales of you, but I gave them no credit."

"And what tales are these? I am sure they hold at least half-truths. Come, Dacre, sit here and do not spend so much time worrying about your beauty."

Dacre laughed and sat in the chair beside Ranulf's, dismissing the servant with a wave of his hand. "It is not for me to question the ways of our Lord, but at times I wonder that He gave you the look of a devil and the temper of an angel and me the body of an angel and the character of a devil."

Ranulf sipped the mug of hot wine. "There are many who would disagree on which is the devil body and which is the angel body."

Dacre's laughter roared. "So you do agree on who has the temper of an angel. I would have thought as much."

Neither man noticed the young serf girl who stayed so close to the back of their chairs. Maude thrust a large basket with a little broom and shovel in it at Lyonene and motioned for her to go and clean the hearth. She did not reason with Maude that it was not her duty as Ranulf's serf, but was glad to be able to hear the conversation between Dacre and her husband.

Dacre continued. "I would know the truth of one tale though—that you married, a young girl but poor."

Lyonene wanted much to turn and see Ranulf's face but busied herself with the hearth ashes.

"It is true," came Ranulf's quiet answer at last.

"And I heard she has some silly name for a lioness, named so at birth for her wide flat face, big nose, no lips . . ."

"You heard wrong!"

Dacre laughed at the vehemence in his friend's voice. "Well, tell me of her then and what possessed a father to name a child after a lion."

Ranulf leaned back against the carved oak chair. His voice was quiet, as if coming from a great distance. "She has tawny hair the color of a lion's, a great thick mane of it. Green eyes that would put an emerald to shame, a tiny nose and a full, soft mouth. When she is angry, one eyebrow . . ." He stopped abruptly and looked into his wine cup.

"Go on. You must tell me more of this woman. What of the rest of her? Is she thick-waisted and what of her legs?"

"Dacre!" Ranulf's voice was angry. "You go too far. This is my wife of whom you speak. She is not a serving wench to be shared."

"I understand. She has legs the width of the Frisian's neck and a waist the size of yours. Had I such a wife I would not speak of her either."

"She is . . ." Ranulf's laughter came to Lyonene, a sound she had heard too seldom. "I will not rise to your bait. You must come to Malvoisin and see her."

"Or ask Corbet. I am sure he can give me a true opinion of this unknown wife of yours."

Ranulf frowned into his cup. "Corbet talks overmuch at times."

"Mmm. Jealousy so soon! She must indeed be beautiful. You must tell me what possessed you to marry her. I had thought Isabel soured you for all time."

Lyonene listened breathlessly for Ranulf's answer, the reason he would give for the marriage.

Too much time elapsed and Lyonene knew Ranulf would give no answer. She returned to the dirty job of removing ashes. At least it was warmer before the fire.

"Remember that red-haired wench in London Town? The one Corbet and Sainneville fought for?"

Ranulf laughed again. "They were well into their cups and . . ."

"Neither you nor I were too sober. Thank the heavens for Hugo Fitz Waren."

"Aye, Hugo helped to pull them apart when I could not. I did not care who got the woman."

"She was a smart one. She knew then who was the earl. I shall never forget your face when she plastered that plump little body to you, sobbing that you'd saved her life that she owed you everything. Such eye-rolling at the mention of 'everything.' "

"Her 'everything' was not so bad after all."

Dacre fair shouted. "And how would you know what she had to offer, for she came to me that night."

"To you! Why would she want a weakling when she could have a man!"

"A weakling! Why, that little honey-fruit whispered that you frightened her more than the Devil himself."

"And she said to me she would as soon spend the night with a girl as one of your prettiness."

"Such prettiness I will show you!"

Lyonene turned to see Dacre leap at Ranulf's throat, and then the two men fell together to the rushes, massive strength pitted against the other. Lyonene was disgusted. That two grown men should wrestle one another on the floor in such a manner, and worse that it should be over a woman! They rolled to her feet, locked together, and as their faces were only inches apart, she calmly dropped the nearly full basket of ashes from her waist to the rushes, very near their faces. She did not wait to see the damage she had done but sedately walked away from them. She smiled slightly when she heard their struggles cease and their coughs and curses begin.

Maude seemed to appear from nowhere, and she clasped Lyonene's slight form to her much larger body, forcing her head to her ample shoulder.

"I will kill the wench," Dacre bellowed, his voice very near where Maude stood holding Lyonene. "Maude, let her go. I have my own manner of punishment for her."

"You scared the poor girl half to death." Maude stroked Lyonene's hair, completely hidden under the woolen veil that flowed down her back. "She is young and not used to the rough play of the king's earls." Her voice held such a sarcastic edge that Lyonene began to silently laugh, her shoulders shaking. Maude gave her a reproachful look. "You see, she is trembling with her fright." This made Lyonene laugh harder and a sound escaped her that was surprisingly like a sob.

"That is the one you teach to dance, Maude?" Ranulf's voice was gentle.

Maude nodded.

"Then keep her with you in the kitchen and send someone with water that we may remove this dust."

Maude pushed Lyonene's head back to her shoulder for the girl much wanted to see the havoc she had caused, feeling they wholly deserved it for their talk of tavern wenches. As Maude led her toward the kitchen, Lyonene heard Ranulf speak.

"Maude is teaching that one to dance. She says she is very good and will be ready to perform by the time we reach Wales."

"Well, then, let us see her. We can forgive her if she dances well."

"This one is mine, Dacre. She is young, too young for the rewards you have in mind. In a few years, when her dancing is better, then mayhaps you can 'forgive' her, but not yet."

Maude led Lyonene into the kitchen and gave her a pile of onions to chop—punishment for her behavior. She chopped and slashed with a vengeance as she thought of Ranulf's words about the London barmaid. She also remembered him saying, "This one is mine." How many other women had Maude taught to dance for him? She did not know when the onion tears and the real ones began to mingle.

Lyonene felt that Maude made an effort to separate her from Ranulf, for there were always jobs to do that required her presence far from him. She was thoroughly exhausted when she fell onto the mattress before the fire.

The straw was uncomfortable and she longed for the comfort of the feather mattresses of Malvoisin.

Morning came too early and she sleepily mounted her little donkey.

"This might well be the night, for tomorrow we reach Wales."

Maude's statement drew Lyonene awake, and all day she tried to dissuade herself from going ahead with the dance. When they stopped for dinner and she saw first one of the women running her finger down Ranulf's jaw and then Ranulf holding the woman's hand for a brief moment, Lyonene was decided. She would not think of the consequences of this night; she only knew she wanted him to see her, to hold her hand and no one else's.

As Ranulf's tent was erected, Lyonene saw Maude talking to him and knew he had agreed to the old woman's suggestions. Her heart began to beat rapidly.

She had no time to think as Maude pulled her into the seclusion of the trees. The beginnings of a protest were stifled as her clothes were removed. Soon the silken dancing costume encircled her. It was as if she were no longer Lyonene but someone else: a dark beauty, a Saracen who had been trained from childhood to tempt and entice men with her fluid body motions. She could hear the strange music in her head and her hips began to move slowly, a secret smile on her face.

Maude took a silvered piece of glass, a mirror, from the wooden box and a jar of black powder. She applied the kohl to Lyonene's eyelids, upper and lower, and darkened her eyebrows. There were transparent veils, soft, gentle colors, added to the costume, then one about her hair that hid the lower part of her face.

It was a different woman who stared back at her from the little mirror, and the dark, sultry eyes promised things Lyonene knew too little of—promises of passion and satin skin. She walked with ease and confidence to the candlelit tent.

Ranulf half-reclined on a low cot and did not see at first the dark girl who entered his tent, only hearing Maude's music, joined by a flute and little vibrating instruments like drums. He was instantly surprised by the confidence exuded by the girl, her movements sure and seductive. He then forgot that he knew this to be a serf girl, for somehow she was transformed into such as he'd not seen since his years in the Holy Lands.

Each slow undulation was a gesture of love, and he began to feel that this girl danced for him alone in a way no other woman ever had. Her hips moved toward him, her arms beckoning, her smoky eyes caressing him. Always the dances that Maude knew so well had excited him, but this girl was more, giving him a feeling of longing as well as lust. A veil fell at his feet, revealing one long slim leg hidden and yet revealed beneath the silk trousers. The music increased its speed and the girl turned her back to him, glimpses of her hair showing through a dark veil.

Another scarf drifted through the heavy air and he saw a curved hip, the gold belt flashing in the reflected candlelight. Her hips moved faster, the tiny bells tinkling in rhythm to her movements. The exposed hip was golden, creamy, while the other teased his bewildered gaze as it moved from behind a folded veil and then disappeared.

She turned to the side, the shape of her body showing through the silks. Her breasts rose again and again as her hips moved forward and back, and always her eyes entranced him, smiling, frowning, tempting, shunning, ever changing. Her fluid arms emphasized her liquid movements.

Another veil fell and he saw more of her beautiful body. Her stomach undulated, showing the lovely secret of her navel. Ranulf was frozen where he lay, unable to break the paralyzing spell of desire and fascination she wove about him.

The music's speed increased and his breath deepened as yet another veil fell to the floor. Her breasts rounded above the silk, gleaming, moving, quivering as she danced and he heard her low, throaty, lusty laugh, growling, filling his own body with tremors of unfulfilled passion.

He was afraid to move, afraid she was an apparition of pleasure that might disappear at his merest breath. She moved closer to him, slowly, tortuously, exquisitely, her skin giving off a delicate perfume. With fear but uncontrolled longings, he put out a hand to touch her. A brief whisper of creamed satin skin against his fingertips and she drew away, her head falling back as she near drove his senses mad with that laugh, so low, yet permeating him with its promise.

Her arm grazed his face, close to his lips, exciting him further to depths of what seemed to be a new part of his being. Then, abruptly, she moved away from him, far away, to a darkened side of the tent; her dark eyes and golden body were radiant against the cream-colored silk walls. He could not bear the void she had left behind. The music was reaching a frenzied peak and her eyes challenged him now, her hands reaching out, daring him, as her body increased the pulsating movements.

One powerful hand swept her to him, clasping tightly the deep curve of her waist, the other crushing her to him. The tent was dark, much too dark as he looked into her half-closed eyes, but he saw the mouth that waited below the veil, and the hunger it showed more than matched his own.

Enjoying and prolonging each exquisite moment, he stroked her skin, slightly damp from her dance, as was his own. She seemed to purr, a low, throaty sound, as he touched her. For only a very brief instant did her eyes open to meet his as he pulled the veil away and sought her lips, and then his eyes were closed too.

The music from outside the tent slowed to a sensuous rhythm as if sensing what was taking place inside.

Lyonene allowed her body to be supported totally by Ranulf's strong hands. His lips touched hers gently, savoring the feel of them, the taste of them. His tongue ran across the edge of her teeth, delighting in the tiny chipped place. The agonizing slowness with which he took his pleasure of her weakened her body; she felt almost as if she were dying under his sweet torture. He ran his teeth along her lower lip, tasting the firmness of it, relishing its special flavor. The corners of her mouth received his unique attention, and then his urgency enveloped her, his lips crushing hers, moving as he delighted in the nectar of them.

Lyonene pulled him to her, closer, ever closer, and ran her hands across the great muscles of his back, glorifying in the reserved power they held. The feel of his fingers caressing her bare skin made her mad to feel his dark, smooth skin under her hands. His lips moved to her ear, and soft words came to her, unknown words, meaningless yet all-meaning.

It may have been a discordant sound from the music that made Lyonene return to herself, to know that she was Ranulf's unwanted wife and not a serf girl as he now believed. He made love to a serf girl, a girl who danced for him, but he did not hold and caress his wife. Her pride, the pride of a lioness, returned to her and she knew that she could not continue with their lovemaking when he thought she was another.

She steeled herself and refused to hear the words of love, and harder still, to feel the lips that traveled along her throat. She released him so quickly that she had a second before he realized she had fled the tent. She ran as hard and as fast as she was able before stopping. The built-up tears poured forth in a violent torrent. She cursed herself for a hundred times a fool. Her mind rang with her confusion. How could this man's touch inflame her so, and how could he make such sweet love to one he thought to be only a serf girl, someone he cared for not at all?

Maude found her and helped her to bathe her swollen face and change her clothes. No words were spoken as they made their way to the camp, and the old woman carefully shielded Lyonene's view of Ranulf's dark tent, silent now from the rages of an hour ago. Only Maude's long understanding of Ranulf had been able to calm him from the anger he carried toward the girl. Lyonene breathed a ragged sigh in her sleep, and Maude shook her head in disgust.

Maude sent Lyonene away from the camp for water early the next morning. Ranulf would appear soon, and he would easily know which of the four women had danced for him the night before. All she could do was prolong the inevitable.

Lyonene's thoughts still warred within her as she pulled the heavy bucket from the water. So loud were her thoughts that she did not hear the horses approach. Before she could protest, strong arms pulled her against a bony body, hands groping her beneath her serf's garb. A mouth that gave a foul odor found hers. She began to kick and claw.

"Sir Henry!" a familiar, laughing voice called. "I don't believe you know how to treat a lady."

The old man released her and she spun around, her back to the voice. Keeping her head down, she raised a cautious glance to see Geoffrey before the man who had just attacked her.

"Lady?" Sir Henry spat. "She is but a serf girl."

Geoffrey's voice hid his contempt. "May I suggest, sir, that all pretty young women are ladies."

Lyonene felt the gratitude rising in her breast.

Sir Henry laughed. "I see what you mean."

"You do not mind if I try?"

"My experience bows to your pretty form."

Without even looking at her face, Geoffrey whirled Lyonene into his arms and began to kiss her. She was aghast that he would do this to her. He had no more respect for her than Sir Henry had.

"I see my little brother has found entertainment that pleasures him. Mayhaps you can excite this one more than I, for she runs from my caresses. There are some young women who prefer pretty boys rather than men—Dacre has proven that."

Geoffrey looked up to see Ranulf astride Tighe's broad back and lazily smiled. "She seems to find me acceptable enough, and my thanks for the comparison to Lord Dacre." He looked down at Lyonene's face, her jaw set against the inevitable exposure of her identity. Geoffrey stared at her in horror and turned her to face Ranulf.

Ranulf's look of pain before it turned to blackest hate startled her. He sneered at her. "I see now why she finds you so . . . acceptable. You must ask her to dance for you. She is . . ." The pained look crossed his face again and then he turned his horse and left them.

Chapter Nine

"Lyonene, what is the meaning of this? No, do not tell me, for I am sure it is Ranulf's doing. Is he so unbearable to live with?"

Lyonene could only shake her head, for a great lump was forming in her throat and she could not speak. Maude appeared from nowhere and took Lyonene away to the little donkey. She was too distraught to notice that Geoffrey rode to his brother.

"Ranulf," Geoffrey implored his stone-faced brother, "what has caused you to treat her so? Why is she dressed as a serf and made to ride a donkey?" He waited for an answer but none came. "I cannot understand your treatment of her. She is beautiful and desirable; how can you shun her?" Still no answer was given him and he sighed in exasperation. "I go now to Sir Tompkin. We are off to Cornwall this day. Remember, Ranulf, she is your wife."

"It is she who forgets."

Geoffrey frowned up at Ranulf. "Do you hint that she had a hand in what happened this morn? That she perhaps desires the attention of other men?"

Ranulf shrugged in answer.

"If I were not your brother and loved not life so well, I would challenge you for that. Any lady who is falsely accused and forced to act as a serf deserves a champion."

"You are so sure she is falsely accused? What proof have you of her innocence?"

Geoffrey smiled. "Because I know you. You care for your possessions and on that island of yours you would know when she sneezed or no. And that Black Guard would kill any man who came near to Lady Lyonene. I am correct, am I not? You have always known of her whereabouts, even to each minute."

"Aye. Until we left for Wales. She was clever in hiding."

"Hiding! Then you are indeed fortunate to have a wife who loves you so that she will dress as a serf to follow her beloved. Tell me, would any of your court ladies so love their husbands? I worry overmuch. Lyonene will have her way, and if that way includes a glowering, angry, accusing . . ." He laughed at Ranulf's black look. "There is no understanding women. I cannot fathom her choice of such a husband. I would give much to be chosen by such as she." Geoffrey frowned at the fierceness of the look given him by Ranulf. "I go now. Mayhaps I can leave Cornwall and return to Malvoisin later this year. Go in peace, my brother."

Lyonene was unaware of Geoffrey's going; in truth, she was aware of little around her. Her own thoughts raged with one another.

She did not even hear the thundering hoofs of Tighe as Ranulf rode toward the little donkey. She only felt herself being lifted into the air, coming to rest, sidesaddle, on the Frisian's back, held firmly in Ranulf's arms. She knew he was angry but she did not care. At least for the moment he held her close. They rode to the head of the line of people. Ranulf roughly tore the russet cloak from Lyonene, flinging it to the ground. Then he thrust his hands in her hair, pulling her head back, her face toward him. In spite of the pain he knew he caused her, she smiled up at him, her eyes shining.

"Hear me now, wife, and hear me well. You are mine and I do not share you."

Her eyes held his. "I have never been other, my Lion."

He stared at her for a moment and then looked away. She leaned back against him, and they traveled in silence.

"And now tell me what I am to do with you." Ranulf's voice was harsh as he stared at her, the silk walls of his tent surrounding them. "Did you think I rode to Wales for pleasure? Tell me, have you always had your way, so that a man who goes to war must have the added burden of a woman to succor?"

"War? There is no war," she replied hotly.

He glared at her. "You think I lie? The Welshman Rhys has decided he would be king. He rides north of here. King Edward sent me a message to find the man and stop his rebellion. Did you think I left my isle to travel to this cold country so that I might enjoy the scenery? Do you not think I have enough to care for in my men, but now I am also saddled with a noblewoman."

"Nay, I did not think—"

"That is it! You did not think. Now you have had your fun, you have dressed as a serf and deceived me. But tell me, mistress, what purpose did you have in mind in all this? If my memory still serves me, we last spoke of your returning to your parents."

She deserved all of this, she knew. She had not thought when she had taken the disguise. How many times had her mother punished her for just such waywardness?

"Speak up, woman! I know you have a tongue."

She lifted her chin and was glad anger was replacing her guilt feelings. "I did not want to . . . to leave. I wanted to . . ."

"Go on, I am listening."

She stood and touched the silk, glad to have removed the rough wool mantle. She whirled to face him, eyes alight and hair in wild disarray. "You are my husband and I love you." She waited breathlessly for his answer.

His black eyes did not soften. "You have an odd way of showing your love. You rob me, you—"

"Cease!" She put her hands over her ears. "I know it all. Have I not lived it, every horrible moment of it? Have I not been caught day after day between threats and rage? We had two days of love and we married because of that love. Is there no way I can bring about a return of love? Is there no way I can prove myself?"

He watched her and then moved closer to her, his hand touching her cheek gently. "I do not know," he said quietly.

The sound of iron striking iron brought Ranulf's head up.

"What is it?" Lyonene gasped.

Corbet burst into the tent, his eyes only briefly flickering over Lyonene. "Rhys attacks," he said bluntly.

"Guard her!" Ranulf commanded as he grabbed his shield and went outside the tent into the ever-increasing noise of a full-fledged battle.

"This way," Corbet said as he slit the serge of the tent at the back, and she followed him, her eyes constantly looking over her shoulder.

The sunlight was bright outside, and already the smell of blood was strong, mixed with dust and the horrible noise of men's screams, their dying gasps, the thundering of the horses' hoofs.

She saw Ranulf immediately, in the midst of the battle, on foot, having had no time to straddle his horse. She saw the glint of the sword as he swung with a two-handed grip at a man riding at him hard. Her breath stopped and the blood seemed to leave her body.

Corbet roughly jerked her arm as he pulled her forward. She stumbled and fell to her knees, grasping at a tree trunk to steady herself. The guardsman again pulled her, but she could not take her eyes from her husband or stop the deafening roar of the battle that surrounded her. Ranulf was covered in blood now, yet still he fought.

An arrow whistled into the tree, inches from her hand, and she stared at it incredulously. Vaguely she was aware that Corbet fought a man behind her, and still she stared at the arrow. Her fear began to make her tremble.

A movement in the tree above her caught her eye and she saw a man hidden in the leaves pulling back on a crossbow and aiming an arrow at Ranulf. She screamed, but no one heard her.

"No," she whispered, "no." She began to run, straight into the thick of the battle, toward Ranulf. She ran toward him and he stared at her in disbelief, his face smeared with sweat and blood.

She reached him at the same second as the arrow. Her arms went about him and her right shoulder covered his heart. The arrow slashed through her skin and muscle as it made its way to Ranulf's mail-covered chest. The steel tip pierced the iron armor, the hacketon, the linen and Ranulf's flesh, but Lyonene's body had slowed it and it went no further. She looked up at him as their bodies were held together by the thin piece of wood.

"Lion, I . . ." she whispered and then fainted.

Ranulf held her so she would not fall, and then he put his head back and gave his battle cry.

Sainneville did not at first see the little form so hideously attached to his master.

"Break it off, man! Do not stand there," Ranulf said, his voice harsh and shaking.

Hugo appeared, gave one look at his lady and turned away to guard his lord's back. Sainneville broke the feathered end of the arrow off, trying not to look at Lyonene's lifeless face.

"Can you get it out of the iron? It binds us together."

"Aye, my lord." Sainneville lifted trembling fingers.

"Fitz Waren!" Ranulf commanded. "Come and do this. Quickly! She begins to rouse. I do not wish her to feel more pain."

Hugo deftly put his fingers between Lyonene's shoulder and Ranulf's chest. The arrow was embedded deeply and intertwined with the mail links. To twist the arrow out without also twisting the shaft, was very difficult.

"Here, my lord," Hugo said at last. "Let me have the girl and I will pull her off the thing. Hold the arrow and do not let it move."

Ranulf did as his man bid, and Hugo carefully pulled Lyonene away. Ranulf jerked the steel point from his chest and angrily tossed it to the ground. Then he picked Lyonene up in his arms, her blood flowing on him.

"Ranulf," she whispered. "It hurts. My shoulder hurts. You are well? The arrow did not harm you?"

He did not answer her but strode quickly to his tent.

"What is wrong? She has fainted?" Maude asked, then gasped at the blood that covered both Ranulf and Lyonene. "I will care for her," she said as Ranulf carefully put his wife on the bed.

"Nay!" Ranulf said. "Go. I need no help. Bring me water and clean linen and then leave us."

Maude went out of the tent quickly, and Ranulf gave his whole attention to Lyonene. Her eyes were open but she didn't seem to see. He took an estoc from its sheath and slit her clothes away, tenderly covering her with the velvet bedclothes. When Maude brought the water he washed and bound the wound. Only then did he sit quietly and look at her.

"My lord?" Hugo stood at the doorway. "She is well?"

Ranulf turned to him, his eyes bright, his face and body still covered with the dirt and stench of battle. "She is well for a child who protects her husband with her own frail body. The Welshman who shot the arrow—"

"He is dead. Maularde saw to him. The battle is ended and won." He looked at the pale woman on the bed. "We will pray for her this night."

Ranulf nodded and the man left. Night came, and he stayed by her bed, on his knees, his prayers constant. He neither saw nor heard Maude set candles throughout the tent.

"Ranulf."

His head came up at Lyonene's whisper. He stroked her forehead, noticing for the first time the excessive warmth there. "Be still, love, do not speak."

"You still wear your armor," she whispered as she touched the iron links on his wrist.

"Aye. It does not matter."

"You are not angry with me?"

"Aye, I am angry with you, but I will wait until you are well to scold you."

"I did not mean to disobey. I saw the man and knew he meant to shoot you. I screamed, but you did not hear me."

"So you used your own body as a shield," he said flatly.

She moved so that her left hand touched the spot over his heart where the mail was torn and covered with dried blood. "Had I not done so you would have died."

"Yes, my love. You have saved my life. For what reason I do not know."

"Because I love you, my Lion, because I have loved you from the first moment I saw you, because I shall always love you."

By morning, Lyonene's fever raged. Ranulf often had to hold her to keep her from tossing about the narrow cot.

"My lord, you will eat," Hugo commanded his master, after two days of food hardly touched. "You do not help the girl any by your fast."

Absently, the earl ate, never taking his eyes from his wife.

Ranulf had hours, long, painful hours to think about the girl who lay before him, her face red and hot with fever. How many times had she told him she loved him?

And how often had he jeered at her for her avowals of love? He knew she was a woman of much pride, yet she had swallowed that pride to follow him after he had struck her and said he wished to cast her aside.

He dipped the cloth in warm water and wiped her forehead, touching her mouth gently. He remembered vividly the blood on her lips when he had struck her, and his stomach tightened in disgust and remorse.

She did not move, but lay there perfectly still, deathlike. He lifted the small hot hand to his lips. She had asked what she had to do to prove her love.

He had loved her once. No, he thought as he rubbed her hand against his cheek, he had loved her at once, from the first moment he had seen her, when she had stared up at him with sparkling green eyes. Why had he forgotten those first few days?

He remembered Giles and his first wife, Isabel, and it suddenly seemed so clear to him. Giles had been mad. He had willed his own death, using Ranulf as a means, and Ranulf had believed the boy over his wife's words. Yet he had only to look and he would have seen the unnatural light in the boy's eyes. Had not Lyonene seen pain in his eyes when they first met, the same pain as he was sure she had seen in Giles's eyes?

He began to realize how much he had wronged her, and the pain and fever she bore now set more heavily upon him. She was no more like Isabel than he was like Geoffrey, and he had been wrong to compare them. Never had Isabel given him any avowal of love. She had given nothing but hate.

"She is the same?"

Ranulf had not heard Hugo enter the tent. "Aye, she is the same."

"The men pray for her. They have already come to love her and admire her courage."

Ranulf turned a black face to his man. "And what good does their love do her now that she lies so near death? Why did they not 'love' her in the thick of battle, when she must protect her husband with her own frail body? Why did not someone stop her from coming on this journey? Why—?"

He broke off as Hugo put a hand on his lord's shoul-

119

der, and Ranulf buried his face in his hands, giving way to the tears long buried in his breast.

"Water."

Ranulf sat still, his eyes half-closed, and did not hear the faint whisper. For five days he had not left the tent and he had eaten nothing in the last three. Now he was weak, his grief having worn him away.

"Water," Lyonene repeated.

Ranulf jumped and stared with disbelief at his wife's open eyes. It was seconds before he recovered himself enough to take her in his arms and lift a cool mug of water to her lips.

"I do not remember. Why am I here?"

He held her close to him, feeling his heart pounding. She would be well! "Hush now, love, do not speak. You took an arrow meant for me." He blinked back tears and worked hard to keep from crushing her to him.

"You are unhurt?" she whispered.

Suddenly, he felt joyous because he'd have a lifetime to love her, to make her forget his anger and hostility. He pulled back and smiled at her. "Unhurt! I am more than unhurt! You have saved my life and I owe all to you. And you, my sweet Lioness, will be well. And now you will eat."

She managed to smile at him. "And if I do not?"

He lifted one eyebrow at her. "I had not thought on it, but knowing your constant disobedience, I shall probably have to force you to eat."

She put her hand on his. "I wish . . ." she said quietly.

"Aye? What is it you wish?"

"This morn is different. It is as if we were at Loran-court and you were the man I met and there were no more hate between us."

"I would also that the hate was gone," he said quietly. No other words he could have said would have meant more to her.

What followed were, for Lyonene, blissful days of learning to know her husband, of laughter, of surcease from the fear she had grown to feel.

"My lord!" Corbet shouted. "A messenger is come from King Edward to cry a tourney."

"A tourney?" Lyonene said from her seat on the mossy bank. "It is safe? What of this man Rhys? If he wishes to take the king's place, is it safe to be so near?"

"Rhys and his three sons were killed in the battle. His men will cause no more harm with no leader." He stared down at her. "You would care to see the court and a tournament?"

"Oh yes, Ranulf, oh yes, I would much like to go."

He knelt and put a hand on her shoulder. "Then we shall." He turned to Corbet. "Tell the messenger that the Black Lion and his Black Guard challenge all."

Corbet grinned. "We have done so, my lord."

Ranulf's face hardened, but before he could speak, Lyonene laughed. "It is good your men know their lord so well, is it not?"

He stared for a moment and then relaxed. "Aye, that it is. Go now and ready yourselves. We leave on the morrow."

When they were alone, he turned to Lyonene. "You are well enough to travel? The wound does not plague you overmuch?"

"Nay, it does not." She held up her hand for his and pulled him to sit down beside her. "Tell me about the court and the king and the queen and the other earls and—"

"You go too fast. Be still and I will tell you all I can about a round table."

"A round table? As in King Arthur's tales?"

"Aye, the name is the same but it describes three days of games, jousting and eating. Think you can survive the excitement?" His eyes twinkled.

She knew he teased. "Tell me of the queen, is she a great beauty?"

Ranulf laughed and began to talk of a life so familiar to him, so new and awesome to his wife.

Chapter Ten

Lyonene and Ranulf had been at the new Caernarvon Castle for six days, and she had spent the time in getting to know the people of the court and Queen Eleanora. The queen was a short, quiet woman, much more interested in her children than in state politics. She and Lyonene got on famously. The king was a formidably tall man with red hair and enormous energy. To Lyonene he never seemed to sit still for very long.

In the evenings Ranulf and Lyonene sang duets, she playing a psaltery, he a lute. They were much favored by the many guests, who began to arrive in great numbers. Each guest was treated according to his rank. The carls were given first priority and the finest that could be had, while the lesser knights, the mercenaries, were given a place to stand their tents, fodder and the privilege of one meal a day with King Edward.

The growing excitement affected Lyonene and she enjoyed herself. Queen Eleanora came to depend on her, and Lyonene found herself to be an easy hostess.

"You spend much time with these men." A strong arm encircled her narrow waist and pulled her into a dark corner of the house.

She had stiffened at first, but relaxed when she realized she stood so closely, so intimately, pressed to Ranulf. Her teeth showed clearly in the dim light as she grinned up at him. "I would but make them comfortable. There was a lady, a Lady Elizabeth I believe, who seemed overinterested in the cut of your tabard, especially your shoulders and arms, at least it looked so from the manner in which she ran her hands over your . . . ah, tabard."

He pulled her tight against him till she could hardly breathe. "Mayhaps she felt me to be neglected by my own wife. I have not seen you much these past days. Mayhaps I should pretend to be a guest to get your attentions."

Her heart beat rapidly and she could feel his under her hands. She worked her arms away until she clasped the great bulk of his chest. "Of course, my lord, you are most welcome to Caernarvon Castle. And, pray tell, what would you desire of our meager assets? Could I fetch wine or food or . . ."

"A dancer. I would have a veiled Saracen dancer for my room. One who entices and shows her tawny body as she casts away the veils. Do you think such could be found? Mind, I want only the best."

"You did like my dance then?"

In answer, he kissed her, a fierce, demanding, crushing kiss that made her draw him closer to her and answer with equal fire.

"He is here!" A voice near them called. "I find my friend has changed little, for all his marriage to a baron's daughter. Leave the girl, Ranulf, and come talk to me. The night is young and she will wait for you, no doubt."

Ranulf pulled away from her, and she felt him to be as reluctant as she.

"There are times, Dacre, when you are more a curse than a friend."

The handsome blond man placed hands on hips, legs apart, and his laughter rang, causing many people to turn and stare. They clasped one another, each seeming to try to break the other's ribs. They smiled at one another with the special look of old friends who had seen much together.

"I hear of this marriage of yours and not two months later, I find you locked together with one of the castle ladies. I said you should have brought her with you to Wales. At least I hope this one is not so well-used as Lady Adela whom you bedded so often last year." He stopped at Ranulf's scowl.

Lyonene had stood behind Ranulf as he talked to his friend and now Ranulf pulled her to stand beside him, holding her forearm and hand possessively in his two hands.

"This is my wife, Lady Lyonene. And you, I believe, have met Lord Dacre."

123

"What story is this? I would remember this beauty had I met her."

Ranulf smiled from his friend to his wife. "She followed me to Wales in my train, dressed as a serf." His voice was proud.

"I find that a tale not to be believed. Even dressed as a serf, this beauty could be recognized. She would be a lady no matter what she wore. My lady, you have a fool for a husband. You should have married me and I would know you even should you dress as a man."

Ranulf remained smiling. "Remember the night at your castle as we talked and a serf girl cleaned the hearth?"

Dacre looked in astonishment to Lyonene, who looked away, the blood beginning to rise to her cheeks.

Dacre's laugh roared out again. "Then it was you who dropped the basket of ashes in our eyes!" He snatched her from Ranulf's grasp and lifted her above his head. "I vowed you would be punished for that and so you shall."

"Do not!" Her frantic words were directed to Ranulf. Dacre recognized the warning in her tone and, his hands still on Lyonene's waist, hastily turned to Ranulf.

Dacre frowned for a moment at the Black Lion scowl on Ranulf's face and the half-drawn anelace. He released Lyonene and clapped a heavy hand on his friend's shoulder, his lips twisting into a half-controlled smile.

"I do not jest, Dacre. She is . . ."

The people in the Great Hall had stopped their talking, the musicians in the gallery had fallen silent. Not many men had seen the Warbrooke wrath and lived. Lyonene put herself between her husband and Lord Dacre.

"So that old affliction has finally taken you, and now you wish to tell me a noble speech of how you will protect your wife with your life," Dacre teased.

Ranulf's body relaxed and his hand left the scabbard. He looked away, a sheepish expression on his face. "It is true; I would protect her."

"Well, then, my friend, if I promise not to spirit her away, may I look more clearly at her?"

Ranulf returned his friend's grin and pulled Lyonene into the light. The guests went back to their talk and the music resumed.

Lyonene tried to control her anger as Ranulf turned her in the bright candlelight. She felt as if she were a piece of horseflesh that they were considering for purchase.

"You have done well, Ranulf." Dacre clapped Ranulf's back. "That much hair alone was worth losing your freedom."

Lyonene whirled on them, her emerald eyes flashing. Her voice held contempt. "If you gentle knights have finished your inspection, the cattle of this castle have work that needs to be done." She turned on her heel in midst of a swirl of tawny hair and angrily stalked away. She heard Ranulf's low voice, but not his words as he spoke behind her. She clenched her hands into fists at Dacre's answering laugh.

Dacre and Ranulf were quickly forgotten as Queen Eleanora introduced her to Berengaria. Lyonene had never had many friends as a child, every visitor to Lorancourt being either too old or too young, yet when she saw Berengaria, she knew she had found a friend. Queen Eleanora introduced them to one another and they clasped hands like long lost friends.

"I think you feel as I do, that we have been friends for long. We shall cause a stir wherever we go, you and I."

"What do you mean? I can see no reason why there be any confusion?"

"You are an innocent babe! Look about you at the men in the room and the narrowed eyes of their wives. And look at that great handsome husband of yours as he watches you. He looks ready to spring in attack if any man so much as speaks to you."

"But why . . . ?"

"I will not explain, for you will learn soon enough."

Ranulf did indeed watch his wife, for her beauty was suddenly enhanced by that of Lady Berengaria. The two women were of a height, one fair with tawny locks that hung past her waist in a profusion of fat curls, the other with dark auburn hair and eyes the same color. Her hair fell a few inches short of her waist and gently rolled under in a perfect curve. There were three tiny braids on each side of her forehead, pulled to the back of her head and fastened with a long red ribbon embroidered with tiny white seed pearls. The silk tunic that outlined her voluptuous figure was the color of her hair, covered by a spotless white velvet sleeveless surcoat.

Lyonene wore blue, a blue-green tunic that reflected in

her eyes and a rich darker blue velvet surcoat. The two women, both extraordinarily beautiful, delicate, their exchanged words quiet, were indeed causing a stir in the Great Hall, a stir of envy, jealousy, desire, and from two husbands, a wary protectiveness.

"Come, let us sit here." Berengaria motioned to a bench along a wall where they would have a clear view of the people in the hall. "You must tell me how you captured Lord Ranulf, for there have been many women who have lusted for his money and that handsome form of his. Although I have heard that he is willing enough to share one of those."

Lyonene shook her head. "Do not tell me which, for I vow every woman but the queen has told me of my husband's past adventures."

Berengaria laughed, causing several heads to turn, heads which had been waiting for a chance to gaze again at the loveliness of the two women. "I can well imagine their words. But you did not answer what magic potion you used to snare him, and, if the gossip be correct, in but two days."

Lyonene shrugged. "I did but make him laugh."

Berengaria considered this for a moment, then nodded. "Yes, I can see why he would love the woman who made him laugh."

Before Lyonene could protest, her friend continued. "Is it wondrous to be so very rich? Do you have twenty maids to see to your every whim, to bring you hummingbird's tongues roasted in three sauces?"

Lyonene laughed aloud. It was good to be near someone so honest, someone who did not say one thing and mean another unpleasant thing. "You will not believe this, but I have no maid at all."

At the disbelief on Berengaria's face, she told of taking Kate's place on the journey to Wales and, since no mention had been made of a maid, she had not requested one. There seemed to be hundreds of servants about Caernarvon with little to do, so all her needs were cared for.

"I can see we will be good friends, and I long to tell Travers that I am not the only woman who perpetrates misadventures. He swears that it is only I who still gets into mischief; all other women are the height of decorum at all times."

"Ranulf was very angry, but Queen Eleanora was pleased that I came and scolded Ranulf for forcing me to go to such extremes to get here."

They laughed together.

"We are most fortunate in having such a queen. My father still tells horror stories of the last one."

"This Travers is your husband?"

Berengaria's face lit at the mention of her husband. "Look you about the hall and see if you can guess which man is my Travers."

Lyonene guessed several men, all handsome men, and Berengaria snorted at each one, giving some derogatory quip, such as, "Beats his wife," "Does not like women" or "Greedy," and wiggling her brows. When Lyonene surrendered, Berengaria pointed.

"He talks now to Lord Dacre," she said and watched Lyonene with twinkling eyes as she saw the expected reaction on her new friend's face.

The man talking to Lord Dacre was the ugliest man Lyonene had ever seen. He was of average height and seemed to be built of stone, so square was his form; there was no grace or ease of movement about him—only an unshakable solidity. But his face was what was almost frightening. His ears were huge, his hair a faded mixture of nondescript colors, an unruly, wiry mess. His forehead overhung his eyes by what seemed to be several inches, the brows grown into a single line. Deep creases ran beside his nose to a lipless mouth. His eyes were mere slits.

She tried to compose herself as she turned back to Berengaria. Surely the woman only jested.

Berengaria grinned at her. "Is he not a troll? But I will tell you that I have loved him since I was but three years and I shall continue to do so until I die."

"Tell me of this, for I sense a good story here."

"I tell it gladly, though to few people. My family is a large one. I have six brothers and five sisters. My father has always been glad that his daughters are pretty and docile, his sons handsome and independent. But for me. From my birth I seemed to be the wrong sex, for I ever did things a young lady should not.

"One day when I was a little past my third birthday, I walked with my nurse in the fields by our castle. When she looked away for a moment, I hid from her in the tall grasses and watched as she searched and called for me."

"How can you remember a thing so long ago? I do not recall events of when I was three."

"I remember no others, but this could have been last week, it is so clear. When my nurse returned to the castle path to search for me, I made my way to the duck pond, a place she ever refused to take me. Silly woman! She constantly feared I would end myself in every conceivable manner, so she kept me from most pleasant things. When I got to the pond, a face peered at me from the reeds. I indeed thought it was a troll at first, but I kept staring at it even when it stepped from the reeds and I saw it was but a boy. We stared long at one another and an overpowering feeling came to me that this boy was mine and would always be so. He was twelve years then and near as big as he is now.

"I put my arms up to him and he lifted me. He carried me for hours, talking to me and showing me birds' nests, little crawly things and sharing his bag of food with me. Neither of us thought of time and so it was late when we returned to the castle.

"Everyone was frantic by then and sure I was dead. My mother came to take me from Travers, but I would not leave and when my father finally pulled me away, I kicked and screamed until Travers came and kissed my forehead and told me to do what was wanted of me."

"Your parents must have wondered greatly at your behavior."

Berengaria shrugged. "I have ever demanded my way. All the next day I refused to leave Travers's side. I rode with him on his horse as his father and mine inspected a piece of land my father wished to sell. On the morn I knew he was to leave, I cried and said I loved him and that he must not grow and instead, wait for me. He kissed my forehead and said that when I was ready for marriage he would come for me."

"You cannot tell me that that is just what happened!"

"Aye. When I was ten and five my father brought a young man and his father to me and said I was to marry the man. I knew my father thought to have his way so I said before all that I was secretly married already and now carried my husband's child."

"You did not! Of course it was not true!"

"No. It could not be, for I had not seen Travers since that one day, and I would allow no other man to touch me."

"Your father must have been very angry."

Berengaria rolled her eyes. "That is a mild statement for my father's temper. He had a midwife examine me and found I lied and then he locked me into a tower room with only bread and water to eat. I pleaded great illness and my old nurse brought me pen and paper to write my will. I wrote Travers that it was time for him to come or else my father would marry me to another. I tossed the letter out the arrowslit with a gold ring to a serf boy."

Lyonene began to laugh. "I believe my story of dressing as a serf is mild. Tell me the rest of it!"

"Travers came within three days with an army! Over three hundred men approached my father's gate and my father, to tell the truth, was well pleased by so forceful a son-in-law. He said later he thought it would take such a man to be able to live with me, for he found it an arduous task."

"But what of you? You had not seen Travers since you were little more than a babe. Did you feel the same about him after all that time?"

"Oh, yes. I ran to him when I was released from the tower and he held me and kissed me, only not on the forehead." Her eyes twinkled. "Had I any doubts before, that kiss would have dispelled them."

Lyonene leaned against the wall and sighed. "And now you live in sweet contentment."

"Hah! There is naught sweet about my Travers. He has a temper as ugly as his face. If you could but see his arm you would see where I slashed him once."

"I do not understand. If you love him . . ."

"Real love is not the pretty stuff of the jongleurs. It is a feeling inside that you are one with this man, no matter what he is. Were Travers to sell his soul to the Devil, I would still love him and mayhaps I would bargain for a good price myself."

Lyonene knew she should have been shocked at this, but instead, she stared at Ranulf and felt again the pain of the Welsh arrow in her shoulder. "I fear I would join my Black Devil also."

Berengaria smiled. "Come, let us eat and no more talk of devils. I fear the penance now for my sins will be too high."

They walked together to the tables.

Later, Lyonene and Ranulf were alone in their room, Ranulf soaking in a hot tub.

"I have wanted to ask you something," Ranulf said. When he was quiet, she stopped her washing and looked at him. "Could it be so terrible?"

"Some think so. Henry de Lacy has asked me to take his youngest son to page. The boy is only six years and should wait another year before leaving his home . . ." He paused and when she did not speak, he continued. "It would, of course, be for you to say, for a page is the woman's responsibility until he is of an age to be a squire."

"What is this child's name and why do you seem to think I should object?"

"He is Brent and although young, he . . ."

"Brent! Is he not the boy who tied old Sir John's leg to the table at dinner?"

"The same."

"The boy who loosed the pigeons in the monks' study? The boy who . . ."

"He is the one responsible for it all and I can see your answer to my request."

"So now you have turned sorcerer and know my thoughts! Then you must know I love the boy well already. He has but high spirits and his parents try too hard to still him."

She began to lather his face as she prepared to shave him, a new task.

"You cannot know what you say, for the boy is a devil. He is the last of that great litter of de Lacy's, and the parents are tired and need a rest. From what I see, Berengaria was enough to put them in their graves."

"What has Berengaria to do with my Brent?"

"Your Brent! So now you adopt the boy already. He is your friend's little brother. Did you know she was an earl's daughter?"

She scraped a patch of whiskers. "Being only a lowly

baron's daughter, I know little of the hierarchy of court," she said loftily.

Ranulf understood well her dig at his words. "You know little of raising children and yet you are anxious to take on this one. Could you know that four women have refused him so far? It is said that one of them near fainted at the mention of the little monster."

She could not shave him as he talked. "First you ask me to take him and now you work at dissuading me, and what is this you say of my lack of knowledge of raising children? I do not see that you have any great experience in this matter, yet you do not shrink from the idea of taking Brent."

"Aye, but I can always beat him if he misbehaves," he said smugly. "I doubt if you are even as strong as the boy."

She gave him a look of disgust. "You talk overmuch of beating, first your weakling wife and now a boy who is not as big as . . . as your swollen head. Now stop arguing with me so that I may finish shaving you, and concentrate your arrogant thoughts on whether or not my hand slips and cuts your smug words from your throat."

He took her wrist as she brought the sharpened steel near his cheeks, his eyes showing his pleasure at her. "I begin to pity a poor child who must have a lioness for a mother. He will ever think he has had his own way, but in truth she will always win."

"There is only one prize I have ever wanted to win and I have done so." She smiled down at him.

He leaned his head back against the tub. "Finish my shave, wench, and contradict me no more."

She smiled at his closed eyes and finished the shave.

They entered the Great Hall together and smells of food reached them. Ranulf introduced Lyonene to Henry de Lacy, Earl of Lincoln and Salisbury, the father of Berengaria and Brent. When the men began to talk of estate management, she went to sit alone on a bench by the wall. Brent came to his father's side and the man pointed and sent the young boy to her.

"You are Lady Lyonene?"

"Aye, and you are Master Brent?"

"I am, my lady."

She patted the seat and he sat near her. He stared at her with wide eyes and then with a curious expression at her hair. One small hand darted out and heartily pulled a lock.

She quickly put a hand to her head against the pain. "What is your reason for that?"

He looked little surprised at himself for his action. "I but wanted to see if it was real. I heard two ladies say it was not and another said you should cover it."

Lyonene smiled at him. "And what think you?"

He shrugged. "It is no matter to me. I cannot interest myself in women's hair, for I am going to train to be a knight." He squared his little shoulders.

"But is it not good for a knight to care for his ladies? Would you not protect me from danger if need be? For you have chosen to train at Malvoisin, and since I live there . . ."

He relaxed again, pleased that she gave him a reason to be near her, for he liked her.

"You are glad that you go to Malvoisin?"

"Oh, yes," he answered. "You are a good lady, for you are not old or ugly."

"I thank you for the compliment," she smiled. "Now, tell me of these tricks I hear of you. Are they true?"

He shrugged again. "See those girls? I made them cry yester eve." His voice was proud.

"And whatever did you do to make them cry?"

"I told them a story of a dragon who flies through walls and eats girls, only girls," he said grinning. "I heard their mother say they did not sleep all the night." He gave her a sideways glance to see her reaction.

"Silly girls! They should have told you worse stories and then you would not have slept."

He gave her a look of disdain. "No girl can make worse stories than I."

She leaned close to him. "I can, and when we are at Malvoisin I shall. I will not only write them but I will put them to music and sing them." She made the last words seem like a horrible threat.

He looked at her with new respect. "And what if I should put a dead rat under your pillow?"

"I should chop it up and serve it to you for dinner and only tell you after you had eaten it."

His eyes widened and he made a face as if he imagined the taste of such a meal. He settled back against the wall, satisfied for the moment with her bravery. "My father has told me only that I am to live with you, but I do not know your husband, who is to be my master."

"See the man talking to your father? The man in black?"

The little boy sat bolt upright, his shock portrayed on his face. "But that is the Black Lion," he whispered.

She looked at him in puzzlement. "Do you not wish to be page to Lord Ranulf?"

He gave an involuntary shudder and his voice was strained. "My cousin told me he chops boys my age apart for practice, to keep his sword edge sharp."

She grabbed his shoulders. "That is horrible! As you created a story for the girls, so your cousin made up the tale of my husband."

He looked at her in awe. "Are you not afraid of him?"

She smiled. "In truth I am at times, but when I am, I make sure he does not see my fear. And you also must not show your fear."

The boy looked as if he might cry. "Or he will . . ."

"Do not say that! Do not think it! Here, stay here and I will fetch him. You will watch and see how gentle he is. If I, a mere girl, am not afeared of him, certainly a knight's page will not be."

Brent tried to lift his shoulders again, but his lower lip still trembled. "That is true."

Lyonene muttered some words about men starting young with their arrogance and made her way to Ranulf. He was engrossed in talk with Henry de Lacy, and when she put her hand on his arm, he merely held it, caressing each of her fingers. Lyonene stepped back so Brent could see, and the boy watched with fascination.

"What is this you do?"

"I beg your pardon, Lord Henry, but I would speak a few words to my husband."

"Young pup already giving you trouble? Well, if you want to go back on the agreement, I will understand."

"Oh, no," Lyonene said at once. "I am most pleased with the boy and do not wish to relinquish him."

Henry laughed. "Well, you may wish you had answered differently in a few months. After twelve children, one would think I would be ready for all things, but that boy is beyond me. Mayhaps I am just getting old. Well, it is good speaking with you, my boy." He clapped Ranulf's shoulder and left.

"Now, what is so wrong with the boy?"

"It is not the boy, it is you."

"I? But I have not spoken to him."

"He is terrified of you. A cousin has filled his ears with horrible stories of you."

He gave her a half-smile. "And do you know they are not true?"

She told him Brent's story and Ranulf's upper lip curled in disgust. He walked toward the boy and Brent nearly leaped from the wooden bench.

Ranulf looked down at the bowed head and saw that the boy trembled. He stretched out a hand to touch the sandy-colored hair, but did not. He sat on the bench.

"I am honored, my lord, to be your p-p . . . page." The boy's voice was barely audible.

"And, I am most honored to have you. So, you fear the Black Lion?"

Brent did not answer, nor did he look at Ranulf, and his trembling increased.

"Tell me, Brent, do you think the Black Guard fears their liege lord?"

"Oh no, my lord." His head came up. "For they belong to you; they also . . ." His fear increased at the memory.

Ranulf's voice was quiet, soothing, reassuring. "If it is as you say and they have no fear because they are part of my household, then you should not fear me. My page belongs to me just as do my Black Guard. Mayhaps you will be known as the Black Page."

Lyonene could see the boy's face work as he digested this information; then a smile began to form, then a question. "How can I be the Black Page when I do not have black hair? All the Black Guard has hair of your color."

Ranulf held out his hand to the boy, showing him the back of it. "You see, I have enough black hair for both of us."

Lyonene could not help laughing. "It is true. His whole body is covered with black hair."

Ranulf gave her such an intense look that she felt the

blood rush to her cheeks, and she turned away to become uncommonly interested in the figures of a tapestry opposite her.

Brent did not yet dare to touch the hand held out to him. "Am I really to be your page, my lord? I may see your black stallion and meet your guard and touch your sword and . . . ?"

"Aye, all that and more." Ranulf's eyes twinkled. "We go to supper now, but as soon as we are finished, you may come with us to the stables and see my horse."

The boy stood perfectly still, but somehow he gave the impression of jumping a few feet in joy. He grinned at Lyonene, turned and ran to a group of older boys on the other side of the hall. Within seconds, all the boys turned open-mouthed stares toward Ranulf.

Lyonene whispered to her husband. "I have no doubt he tells them you eat three boys a day and he is chosen to help you in your gruesome slaughter."

Ranulf stood and held his arm for her. When she stood beside him, he gave her the same intense look of a moment before. "I am more concerned with your interest in the black hair that covers my body. Mayhaps you can demonstrate some of this interest to me."

"Mayhaps," she said, looking at him with half-closed eyes.

He pulled her arm closer to his body, as if he were afraid she might vanish. "Come, we must show the boy to Tighe, but later, Lioness," he murmured, kissing her hand, "later."

Lyonene woke first the next morning and, donning her green robe, went to stoke the fire into life. Ranulf still slept as she looked down at him, the care lines in his face smooth in his sleep. She touched a sable curl as it curved toward his eye. His hand caught her wrist and she gasped in surprise.

"Come to me, Lioness." His voice was a commanding growl.

She eagerly sought him, cursing the coverlet and robe that separated them. His lips did not tease this morn but demanded, and he pushed her beside him, his weight pressing her into the feather mattresses. Her arms tightened about him and she greedily returned his kiss.

A knock sounded at the door, and the oath Ranulf uttered was so vile that it caused her to shudder. He did not seem to notice her trembling as he bellowed for the person to enter. A white-faced Brent carried a heavy pitcher of hot water.

"I brought washing water, my lord." His voice quivered.

Lyonene saw the black scowl on her husband's face and plunged a sharp elbow into his ribs. He grunted and turned the scowl on her. She gave him a sweet smile. "Your page has brought you washing water and means to help his lord dress for the procession to the lists." She kissed the corner of his mouth, which was a hard, grim line. He immediately grabbed her and threatened to push her back on the bed.

"Ranulf!" she cried and pushed against his chest. He seemed to recover himself, released her and stepped from the bed, wrapping the loincloth about his hips.

Brent stopped before Ranulf and stared up at him in awe. "You are the Black Lion all over!" He did not understand the laughter he caused from his lord and lady, for he did not know that those were the very words said by Lyonene when she first saw an unclothed Ranulf.

It was a while before Ranulf was readied for the procession, this day wearing the silver-coated mail that was used only for ceremony. Lyonene had to give Brent a hand in lifting the mail and, although the boy was not yet a squire, Ranulf allowed him to help.

"I will see to the horses, and I will return for you in one hour. See that I am not kept waiting."

She tossed her hair. "I am not in the habit of causing you delay."

"Do not play the Lioness with me. Come here and kiss your knight."

He lifted her from the floor with one arm as he quickly kissed her, nearly crushing her ribs. He dropped her abruptly and winked at the staring Brent. "See you how to kiss women; let them know they kiss a man."

Little Brent nodded solemnly, as if he'd just learned an important lesson.

"Come, Brent, we have had enough lessons on women this day," he said, hastily ushering the boy from the room and giving Lyonene a broad grin before she slammed the door on him.

She had arranged for a maid to help her dress for the procession and was careful with each fold of her green silk tunic, velvet surcoat and green, sable-lined mantle. Most of the women wore their husband's colors or the colors of their liege lord, but too often they made the garments too gaudy for Lyonene's taste. The maid sewed Lyonene's tight silk sleeves in place. Many of the other women made their sleeves so that the top of the forearm was one color and the underside another color; then the rest of the tunic would be a third color. Lyonene thought the resulting multicolored costumes obliterated all color.

The maid made tiny braids at Lyonene's temple and loosely tied them in back with several green silk ribbons. She had liked Berengaria's hair arrangement and hoped her friend did not mind her copying it. She opened a little box in the bottom of the trunk to assure herself that the ribbon was still there. It was a copy of the lion belt and she would present it to Ranulf at the joust, to wear on his helm. She had loved making every stitch of the black and gold lions.

The maid scurried from the room as Ranulf entered. He stopped and stared at his wife.

"Do I please you, my lord?" she curtsied.

"You wear the colors of Malvoisin."

"What other colors would the Countess of Malvoisin wear?" she asked haughtily.

He sat on the unmade bed. "Turn so that I may look at you. Is not that tunic overtight?"

"It is loose, see?" She made as to move the fabric and show him, but her maid had laced the silk too securely. She looked up at him and laughed, then shrugged her shoulders. "It is the fashion. I dare say Lady Elizabeth's will be as tight."

"Elizabeth is not my wife and I care naught how many men gape at her."

"Do you think men will gape at my poor form?" she asked in mock innocence.

He squinted at her. "Do you try to make me jealous?"

"And if I do?"

"Then I would say you should not. I fear I need no aid. Now come below, for we begin soon. I have obtained a black horse for you. You will not mind not riding a white one as the other ladies?"

She knew she would get no compliment from him. She put her hand on his mail-covered forearm. "The wife of the Black Lion cannot ride a white horse; it would not fit with the rest of her men."

His eyes glowed as he looked down at her, and he touched the gold lion brooches that fastened her mantle, the emerald eyes matching hers. He kissed her cheek tenderly.

The Black Guard waited below, and they were resplendent. They stood in order, ready for the procession to the lists. Hugo Fitz Waren rode first, his mail painted green, his tabard black with the rampant black lion on a green field. The Frisian and a black mare stood ready for Ranulf and Lyonene.

When she stood before her horse, Ranulf took something from his saddle pommel. He removed the customary gold circlet from Lyonene's head, tossing it to a castle servant. In its place he put a coronet—gold, with emeralds and black pearls. "A countess cannot appear as an ordinary lady," he said, smiling at her.

She pulled a green ribbon from her hair and tied it to his upper arm, the silk showing well against the gleaming silver.

He lifted her onto the horse, and she adjusted her leg to fit the sidesaddle. Her hair spread about her, grazing the horse's rump behind her.

They slowly made their way to take their places in the long line of people. Hugo Fitz Waren held the black and green banner of Malvoisin aloft, the snarling lion vivid against the emerald ground. His black tabard swirled against the green serge trappings that covered his horse.

Ranulf headed the double line that followed the chief of his Black Guard. Both his tabard and Tighe's coverings were of the darkest black. Behind him rode Corbet, with green clothing and black horse drapes. The colors alternated down the line. Lyonene was totally clad in green as was her horse, with the men that followed her also alternating in color.

Ahead of her and behind her waved the banners of the king and his earls. There was Lord Dacre's blue and gold unicorn, Humphrey de Bohun's six lioncels, Robert de

Vere's three crowns, John de Montfort's sable markings—and the three leopards of Edmund, the king's brother. The colors and the jewels sparkled, and the horses felt the excitement and pranced, threatening to overcome their riders.

Lyonene thought of Brent and knew he rode with his father. She wished there had been time to sew him a garment of the Malvoisin colors.

The great oak gate to the new castle walls was lowered, and the procession began. The noise of the waiting people drowned all thought as the riders slowly made their way to the lists. For weeks the people had been arriving: freemen, serfs whose masters attended the celebrations, women whose profession was to entertain, and merchants—hundreds of merchants.

The lists themselves stood atop a small rise, and they were alive with banners and buntings. Two sets of raised benches had been built on either side of the barrier fence, one for the nobility and canopied in a red and white striped serge, the other for the ladies of the lesser knights who entered the contests, with its roof open to the spring sky. At each end of the long, narrow field were tents. One end held the tents of the challengers, the other the comers. Lyonene could see the pennant of the Black Lion among the challengers' tents.

Behind the wooden seats and the tents were the small tents and wagons of the merchants, the guild pennants easily discernible. Among the cheering crowd were many men with flat boxes strapped to them that held food, drink, cloth, saints' relics, medicines guaranteed to cure all and ornaments from the world over.

The fences threatened to break with the teeming masses that strained against them to see the richly clad men and women. As Hugo Fitz Waren entered the gate, his horse stepping onto the soft, sand-covered field, a cry went up for the Black Lion. Lyonene was especially pleased and smiled at the people, but a quick glance at Ranulf showed he did not acknowledge the cheer. In truth, he was more than a little formidable in his black attire, his back straight as a steel rod.

The next group waited as the Earl of Malvoisin rode with his wife and his men around the edges of the jousting field. It seemed to Lyonene that the people cheered louder for them, but of course, she chided herself, that was her vain pride telling her so.

They left the far gate and entered the tent grounds at the far end. This area too was enclosed, reserved for the use of the king's chosen men only.

There were three tents sporting the Malvoisin colors, two for his men and one for Ranulf. It was the largest tent that the Earl and Countess of Malvoisin now entered.

Lyonene could not help the memories of her dance that filled her at the sight of the cream silk walls. Ranulf stopped his undressing to stare at her. Then a slow smile curved his lips. He began humming a tune from that night.

Lyonene laughed. "I think you have forgiven me for hiding away and coming to Wales."

"I have said I would forgive you aught."

She did not like his smugness. "I should test that."

"Do not dare," he growled and then saw she teased.

Brent burst into the tent. "I come, my lord, to help you dress. Is it proper that a lady be present in a knight's tent?"

Lyonene narrowed her eyes at Brent's back.

"It is an honor, Brent," Ranulf said to the boy. "No knight may go into battle, even mock battle, without his lady's favor. Now, come and help me prepare for the wrestling. You may help apply the oil over my body."

Lyonene muttered something about pages having most delightful duties and turned away when Ranulf stared at her. She called out when she heard Berengaria's voice, and her friend entered.

"I have ever wanted to see this tent." She fingered the silk of the walls. "Lord Ranulf, I think you take the wrestling this day."

"Aye. I have had Edward make eight gold cups, each set with emeralds for the prizes."

Berengaria raised her eyebrows to Lyonene, who smiled in answer.

"My lord, is it an honor for *two* ladies to be present?" Brent's voice was exasperated.

Berengaria laughed. "He is a de Lacy, ever impatient and rude. You have taken on a monster, Lyonene. Come and let us find a seat and watch your husband's triumph.

"You may sit with my wife in the section for Malvoisin. I do not think you will find it difficult to see from there."

The two women left the tent. "How do we women bear such arrogance?" They looked at each other and laughed.

Ranulf had been correct; green and black ropes sectioned off a good piece of the tiered benches. There was room for about a dozen people. Lyonene and Berengaria took their places on the front row. There would be a while before the wrestling began, so they purchased flawns, a kind of cheesecake, from a shouting merchant.

The trumpets sounded and split the air; the people hushed in anticipation. The men began to come from both ends of the lists, dressed only in small white loincloths. Lord Dacre with his five men caused no little commotion —his body a light gold color, his chest lightly covered in fair hair.

When Ranulf entered the field, followed by his seven dark men, Lyonene gripped Berengaria's arm.

Berengaria exclaimed, "I can see why you love the man—he is magnificent!"

Lyonene smiled proudly.

Favors from the women in the stands rained upon the field—flowers, ribbons, sleeves. Around her, Lyonene heard shouts of the names of the men of the Black Guard, especially those of Corbet and Maularde. Corbet acknowledged all shouts with thrown kisses and tossed all favors to a waiting servant. Maularde took only one ribbon tossed to him and smiled to someone behind Lyonene. She turned to see a young girl dimpling prettily at the guardsman's attentions.

Ranulf nodded to her, and she saw that her green ribbon was tied about his upper arm.

"Travers would never allow such men near me. It would not be easy to choose one of them."

"But my Ranulf is by far the best, do you not agree?"

"It is said that love is blind, but it is not so in your case."

Dacre did not wrestle against Ranulf as the Black Lion had hoped, for he had wished to best his friend, but the two earls and their men challenged all comers. First the men of the guard fought the comers. If any bested the king's men, he went on to fight Ranulf or Lord Dacre.

The matches began with Ranulf and Dacre looking on as five groups of men circled one another. Their oiled bodies glistened in the early sun and the cheers of the many people urged them on. One of Dacre's men was thrown and held until a king's official declared him bested. Lyonene saw Ranulf punch his friend heartily.

The three men of the Black Guard easily won their matches, and Lyonene knew that the other men could not have been as trained in wrestling as her husband's men were.

The trumpets sounded again and eleven men entered to challenge the knights. Lord Dacre and Ranulf looked on again and saw the comer who had bested Dacre's man easily felled by Sainneville.

The second round was won also, and Lyonene could see the smugness on Ranulf and Dacre's faces, their mock yawns.

The trumpets sounded again and the field cleared, but there were no new comers. Ranulf and his friend stood straighter as the trumpets blared again and again. The gates at the far end slowly opened, and two covered litters were carried into the midst of the lists.

A hush fell on the crowd as every eye went to those litters, their contents secret. Two men ran from behind and blew more horns, and the serge of the litters fell back, the dark interiors revealing nothing. The men shouldering the carriages lowered them and two men stepped from them—enormous men, powerful men, their heads and bodies completely shaved and oiled to a slick sheen. The litters were quickly taken away, and the two men stood with legs apart, hands on hips. "We are from Angilliam, the brothers Ross, and we challenge Lord Dacre and Lord Ranulf to a fight until one cries, 'Peace.'"

The cry from the crowd was deafening, a roar that vibrated the benches. Berengaria laughed and clapped her hands, then looked toward Lyonene's pleased smile.

"You seem confident of the outcome of this match."

"Ranulf will win, but he will need to work hard to win. I am glad he does not receive his gold cups without effort."

"Oh, I trust he will make an effort to win from those men."

They watched as Ranulf circled the enormous man, and Lyonene was pleased to see that her husband equaled him in size. The first hold brought Ranulf to his back with a loud thud. She saw his muscles strain as he pushed the man from him, their legs locked together, Ranulf's darker skin prominent. They broke their holds and circled again, but this time Ranulf got in the first grip. Ranulf's arm encircled the man's neck and she saw Ranulf's back as the strong man freed himself.

Their muscles strained as they pushed, each taking a hold or using his massive strength to break the other's hold. They stood and locked arms, their legs pulling-pushing, expanding, as their bodies wrestled together. There were whole minutes when neither moved, and had it not been for the expanded cords in their necks, the knotted muscles in their backs, one would have thought they but rested.

"The man Ross is tiring," Berengaria said. "His legs begin to quiver, but your Ranulf's do not. He must be trained well for this match."

She merely smiled, for all her attention was on her husband and she could only guess at the pain he felt at this long, long match.

They broke the hold and the crowd cheered, for the bald man showed visible signs of weariness and Ranulf took advantage and attacked.

"Lord Dacre does well, also, though his brother Ross is smaller than the one who fights Lord Ranulf."

The two men continued to strain against one another until Ranulf brought the man down with an ankle locked about his opponent's calf. The man could not break the fierce hold. The cry of "Lion" filled the air when the man cried, "Peace." Ranulf stood and solemnly helped the bald man to stand beside him. He left the field and Ranulf stood in triumph. It was but a moment before Lord Dacre joined him, and together they strutted around the field.

Ranulf paused before Lyonene, and she kissed a ribbon and threw it to him. He caught it in the air and kissed it as he looked at her, a look that made her blush. He looped it and stuffed it into the side of his loincloth, the ends hanging down his hip and thigh. He gave her a one-sided grin, almost a leer. She covered her face with her hands as the crowd, and the men and women around her, cheered his gesture. She did not look up again until he was gone from the lists.

"You may show your face again, for he is gone and the trumpets sound for dinner."

They joined the line that began to leave the tourney grounds.

"My lady. My Lady Lyonene." She turned to a breathless, starry-eyed Brent. "Is he not the strongest knight? Did you see him?"

"Aye, I did." She did not know her expression matched his.

"He bids you come to him, to his tent, for he dines there. He says he must not dress yet; there may be more men such as the brothers Ross to fight." His face fell. "I must dine with my father."

Berengaria laughed. "I fear our father is a poor substitute for the Black Lion. Come along, Brent, mayhaps you can make do with my poor Travers."

Lyonene hurried to Ranulf's tent. She did not see him at first, he lay so still on the cot.

"Lyonene?" he whispered.

She hurried to him. "Ranulf! You are hurt!"

"I am more than hurt, I am dying," came his muffled reply. "There is naught of me that does not pain me. Neither of the ax wounds in my arm and leg, nor both together, caused me so much pain."

She stroked his sweat-dampened hair, laughter in her voice. "But Brent has said you ready yourself to fight other men, men, of course, more fierce than the little one just finished." She laughed at his groan.

"You are cruel. What would the boy say of me 'twere he to see me like this?"

"At least you do not think I needs must be impressed." She tugged on the green ribbon that hung from his loincloth and his hand instantly covered hers, but not without his groaning in pain.

"That is mine; I won it and do not make me need to wrestle you to keep it."

"Hmph! You could not even whip me now."

His arm encircled her waist, and amid squeals of laughter, he pulled her down beside him on the cot. He threw one heavy leg across her thighs and an arm across her breasts, his face snuggled near her ear. "You delight in causing me pain. First I must strut before my page and then I must prove again my strength to my wife. Lie still and do not plague me."

She did as he bid and was content with his nearness.

"Good morn, your lordship." Brent greeted them below stairs, the next morning, his face solemn.

Ranulf frowned at the boy. "I seem to be somewhat weary this morn. Mayhaps you would oblige me and rid me of this burden until we are at the lists." He unbuckled the long sword that hung in front of him.

Lyonene thought the boy's eyelids might turn inside out, so wide did he open them.

"Oh, my lord," he whispered. "This is the sword you used to kill the infidels in the Holy Lands?"

"Aye, it is."

"And what is its name?"

"Challouns. It is written here," he said, pointing, "on the blade. There is a splinter of the true cross in the glass ball on the hilt, and this emerald is said to come from King Arthur's crown."

Brent reverently held the sword before him, his head back and his arms lifted.

Lyonene and Ranulf followed, and she squeezed his arm. "You are most kind to the boy. I can see why he near worships you. My father has never spent so much time with his pages, or even his squires."

"I like children." He looked pointedly at her stomach. "Mayhaps you could give me a few."

"I shall fill every nook at Malvoisin with lion cubs."

He grinned mischievously. "If I but last through the nights required of me."

She tossed her hair and refused to answer him, which made him laugh and kiss her cheek.

At the lists, the benches were already full and several of the Black Guard occupied the section set aside for the Earl of Malvoisin; they rose until Lyonene was seated. She spoke to each of the four men and congratulated them on their win at wrestling the day before. Corbet and Maularde sat apart, each beside a pretty girl. To her surprise, Hugo Fitz Waren did also. She nudged Ranulf.

"Hugo is so solemn, I did not think him to be . . ."

Ranulf's eyes sparkled. "None of my men find it difficult to have a woman. They are most honored to be of the Black Guard. For all the bragging of the others, Hugo has many women who work to bind him to them."

She sat near Ranulf, their thighs and arms pressed close. "As I have bound you to me?"

He pushed a strand of hair from her eyes. "Aye, as you have done so to me."

The blaring of the trumpets turned their attention to the sand-covered field. The jumping events occupied the morn—jumping high hurdles and across long distances. Lord Dacre's men took one of these events.

The trumpets again sounded to announce that dinner was served. For this meal, Berengaria sat at Lyonene's left and Ranulf at her right. They were pleasantly entertained by three young girls who played and sang.

King Edward stood, and the room was silent. "I have an announcement . . . this day. We strove to conquer Llewellyn and did so, yet all . . . know the story of his traitor brother, David. When David was . . . captured, his family was taken to Rhuddlan Castle. There were two sons and s . . . seven daughters. The sons, twins of three years, have been g . . . given to my knights to raise. The . . . daughters and wife all asked to go to nunneries. The . . . wife and four of the daughters I have allowed to do so. . . . Now I have tried to wed the other three. One killed herself."

The crowd gasped at the horror of this mortal sin.

"The other daughter I married to Sir John of Bohum. Some of you may have . . . known him. The girl killed him on their . . . wedding night and then herself."

The hall was totally silent, each face a mask of horror.

"Now I try to . . . keep the last daughter from a wasted life." He motioned to a man near the door, and everyone turned to watch.

Two enormous, mail-clad men came into the room with the sounds of a dragging chain behind them. The girl was almost too small to be seen at first. Her head was down, face hidden, but her black hair cascaded over her blue velvet surcoat.

"You may . . . wonder at my chaining so small a girl,"

Edward continued, "but she has killed one of my guards, and you can see the wounds born by these men."

Lyonene noticed the long furrows on the men's faces where she had raked them with her nails.

Berengaria nudged her friend. " 'Twere I in her place, I would act just so. I hear the Welsh do not think their David a traitor."

"Her . . . name is Angharad, and I now offer her in . . . marriage to any knight worthy of the woman's rank."

At this the girl lifted her face and the crowd exclaimed at her beauty. The black hair framed a pretty face with a small nose and full lips, but her eyes were what was startling, for they were a brilliant, vibrant blue. They burned now as if from a fever, and her look of defiance and contempt was easily read.

Berengaria directed Lyonene's attention to Lord Dacre, a few places from them. He stared at the girl open-mouthed, his eyes glazed as if there were no reason left in his brain. Lyonene nudged Ranulf so he could see his friend.

"Dacre has more sense than that," he whispered under his breath.

Even as he spoke, Dacre threw back his chair, the loud sound it made as it struck the floor causing many of the guests to jump. He bounded across the table to the girl, startling her so that she could not react. He grabbed her to him, crushing the chained hands helplessly between their bodies as his lips came down on hers.

Dacre drew back with a cry of pain, and everyone could see the drop of blood on his lip.

"You will regret that lost blood in future, for I swear before God that someday you will love me more than your own life. You are mine!"

She screamed at him in a torrent of words of the Welsh language. The silent diners gasped when she spit on him. Dacre but grinned at her and rubbed his wet cheek against hers. She tried to move her arms, but could not.

Dacre turned to his king. "I claim her now, and if a priest is not come soon, I bed her unwed."

The tension was broken as the crowd laughed.

King Edward nodded toward a man at a far table. "Stewart! Draw up the p . . . papers. There is no dowry, for her father lost all for his traitor's deeds."

Angharad lunged toward the king and he drew back, although Lord Dacre held her fast. "My father was no traitor!" Her words were oddly spoken as she struggled with a language foreign to her.

"Take her L . . . Lord Dacre, and I do not envy you. See that she does not kill you on your wedding night also."

Dacre lifted her to his arms, her violent struggles effortless against the man's strength. He smiled up at his king. "Have no fear for my life. She is but a woman who has not met a man. This night she will, and she will be tamed."

The crowd broke into gales of laughter as Dacre took the struggling girl from the hall. All agreed that naught had ever so enlivened a meal before.

"What think you of your friend now?" a laughing Lyonene asked her husband.

"Dacre has ever had little sense about women." He took her small hand and kissed it. "I have fought in two wars and I do not care for the constant battle. I wish for peace in my own bedchamber."

"And you find our encounters . . . peaceful?"

The laugh rumbled in his throat. "Nay, my Lioness, I find your nearness aught but peaceful. 'Twere it not that I must participate in Edward's games, I would join the sport Dacre enjoys this day."

She felt her cheeks redden and looked to see who listened to his words. She returned her hand to her own lap. "Many will wonder at our actions and think we are but just married. After so long a time, we should by now be tired of each other and turn to lovers."

His hand clenched her wrist, causing her pain. "Do not say such!"

"Ranulf, I do but jest. Do not hurt me. I will not look at any other man, I swear it. Can you not see I jest?"

He released her. "I am sorry I hurt you, but I cannot laugh at such things."

"You will tell me someday who has hurt you so to give you such pain?"

He looked away, not answering.

They were silent for the rest of the meal, but by its end, Ranulf's good humor was restored. She walked with him to his tent at the far end of the lists. Brent waited impatiently for his lord. Ranulf gave her a chaste kiss as she left to join Berengaria in the stands.

The lance casting came first. Gilbert de Clare, another earl, and a knight of Robert de Vere's took the event.

Ranulf appeared in a short garment of the Malvoisin colors and demonstrated the longbow. It seemed to Lyonene that there were too many female exclamations of joy near her. Berengaria laughed at her friend's intense frown. The crowd of serfs and free men were not restrained by the rules of chivalry, as the knights were, and their cheers at the speed and distance of the new longbow were thunderous, for Ranulf was among their favorite knights. He waved to them, enjoying their adoration.

After the exhibition, Lyonene joined Ranulf in his tent.

"You were pleased with my shooting?" he asked, grinning at her. "Brent is torn between his father's words and his new lord. I think he will see my way, do you not?"

"I am sure he will, for have you not won me to your way of thinking?"

He pulled her to his lap, kissing her. "I am more pleased with winning you than my page. What say you we miss dinner and stay in my tent?" He muffled her protests with his lips, and she could aught but submit as his lips slowly worked their way down the side of her neck.

Their lovemaking was as passionate as if they had not been together for months instead of for just a few hours. Later, Lyonene and Ranulf lay together, their bare flesh moist and satisfied.

"You have bewitched me. How shall I win the joust on the morrow when my mind is ever on you?"

"I do not care if you enter or no. Stay all day with me and we will watch from the stands."

He grabbed her shoulders and held her away from him, frowning into her eyes. "You would dishonor me. The Black Lion must fight or he will lose the men who follow him." He dismissed the subject. "I wonder how Dacre fares with that new wife of his."

"Did you think her pretty?"

"Beautiful."

"More so than me?"

"By far. You are a slug compared to her." He only laughed when she struck his chest.

Lyonene woke early the next day, and she slowly turned her head to look at Ranulf as he slept near her. One of his hands was tangled in her hair, another held her firmly by the waist. She smiled as she thought that even in sleep he would not loose her.

"You seem to plan some devilment this morn."

"Nay, I but look at you." She moved closer to him, putting her arms around his neck. "We will return home soon?"

"I think you grow as weary of court as I. What say you we leave early on the morrow.

She gave him a quick kiss. "I look forward to the journey."

He pushed her down on the mattress and rolled on top her. "And what entertainment do you plan on the return? It could not equal the dance."

She shot him a wicked look with her emerald eyes. Her hands ran down his body until she found what she sought. "Think you not?" she whispered before speech deserted them.

At the lists, Lyonene looked with trepidation at each of Ranulf's opponents. Ranulf himself was splendidly clad in his silvered mail, with her ribbon, the copy of the lion belt, tied to his helm. Three charges with each man were allowed. The thundering of the horses' hoofs, the splintering lances, the cheers and jeers of the crowd were overpowering. The man who so confidently sat astride the great black horse was a stranger to her. Gone was the smiling, teasing man she had spent so many hours of pleasure with and in his place was the intense, dark face of the king's champion—the Black Lion. She did not wonder at the fear he instilled in so many men.

The jousting was not stopped for dinner; instead, servants brought food to the stands, and the spectators ate and drank heartily as they cheered their favorites. Lyonene could not help her flush of pride that none of the Malvoisin men were bested.

The mercenary knights required large ransoms of the men they felled, and more than one poor knight made no little fortune on this day. Occasionally Lyonene spotted Brent, an exhilarated, tired, dirty boy.

Lady Aleen, Brent's mother, came to express her appreciation that Lyonene had taken her burdensome son. She laughed as she recounted the boy's tales of Lord Ranulf and told of his complete adoration of the knight.

It was late when the jousting ended. Lyonene and Berengaria laughed over the sight of several young girls who wore only their tunics, having torn their other apparel and cast it as favors to their favorite knights. Already the tents were being dismantled as the two women made their way back to the castle.

Lyonene heard the sound of water even as she opened the door to their bedchamber. Ranulf sat in a large tub of steaming water.

"Come and wash my back. I am glad I can now turn my mind to other matters.

"Do you not fear to wet your clothes? I did not think only of the sleeves." He grinned at her.

It was but minutes before Lyonene found herself pressed to Ranulf inside the tub, the water flowing over the sides onto the floor. They laughed as they ran soapy fingers over one another, exploring sensuous places.

There were two very clean people who joined the other guests for the feast at the end of the tourney.

Edward's chief falconer had brought several hawks into the hall, and after the first two courses the trumpets blared. A dozen enormous pies were brought from the kitchens, each pie taking two boys to carry it. As the pies were cut, live birds flew into the air, the flapping of their wings filling the hall. The clapping and cheers of the people added to the general confusion. As the hawks swooped down on the birds, the guests covered their heads, peeking through their arms at the slashing hawks.

Some time later, the birds were removed, but the excitement remained. Dancing girls were now brought in and the jesting became louder and cruder.

Too much wine made Lyonene's head spin. She asked for water to dilute the intoxicating beverage.

"Hear, my L . . . Lord Ranulf, give your wife s . . . some water." King Edward's eyes twinkled as he handed a silver pitcher to his earl.

Ranulf hesitated for a moment, then grinned roguishly

at his king. "I see your meaning. Mayhaps a little water will help."

The watered wine did not seem at all weaker to Lyonene, but the dizziness was not unpleasant. She looked at Ranulf and seemed to forget the presence of other people. A quick movement caught her eye and she saw a knight grab one of the dancing women and tear her tunic away, burying his face in her too full breasts.

It seemed to Lyonene that all her senses were on fire. She raked her tongue across her teeth, enjoying the sharpness. Her fingers were tingling and they seemed more sensitive than they had ever been. She studied Ranulf's profile and felt an incredible hunger to taste his skin beneath her mouth. She had never felt so strange.

"Warbrooke!" someone called above the general din. "See to your wife. I think our king's 'water' has not quenched her thirst."

Ranulf turned startled eyes to his wife and then a slow smile overtook him. He lifted her fingers to kiss them. He turned serious when she ran one finger firmly across his lips. He did not hesitate. He lifted her in his arms, ignoring the howls of laughter behind him, and carried her to their bedchamber.

Lyonene, later, did not remember too clearly all the events of that night. It seemed that they were instantly without clothes and on the bed. She remembered that she fought Ranulf and that he let her win. She satisfied herself at last by hungrily running her mouth over his entire body. When he sought to pull her to him, she pushed him away until she was ready for him.

She growled and laughed because she knew she had power over him, that she had bested the Black Lion as no other could. She ran her hands over his body, using her nails as she explored every inch of him.

Almost violently, he threw her down beside him. Their lovemaking was angry, turbulent, crashing waves of a raging storm, lightning causing fire as she ran her nails across his back, the inside of his thighs.

The storm abated with the same violence as it had begun. They rolled away from one another, not speaking, not touching, content, and slept.

Chapter Eleven

Lyonene tried to still her aching head the next morn, but Ranulf's jests did not help. She looked away when he teased her for her actions during the night. Her stomach turned over several times when he pulled her from the bed and clasped her to him.

"Edward ever likes his tricks. He gave me white wine to use to dilute your red. I must thank him, for the results were . . ." He bit her earlobe. "There is not an inch of skin left on my back. How will I explain such wounds to my page?"

She could feel the hot blood flooding her face, and she refused to meet his laughing eyes.

"Mmm, my Lioness." He buried his face in her neck. "I regret the time we have lost. I know you are not well, but are you too ill to begin the return journey to Malvoisin?"

In spite of her head and her stomach, she managed a timid smile. "Aye," she whispered, "I am ready to return home."

It was late in the day before they could begin the journey. Clothes, food, weapons, armor, tents had to be packed in wagons, Maude and the other two women from Malvoisin found and good-byes said. Lyonene regretted leaving Berengaria, and they exchanged promises to visit one another.

Brent gave one mournful look to his mother, and then even a hint of sadness left him as Ranulf led a solid-black pony into the courtyard and handed the reins to his new page. Henry de Lacy laughed and accused Ranulf of spoiling the boy, but Ranulf stated that all his men were treated with honor, as they deserved. Lyonene hid her smile at the solemn man-face on the six-year-old child.

A quick glance at the Black Guard showed Corbet and

Sainneville to be in much worse shape than Lyonene. Ranulf heartily slapped both men on the back and asked if they did not think it a lovely day. He winked at Lyonene, who could not see the humor of the jest since her own stomach refused to remain still.

The return journey to Malvoisin was slow, taking a full week. They stayed at no castles, preferring to pitch their tents and spend the night with just a thin sheet of fabric separating them from the warm spring air. They often walked hand-in-hand among the trees, laughing, kissing, enjoying.

From the time they crossed the ferry to the Isle of Malvoisin, Lyonene felt a tense excitement. When the first sight of the pennants came into view, she and Ranulf exchanged looks and secret smiles, then spurred their horses ahead. They entered through the west barbican, as before, only this time Lyonene bent to touch the offered hands also.

There was only one blot on their joyous homecoming: the sight of a knight who glared at them, half-concealed by the stable walls. She remembered having seen him once before on guard duty. He gave her a smirking look, and she turned away quickly.

Ranulf swung Lyonene from her horse, his hands lingering on her tiny waist. He held her aloft a moment and they smiled into one another's eyes.

"My lady, you are returned! I near died of fright every moment you were away." Lucy waddled toward her mistress.

"Her fretting does not seem to have affected her appetite," Ranulf whispered as they both saw that Lucy had added weight.

"And this baggage! It seems she helped you in your wicked plot." She tossed her head back to the maid, Kate, who smiled nervously. Lyonene knew that for all Lucy's words, she would never be mean to Kate or anyone else. The old woman turned to Ranulf for the first time. "You seem to have come to your senses," she sniffed, eyeing the ease between them, the touches.

Ranulf did not smile but Lyonene could see the amusement in his eyes. "If you mean about this Lioness, I had no choice. She spent many hours working at ways to seduce me. A man can resist only so long."

"Ranulf!" Lyonene gave him a horrified look.

Lucy looked from one to the other, serious. "I have told her to do so. A woman should not need to depend upon the infrequent thoughts of a man to get what she wants."

Lyonene could not speak, she was so embarrassed.

Ranulf grinned then and took Lyonene's hand and held it to his lips, his eyes never leaving Lucy's. "She has gotten what she wants now. But it has not been easy for me —all day and all night." He ignored Lyonene's half-scream, holding her hand firmly to him.

Lucy grinned. "It certainly looks as if her wants have agreed with you."

Lyonene gave a violent jerk to her hand and drew it from Ranulf's. "I will not be discussed like a . . . tavern wench!" Her head held high, she marched to the front door of Black Hall. She had to use all her strength to keep from losing her slight composure when she heard Ranulf say something about, ". . . best tavern wench I've ever had . . ." and Lucy's giggle of delight.

Brent, his excitement at the unusual castle no longer contained, burst past her. She was happy to show the boy all the beauties of Malvoisin, and experienced anew the wonder of glass windows, tapestries and carpets.

The day was spent in hearing reports of happenings in the near two months they had been away. William de Bec, the steward, reported problems at Lyonene's dower castle, Gethen. It seemed a neighbor had decided to declare that a large portion of the estate belonged to him. Ranulf sent William and six garrison knights to report on the matter.

The days lengthened and ran together in a blur of happiness for Lyonene. She and Bassett, the gardener, worked together to fill the Queen's Garden with roses, lilies, marigolds, poppies, daffodils and many herbs. Espaliered cherry, apple and peach trees covered the walls. On the warm nights, she and Ranulf often sat together by the tiled fountain and talked or sang.

Ranulf spent near two weeks tending to his other manors. When he returned, their reunion was joyous. They spent many hours together in the solar, drinking from one another's cups, telling stories of their separate happenings.

It was in late June as they sat in the solar, Brent drowsing on a sun-warmed carpet, wrapped around the puppy

Ranulf had given him, that a servant announced a fire in the village. Ranulf went immediately, Brent not far behind.

It was late when the Black Guard returned with their master, their bodies blackened by the smoke.

"We could not save the houses, but the people are alive, although burned. Could you see to them?" he asked tiredly as the men wearily walked to the river to wash.

Daylight saw a lord and his lady who had not slept at all through the night. The climbed the stairs to their room, arms locked, eyes barely open.

"Here you go." Lucy handed Lyonene a basket, which she took only because of a remembered response. "No one will let you sleep here. Soon the whole castle will awake, and then William will have a problem that desperately needs solving and then Bassett will ask for her ladyship's help. You must go. I have prepared you food and that mean, devil-horse of yours is saddled, so off you go. I do not wish to see you until nightfall."

Ranulf seemed to shrug his weariness away easily. He ran a hand down Lyonene's back and firmly cupped her behind, grinning impishly when she jumped. "Lucy, you are after my own heart. I am so pleased that I do not even defend Tighe's abused name. Come, Lioness, I know a glade that you will enjoy." He took her hand and near pulled her to the door. She had only time for a smile of gratitude to Lucy.

The glade proved to be more than Ranulf had promised. It was sheltered and private, the ground soft with moss and tiny pink flowers.

Lyonene wore only her linen undertunic and Ranulf his loincloth. He leaned against a tree and Lyonene snuggled her back against his chest, his arms encircling her.

"You are no longer unhappy you married me?" she asked.

"I was never unhappy."

She smiled and moved closer to him, her hand running idly along his thigh. "You are pleased also with Brent?"

He turned her to look at him, lifting one eyebrow. "Why all these questions? Has aught displeased you?"

"Nay." She lay back against him. "I am happy. I but wondered how you felt towards me and towards . . . children."

156

He snorted. "You are a troublesome baggage, but men must make do with their wives. As for children, or at least Brent, I grow fonder of the boy each day. Brother Jonathan says he is most bright and can write his own name. Corbet has been teaching him . . ." He stopped abruptly and turned her again to face him, a black scowl on his face. "Why do you ask me these questions?"

She put a hand on his chest and laughed. "I am not your enemy, Ranulf, that you must turn such a face on me." She winced. "You hurt me!" He released her so quickly she almost fell backwards.

She smiled secretly and took her place against him again. "To answer you, I am but curious." She felt him relax against her. "Whatever did you think me to mean, my lord?"

He took a deep breath and sighed, totally relaxed. "You startled me, 'tis all. I thought, for a moment, you meant to say you were with child."

"And if those were my words?"

He tightened again and then relaxed. "I would force myself to bear such news with the courage that befits a knight and an earl."

She was glad he could not see her expression. "And what courage could you speak of? I see no great feat for a man to create a babe."

"It is not the creating, but the eternal responsibility. A child is a serious undertaking."

"And you would bear the news with the gravity that befitted the occasion?" If he could have seen her eyes he would not have fallen into her trap so readily.

"Most assuredly. All in all, I am glad you are not breeding, for I have not had the time to think on the duties of being a . . . father."

Her heart fell somewhat. "But what of your daughter?"

Ranulf was quiet. "I was young then and . . ." He paused. "Let us not talk of this more."

She turned to him then. "But, my husband, we must speak of this, for at Christmas, I plan to present you with a most special gift."

He grinned. "And what can it be? There is naught that I do not have."

She shook her head at him. "Mayhaps I should have Brother Jonathan create a mind for you from paper. It could not be of less substance than the one you now attempt to use."

He frowned at her and then all color drained from his face, his eyes wide.

She looked down at her hands. "Please do not say you are displeased. I do not think I could bear it."

They sat in silence for what seemed to be hours, and then Ranulf lifted her chin with his fingertips. She could almost swear that the strong, masculine hand, the hand of the Black Lion, king's champion, trembled. His eyes held a strange expression.

"This is true? You will bear me a babe?"

She nodded, not sure what she saw in his face. He dropped his hand and stood up with lightning speed, his legs wide apart, hands on hips, and threw back his head, giving the loudest, ugliest, most terrifying war cry she had ever heard. She covered her ears against that hideous sound, which sent tremors of unknown terror through her body.

The sound carried for a long way, and those who heard also shuddered at the sound, never before given off a battlefield.

Lyonene still sat with her hands over her ears when Ranulf looked back at her. He pulled her to him to study her face and then kissed her mouth, hard.

"I may take it that the news does not cause your displeasure?"

He swung her into his arms. "No man has ever been happier."

"You do not think of responsibilities and duties?" she teased.

"Your fun of me is at an end. I should like a son first and then a score of daughters. I will need a boy to help me protect my beautiful daughters. And I shall never allow them to marry, but keep them by me always to fetch my slippers and tend to my wine." He paused a moment. "Of a surety, Edward will take credit for this."

"What has the king to do with our child?"

"If it is to be born at Christmas, then it had to have been created at the Round Table." He gave her a mocking look. "My poor brain has always been good at arithmetic, if not at women's riddles. Edward will say it was the white wine he had me mix with your red. Of course everyone else would agree, for you had an unwholesome look on your face when I carried you from the hall."

"You did not carry me!"

"I most assuredly did. There were great cheers and not a few suggestions as to how to proceed from there, but I fear you outdid any suggestion a mere man could create. Yes, I am sure 'twas that night that made my child."

He laughed when her fist pelted his naked chest. "What will our boy say of a mother who beats his father?"

"He will probably join me, or it would be my good fortune to bear a braggart just like you. His first steps will no doubt be a swagger, his first words a boast."

Ranulf laughed hard and hugged her to him. "Then you must indeed have my daughters, for who else will listen to us?"

"I am sure you will find someone."

"That is true, but they all sit in rapture of me. No other woman makes me work so hard to make an impression or beats me when I go too far."

She laughed with him and put her arms about his neck. "I shall bear you hundreds of whatever you wish." They kissed, quietly, sweetly. "You are glad then, truly glad?"

He nibbled her ear. "You are hard to persuade. There is naught I can say. I look forward eagerly to my first child. Now I should like to return to my house and put you to bed and then go and brag to my men."

"Release me and do not act such a fool. I am well, and the strength I build each day flows to the child and gives him strength."

He set her down carefully and seemed to consider her words. "I do not know . . . Lucy and Kate will care for you and keep you from building too much strength, as you say. Now dress that we may return." His eyes widened. "Should you ride?"

She kept her face perfectly calm. "Nay, I should walk back to the castle."

He narrowed his eyes at her. "Do not grow too saucy, wench. There are ways to punish you that will not harm the babe."

She tossed her hair over one shoulder. "And how may that be, my lord?"

He grabbed her arm and with deadly seriousness began to tickle her until she cried. They fell together on the ground, Ranulf ignoring her pleas for mercy. The under-tunic, caught beneath his knee, tore away and revealed her breasts. His attentions turned from thoughts of revenge.

Their lovemaking was sweet and gentle, a fitting crown to the news that bound them together, each of them aware of the life they had created in their joy of one another. In a state of sensuous rapture, they fell asleep amidst the moss, the flowers, the trickling water, the lazy drone of insects and the soft warm summer breeze.

Lyonene sat quietly in the solar, a new tabard for Ranulf under her needle. The sounds of the Black Guard from the Great Hall made her smile, for the cheers were loud and growing louder. The comradeship between her husband and his men was a deep friendship, built over years of war, battle, pain and joy, and, she guessed, no small number of kegs of wine.

She was in bed when Ranulf returned, loudly undressed and fell onto the mattress beside her. He roughly pulled her to him as if she were a rag doll and caressed her hardening stomach. He gave a grunt of contentment and fell asleep, his face covered with her hair.

It was two weeks later when the storm began. They woke to a gray sky, lightning flashing in the distance, the air cool and clammy.

Ranulf stood with his men in the courtyard and studied the ugly sky. "I think we should make preparations." He turned and saw Lyonene's worried face. "Malvoisin Isle has terrible storms and I think this may be one of the worst. My men and I must prepare the villagers. See you that inside the walls all is secure; I do not wish loose boards flying about the stables or the mews. Assign a boy to each horse to stay the night and calm him. Find William and give him my orders."

"I am here, Lord Ranulf, and I have begun preparations." The steward's voice showed that he needed no one to give him orders. "The shutters are being nailed over the windows."

Ranulf merely nodded and was gone.

The atmosphere inside the castle changed from its usual noisiness to an eerie quiet. The people seemed to walk on their toes, their voices whispers. The master carpenter and his apprentice carried the tool box about and put extra nails in worn partitions. The horses sensed the coming storm and became nervous and skittish, the boys calming and soothing them.

The garrison knights saw to firewood piles and the storage of food in the stone towers. Leather goods, fabrics, small animals were all taken inside the towers. The courtyards and walkways were thoroughly cleaned to prevent the rain from mixing with the filth, thus turning everything into an open sewer.

The first heavy drops of rain came in the late afternoon.

"Lady Lyonene, you must come. Lord Ranulf said you were not to be outside after the first sign of rain." Kate, who took her new responsibilities as Lyonene's maid very seriously, near pulled her mistress to the safety of the stone house.

Inside, it was dark. The windows were all completely shuttered.

"Hodder, please see that a fire is lit in the solar, and fetch towels and robes for Lord Ranulf and Master Brent. They will be wet when they return. And see that Dawkin keeps food and wine hot."

"Yes, my lady."

Even as Lyonene mounted the stairs, the storm grew worse. The thunder cracked above their heads, the lightning felt rather than seen. She thought of Ranulf, Brent and the Black Guard outside and she shivered.

The solar was warm and dry, yet each fresh rage of the weather brought a new frown to her face. She could not look out, for the shutters were on the outside, protecting the precious glass windows.

"I cannot work on this!" she said, putting down her sewing. "Why do they not return? Go again and ask Hodder if there is word," she told Kate.

"My lady, I have but returned. The island is large and they must see to many people. All the watch towers must be lit."

"What is this? Why must there be a light?"

"To warn any ships of the island. There are many shipwrecks at St. Agnes' Point."

"Shipwrecks?" she asked quietly and sat down again.

"Aye. Then the men, Lord Ranulf's men, must go to the point and look for survivors."

"Why must he go? Are there not other men?"

"Oh yes, my lady," Kate answered. "But they are not as honest as Lord Ranulf." She saw Lyonene did not understand, so she began to explain. "It is the law that whoever finds a ship with no survivors may have the cargo of that ship. If even one person survives, then that person owns the cargo, not the finders."

"I do not yet see how this affects my husband."

"Too often the finders will kill the survivors rather than give up their booty. Lord Ranulf goes to see they are not killed."

"Oh." She leaned back and digested this information. "But is it not dangerous to go in a storm and search for these near-drowned people?"

"Oh, yes, it is most . . . " Kate caught her words when she saw the wild look in her mistress's eye. "Lord Ranulf does but give orders," she lied. "It is not so dangerous for him. There are others, men who use a boat well who look for people."

Lyonene was relieved somewhat by the girl's words, but not enough to continue sewing. "You do not think there is a shipwreck now?"

"No, word would have been sent to us. The whole island knows when there is such an event, even in a storm."

The hours dragged and Lyonene walked again and again to the windows, forgetting each time they were covered. She heard noises and ran to the stairs to see only darkness below.

It was late when she heard unmistakable sounds of doors and people. She barely touched the stairs as she ran below. She flew to Ranulf, mindless of his wet clothes. He held her to him, aware of her pounding heart.

"Here, I am near drowned and you wet me more." He kissed her tear-covered eyelids. "Let me go by the fire, for the cold and wet has gone to my bones."

"Brent! Where is he?" she demanded.

"Corbet took him. Their women will care for him."

She could not help a pang of jealousy.

Ranulf saw it. "You have not enough with me? You let me stand here and turn to ice? Mayhaps I should have followed my page?"

She grinned at him and pulled him up the stairs, where she dismissed Kate. She hurriedly helped Ranulf peel off his sodden clothes and rubbed him briskly with the towels. Hodder brought a warm robe, fur-lined slippers, hot wine and a charger of soup and roasted chicken.

Once warm, Ranulf attacked the food and drink.

"This is one of the worst I have ever seen," he said through mouthfuls of food. "I saw the wind lift a dog and carry it a cloth-yard away. Brent was holding onto his saddle with both hands. Hugo pulled him to the front of him and led the pony. The rain slashed so hard we could hardly see. We shall spend months repairing roofs after this. You prepared the castle properly?"

She rubbed his calf muscles with the towel. "Aye, I am glad for the shutters. There is no sign of a ship?"

He paused an instant over a chicken leg and then continued. "Nay. The fires are lit on all the towers and I have sent more men to St. Agnes' Point. They are to ride at once to me to tell if a ship is sighted."

"You must go? You cannot send another to give your orders?"

He lifted one eyebrow. "Nay, no one else can . . . give orders."

Even as they spoke, Herne broke into the room. "There is a wreck and it looks to be a big one. The rest of the guard are dressing now."

Ranulf rose abruptly and strode into the bedchamber. Lyonene followed, watching silently as he pulled clothes from chests.

"You cannot leave this to your men?"

He turned a face to her as violent as the storm outside. "Nay, I cannot. Do not say so to me again." His voice was low and deadly. He pulled on thick woolen chausses, then the linen undershirt.

"Come here," he finally said. "Do not look so at me. I must go and I do not wish you to plague me."

She stood before him, silently.

"Where is my Lioness?" he demanded. "Fetch me my heavy woolen mantle. Are you not worth all the gold I spend on you or the food I feed you?"

Her head came up then. "Mayhaps the rain will mold you into a chivalrous knight."

When he was dressed, he clutched her to him, his

strength near cracking her ribs. "If you wish to help, go to the chapel and give us your prayers. I do not wish to fight the sea unaided."

As he ran down the stairs, he bellowed back at her, "And see the water wiped from my floor. I will not have my house harmed for a hundred storms."

She heard voices and then the heavy front door slammed. She stood silently in the vast emptiness, the rain blasting the roof, the wind threatening even the heavy stones of the house, before his words came to her—" . . . to fight the sea . . ." He meant to join the men in the boats.

Her mind moved rapidly. Of course! How else could he know whether there were survivors? Unless he was there, the men in the boats could easily remove any traces of people found alive. No one would ever know.

She ran back to the bedchamber and tore through chests to find the wools she sought. In seconds she was dressed, near swaddled in the thick garments.

There was only one horse left in the stable in the inner bailey, an unruly black stallion that she would normally have been afraid to ride. She talked to the sleek animal as she saddled it and it rolled its eyes at her but did not nip at her or kick.

"You must run for me this night. We must forget our prejudices of one another, for Ranulf needs us. I must stop him from what he plans."

She led the big horse out of the stables and cast herself into the saddle. The horse made one small protest, but she jerked on the reins and he quieted.

"There is no time for play. We must go."

The stallion did run for her, and the rain and wind cut them, lacerating the rider and horse that had become as one, their purpose agreed upon.

There were many horses and men overlooking St. Agnes' Point. Lyonene knew if she were seen, one of the Black Guard would return her to the castle. She left the horse near some rocks, not tying it, knowing it was trained to stand.

No one noticed the dark form that followed the cliff wall down to the beach. When a streak of lightning showed her the boats, she saw she was too late. Three boats were already upon the turbulent water, Ranulf easily discerned in the farthest boat.

She knelt in a shadow of the cliff and began to pray with more fervor than she had ever thought possible. The storm continued, soaking her, lashing her, pulling and plucking at her clothes, but she did not notice. She only prayed, keeping her face turned toward the black sea.

It was hours later when she first saw the light specks of the returning boats. She ran to the shore, the salt water spraying her, heedless of the men who ran toward her. Someone's arm went about her shoulders, but she did not look, for her concern was only on the returning boats.

She saw instantly that he was not there.

She began to run into the sea, but something about her waist stopped her, held her.

The boats came near her and still she could not move.

"I am sorry, my lady," one of the men yelled over the fury of the storm. "He saw a head and fell over trying to save the bloke. We searched for hours but could not find him."

Strong arms pulled her around, and her face was buried against a wet shoulder, hands stroking her back, comforting her.

"Nay!" The word bubbled inside her, boiling, festering. She pushed hard against the man who held her, and when she turned to the boatman again, the man took one step backward. The woman had gone mad! Her face was distorted with rage.

The sweet-voiced Lyonene was no longer present. The voice that bellowed across the wind and rain was not even that of a woman.

"You will know hell on earth do you not find him and return him to me—alive! There are no tortures even in Castile that will equal what I will do to you." She stepped forward and the men around her retreated. She was possessed by something they did not wish to fight.

"Are my words heard? Do not return without him."

No man protested as they returned to their boats and vigorously began to row themselves out into the death-giving sea.

There were no protecting hands now as Lyonene sank to her knees, but all hands were clasped together as they followed suit of their mistress and began to pray.

There were watchers from the hill above, and the sight of the tiny girl kneeling in the sand and surf, surrounded by seven dark knights, also on their knees, made them forget the wet, the cold, and they joined in the prayers for the return of their beloved master. No one of them moved or lost fervor even when a faint light began to show and the storm lessened in its fury. There was not a man in the returning boats who did not cross himself and offer a silent prayer at the sight that greeted them.

A hand on her shoulder made Lyonene look up to see the boats. Other hands helped her stand. She did not see him at first, his head bent low. When she was sure he was there, she collapsed, her face buried in her hands, the release making her shoulders droop, her body weak.

Someone knelt beside her and put an arm about her shoulders. When she meant to rise again, she was supported.

She walked to the side of the boat and saw Ranulf, intent upon a long, wet bundle across his lap. When he saw her, he was startled and then angry. He looked up at the man next to her.

"She should not have been allowed here."

"She has saved your ungrateful life, so do not speak of her so!"

Ranulf was even more startled at the tone of his man, for none had ever dared speak to him in such a manner. "We will speak of this later. Take this." He handed the bundle to Sainneville. "It is a girl, so treat it with care."

The rain had dwindled to a drizzle, and the sun made a valiant effort to show itself. Ranulf stepped from the boat his clothes soggy and cold. He looked in puzzlement at the rather skittish behavior of one of the boatmen towards his wife. The man acted almost as if he were afraid of Ranulf's little wife.

"What have you done in these few hours that has caused my man to rebuke me and these others to fear you?" he asked, frowning.

"Ranulf . . ." Her lip trembled and then she was in his arms, her sobs racking her body with their violence. He held her to him, frightened himself at the fierceness of her emotion. He pulled the hood away and stroked her wet hair, soothing her.

"Come, my sweet. I am well. I am returned. Do not

cry so. Please, you must cease; I can bear it no longer!"

She sniffed and tried to calm herself. "When they returned without you, I could not bear it, I could not think ... Oh, Ranulf, they would have left you."

He looked around at the men near him. "What is this? They would have left me to drown?"

"Aye," Corbet laughed. "We thought you done for, but your lady had other plans for you than a watery grave. She is tame now, but there has never been a storm to equal her. I vow she made my blood freeze with fear."

Ranulf frowned, for he knew Corbet jested, but there was a ring of truth in his words. Then he grinned, flashing straight white teeth. "She is a Lioness," he said proudly as he swept her into his arms and carried her to the top of the hill.

He set her down and left her for a moment to see to Tighe, who had stood faithfully by throughout the storm. Lyonene walked a few feet away to retrieve the waiting stallion from the rocks.

"My lady!" She looked in astonishment as Maularde made a leap for her. She jumped back and avoided the powerful body that flew towards her and landed heavily at her feet.

"Lyonene, be very still."

She looked in puzzlement at Ranulf and the men staring at her, Ranulf advancing slowly, stealthily. She sensed some danger, mayhaps a wild animal near and so did not move. She was stunned when Ranulf made one quick leap and did but grab the reins of the black horse from her hands.

The horse threw his head back and neighed, his front feet prancing.

"What is this you do?" she demanded. "You frighten the poor animal." She took the reins and stroked the horse's nose to calm it, and the animal lowered its head to nuzzle her shoulder.

She looked back at her husband and his guard. There was open-mouthed astonishment on their faces and then, while she watched, all eight men began to laugh. It started slowly, but soon built into a torrent, gales of laughter. First one and then the other fell to their knees, holding their stomachs as they laughed. Eight men rolled about on the wet, mushy ground at her feet.

"Pardon me, my lord," Sainneville gasped, his eyes tearing, "but you will frighten my horse."

"The horse's tail weighs more than she does." Herne dissolved into more laughter.

"The boatman's face!" New laughter.

Ranulf was louder than all of them. "She really did it? Edkins looked terrified!"

"I was also! I vow she was twenty feet tall and the storm was silent compared to her booming voice!"

"My lark?" Ranulf gasped. "I called her a lark to Edward. Would he could have seen her!"

Lyonene knew they laughed at her. She had done nothing laughable! "I do not wish to keep you from your fun," she said icily, "but I return to my home and a fire."

The men began to sober and sit up. Then each of them tensed and quieted as she first put her foot into the stirrup. When she sat atop the horse and gave them what she hoped was a quelling look, she felt disgusted when they fell again to the ground, their laughter harder and louder than before. She squared her shoulders and left them.

"Lyonene!" Ranulf thundered to a halt on Tighe's back beside her.

She refused to look at him. "I hate you! You use me as a jest for all your men! You are detestable!"

"Do you not know the reason for our jests?"

She refused to answer him or look at him, urging the stallion ahead of Tighe. Ranulf moved beside her.

"Do you know of the horse you ride?"

She frowned at him, further angered when she saw his amusement. "It is from the stables. I have seen the horse before, 'tis all. I am sorry if I took someone's personal horse, but there was no other available." She gave his wet form a scathing look. "Had I thought twice of saving you, I do not think I would repeat the action."

He chuckled. "But you have never seen the horse ridden?"

"Nay, I have not. He is a smooth-gaited horse, and I wonder now why he is allowed to grow fat."

"The reason, my sweet, is that Loriage has never allowed anyone on his back for more than a few moments."

"You jest! He has spirit, but is otherwise gentle."

Ranulf took her hand and kissed it. "As you have tamed the lion, now you tame this beast. He is Tighe's son, and I believe I promised you one of his offspring. Of course I did think more in the way of a pretty daughter— not this hellion of a son. I had already decided to geld him."

As if the stallion heard, he lifted his forefeet from the ground, but Lyonene easily controlled him.

"You hurt her, you ugly beast, and I myself will break your neck," Ranulf warned, seething.

Lyonene giggled when the horse rolled its eyes at Ranulf.

"I am forgiven?"

She gave him a slight smile, not sure yet if he deserved forgiveness.

"You must see the humor, when we saw you leading, as if he were a lamb, this animal that has hurt several men."

She leaned forward and stroked the animal's velvety neck. "I have ever had success with the taming of great black animals. Come, Loriage, let us show these old men how fast youth can travel."

They arrived at the castle gates at the same time, the speed of Loriage more than the heavier Frisian's, but Ranulf's dexterity and knowledge of his horse greater.

He swung her to the ground. "Do not ride so fast that you injure my babe," he warned her.

She could not help smiling at him, pleased that he spoke of their child. He took her hand.

"Come and let us see what the sea has given us, or did you forget why I went bathing this morn? And then I am for sleep." His eyes raked her. "Or other activities beneath the sheets."

She squeezed his hand. "I am glad you are here and not . . ." Her eyes misted.

"You would miss me?"

"Never!"

He grinned and threw back his shoulders, looking ahead to the house. "You lie always."

Chapter Twelve

They forgot the girl Ranulf had dragged from the sea.

"My lady," Kate said as she met them. "We have put her in a spare bedchamber. Should we move her to the servants' rooms?"

Lyonene was puzzled for a moment, then remembered. "I will change my wet garments and then see to her myself."

"You cannot tend the girl. You have had no sleep for many hours. Send her to Jewel Tower."

"Have you no interest in this child who near cost you your life?"

He shrugged. "Nay, I have interest in only one matter at the moment."

She moved from his grasp.

He yawned and stepped into the soft bed. He was asleep before she finished dressing. She gave one last, longing gaze to his still form before she left the room.

The woman lay asleep on the wide bed; Lyonene saw instantly that she was no girl in spite of her slight form. She was pretty in a timid way, with pale blond hair and pale brows and lashes. There were sunken places beneath her high cheekbones and little color in her rather thin lips.

"She sleeps now, my lady, but I have given her some hot broth. She is very thin, almost like a boy. A shipwreck could not make the meat all leave one's bones, could it?"

Lyonene laughed. "Nay, it could not. It is fashionable to be slim. Mayhaps the lady comes from a land where the fashion is carried too far. See that someone is with her always. I go now and sleep. Tell William to keep the castle quiet."

She removed her clothes and slipped in beside Ranulf. He moved closer to her and sighed in his sleep. Content, she also slept.

The last rays of the sun were fading when they woke, the warmth of the bed making them drowsy and languid. As Lyonene made to rise, Ranulf pulled her back to him.

"You have escaped me once this day and you will not do so again. I will reward the one who saved me from an early death."

His lips were on her neck, savoring the shape and texture of her smooth skin, as she murmured, "I am glad Hugo did not rescue you, for he would not enjoy your rewards half as much as I."

Ranulf silenced her words with his lips. A loud knocking at the door interrupted them. Ranulf loudly cursed the knocker and returned his attentions to his wife. The noise continued.

Angrily, Ranulf flung himself from the bed; only Lyonene's voice made him don the loincloth before opening the door. Kate stood there, craning her neck to see her mistress.

"I do not mean to disturb you, my lord, but it is the woman you found."

"What woman?" He scowled at the already frightened girl.

Lyonene donned her robe and stepped before Ranulf, giving him a look of rebuke. "What of the woman, Kate? Is she not recovered as you thought?"

"Oh, yes, my lady. She has more than recovered. She is sitting in her bed and demanding to see his lordship."

"Demanding?" Ranulf stepped forward. "I near die dragging the worthless piece from the sea and now she makes more demands of me? She should say prayers of thanks for me and her delivery from the sea."

Lyonene tried to stop him as he pushed past her to stride angrily to the bedchamber. She was close behind him.

"Now, woman, what is this you demand of me?" His voice was quiet and heavy with sarcasm.

Lyonene looked at the woman's pale-blue eyes and saw them widen at the sight of the near-nude Ranulf. The eyes were odd, searching, calculating, and now they narrowed shrewdly, seeming to figure a method of approaching the handsome man before her.

"Oh, my lord," she said, pressing a tear from the corner of one eye. Her voice was high with a strange sing-song quality to it. "I do not know what the maid has told you. I did but ask who was my rescuer. I owe you my worthless life."

Lyonene looked at Kate's startled face and knew the woman lied. Ranulf went to sit by the woman and took her hand. "You are safe now and there is no reason for tears."

She leaned toward Ranulf and put one hand on his chest, the fingers twined in the thick hair. She looked up at him, her eyes wide and innocent. "I will ever be in debt to you. I cannot repay you, for all my worldly goods went down with my father, the Duke of Vernet."

"Your father is a duke? Then you must be Frankish." She nodded and another tear came.

"Then we are honored by your presence. You may stay with us until you can notify relatives of your whereabouts."

She leaned even closer, her head almost touching Ranulf's shoulder. "Alas, my lord, I do not have more relatives."

"Well," he responded, patting her hand, "you are welcome at Malvoisin for as long as need be. Now you must rest." He rose. "Your name, my lady?"

"Amicia."

"I am Ranulf, and this is my wife, Lady Lyonene."

The pale woman gave Lyonene her first look. It startled Lyonene by the coldness of it, and then the little smile made chills on her arms; it was almost deadly. Lyonene gave the woman a brilliant smile in return, but the eyes that met hers held a challenge, a dare.

When they were alone in their room, they began to dress.

"The woman has missed her call. She should be in London. She is far better than any other mummer I have seen."

"Of what do you speak?" Ranulf asked.

"Why, our Lady Amicia, most assuredly. If she is a Frankish duke's daughter, then I am Queen Eleanora's sister. I especially liked the 'my worthless life' part. Tell me, did you like those skimpy tears she managed to produce?"

He grabbed her arm and pulled her to his lap. "You are jealous."

"Nay, I am not, for there is little substance on which to base a jealousy."

"Oh! I think I like this. Tell me more. Did you not like the way her little hand touched my chest?"

"Ranulf, I am serious! The woman is bad; she is not as she seems to you. Already she has lied about Kate and . . ."

He pushed her from his lap and returned to dressing. "How can you judge her so harshly after but a few words? I found her but an ordinary woman, but she says she is a duke's daughter, so she must be treated with respect. Now see to our food and do not complain to me of her again. She is but a woman. What harm can she do?"

Lyonene went to the kitchen herself to order food. Ranulf was unreasonable! She knew there was naught she could do to persuade him that the woman's words were all mummery.

Dawkin met her at the door. "My lady, she is not to be pleased. She has sent her food back three times—it is not cooked enough, it is overcooked. Kate has near flooded my kitchen with her tears."

She tried to calm the chief cook as best she could. "I will speak to her, but do not take this to Lord Ranulf." She remembered his reaction to her complaints. If more were said against her, he would perhaps ask her to make Malvoisin her permanent home. She took a large tray of food and carried it to the solar for herself and Ranulf.

To her chagrin, Amicia sat near the fire, wrapped in a fur-lined quilt.

"Oh, Lyonene," Ranulf said, taking the tray, "Lady Amicia has decided she is well enough to join us for the evening meal."

"How thoughtful of her." She met the woman's eyes briefly.

"Tell us of your homeland. I have not seen France for several years."

"Then you have seen it. I knew you to be an educated man when first I saw you. It is something in your eyes."

No one saw Lyonene's lip curl at the woman or her disgust at the way Ranulf reacted to the syrupy words. She listened as they talked, watching how the Frankish woman leaned toward Ranulf at every opportunity and touched his arm often. The only consolation she had was that never once did Ranulf smile at the woman or laugh at her statements.

Kate came and escorted Amicia back to her chamber. "You hardly spoke during supper. I do not like your being so rude to our guest."

"I was never rude. I am sure I spoke whenever there was a chance to insert a word."

"Come here." He pulled her to his lap. "I am not so sure I like this much jealousy. I have never seen you treat another so. Even Lady Elizabeth at court did not cause you so much anger."

"You do not understand. This Amicia is not as they are. They cared for you, in a way. This woman cares for naught but herself."

"How can you say such when you have but met the woman?"

She sighed against him. It was hopeless to continue. She had heard her mother spend hours trying to persuade her father of the character of a person, a person just met, and Melite had always ended in failure. She seemed doomed to wait until Ranulf slowly came to the same conclusion that she had already reached. She just hoped it was not long.

The morning dawned bright, the sun hot, as the earth tried to repair itself from the damage of the storm.

"I will spend the day with my men and will not return until supper. See you that our guest is made welcome."

She grimaced but nodded that she would attempt the task.

When Amicia arrived in the solar, she wore Lyonene's clothes, and the countess wondered at her boldness, for she had never been asked for the loan. Amicia's eyes dared Lyonene to question her use of them, but Lyonene merely laughed, for the clothes hung on the woman's boyish frame.

"It seems we must spend this day together, for my husband's escapades of yester eve have torn his clothes badly. Would you care for the wherewithal to embroider?"

Amicia did not deign to look at Lyonene. "Nay, I do not sew. A lady has servants to perform those duties for her."

"Of course. I must then inform Queen Eleanora, for she ever embroiders her own clothing."

Amicia shot her a quick hateful look before turning to the window seat, her finger running along the diamond-shaped panes of glass. "Lord Ranulf is the Black Lion, is he not?" She did not wait for an answer. "I have heard of him even in France. My father, the duke"—she made sure Lyonene heard the words—"often spoke of him. He even once considered him for my husband."

Lyonene did not look up from her needle. "My husband is an amiable man and might have agreed to the marriage, for he proved in his first marriage that he does not object to a wife older than himself."

There was silence between them.

"You seem secure in your marriage . . . Lyonene, is it not? An odd name. I suppose you brought his lordship an enormous dowry."

"In truth, I did not, but I do not see that that is something for us to discuss."

Amicia ignored her. "Then it is a love match."

Lyonene stopped and considered. "I believe it to be."

"Lord Ranulf does not swear his love for you each moment of the day, then?"

"You are a guest in my house and I must treat you so, but I will not discuss the private lives of my husband and myself with you." She tossed the sewing down on the nearest stool and left the room. She did not hear the little laugh of triumph Amicia gave.

Lyonene went toward the Jewel Tower, intending to see if there were any people hurt in the storm. Amicia had put a seed of doubt in her mind that had never been there before. Of course Ranulf loved her; had not theirs been a love match? But he had never said the words. She was a silly woman, she told herself. Words were not important. Of course he loved her, just as she had told him many times of the love she bore him.

She shook her head and made herself attend to her work, but the question plagued her: Would he care for her when she was old and ugly?

Amicia joined them again for supper. She was all smiles and apologies for all the work she caused and hung on Ranulf's every word. He did not discourage her.

Alone, at last, in their room, Ranulf asked after her health.

"The babe does not trouble you overmuch? You seem quiet."

She pulled away from him. "The babe troubles me naught. I sometimes think he is the only perfect thing in my life."

He held her close to him, stroking her hair. "What troubles you? I would make it well if I could."

"Would you? Would you make me able to bear your son and not grow fat, or grow old with the years?"

He smiled down at her, his thumb brushing the corner of her eye. "You do well to be concerned. I detect a fold in your skin already."

She pushed away. "I do not jest."

He frowned at her. "There is something which troubles you. It could not hurt to share it with me." He saw tears in her eyes. "I have never seen you like this. You are ever of high spirits, even when I am not so pleasant to be with."

A faint smile began to appear through her tears. "I am most happy to hear you say what I have always known."

"Come to bed before I beat you as you deserve." He pulled her to him, his hand rubbing her bare stomach, as if he inspected the growth his child made each day.

"And what will you think when my stomach sticks out to here?" she whispered.

"I will hope for twins," he murmured as he fell asleep.

When Lyonene said she was to ride to the village the next morn, Amicia declared herself well enough to ride with her.

Since the stable boy was afraid of Loriage, Lyonene had to saddle him herself.

"You do not have him whipped?" Amicia asked in astonishment.

"He is but a boy. Later I will show him Loriage is gentle if spoken to correctly."

"I am sure he is easy to ride and you but create the story of his fierceness. I may show you?"

"Certainly." Lyonene stepped back.

The black stallion did not even allow the woman to

sit in the saddle, but reared and fought her as she slipped one foot into the stirrup. Angrily, she walked away.

They paused in the outer bailey to greet one of the cooks, who held some especially fine cabbages for Lyonene's approval. Off to the side skulked the man Lyonene instinctively recoiled from.

"Who is that man?" Amicia asked.

Lyonene turned toward the knight. "I forget his name. He seems ever to be idle and his ways are too insolent to my taste."

"You do not think him handsome?"

She did not look back at the smirking man. "Nay, I do not." She spurred the stallion ahead.

Many serfs gathered around their mistress in the village, and she gave her attentions to new babies, flooded fields and the egg production of some famed hens. She looked up once to see Amicia in deep conversation with the garrison knight from the castle. They deserve one another! she thought.

It was well past dinnertime when the two women returned to the castle. Ranulf stood with the Black Guard in the courtyard and introduced the seven men to "Lady" Amicia. Lyonene noticed that Hugo and Maularde regarded her honeyed words with the same suspicion that she herself felt.

When Lyonene entered the hall, the first person she saw was Brent, absent from her for two long days. She had not realized how much she had missed the boy. "Brent!" She knelt, holding her arms out to the child, and he ran to her, giving her a rather fierce hug to show his growing love for her.

Remembering his manly status of page he released her as if disgusted by her embrace. He looked quickly to see if his Lord Ranulf had seen his lapse, but the Black Lion stared intently out a window.

Lyonene stood, not allowing herself to further caress the boy. "You have spent the days in the Great Hall of the Black Guard? You must tell me of it, for I have never entered it."

"You have not?" Brent was astonished.

"Nay," Ranulf answered. "Only men are allowed in my guard's hall."

"But there are women in . . ." He stopped at Ranulf's broad wink. "Oh, aye. No lady-wives are allowed."

Lyonene smiled innocently. "Then you must tell me about the place. Is it dark and dirty and full of spiders?"

Brent walked proudly ahead of her and then tossed over his shoulder, "Only a few, but I did not notice them."

Lyonene wanted to share her laughter with Ranulf, but saw he held the same expression as the boy. She rubbed her stomach and gave a silent prayer asking for deliverance from bringing a third such braggart into the world.

Brent stopped at the doorway of the solar, where Amicia already sat. "Who is she?" he whispered to Lyonene.

They both watched as Ranulf went forward to greet the woman. "Lord Ranulf saved her from the sea. Did not the men tell you?"

"Oh, yes, Martha said that Lord Ranulf saved her and you saved Lord Ranulf. Is that true? You are too small to save him. The Black Lion needs no one to save him."

"I am afraid you are wrong, Brent," Ranulf said to him. "Come and meet Lady Amicia and I will tell you how my tiny wife quelled over twenty men, and even made a storm abate to appease her wrath."

Brent hardly noticed the pale woman to whom he was introduced, but waited intently for the promised story. Ranulf began, ignoring Lyonene's whispered question of, "Who is Martha?" He was a good storyteller and created a colorful tale from what Lyonene considered rather ordinary happenings.

Brent watched her with awe. "Can you do it again? Can you make your voice so loud it will crack the stone walls?"

"Ranulf! The boy believes your lies."

Both Brent and Ranulf were indignant. "A true knight does not lie," they both exclaimed, echoing one another.

She could not help laughing; they were so much alike. Amicia, ignored for so long, destroyed the gaiety. "I must not intrude on so happy a family scene. I am feeling a bit weak and must retire."

"Pardon our rudeness, Lady Amicia," Ranulf answered her. "Supper will be served in here and you must dine with us."

"You do not set a table with your retainers?"

"Nay. They each have their own homes. I grew used to being a bachelor and still keep to my old ways."

The woman's light eyes were only on Ranulf's dark, somber ones. "You have been married recently, my lord?"

"Aye, it is now . . ."

"Six months," Lyonene supplied.

Ranulf turned and grinned at her, and she looked interestedly at the window.

"Oh, Hodder comes with the food. You will join us?"

"How can I not when so pleasantly asked?"

Lyonene saw Hodder sneer as he set the table. She rarely agreed with the pompous little man, but in their opinion of this woman, they did. For the first time ever, their eyes met briefly in accord.

Amicia talked throughout the meal, complimenting Malvoisin, pleading for Ranulf to tell her of his trials on Crusade, praising his superior talents in designing such a castle as Malvoisin. Brent listened raptly to Ranulf's stories, but Lyonene thought she glimpsed a surreptitious look at Amicia now and again. It did not help matters to know that even a six-year-old boy could see through the woman.

Early the next morn, Ranulf stormed back into the house. "Hodder!" he bellowed. The house rocked as he thundered up the stairs, two at a time. "Where is that man! Hodder, if you value your life, you'll come this instant!"

"What is it? Ranulf, why are you so angry?" Lyonene asked.

He jammed clothes into a leather satchel. "Pack my mail and all my armor and make haste!" He threw the words at Hodder as the man entered the room. "No, not the silver. I make war, not merriment."

Lyonene felt her knees weaken. "What is this talk of war?"

"That damned blackguard! William's threats were not enough. Now he sends serfs to farm my land."

"What land? What is this you speak of?"

"Gethen Castle, your castle! My steward, your steward, hell! I do not care who owns the place. Sang de Dieu,

179

I will kill the man with my bare hands. He dares to question my boundaries."

Lyonene was almost afraid of her husband and wondered at Hodder's steady hands. She watched with a stomach that churned as he pulled mace, flail, battle ax and war hammer from the walls.

"Ranulf, could you not talk with this man?"

"Talk! The time is past for talk. He should hope his castle is well provendered, for I may hold siege. We will see how long this lowly baron holds against the Black Lion. You will see to the castle while I am gone. I take my guard and a hundred garrison knights. Should I need more, I will send a message and you will send them. You understand your duties?"

"I am well trained," she said icily.

He gave her a quick look, but his anger did not abate. "Brent goes with me." He stood dressed in the sturdy travel clothes. "Now come and kiss me that I may remember it for a while, and give me no cause to worry for you. It is your castle I defend."

She did not tell him her thoughts—that she would not give one day of his company in exchange for the unseen castle. She held her tears, and her protests, as he kissed her, his anger and urgency creating a violent, bruising kiss.

"I will send you news of our happenings." He ran down the stairs, Lyonene trying to keep pace.

"Wait! Wait!" She ran back up the stairs and hurriedly found the jeweled and embroidered ribbon she sought, the copy she had made of the lion belt. Ranulf was already in the courtyard, his men waiting. She put her arms about his neck, then put one hand inside the fitchet opening of his tabard, looping the ribbon over his leather belt. What else she did with her hand made him gasp and push her away.

"You forget yourself." But his eyes twinkled.

"Do but remember me," she whispered, blinking hard to restrain the tears.

"I could do naught else," was his equally serious reply.

As he rode from the courtyard, her sobs were echoed by four women standing in the doorway across the way, the entrance to the Black Guard's hall. The women looked at one another and did not speak, but there was a comradeship between the lonely women, doomed to wait and pray for men gone to war.

Lyonene and Amicia spent the afternoon in the solar, the countess with her sewing, the other woman's hands idle.

"I envy you, Lady Lyonene, your serenity, your apparent peacefulness. I am sure I could not be so in your situation."

"And what, pray tell, is your meaning?"

"I believe you carry Lord Ranulf's babe. I assume it is his, but then one can never be sure."

Lyonene gave the older woman a brief, cold look.

"I do not mean to offend. It is only that Lord Ranulf is such a handsome man. I am sure he must be quite popular with women. I know I find the man thoroughly fascinating."

"I will not have my husband discussed so."

"Pray forgive me. I do not, in truth, speak of your husband. I but wonder at you. 'Twere I soon to grow heavy with child, I would worry that my handsome husband is miles away, alone with men who are sure to introduce women—of the lower sort, of a surety, but women nonetheless—into the camp."

"Lady Amicia, if lady you be, your hints are quite unsubtle and I do not like them at all. I request that you keep such thoughts to yourself."

"I agree with you. I would not wish to be reminded of my plight, either."

Lyonene merely looked at her.

Amicia smiled and ran her hand across a tapestry. "Even from my brief contact with him, I find Lord Ranulf to be . . . most susceptible to even the merest hint of . . . romance, shall we say? Tell me, Lady Lyonene, of your courtship. Did you find him a difficult man to bring to terms, or was he quickly snared? It would interest me much to know this. Did you know one another for weeks, months before the betrothal?"

Lyonene stared at the woman, speechless.

"I find it has taken but a matter of days . . ." She covered her mouth. "I am sure Lord Ranulf is not the sort of man to fall in love quickly; he is too serious for that. Oh, my pardon, you did mention that Lord Ranulf has not declared his love for you. Mmm. I wonder what the kitchen people have prepared for dinner? I am feeling a bit weak and shall retire to my room. Good-day, my lady. I do so hope I have said naught to offend you."

Lyonene sat stunned, and then shook herself. She had known the woman was evil and should not have been surprised when she was offered proof of it. What if Ranulf did take a woman while he was away from her? Most men did. It was natural, and she must accept the idea.

"Oh!" she cried aloud when she stuck the needle into her thumb. She looked at the new tabard she sewed and stuck the needle into it with vigor several times. No! No! No! her mind cried. She would not accept another touching her Ranulf.

Ranulf had been gone but four days when the first messenger arrived. She saw him from the solar window, saw that his horse carried a pouch stamped with the lion of Malvoisin. She ran down the stairs, almost tripping once in her haste. She did not notice Amicia close behind her.

The boy held two pieces of paper, each sealed with the Warbrooke lion. She near tore them from his hands.

"You are Lady Lyonene?" He held her hand from tearing open the missal.

"Aye, I am."

"And who be Lady Amicia?"

"I am Lady Amicia."

Lyonene stood still as the boy took one of the papers from her hands and gave it to the pale woman.

"Go . . . go to the kitchen, and take what you need." Her first spurt of joy was dulled. Ranulf could not have written to Amicia! She watched as the woman eagerly tore the seal.

"He is well," she murmured, then looked to Lyonene, holding her letter to her breast. "You do not hasten to open your letter?"

Lyonene walked past her and went to her bedchamber. Her first impulse was to toss the letter, unread, into the candle flame, but she could not.

It is a siege and I fear it may take months. I have sent men to Malvoisin for carpenters to build our weapons. I have offered the man every retreat, but he refuses me. I grow bored with this already. I have become soft in the last months and now wish only the comforts of my home.

Brent is well and we talk of you always. The ribbon never leaves me.

Your loving husband and weary knight,
Ranulf

She sank onto the bed and cried. The letter was so gentle, with none of the arrogance he usually displayed, and she knew how lonely he must be. She cursed herself, in a very limited vocabulary, for doubting him for an instant. It took a long while, but she was at last purged and smiled again for the first time in days. She took time to write her return letter to Ranulf, assuring him of the health of herself and their child, telling him of the castle happenings. Only at the last did she add some of what she felt:

Kate worries that I become as you once were, for I find naught to make me smile.

Your Lioness

Her mood had lightened by the time she went to the solar to dine, Amicia her only company.

"Your letter contained pleasant news?" the woman asked.

"Aye. I fear there is to be a siege and Ranulf may be gone some time."

"Oh, yes, there were four meetings with the baron, but none were successful and now tunnels are being prepared and . . . You must forgive me. I am sure he wrote you much the same."

"I do not seem to know quite as much as you do. Perhaps the man who wrote you is a more prolific writer."

"Aye, Lord Ranulf wrote me a great deal."

"Ranulf! What is this you say?" Lyonene demanded.

"Why, my lady, I assumed you knew. You assured me my hints were most unsubtle."

"Are you making an attempt to tell me that my husband sends messages to you?"

"You cannot blame a man if he is attracted to another woman."

She rose from her chair. "I believe you not. You must show me this letter."

"My Lady Lyonene, I can see this must be your husband's first . . . infidelity, shall we say, and I do not wish to repay your kind hospitality by showing you something that will surely cause you distress."

"I will go to my husband and he will deny your lies."

"Most assuredly he will. You would not expect him to boast of his women to you? You did not think him to be a monk before his marriage, so why ever should he change just for a few vows before some witnesses? And he has fulfilled those vows; you certainly seem to have all a woman could desire. Please, you must eat. You must think of your child, who grows larger each day."

The food stuck in Lyonene's throat. She would not believe the woman's words! She would ride to Ranulf and . . . Would she believe him if he denied an interest in this woman?

Amicia chattered about the food, the insolence of the Malvoisin servants, but Lyonene heard not a word, her thoughts too desolate to allow her to hear aught else.

The next day Lyonene donned old clothes and spent hours working in her garden. She pulled at weeds viciously.

"There you are, my lady." Amicia's voice made her carelessly grab another bunch of weeds, only to find her hand cut and bleeding from a sturdy thistle. She sat back on her heels and wiped the dirt from her palm.

"I do not know how you bear the dirt and sweat of gardening. I would have thought a lady . . . oh, yes, you are but a baron's daughter, are you not?"

"I do not have time for your insults this morn. If you have aught to say to me, do so, but get to your meaning quickly."

"I seem ever to displease you. I came but to the garden to enjoy it. It already holds many sweet memories for me."

"My Lady Lyonene," Kate called. "You must come inside from the sun. Lucy frets for you and the babe."

Silently, Lyonene followed her to the kitchen. She knew Amicia would not enter such a room.

"Lady Lyonene, if your mother saw the way you worked and you carrying a babe." Lyonene thought of her mother as a cool haven. "And Lord Ranulf," Lucy continued, "he would be angry to know you would harm his babe."

Lyonene slammed the mug of ale down. "Lord Ranulf! I hear naught but his name. I will deliver the child he so craves, but I do not know that I shelter his mistresses much longer."

"What do you speak of, child? Lord Ranulf has no mistresses. Why, I have never seen a man love a wife so. The man dotes on you."

"Oh, Lucy." She clung to the fat old woman who had always been with her and began to weep on the ample bosom.

"Come, upstairs you go. You are to go to bed."

Lyonene leaned on the woman and allowed her to undress her and put her to bed. Lucy stroked her forehead, too warm, and noticed circles under her eyes. "Tell me what troubles you, child. Lucy will listen."

"He does not love me. He has never loved me."

"How can you say that? The man never leaves your side when he can prevent it. Was there something in the letter that has made you sad?"

"There are other women."

"Sweet, all men have other women. It is their way, but it does not mean he does not love you."

Lyonene's tears began at Lucy's words.

"Sleep, child, and the pain will ease."

Gradually. Lyonene's sobs ceased and she did sleep, fitfully, feeling worse when she woke to an empty room, an empty bed.

She avoided Amicia for the next few days, taking meals in her own room, keeping from the solar, an exile in her own house.

"She is gone, my lady." Kate came to Lyonene's room.

"Gone? Who has gone?"

"The woman, the Frankish woman. A messenger came early this morn with a letter for her and in moments she ordered a horse saddled and she was gone. She took no clothes. Think you she will stay away?"

Lyonene's heart quickened a bit at the thought of ridding herself of the hateful woman. "I do not know. This messenger, what banner did he carry?"

"Why, that of Malvoisin, the Black Lion."

She could feel the color draining from her face. "Did you see the letter, Kate?" she whispered.

"Aye, my lady. It lies on her bed now, but I cannot read."

"Bring it to me."

With trembling hands, she opened the stiff, heavy paper.

Come to me.
Ranulf.

It fell to the floor.

"My lady, my lady!" Kate ran for a mug of wine. "Drink this!"

Lyonene choked down some of the sweet liquid. It was all true! Every word was true! There was no mistaking Ranulf's bold scrawl or the seal set in the wax. Only he carried the seal of the Earl of Malvoisin, and it never left his person.

Amicia was gone for three days, three days of hell for Lyonene. She was past tears. Kate took care of her, and she was only vaguely aware of people around her. Lucy tried to help by telling her no man was worth so much fuss, that it had been a shock to her when her first husband took another woman but that she had had to go on living.

Another letter arrived from Ranulf, and Lyonene's answer was curt and brief, giving only an account of life at the castle.

"Why, Lady Lyonene, are you ill? I have never seen you look so tired." Amicia greeted her in the hall after her return. "I vow there is naught like a stay in the country to refreshen one, although a tent is a little too warm in summer, do you not agree?"

Lyonene swept past her and left the house. The stable boy, no longer afraid since Lyonene had spent time with him and Loriage, saddled Loriage for her and she spurred the horse to run as fast as he was able, glad of the wind and the exercise. She was already there before she realized that she had traveled to the glade, the sweet place where she had told Ranulf of their coming child. She had been happy then, a happiness she knew she'd never know again. She lay on the mossy ground, her face buried in her arms.

"I love you so, Ranulf, why could you not love me in return?" she whispered.

When she returned in the evening, she had made some decisions. Ranulf had chosen her for wife, and even if he did not wish her as lover, she would perform her wifely duties as expected.

"I am pleased you are feeling better and can join me at table." Amicia smiled at Lyonene. "It is a shame to be so heavy with child in the summer's heat. I just hope I do not find myself in the same state."

Lyonene smoothed her skirts, her stomach/hardly extended at all. "Can you talk of naught else but my husband?"

"But I did not mention Lord Ranulf! Since you do seem interested, shall I tell you of the progress of the siege?"

"Nay, I do not wish to hear it."

"I am sure I understand. We will speak of other things. I say that I grow quite fond of the boy Brent. There are times when he quite reminds me of Ranulf. It is something in the way they walk, I believe. Tell me, how did Ranulf acquire that awful scar that runs from his stomach to his . . . my pardon, my lady, we were to speak of else."

"Amicia, I have taken enough. What my husband does is not my affair, but I will not sit in my own house with your stories of your . . . of your actions. If you do not cease, I shall have you removed to the garrison hall."

Amicia's eyes narrowed. "Nay, my lady, I do not think you should do that. Nay, I would not."

"Do not threaten me. I have the power of the castle in my husband's absence and no one could say me nay 'twere I even to order your hanging."

"Your threats do not frighten me. You would not hazard Ranulf's wrath, and although I have had no occasion to see such anger, I can imagine it is no pleasure. I would suggest you must bear my presence with as much fortitude as you may summon. Ranulf will make his own decisions as to my placement in this household."

The two women stared at one another, neither relinquishing her hold until Hodder came to remove the soiled dishes.

Exhausted, Lyonene fell into a heavy sleep that night. The morn brought a messenger with a letter from Ranulf.

It is late now and I cannot sleep. My page would not think me a man 'twere he to know I pine for a bit of a girl. I sense you are troubled. Would that I were with you now.

Can you not write to me else but of William de Bec? Send me one of your damned roses you think so much of.

There is not a moment I do not think of you.

Ranulf

She held the letter close to her. How could he write such letters to her and then send for Amicia to stay with him?

Could Lucy be right, that a man could truly love one woman yet bed many others?

She forgot Amicia for a few moments and ran to write a return letter. She told of her loneliness, of her journey to their glade, but she made no mention of the hurt she felt that he could turn to Amicia. Had he but hinted that he wanted his wife to come to him, Lyonene felt she would run to him, in her bare feet if need be, but he made no mention of such a possibility and she was careful not to tell him of her feelings. She sent a separate letter to Brent, telling of horses and hawks.

When the letters were prepared, she had Dawkin fill a box with honeyed fruit and a crock of his special, hot pickles. She then went to the garden and fair stripped it of flowers. The messenger boy began a protest, but Lyonene silenced him with one look. The stems were wrapped in damp canvas, then packed in moss and put again into several layers of wet canvas. William de Bec solemnly supplied a hard, molded-leather bag that would protect the huge bouquet on the back of the horse.

She attached one tiny rosebud with wax to the bottom of her letter to Ranulf and then sealed it. For Brent she sent a new leather belt, stamped with the Malvoisin lion, a tiny emerald in its brass buckle.

As the boy rode away, she felt happier than she had in weeks. She did not see the angry face of Amicia as the woman watched from the solar window. "You have had all in your life and now it is time you share some of it. I shall have the rich husband and the love of the servants."

Lyonene was smiling when she started up the stairs, thinking of Ranulf's reaction when he received the flowers.

"You seem well pleased this day. I am happy you are not ill as you have been of late."

"Yes, thank you. I am quite well."

The little object made only a slight sound as it fell from its hiding place under Amicia's skirt. Lyonene bent to retrieve it. To say her happiness left her would be too mild, for she held the ribbon, the copy of the lion belt, that she had sent to Gethen Castle with Ranulf.

"How came you by this?" she managed to choke out from her dry throat.

Amicia tried to take the ribbon, but only shrugged when Lyonene held it fast. "It was given me when I requested it. It is pretty, do you not think?"

Lyonene walked ahead to her room, the ribbon clutched firmly in her hand. Once in the room, she threw the ribbon to the farthest corner with all her might. "I send you flowers and you present my gifts to another. Tell me, do you plan to be so generous with our child?"

She did not cry, but went to the solar and resumed her embroidery. She would not think on the fact that the garment she sewed was for a husband who sent her false words of sweetness and in truth was a treacherous man. When Amicia entered the room, Lyonene smiled sweetly at the woman and Ranulf was not mentioned between them.

Chapter Thirteen

It was three days later when Ranulf's next, longest letter arrived.

> The flowers arrived perfectly. I parted with seven of them to my men, for they seem as weary as I. My head is sore this morn, for I spent yester eve with a barrel of wine and Maularde. I did not know the man had so many words. He loves the girl he met at Edward's tourney and wishes to marry her. I will have them live at Malvoisin, for I cannot relinquish my men.
>
> Even Brent grows tired of this ugly battle. He was most affected by your mention of the hawks. He never is without the belt you sent. He will not bathe and another week and I shall refuse him my tent.
>
> Someone has stolen the ribbon you so prettily gave me. I have torn the camp apart but it is not to be found. Forgive my carelessness.
>
> I had the rose from your letter sewn into my leather hacketon. Do but remember me.
>
> > Your knight,
> > Ranulf

He wrote that the ribbon had been stolen when he knew Amicia had it. The woman could not have gone to the camp and not have been seen by him. Nor was it possible for Amicia to have sent her own messages or have access to Ranulf's seal. Lyonene remembered Gressy's stories of Ranulf's first wife. It was said the woman attempted to kill herself, so unhappy she was. What treachery could make a woman try to commit a mortal sin?

She had been married to him only six months and already he was a master of lies and deceits. What heights could he climb to in three years? A man does not earn the title of Spawn of the Devil for naught.

She took quill and ink and paper into the solar. She would not let him know she knew of his dishonorable behavior. He should have been honest with her and told her he no longer desired her, rather than sending letters of kindness and practicing deeds of deception.

Amicia stood by a window, her letter in her hand. "You write him?"

Lyonene nodded.

"I am to go with the messenger when he returns. Mayhaps I may deliver it myself. I must prepare a few things." She swept from the room.

Her letter lay open on a chair seat and Lyonene could not refrain from walking to it. She did not touch it—there was no need. The last line was quite clear.

I love you, my Amicia.
Ranulf

When Amicia returned, Lyonene was seated again at the little table, but the letter she had begun was crumbled before her. She walked down the stairs to the courtyard, where the messenger waited. Amicia walked ahead to the outer bailey, presumably to obtain a horse for her journey.

"You have a message for me to return?"

"Nay, I do not. Do but tell my husband his child is well and his castle is well cared for."

The boy looked doubtful, but turned and led his horse toward the gate where Amicia had gone.

The woman was gone only one night, and when she returned, she proudly showed Lyonene a beautiful little jar of rock crystal and gold that contained a small, precious amount of perfume. The Frankish woman reeked of the scent.

"It is an expensive gift and, he says, well deserved. I vow I have never had such a night as this last. I do not wonder you are breeding already with such a husband."

"Out! I will have no more! You spend your nights as the lowest of women, yet you brag and display your ill-gotten goods. I will bear no more of your insults. William! Show this woman new quarters. She may stay inside the castle walls, but not in the inner bailey. Throw her to the garrison knights for all I care!"

Even through her blaze of anger, she thought she saw a faint smile on the steward's mouth.

Amicia smiled lazily, knowingly. "You will regret this. It will be you who will leave this fine house and I who gives the orders." She jerked away from William's arm and went down the stairs before him. At the door she stopped, not turning, and laughed, an ugly laugh that filled the hall, making the hearers' flesh crawl.

Almost instantly there was a lightness in the house, now that the woman was gone. Familiar noises returned and servants walked more quickly. Lyonene even thought she saw Hodder smile. She had Loriage saddled and fled to the private glade, where she could be alone.

Dismissing Amicia had not dismissed her troubles. She could still see the letter that told of Ranulf's love, a thing she had come to want greatly, but the words had been said to another. Why did he marry her? It was not for gold, he had proven not for love and he had not shared her bed until recently; what then was his reason?

A slight noise broke through her thoughts, a remembered sound of metal against metal. She turned over and saw that he stood above her, his face grim.

Her heart began to pound wildly. Ranulf was before her, the man she loved so intensely—yet one who gave his love to a woman he had known only a short while, and not to her. "Your . . . siege is finished?" The whispered words near choked her.

He sat down beside her, heavily. "Why did you not return my letter?" His voice sounded almost dead.

"You have journeyed far to ask me this one question? Could you not have sent another messenger?"

"Do not give me more questions, but answer me."

She looked down at her hands. "I did not think you cared for my answer. I am well, as you see, and am carrying your child. William runs your castle quite well."

"Lyonene! What has made you as this? I am tired. I have ridden all night and all this day without stop to come to you, and now you greet me coldly."

" 'Tis not I who is cold."

He pulled the mail coif from over his head and bent to douse his face and hair in the little stream. "I understand naught of this. Have my letters displeased you? I am not used to writing such letters. Geoffrey says I am clumsy with a pen, though my studies have pleased my teachers." He leaned back against a tree, the heavy armor dragging at him. "I did not mean to give offense, however I did so."

Lyonene could not hold her tears. Ranulf was usually so sure of himself. She remembered the last time they had been together in this glade, how he had boasted, how pleased he was at his child.

"The babe does not trouble you?"

She kept her head lowered so he could not see her tears and shook her head.

"Has my blackness grown uglier while I was away that you can bear me no longer?"

She again only shook her head.

"By all that's holy, Lyonene, look at me!" he shouted. "I leave a wife who laughs, one who kisses me, and in a month I return to one who hates me afresh."

Tears blurred her vision, choked her words. "I do not hate you."

"Then why do you send me flowers and a few days later naught but a few short words delivered by a nervous boy?"

"You came just to see why I did such? Just for those few short words?"

The pain she saw in his eyes made her heart tighten as if steel bands bound it. "Nay," he said, seriously, "it was but an excuse. I came because I thought my Lioness awaited me with kisses and open arms. I tire of angry words and battle." He held out his hand to her, palm upward, and before she thought, she was in his arms, the iron mail cutting into her soft flesh.

She cried against him, tears running along his neck.

"You rust my mail," he teased. "Had I known I got but tears for my journey, I would have stayed with Maularde. Can you not spare me one kiss?"

She put one hand on each side of his face and kissed him with a violence she had not known she possessed. He pulled her closer to him, deepening the kiss, lips crushed in one another, their stored desires released in a passion of liquid fire.

He pulled back from her. "You do indeed remember me?"

"Nay, I know you not. You are a great black beast of a man come to make love to me."

He ran his lips along her neck. "You would have me as I am, for I fear that even I quell at the stench I have worked up?"

"Aye, I will have you no matter your smell or your treachery."

'What is this you speak of?"

"Do you mean to waste so much time in talk?" She began unbuckling the heavy sword belt.

"Nay," he chuckled. "I need no more words."

A month apart had raised their desires for one another to fever pitch. They were frantic, clumsy, as they tore their clothes from their bodies. Ranulf, dressed for war, was slower, the iron mail difficult to remove. When Lyonene stood nude before him, the filtered sunlight showing golden on her skin, he paused, and she ran to him. The cold, iron mail bit into her flesh, pinching, nipping, but the slight pain only increased her need for him.

"Nay, do not remove it, come to me."

She pulled him to her on the velvety ground, relishing in the contrast of his warm, sweet-dampened skin against her legs and the massive hardness, coldness, the total maleness of the iron against her soft breasts.

They came together almost violently, Lyonene crying out at the first moments of painful pleasure. Her hips rose to meet his need of her and they soared together to new heights of fury, of storm-tossed seas and a bursting of lights of fulfillment.

They lay together, locked tightly to one another, their hearts thundering, complete in the dewy aftermoments of their love. Ranulf rolled from her, but kept her to him with one leg over her thighs, his hand caressing her cheek, his eyes soft and happy.

"I think you please me more than I remember."

"Thank you, my lord," she smiled up at him. "I would but please a man as powerful as the Black Lion is at this moment."

"You give me overmuch credit. I fear the Black Lion has no power at this moment."

"You are wrong, for the stench of you may lay me low."

Ranulf grinned at her. "A wench who would have me come to her clad in iron is not a lady of delicate sensibilities."

She put her arms around his neck and pulled him to her in a fierce hug. "Nay, I fear I am not a lady when I am near you." She pulled back and kissed him. "I will help you remove this heavy thing and then we may return home. Mayhaps I will share a tub of hot water with you."

"A delightful prospect."

She helped to pull the mail from him, and he pulled her close to him. "You have not told me the cause for your anger at me. Do not say you felt no anger, for I have come to know you."

"Nay, it matters not my reasons. The anger and the reasons are at an end now. You are with me and naught else matters."

"I have become as an old woman since I took you to wife and fret overmuch on too many things. I do not feel your troubles are at an end and will not be unless you tell me the causes. Am I so formidable a husband that I am not worthy of your trust?"

"Nay, it is not your trust in me that plagues me, but mine in you. Do not question me more. It is gone now and we are together. I ask for no more."

He kissed her forehead, not really sure of her answer, but helpless to learn more. He held her at arms' length, studying her body. There was a little more fullness in her breasts, her stomach harder, only slightly rounder. He ran his hands over her, impersonally.

"I hope I meet with your approval and you make your purchase."

He ignored her. "I thought women were ill when they carried children. You do not seem affected by my son."

She shrugged. "I believe some women are. I am glad not to be ill. My husband causes me enough worry without his son adding to it."

"I am a sweet-tempered man and never give you cause for concern."

"Aye, it is me that creates my own troubles."

He frowned at her, her acquiescence more alarming than her anger. He held her against his chest, almost frightened by her strange words. "I will listen, whatever your troubles." His grip on her tightened until she could not breathe. "There is no other man you desire?"

She hit him with all her might, with her fist, just under his ribs. "You have a meager brain and I will not glory your question with an answer. Now dress yourself so we may return home." As he turned away smugly, she could not resist a jibe. "There could be no other man, for you took all the most handsome when you took your guard." His hand gripping her wrist caused such pain as to bring tears to her eyes. "Ranulf, you hurt me! I do but jest. I want no other man. Release me, you great oaf!"

He let her wrist go and then smiled at her, as if ashamed. "I fear there are some jests I cannot see humor in. I have told you I will never share you."

Her eyes blazed intensely. "And what of you, my husband, am I to share you?" Her voice was serious, almost a whisper.

He seemed startled, her question surprising him. "I have not thought of it. I think it is different with a man than a woman."

"Are my feelings of hurt and jealousy less than yours because you are a man?"

"Nay, I cannot answer. I have never considered the idea ere now." He was serious, his brow creased as he concentrated. "All men go to war and there are always women. I do not think it would be the same."

"All women must wait while their husbands are at war and there are always men."

"It would matter to you that I had other women?"

"Think you could bear another man's hands on me? Nay, do not bruise me again, I but use words. I, also, do not like to think of another woman touching you."

He picked her up then, his arms about her waist, lifting her and holding her above his head. "I have heard that lions take only one mate; mayhaps I am a true lion. Your words are new to me and, in truth, the idea had never crossed my mind. Even King Edward . . . nay, I will spread no court gossip. I will think on this novel idea. Now I grow hungry. Can we not find that ugly animal you ride and return home?"

"Loriage is beautiful! You are but jealous that he is docile for me and no other."

"Your words ring true. I hate all men near you, be they horse or even bird. Why could you not be as other females and ride a dappled mare?"

"If I were as other women you would not have me. I am the only woman who neither fears you nor dotes on you. You have been overly spoiled in your life. I wonder what your mother could have been like to rear such as you."

"My mother was a lady, quiet and gentle, not unlike your own mother. I saw Lady Melite shudder more than once at your wayward behavior."

"I was never wayward!" she declared as he helped her into Loriage's saddle. "It was your fawning over me. I could not help teasing a man who looked at me with such great, liquid eyes."

" 'Twere I not exceedingly hungry, I would make you regret those words." His arm flashed out and encircled her, pulling her onto Tighe's back in front of him. "I think I may yet. Now try to play the lady for a few moments."

"Being a lady does not get me such rewards as being mauled by a handsome knight." She wiggled her behind against him.

"You are the mauler, I am . . ."

"Spare me. You are ever kind and sweet-tempered, I have heard before. Tell me how you came by the name of the Spawn of the Devil, then?"

He ran his teeth along her neck and the beginning of her shoulder, causing chills along her spine. "It was not from being led about by an insolent bit of a girl." His arms tightened about her. "I have always been content wherever I was, but now I find I cannot bear to be far away from you. You are like food or drink to me, a thing I must have to live. You do not know how your anger made me feel. You will send no more ugly messages through my boy?"

"Aye, I think I will, for it has brought you to me as no sweetly written words could have."

"You have no respect for the duties of your husband."

She lifted his hand from her waist and kissed it. "A husband has other duties besides war."

They rode together to the towering, gray walls of Malvoisin, content and happy at being together again. As hot water was brought to their chamber, the sky outside darkened and it began to rain. A small fire was lit against the chill.

Lyonene bathed Ranulf, with both of them laughing and enjoying their loveplay. Only one moment marred Lyonene's happiness.

"What has become of our Frankish guest? Do not tell me you gave rein to your anger and slipped a dagger into her? Although I vow there were times when I wished someone had."

"And what times do you speak of? You know her but a few days. She could not have made her character so well known to you in so short a time."

Ranulf looked away from his wife's intense stare. "I have come to know of the woman, but let us not waste our few hours with talk of her. For whatever reason, I am glad she is not here."

Lyonene did not wish to pursue the subject further either, for Ranulf's manner showed he concealed something, and in this pleasant moment she did not wish to break the spell with talk of what had destroyed her peace for the month past.

"When must you return to your men and your siege?"

Ranulf stepped from the tub, nude, wet, his skin glowing in the golden firelight. He pulled her to him, the water from him wetting her clothes to the skin. He kissed her and she moved closer to him. "You are a grand substitute for a towel," he murmured. "I leave on the morrow. Ssh," he said, putting a finger to her lips. "Do not protest and make the leaving more difficult for me. I am not a man to leave my men to fight my causes alone. We have this night together and it is a long while till morn. Let us make the best use of our time. And do remove those wet clothes! You drip on my floor."

She grinned at him and began to peel the wet clothes from her body. They made love slowly, lingeringly, not hurrying as before, but exploring and searching one another's body.

Lyonene was exhausted from the tension of the past

month, and the release from worry, from her concern for Ranulf's wandering affections, gave her a blissful, peaceful sleep. When Ranulf began to move from her, she clutched at him in her sleep. He sighed with pleasure and held her to him.

"Can you know how much I love you, little Lioness?" he whispered to her sleeping form. "Can you know the longing I feel when I am away from you?" He kissed her forehead and slept, his arms tightly holding his wife to him.

Lyonene awoke first and opened her eyes to gaze on Ranulf's sleeping face. The sooty lashes were almost like a girl's, his lips soft and sweet. She moved a bit and kissed the thin scar along his cheek and he woke. He smiled into her eyes, one hand tenderly brushing a fat strand of hair from her face.

"I am happy to see you again," she said quietly. "I began to doubt you remembered me."

"I did forget at times, but a few things were there to remind me of you."

"And what were they, my lord?"

"The sun, the moon, wind, grass, small things only."

She laughed and moved nearer to him. "I would that you did not return to your battle. I am afraid somehow."

"There is no danger, but fear of a drunk hurling a wooden cask at my head."

"Nay. I do not jest, and it is not the battle I fear, but else."

"You should fear the wrath of the Black Lion do you but talk his time away. Can you find no better way to send your knight into battle?"

She turned in his arms and for a while her fears were forgotten, but later they haunted her again as she watched Hodder help his master dress in his heavy chain mail.

"Do not look at me as if 'twere the last time. Go and tell Dawkin to prepare some food to carry back with me."

While she was gone, Ranulf's eye caught a faint glow of something in a dark corner. He bent to retrieve it and saw it was the ribbon Lyonene had sewn to resemble her beloved belt. He frowned at it, not understanding how it could have gotten there, for he had last seen it in his own tent, far away at Gethen Castle. There was something that worried her and she refused to tell him its nature, but he knew the ribbon was connected with her troubles. He sighed and slipped the ribbon into the pouch at his waist. When she trusted him, she would confide her fears to him. Until then he must wait, for he guessed that anything less than torture would not force her to answer his questions.

Lyonene did not cry when he rode away, his guard following, but stood silently in the courtyard. She had a heavy feeling in her breast, as if a weight pressed upon it. She sat alone in the garden for a time, trying to rid herself of the ugly feeling but could not.

A week passed quietly and Lyonene almost forgot her fears. But noise below stairs one day set her heart racing. The solar door burst open and Kate pushed through.

"My Lady Lyonene, forgive me, but she has caused a great ruckus. She says she must see you at once."

"Send her in." Neither Lyonene nor her maid felt they needed to explain exactly who "she" was.

Amicia came into the room slowly, looking about regally, as if appraising the beautiful proportions, the tapestries, the ornaments. She was, if possible, even thinner than before.

"It is as I remembered."

"No greeting, Amicia?"

Amicia smiled. "It is Lady Amicia, I think you recall. Nay, no greeting. The Countess of Malvoisin need give no greeting to barons' daughters."

"You have me guessing at your riddle, for I am both countess and the daughter of a baron."

"Such daughter you will always be, but I am not sure you hold your title as well."

Lyonene felt her anger rising. "Do not hide your meaning, but speak your words clearly. You have something to say to me, so get it done and be gone."

"Lady Lyonene, you betray your fear of me. I have news to give to you and would that we could have a peace between us."

"There can be no peace between us. What news do you bring?" Lyonene's face lost color. "Ranulf! Has aught happened to my husband?"

"Nay." Amicia ran her hand across the mantel. "He is well, most well and vigorous when I saw him last. Your

200

concern shows on your face. Do you love him well then?"

"What I feel for my husband is my own concern. If you have naught else to say, then leave me."

"Nay, my lady, I have much to say. The love you bear your husband concerns me greatly, for it is a love we share."

"I will not begin this afresh. I believed your lies once, but now I do not. Go from my sight." Lyonene rose in anger.

"You will hear me, for your life may depend upon it." Amicia's voice was deadly. "Aye. Your very life may center upon my words."

Lyonene sat down again, unconvinced, but feeling the woman capable of anything. "Have your say quickly and be gone."

"Lord Ranulf has shown himself to be a fickle man, I believe, when it comes to women. Look at how he betrothed himself to you after but one day's meeting with you. I have given you warnings which you heeded not and now you must pay for your disbelief, and most of all for your treatment of me." Her pale eyes glinted like a snake's. "As Ranulf de Warbrooke chose you in haste, so he will discard you in like haste."

"I believe not a word of your sayings. My husband has but left me not a week past. His behavior did not point to his tiring of me."

"You see, I know Ranulf as you do not. I know he needs women, many women, and I am willing to accept such behavior. Are you, Lady Lyonene?"

She could only stare at the woman, hating her, yet listening in spite of all reason, which told her that the words were false. "I accept my husband as he is, as I must."

"Well spoken by a loving wife. Will you feel the same when this husband sets another in this fine hall, puts another by his side at table? What say you when another child is favored over yours?" She near whispered this last sentence.

"What is your meaning of another child? Ranulf has no other children but the one I carry."

"He will soon, my innocent lady, for I carry one now that is as much his as the one you give shelter."

"Nay! I do not believe you! It is another man's bastard—if indeed you do hold a child in that fleshless belly —and you try to convince me it is my husband's."

"I have given you warning and I have shown you proof of your husband's love for me. Shall I show you the letters again, for I know you have seen them? Shall I describe the intimate moment of passion when he gave me the ribbon with the lions that you took from me? Nay, I see you know my words to be true."

Lyonene tried to still her racing heart, calm her emotions and think rationally. When she spoke, it was quietly and deliberately. "Many women must look aside when their husband's bastards are born. I am no less strong than they."

"Ah, a most sensible way, but I think you forget King Edward."

"And what has the king to do with such an ugly matter as you have placed before me?"

"Much, I fear." Amicia watched Lyonene, studying her reactions to the words. "As has been mentioned, you are but a baron's daughter, while I am heir to the Duke of Vernet's properties and fortune. King Edward would like much to have England associated with such lands. Has he not expressed his doubts as to his earl marrying so low-born a woman?"

Lyonene could not answer, but her mind filled with memories.

"Do you know the story of Gilbert de Clare, the Earl of Gloucester? He has obtained his divortium and will soon marry the Princess Joanna. What think you King Edward will say when he finds the Duke of Vernet's daughter carries the child of the Earl of Malvoisin? Think you he will laugh and pat Lord Ranulf's shoulder? Or will he think of the war such a great insult to France might bring?"

Lyonene could not reply.

"What will you do then?" the high voice continued. "Will you sit calmly by as the Pope dissolves your marriage? And what of your child? Your child whom you thought to inherit will be cast aside and mine will become the Earl of Malvoisin. Will you remain here and share Lord Ranulf's bed as his mistress? He seems to enjoy you well. I am sure he will continue to do so, even when you are not tied to one another with a marriage document.

Mayhaps you will return to your parents. Will they not be proud of their daughter? Married once to the renowned Black Lion, his son in tow. You will be a prize, and your father will have little difficulty in finding you another husband. What say you to sharing a bed with another man? Mayhaps he will not be so strong as Lord Ranulf or so handsome, but he will have the hammers and iron to forge new babes."

"Cease!" Lyonene put her hands over her ears. "Leave me! I can bear your presence no longer."

"It is not my presence that troubles you, but the truth you hear in my words. I will go, but you are far from rid of me."

Alone again, Lyonene sat, stunned, unable to make a coherent thought. Kate came and went, her questions unheard, unanswered. The woman's words did indeed have the ring of truth. She seemed to remember every word spoken at court, every hint at her unsuitable marriage to an earl.

What of Ranulf? He seemed to sneer at convention, but he loved his king, and his honor was a matter of great importance to him. What if he were pressured by his king? She knew the answer, knew Ranulf could not disobey his king. Had he not once mentioned Simon de Montfort with hate, saying how the man had risen against his king, tried to overthrow King Edward's father? Nay, Ranulf was an honorable man and would do what his conscience dictated.

She tried to sew again, but could not. What of Amicia's crude statement? The idea of another man touching her brought a shudder of revulsion. Yet could she stay and become his mistress, see Amicia in his bed?

Nay! she thought, she could not.

Food was brought to her but she noticed neither it nor the hands that served it. She paced the floor, then stopped to stare through the glass of a window. The courtyard lay below and the retainers of the inner bailey walked about normally, as if this were not a day when Lyonene's world had shattered.

Ranulf seemed to come to her from every corner, his face, his voice, his words. She had no faith in him! The thought brought new hope to her breast. Perhaps Amicia did lie. The letters could have been forged, the ribbon stolen. She had not seen them together, had no proof of her own that Amicia's child had been fathered by Ranulf. If the child were not his, then King Edward would not force Ranulf to dissolve his marriage.

She must go to him, yes, she must see for herself if there were any truth to Amicia's words. A glance at the window showed it to be late, too late to begin a journey.

Her mind worked quickly and she planned her journey with care. Once before she had used a disguise and she would do so again, only this time she must travel as a man, a boy at least. Clothes, she thought. She would need clothes; not rich ones to encourage robbers, but those of an apprentice, perhaps, on an errand for his master. She would need an excuse to be traveling alone. Once the thought of danger crossed her mind, but she shook it away. Her future and that of her child were paramount.

She rummaged through a chest of Ranulf's and tried on some of his clothes, but they were hopelessly too large and the fabrics too rich for a poor boy.

"Kate, come here," she called. She knew the girl looked with suspicion at her mistress's wild-eyed look. "Kate, you have helped me before and now I need your help again. I must go to my Lord Ranulf, but I must do so in secret. No one but the two of us must know."

"You cannot travel to his lordship without guards."

"Nay, I must. I have to learn something. If I am right, then I will show myself and there will be no need for secrecy, but if I be wrong . . . Nay, I do not wish to think on it. But I must have your help. I need a boy's clothes to fit me, as might befit an apprentice to a guildman. Think you that you can get these? Oh, and make them clean. I do not wish for vermin to infest my skin."

"Aye, my lady. I can get them."

Lyonene waited nervously for Kate's return. She took the offered garments. "You told no one?"

Kate shook her head.

"They look to be of a good size. What else do you hold?"

"They are the boy's clothes I shall wear."

"You? But why should you dress as a boy?"

"When I travel with you."

Lyonene stopped her examination of the garments. "Nay, Kate, you do not go with me. I must go alone."

"I go with you or I will cry to the castle your intentions."

Lyonene's eyes narrowed. "Do you threaten me?"

"Aye, I do."

Lyonene couldn't help her laugh. "Then I must retreat. We will leave early on the morrow. You are sure you wish to risk this?"

"Do not force me to think of your folly," the girl said as she helped Lyonene undress and get into bed.

Lyonene's last thought before sleep took her was that she was cursed with insolent maids. She sighed and gave a silent prayer of thanks for both Kate and Lucy.

Early the next morn, as Kate and Lyonene packed their clothes, Hodder entered the room. The thin man had never really befriended his new mistress, and the two rarely spoke.

"Yes, Hodder, what is it?"

"I have arranged suitable horses for the three of us. They wait outside the castle walls."

Kate and Lyonene exchanged glances and then the countess turned back to her husband's valet. "I do not know your meaning. I have asked for no horses."

"You could not expect to look as an apprentice astride an animal like Loriage. There is not a robber within England who would not attack for such a horse. Do not stand and stare at me, we must go."

"Hodder, how . . . ?"

"Suffice to say that there is naught that goes on at Malvoisin that I do not know of. You belong to my master and he bid me care for you and I will do so. Now finish with your garments. I have spread the word that you go to the village and will not return until dark. That will give us time before a hue and cry is raised."

Too astonished to ask further questions, Lyonene obeyed him.

They did not change into their disguise until they were at the ferry that took them from the Isle of Malvoisin to the coast of England. Hodder kept his identity and said he took the two freemen to Lord Ranulf. Kate and Lyonene carefully hid their faces and passed, unrecognized by the ferryman.

They rode hard for all the day and most of the night. When they stopped, Lyonene wearily fell onto the blanket Hodder spread for her. The ground was warm but hard, and when she awoke, her body ached in several places.

It was near sunset when they reached Gethen Castle, but Lyonene, spurred by a nervous energy, was unaware of the long, exhausting journey she had just completed. As the pennants of the Black Lion came into view, she slowed her horse and every nerve in her body screamed for her to return to Malvoisin; she did not want to know if Amicia's words were the truth.

Hodder sensed her fears. "We can return, my lady," he said quietly.

"Nay. I must know."

The camp was not heavily guarded. The knight who did see the three riders saw there was no threat and so did not challenge them. The Black Lion was famous throughout England, and many people came to stare at his camp, hoping for a glimpse of the earl or his Black Guard. Consequently, Hodder was able to lead the two women to a slight ridge very near the enormous black tent Lyonene knew so well.

Although the knight on watch thought little of the three strangers, there was another man who was most interested. He circled the camp and saw with satisfaction that the horses were indeed from Malvoisin. He studied the backs of the three people and grinned broadly when he saw a tawny strand of hair fall from under the too-large cap and then a small hand push it back in place. He fair ran back to his own tent, which he shared with many other of the garrison knights.

Lyonene was the first to see her. Amicia walked confidently to Ranulf's tent, and Lyonene knew her heart must have stopped along with her breath. So the woman did not lie; she did indeed go to the camp.

"My lady, you must make yourself known. You cannot let that woman go to your husband's tent." Kate was indignant.

"Nay, I cannot present myself, for . . ." She stopped as she saw Ranulf come out of the tent. Her heart lurched at the sight of him, so tall, his dark hair even darker in the fading sunlight, every part of him reminding her of their moments together—such brief moments, she thought now.

Amicia came from behind Ranulf and took his arm,

then turned to look up at him, one hand on his chest, caressing it. The three people could no longer see Ranulf's face as he turned toward the thin woman. Amicia was talking to him and he was listening earnestly. Her arms slid around his neck and she stood on her toes to press her lips to his.

Lyonene rose and turned back to the horses. "I have seen more than I cared to. We ride for home."

The return ride to Malvoisin was lost in Lyonene's memory. The vision of Amicia in Ranulf's arms was all she saw. So it was true! All that Amicia had said was true. She thought her love for Ranulf was strong enough to bear his children from other women, if need be, but she could not stand by and see him marry another—or find herself married to another man.

She allowed Kate to care for her, blindly doing as she was told. She was not even aware when they arrived at Malvoisin, or when Kate undressed her and put her to bed. She slept fitfully, feeling worse when she awoke.

For two days she was aware of nothing, only sitting in the solar and idly staring or making half-hearted attempts to sew. She felt no anger—no emotion of any kind—when Amicia stormed into the solar one morn.

"So, you know."

"Aye, I know."

Amicia grinned slyly. "And what say you now to your fine hopes for the child you carry? Mayhaps Lord Ranulf will allow him to stay and serve my child."

Lyonene only watched, dully.

"I did not think you so selfish as this," Amicia continued. "You seem to give little thought to your child, but brood continually on your own broken heart. Many women have found their husbands to stray, but they at least sought to protect their children."

"I know of no way to protect my son. How can I work against the evil you plot? I am an apprentice to your mastery of devilwork."

Amicia sat next to Lyonene and took her cold hand. Lyonene frowned at the woman, whose face had changed to show great concern. "My Lady Lyonene, I beg your forgiveness in this matter. I know it was due to you that I was saved from the storm and I owe you my life. I did not mean this to happen, but Lord Ranulf, I cannot ex-

plain, the man but looked at me and . . . I see you under-
tand."

Amicia leaned closer. "I was a virgin when he took me
and I could not resist."

Lyonene looked away.

"I have never loved a man ere now and I will say that
I want him, must have him, just as you want him. I have
no right to ask your forgiveness, but there is a way mayhaps I could atone for some of my ill deeds."

"There is no manner in which you could repay me for
what you have done."

"I know, my lady, and I am ashamed. You were
happy before I came and I have taken away your happiness. If I did not carry his child, I would not press the
matter. I would return to France and try to mend my
broken heart, which would surely be the case were I to
leave Lord Ranulf."

"So what way do you plan to give me back some of
that which you have stolen?"

"I cannot save you, but I mayhaps could save your
child. Even now a messenger wings his way to King Edward with news of my presence in England and also tells
him of the child I carry. The divortium, I am sure, will
come soon."

"How will this save my child?" Lyonene asked, her
mouth a grim line.

"If you cannot be found before your child is born, he
will be heir to the earldom."

"I do not trust you. Why would you risk losing a title
for your child by telling me this?"

Amicia shrugged. "I owe you my life and, too, there is
a chance your child will be a daughter. Also, Ranulf
must leave his title to his first-born son. Not so his estates. I do not risk so much as it seems."

Lyonene considered for a moment. She would not have
believed her had she seemed to sacrifice all for Lyonene's
child, but it was true she owed her life to Lyonene and
might wish to repay her in some way. "So, you have a
plan, it seems?"

Amicia put her finger to her lips and silently walked
to the door, searching the empty corridor. She came back
and sat next to Lyonene, her voice a whisper. "This must

be done in secret. No one must know of it, that nosy valet or your maid. Agreed?"

Lyonene nodded.

"I risk much to plan this and I do not wish to be caught. I have heard your father has relatives in Ireland. This is true?"

"Aye, but I do not know them, although my father has talked much of them."

"Think you they will harbor you until the safe delivery of your child?"

"Aye, I think they would if they knew he were in danger."

"Good," Amicia whispered. "Then I will arrange for a ship to take you to Ireland. You will abide there until after the child's birth. Then, when the child is safely delivered, you may return to England, to your father's house. I am sure the divortium will be final by then, but the church will not allow another marriage until you are found. Therefore your child will be first-born and earl."

Lyonene frowned. "I do not understand. If the divortium is final, how will I still be married to Ranulf?"

Amicia looked about her, wildly, for a moment. "It is too complex to explain. You must trust me, for I am the daughter of a duke and I know better the ways of court law. You agree to this plan?"

"I do not know. I am confused. I . . ."

"You are selfish!" Amicia said in disgust. "I offer you some safety, a means to escape the plight ahead of you, that you even stop to consider is an indication of your selfishness. Think you of your son when he is twenty and turns to you and asks why you did not consider him in this matter, but only your lust for his handsome father. Then you will have naught, this husband you crave or your son's love. Will you speak of confusion then, ask his forgiveness when he is little more than a beggar, declared bastard of the Earl of Malvoisin? Mayhaps he will one day see my sons and be reminded . . ."

"Cease! You go too fast."

"There is need to haste, for I believe the siege to be over soon."

"Then Ranulf will return and I may speak with him."

Amicia threw back her head in a high thin wail of what passed for laughter. "You are more a fool than you seem. You would rather hear my words from this man you simper over? Think you he will allow you to go to Ireland and foil his king's plan of his earl's heir being the grandson of a Frankish duke? Nay, my lady, if you leave for Ireland, you do so quickly and before he returns."

"I . . . When would the ship leave?"

"On the morrow."

"So soon? I have had no time to think."

"I have arranged the time just so, so you could not reconsider. I have watched you and know your lust for him will betray you. You must decide now, this moment, aye or nay, and in a short time you will be off."

Lyonene could not think. She saw Amicia kissing Ranulf, thought of Ranulf's relationship with his king and then she thought of their child. "Aye, I will go."

Amicia gave a smile of triumph. "You have made a wise choice, my lady. This night you must pack only what you can carry in leather bags that go on a horse, no more. And you must let no one know of your plans. No one! Do you understand?"

"Aye, I understand too well," came Lyonene's bleak reply.

"I go now, but early on the morrow you must ride out on that black horse of yours. Say the packs carry cloth for the serfs, if anyone asks, but do naught to arouse suspicion. The ship will be gone when they discover you missing." She left the room.

Lyonene did not move, but later, when Kate helped her to bed, she began to cry and did not stop until the sun showed pink through the glass windows. It was to be her last night as mistress of Malvoisin, her last night in Ranulf's bed. She rose late—not until the sun was full up—and hurriedly slung garments into the leather bags. She took no jewelry save the lion belt. As a remembrance, she took a small ivory box of Ranulf's, carved with the lion of Malvoisin. It was made to hold his seal, but now it stood empty.

She gave one last look at the bedchamber where she'd been so happy and shut the door.

Her passage to the ship that waited at St. Agnes' Point was quite easy. Only Kate had mentioned her mistress's swollen face from the long night of tears, but Lyonene easily explained that away with a short sentence about pains caused by the babe she carried.

Her stomach was definitely rounded now and she stroked the curve of it, again hoping she did the right thing in her flight.

She could see the sails of the ship ahead, knew it to be one of several belonging to Ranulf, used to buy and sell goods with other kingdoms. Amicia came to her from her hiding place among some brush.

"You are late and Morell needed to make excuses for not sailing," Amicia said, accusingly.

"Morell?"

"You do not think I could arrange your escape alone? Sir Morell is one of Ranulf's garrison knights, although he should, by rights, be one of the Black Guard. But this is no time for that. Here, you must hide your clothes and your hair." She handed Lyonene a cloak of russet.

Lyonene dismounted and donned the mantle. "You will see to Loriage? That he is returned?"

"Now is no time to concern yourself with your precious horse. Aye, I will see to the beast. We must go, now. Morell is not sweet-tempered when his plans are mislaid. Keep your head down and look at no one. I do not wish the guards to see you."

She followed Amicia onto the ship, standing quietly as the Frankish woman spoke to a man she couldn't see.

"Get her below then," came a querulous voice, and Lyonene looked up to see the man who was to take her to Ireland. She had seen him but few times before, yet each instance was etched in her memory. She recalled the times she had seen him standing in shadows where only she could see him, a smirk on his face. He always looked at her as if he seemed to know more of her than he did, as if he but waited for a time when he would discover all that he desired.

Instinctively, Lyonene turned away, her steps going toward the side of the boat and home.

"My Lady Lyonene." The blond knight held her arm. "Do not be afraid. I will take you to your father's relatives, and I will protect your safety and your honor with my life. Come below. I have seen to your cabin myself, for I would that you were comfortable."

She could not look at him.

"I am Sir Morell, late in your esteemed husband's employ. I say late for I do not think he will care much for me now that I take his wife away, albeit for a good cause. Come with me and be assured that you will be given every consideration."

Lyonene allowed herself to be led below, more unsure of herself each moment. The cabin was tiny, cramped and airless.

"Lady Lyonene," he said to her, moving his head nearer hers.

"Yes." She forced herself to look into his blue eyes. He was handsome in a way, fashionably fair, with brilliant eyes, a thin nose and a straight, firm mouth.

He seemed to understand her scrutiny of him and gave her a one-sided smile. "Lady Lyonene, I must beg an indulgence from you. My men are not knights; in truth, they are not honorable men, and although I would protect you with my life, I fear I have only one life. You are a beautiful woman and I would not like to risk such beauty in contact with the coarse men who ride with me."

"What is your meaning?" She managed to get words out at last.

"I would protect you from my men."

"Can you not order them to stay away from my cabin?"

He smiled, his eyes devouring her, the hair cascading about her shoulders, the rise and fall of her breast, the swell of her hips beneath the coarse woolen cloak. "I fear I am not a man to be feared such as the Black Lion; nay, I am more of a lover than else." He touched a curl along her breast, and a frown creased his brows when she jerked away.

He stepped back from her, seeking to control himself.

"I . . . I wish to leave this ship."

"To leave, so soon? But our journey has just begun— our long, slow journey, I might add."

"There is something wrong. I do not know what, but I have decided that I would rather face my husband than . . . than what lies before me."

Sir Morell strove to control his anger. "My lady, your fears are foundless. There is no one here who seeks other than to help you. I know all concerning Lady

Amicia, and you must consider your child." His eyes went to her gently rounded stomach and she covered herself. He continued, "You have made the wisest decision, and when you are safe again amongst your relatives, you will realize it. Until then you are surrounded by strangers and it is only natural that you have some reservations. I am older than you, have seen more of the world, have seen too many young wives discarded for another. Here, sit, my lady."

He guided Lyonene to the narrow bunk, his fingers running along her forearm for an instant before he relinquished his hold on her.

"I must continue what I began. To assure myself that you are in no danger from my unchivalrous men, I must lock your cabin door."

"You would lock me into this tiny place?"

"It is for your own safety, no other reason. Trust me. I will help you escape what could be a dangerous situation."

"I do not know . . ."

"I have paid homage to Ranulf de Warbrooke, and whatever else you seem to think me, I am a man of my word."

She nodded then, submitting to what the future held for her.

"You will not regret your trust of me. I go now to see to the safe passage of the ship. I will return soon with food, and mayhaps I may join you in your dinner."

He left her and Lyonene heard the key turn the lock. She felt helpless, beyond despair, and she could only lay back on the hard cushion and stare, sightlessly, into space. It seemed that her life was at an end.

Chapter Fourteen

Hodder rode straight through the night and only by chance met the Earl of Malvoisin as he returned home from the long siege. Corbet helped the tired little man from his horse.

"I must speak to Lord Ranulf."

"I am here. What has happened? Why have you traveled without guards?"

"My lord . . ." he gasped, sitting on a rock. The moonlight made eerie figures of the seven dark guardsmen and their even darker lord. "She has gone," he continued, panting to catch his breath.

"Who has gone? That Frankish woman? I am well rid of her."

"Nay. It is the Lady Lyonene who has flown."

Hodder found himself lifted from the rock by his shoulders. Eight faces glared at him, and he couldn't help his shudder of fright. "I could not hear what was said and so did not know her plans. She rode into the village this morn with cloth for some of the serfs, but at sunset she still had not returned. I alerted the guards, and the island was searched. We spent hours, but she was nowhere to be found."

"We ride." Ranulf turned to his men. "Hugo, assign a man to care for the baggage. My guard goes with me to Malvoisin. Hodder comes with us. I would hear more of the searches made."

It was not easy to talk on the long journey back to the island. Hodder's head near burst with the pressure of yelling above the horse's thundering hoofs, but Ranulf showed no mercy to the man. After awhile, Ranulf stopped and put Hodder on the back of the Frisian and the man continued his story.

Ranulf knew that Hodder was an accomplished eavesdropper, but even he was unaware of the valet's expertise. He doubted if there was a word he'd ever said to anyone in his own house that Hodder had not heard.

Hodder told Ranulf all of Amicia's treachery. He told of the letters, the ribbon, the woman's braggings.

"Lyonene did not believe these things the woman said?"

"Aye, she did, but not at first. She was angry when she felt the woman's words to be true, but she believed you meant no ill toward her as your wife."

"That was good of her," Ranulf muttered sarcastically, barely heard above the noise of their fast travel.

"You cannot blame Lady Lyonene. Even I would have believed the woman's threats did I not know you so well."

Ranulf half-turned in the saddle to stare at his valet. "And what reason do you have to believe in me when confronted with such proof?"

Hodder shrugged. "I but looked at Lady Lyonene and then the bony Amicia. I have come to know the type of woman your greedy lust leads you to."

Ranulf would have laughed had not the moment been so serious. "These letters are what caused my wife to refuse to answer my letter. I knew something was awry when I returned home. The woman is a fool, a brainless fool, to think I write words of love to one woman and then neglect my duties when I but think my wife has a low mood. There is joy in a wife, but there is much pain. Think you twice before you take a wife, Hodder."

The valet was indignant. He recovered himself and continued. "She was happier after your visit, but Amicia brought more news."

"What news—more letters?"

"Nay, my lord. She came with the news that she carried your child."

"My child! That any man's seed could take root in that barren ground is a wonder. Lyonene did not believe her?"

"Nay, she did not. She said she would go to you and see that there was naught between you."

"This is the only bit of sense I have heard. She did not come, though."

"Nay, but she did. Kate and I rode with her to your camp."

Ranulf was silent for a moment, cursing the foolhardiness of a wife who would travel across the turbulent English countryside with only a girl of a maid and a thin, weak man for protection.

Hodder understood his master. "We dressed as merchants' apprentices. We had no trouble."

"Why did I not see her then?"

"We sat on a hill by your tent and watched."

"Go on, man! There must have been more reason as to why my wife refused to see me, why she has fled me."

"She saw the woman Amicia in your embrace, my lord."

"Nay, she could not have!" Then he remembered the time when Amicia had barged into his tent and he had gone outside to escape her. There she had kissed him, and he had had to control himself from striking her. She was no better than a bitch in heat. She came often to his camp during the siege, and from the sounds, several of his garrison knights had enjoyed her favors. She had made numerous advances to Ranulf, but he had been repulsed by her—her long thin arms, her whining voice, her false avowals of being a duke's daughter.

The day after the storm Ranulf had sent a message to France to learn of the Duke of Vernet. The answer had arrived only this morn. The Duke had indeed been on the wrecked ship, but the man was near eighty years and had never had a daughter. Amicia had merely used the story for a purpose as yet unknown to Ranulf.

Filled with foreboding, Ranulf urged Hodder to continue his story.

Hodder told of Amicia's last visit, how she said King Edward would force Ranulf to marry Amicia to prevent a war. Ranulf could only shake his head in amazement that Lyonene could believe such a story.

"What of the rest of it? You have not explained where or why my wife is hiding. Have you searched all the cabins, the glade?"

"Aye, everywhere, and she is not to be found."

"I shall shake her teeth from her body when I find her," he said through a clenched jaw.

"I believe the woman Amicia had some hand in planning Lady Lyonene's hiding."

"I do not understand you."

"The woman is most clever. I could not listen longer

for she routed me from my place and fell into whispers. I should have guessed her intentions."

They rode on, silently, to Malvoisin, Ranulf alternately cursing and praying for his wife. His pride wounded, he berated her for her lack of trust, for believing that he would choose such a woman as Amicia for the reasons that had been given. He cursed himself for leaving her to such a villainous woman, for not forcing her, when he had returned to Malvoisin, to tell him what plagued her.

Hodder repeated more of Amicia's words concerning the babe; how Ranulf intended the child to be servant to Amicia's and how Lyonene's child would be known as bastard. Finally, he revealed Amicia's offer of the earldom to Lyonene's babe.

Ranulf began to see what had caused his wife's fears. She knew little of court laws. Ranulf could choose what son or even adopted son he desired to pass on his wealth and title to. It did not go by birth, as Amicia had insisted.

The ferry to the island seemed to go tediously slowly, and the expressions on the faces of his men were as grim as Ranulf's. He told them briefly of the treachery that had been wrought in his absence, for he had begun to suspect a plot from Hodder's story. The men were divided into pairs and given areas of the island to search. Before the ferry came to rest, men and horses were already wading ashore.

The Black Guard went first to the castle to change horses, but Ranulf stayed on Tighe, the horse having been bred for stamina and endurance.

The entire island was roused, torches lit, and not one person was not called into the search. Beginning to fear that she had been taken to be held for ransom, Ranulf sought to find the hiding place of her captors.

No one had crossed the ferry to the coast of England who could have been Lyonene, so he did not believe her to have left the island. The hounds were brought into the search and given free rein in following the scents they found.

Dawn came and still no sign of her or of Amicia. The beginnings of fatigue and blind grief blurred his thoughts and his vision. He went into the chapel at Mottistone and began to pray, the only course he knew to take to clear his cobwebbed brain. After a few moments' meditation, he knew—knew the island search to be fruitless, knew there had been a ship that had taken her away, knew for sure that this was no simple case of a jealous wife running away, but the result of a careful plan.

He left the altar, grateful to the saints for giving him the answer.

He rode quickly to St. Agnes' Point, tearing up the stone steps to the guard's post at the top of the stone tower.

"Did a ship leave here this day?"

"Aye, my lord." The man was more than a little frightened at his master's black, stormy face. "Two ships; your own, both of them."

"Two! There are no ships that should sail today. What excuse was given for my ships sailing unbeknownst to me, and who sailed them?"

"William de Bec sent one to France with the cargo of wool to be woven; the other went to Ireland to buy more cloth."

"What cargo went to Ireland?"

"None, your lordship. It sailed empty."

Ranulf's eyes bored into the man, his voice deadly. "Have you ever known one of my ships to either leave or return empty?"

"Nay, my lord, but Sir Morell said you were in a great hurry to purchase more finery for the new wife you dote on. He said . . ."

"Sir Morell!" Ranulf sneered. "The man has ever plagued me. Who went with him?"

"Only his crew, my lord, and some serfs and . . . that Frankish woman. She went to choose the colors, they said."

"They said! You have proven you have ears but naught between. They found you an easy mark. Go from my sight before I remove you from the earth. They have taken my wife on their empty boat, no doubt dressed as a serf. A moment more and you shall answer for your indulgences."

The man near fell down the stairs in his haste.

Ranulf whirled when a hand touched his shoulder. Herne stood there.

"We have all come to the same answer. You agree with

the stench of this matter? Have you found aught that is useful?" the guardsman asked.

Herne nodded at Ranulf's answer, then continued, "We must go to prepare, for I do not think you wait for a message of ransom. We travel soon. I hear tell Ireland is a small place and so will be easily searched."

Ranulf spent a day in preparation, allowing his men to rest and sleeping himself for a few hours. He knew little of Ireland, but he knew Dacre had cousins there. He sent messages to his friend and to Lorancourt. He thought he remembered his father-in-law mentioning relatives in Ireland. If Lyonene managed to escape, she would go to her kinfolk and Ranulf must know where they abided.

Through all his actions was a slow deliberateness, knowing the long battle that lay ahead for him and his men. He was no longer angry at his wife, but felt there was some flaw in him that made her doubt him.

The Black Guard met him in the courtyard, clad in their heaviest chain mail, their coarsest wool tabards. The heavy weapons of war hung from the saddles of horses that were also covered in the iron-link armor. There was neither word nor acknowledgment of one another as Ranulf mounted the enormous black Frisian. Their purpose together was united and held by a deathly bond.

It took them two days to reach Dunster, and there the answers to Ranulf's messages awaited. Dacre offered help, if needed, and the names and places of his kin. William Dautry also gave the name of his daughter's cousins, and Melite sent her word of continued prayers.

The ferry took days to reach Waterford on the coast of Ireland. The sight of the unknown land only heightened Ranulf's fears, for it seemed impossible to search the entire island. He and his men broke into four pairs, Maularde beside Ranulf, and began the search.

The ship began to move and Lyonene felt the uneasiness in her stomach almost instantly. The nausea kept her mind from thinking of what she had done. She stretched out on the little bed, and Ranulf seemed to come to her from everywhere. She might never see him again or be able to touch him. Their child would be born and Ranulf might never even see the babe. A sharp pain in her stomach kept the tears from filling her eyes. Would the child be dark like Ranulf or have her light locks?

The door to the little cabin unlocked. "I have brought you food and wine." Sir Morell paused, a frown creasing his brow. "Do not tell me you are given over to the sickness of the sea?"

Lyonene could only look at him, her stomach moving in waves of revulsion. The contents of her stomach rose in her throat, and she swallowed to keep it down, her hand covering her mouth.

Morell's eyes turned hard, his mouth ugly as he glared at her. He angrily threw the charger onto the table, the wine upsetting and spilling, the smell of it sending new shudders through Lyonene.

"Amicia!" Morell threw open the door and bellowed.

Even through her pain and her ardent attempts at controlling her nausea, Lyonene was surprised, for she had not known the Frankish woman sailed with them. She was too ill to think more on the puzzle.

"How may I be of service to you, my sweet knight?" Amicia ran her hand across Sir Morell's leather-covered chest.

"You may care for that sick woman you brought with you."

"Sick! She is not ill. It is not the babe too soon?"

"Nay, it is but the motion of the ship. I had other plans for her than seeing her toss her stomach into a pot. Part of the plan was that I have her."

Amicia cast a worried look past Morell to Lyonene, who lay curled almost into a ball on the bed. "We have a way to go yet, and I would keep our secret from her. She will be more docile if she knows naught of us. You will have her, soon, I swear. It takes twelve days to reach Ireland. This sickness will last but a few of them. Do not be so greedy."

Amicia ran her hands across Morell's shoulders, her arms going about his neck. "I do not see why the woman interests you so. There is naught she can give you that I cannot. Come and let me show you."

He pulled her arms from his neck. "I do not like my women so well-used. Now see you to her and see that she is recovered quickly, or I shall lock you in your cabin and allow none of my crew near you, for opposite reasons than I lock away this lady."

"You insult me and ask me to care for the woman you plan to bed, in the same breath?"

"Nay. I do not ask. No man should ask aught of such a woman as you. Now do as I say or I shall carry out my threats." He roughly pushed her toward the huddled figure of Lyonene and quickly left the room, his revulsion of the sick woman obvious.

Lyonene could not remember much of the next few days, but she was aware of hands pushing at her, words that cursed her and, above all, a stomach that pained her greatly. Food was forced down her throat, and she felt it rise again almost instantly. Then there were more curses, sharp slaps on her hands and arms, a harsh cloth wiped across her soiled mouth.

She awoke one day, sane again, thinner and very weak, her head hurting. It took a few moments to remember where she was and why she was there. "Ranulf," she whispered as she thought of the husband that she would never know again.

The whispered word came from a dry, parched throat and she looked about for some water. An aquamanile stood on the other side of the cabin. What had once seemed a tiny space now loomed enormous before her. She sat up slowly, her weakness making her head spin. The front of her tunic was soiled, encrusted with days of sickness. She sneered in revulsion at the filth, but was not strong enough to consider changing the gown. Her only thought was to slake her burning thirst.

She swung her legs over the bunk and put her bare feet on the oak floor. Supporting herself from one object to another, she slowly made her way to the pitcher of water. She was triumphant as her shaking fingers touched the handle and found it cool to touch, moist to her dry fingertips. She pulled it to her with difficulty, but knew it was empty before she brought it before her eyes. She turned it up over her tongue, one drop doing nothing to relieve the pain.

A burst of laughter, almost beside her, made her laboriously turn to the door. It was not quite closed and the laughter came from somewhere outside it. Maybe someone would give her a drink. She clumsily put the pitcher back on the shelf and made her way to the door, her feet scuffling, arms almost giving way once in their support of her.

The door swung open easily and she walked the few feet to the doorway next to her cabin. Light shone from within, and she could see two people sitting around a table, the coveted mugs of liquid in their hands. She watched greedily as Amicia drank from a sweat-coated vessel. She lifted her hand to push the partially opened door wider.

"To the Lady Lyonene!"

The sound of her name stopped her, and she blinked rapidly to clear her thirst-crazed mind. She recognized Sir Morell as the speaker.

"To a plan of such perfection that we have been able to snatch the wife of the Earl of Malvoisin from beneath the husband's nose. No other man has penetrated the barriers of that guarded island."

"Do not forget to include woman in that, my good sir, for I do not believe you were alone in the execution of the plan."

"Ah, but Amicia, you were but an instrument. It was I who watched her for months, I who planned every step. The day I saw her atop that hill outside his tent, I could not believe our good fortune!"

"She was an easy mark. She is so lovesick for the man I knew she could not bear the idea of another woman near him." Amicia took a sip of ale. "I can see why she favors the man. I have heard her cries at night."

"And you wished much to experience the joys she found, also, did you not? When he repulsed you so readily, I knew I had found a partner for the drama I planned."

Amicia threw him an ugly look. "Now that we have her, what do we do with her?"

"That is arranged. I have a friend in Ireland, a widow who would do much for me. I will take her to my friend and there the little countess shall await her husband's ransom. It will take him months, if not years, to collect what I will ask."

"And what do you plan for her in the years it takes?" Amicia's voice had a hint of laughter.

"This illness of hers plagues me much. I grew up always surrounded by illness and cannot abide it now. I do not see why she is not recovered from this sickness yet. We are but four days from Ireland. Do you add something to her food to prolong her sickness?" He grabbed the front of Amicia's surcoat.

She easily brushed him aside. "Food! The woman keeps naught down but heaves it up again. It may be the child that causes this, although I have not heard of her having pain from it before."

"That is another point. Although the child will bring a higher price in ransom, I will regret the loss of time when she will not share my bed."

"You are too womanish in your ways. Why should a swollen belly keep you from what you have risked your life for?"

"You disgust me, Amicia. I have no desire to flounder about on top another man's leavings. When she is free of her burden, she will be mine, but do not think on it. She will be well again soon, and there is time before she grows shapeless."

Amicia raised her mug to him. "I hope she is worth all the effort you have given to having her."

They both drank deeply.

"Now, go back and see to her. You have been away long. See if you can get some food to stay down her."

Amicia reached for the pitcher and refilled her mug. "There is time. I do but watch her toss about and moan. She does not even heave now, but just lays there, calling his name o'er and o'er."

Morell frowned and refilled his cup.

Lyonene leaned back against the wall, her heart pounding weakly. She began to edge back along the rough boards to the open door of her own chamber. She made her way to the bunk and collapsed on it. Had her face and body not been so dry she would have cried, but there was no moisture left in her, only the bleak, desolate knowledge of how she had fallen prey to an insidious plan.

Lyonene heard Amicia come into the room and carefully kept her face averted. Even in her illness she had only one thought—she must remain ill or the fate that awaited her would be worse than a sick stomach. She must feign illness and somehow escape her captors, and above all, she must not think of the past. "Forgive me, my sweet Ranulf," she whispered.

"Here, you filthy gutter rat." Amicia roughly lifted Lyonene's head and pushed a pewter cup to her lips, the metal striking her teeth. She drank greedily of the stale water. "A fine lady you be. Would that that husband could see you this day. Mayhaps he would think twice when he got within a yard of your stench. Here! Do not drown yourself." She jerked Lyonene's head up and stared into her eyes.

Lyonene forced her eyes to go blank, lose focus.

"It was too much to hope I would rid myself of the burden of you. Morell desires you. Men! It is all in their heads. One woman is the same as another, just as men are much the same." She dropped Lyonene's head and she fell back to the hard bunk.

"At least you drink now, so I'll soon get some broth down you."

For Lyonene, the hardest to bear was the filth and slime of her clothes. The smell made her weak stomach churn against holding even the water she had drunk. She would have to let Amicia know she had some semblance of coherence again, for she'd need the chamber pot soon. When the Frankish woman returned, she turned to look at her.

"So, you are awake. It has been many days."

"How many?" Lyonene whispered.

"Ten."

They were within two days of Ireland, then. "I have been a burden to you."

"Aye, you have."

"I did not know you traveled to Ireland. Should you not be . . . at Malovisin?"

"Do not start your tears again. I have had enough of them. You must have had a fever caused by more than just the motion of the sea, and you have raved every moment you were ill. There is naught of you or Lord Ranulf I do not know. Now we will leave this ship soon and Morell would have you well. You must drink this and then sleep." She thrust a warm mug of soup into Lyonene's hand.

Try as she would, she could not lift the heavy cup. Her

fingers trembled and her arms would not obey her commands.

"Here!" Amicia angrily lifted the mug, forcing Lyonene to drink. She tipped the cup and the invalid's head back too far, and some of the contents spilled down her tunic, adding to the dirt-encrusted fabric. "You are no better than a babe. I have had to tend you as one, and I am fair sick of it. The smell of you puts me off, and there is little resemblance to a woman about you. If that child fled your belly, I would not blame it."

Lyonene put shaky fingers to her stomach, aware that it had increased in size in even the last few days. "My babe is not harmed?" she asked anxiously, fearful that something was wrong.

"Nay. It sets in there firmly. Now I must go to Sir Morell. He wished to know when you woke."

Lyonene lay back on the cushionless cot, feeling as tired as if she had climbed a mountain, mayhaps several mountains. In spite of the discomfort of the horrible scratchy clothes, the smell, the matting of her hair, she was nearly asleep when Sir Morell opened the cabin door.

"Mon Dieu! Amicia, I cannot enter this room! Take her from here and clean her, for I see you have left her in her own filth. I will see that the cabin is cleaned. You are an animal to treat any woman so. Get from my sight!"

There was quiet and Lyonene felt the waves of sleep overtaking her again. Rough hands picked her from the cot.

"I don't mind her so badly. I have seen whores who were worse."

A harsh male voice boomed above her. She opened tired eyes just enough to realize she was being carried from the room.

"Nay, she is not bad. Her eyes are the color of a jewel I once saw his lordship wear."

"Ranulf?" Lyonene whispered.

"Aye, Lord Ranulf it is I speak of. Now, you need not worry, for he will buy you back. Nay, he would not let you go."

"Keep your mouth closed, sailor!" Sir Morell's voice came to her through a haze. She must not let them know she was aware of their plans. "Ranulf?" she whispered again.

"See, she knows naught of what I speak. The lady's too sick to hear me. She weighs no more than a feather, for all she carries a babe."

"Just tend to your duties and say no more to her. She may remember your words later."

"Aye, sir."

Lyonene was deposited in a hard wooden chair, too tired to even open her eyes. She was aware of dampness and heat near her, increasing her need for sleep.

"Nay, you cannot sleep now. My fine knight would have you bathed. I do not believe in so much washing as he; it is not good for the skin. Now here! Do not fall! He will make me answer for your injuries. I cannot believe you could smell so horrible in but ten days."

Lyonene felt cool air as her clothes were torn from her.

"Now, step up, higher."

The water felt wonderful, wetting her skin, filling her parched pores as no amount of water drunk could have. She even enjoyed the roughness of Amicia's washing of her. She wanted more than anyone else to rid herself of the ugly grime of her illness. Her hair was washed, the woman's fingers scouring Lyonene's scalp, removing days of filth.

Lyonene felt almost alive as she stood in the tub while Amicia poured hot water over her. A thin towel was rubbed briskly over her, and the clean linen touched her skin.

"No more fine silk hose for you, my lady. The clothes are warm and loose and will allow for the growth of the babe. It seems to be growing fast." She laughed at a private jest. "Morell will not like that."

Lyonene gave no hint that she understood the woman's words, reveling for a moment in the freshness of clean skin and unsoiled clothing. The pale woman opened the door and a large man entered, dressed in coarse wools, his long hair matted and dirty.

"She looks to be a real lady now, like when she rode beside Lord Ranulf."

Lyonene closed her eyes and feigned an insensibility she did not feel. The sailor carried her back to the little room that was her cabin and gently deposited her on a fresh-smelling bed, the sheets hinting of salt water and sunshine. She relaxed on them gratefully, taking a perverse pleasure in such purely physical comfort, which belied her true situation.

"She is pretty. Did you know the Black Guard calls her their Lady Lioness? I tried to speak to her once but that Corbet drew a sword on me. They let no one near her but the favored of his lordship."

"Leave her, you oaf! I do not need your calf-sick stories to entertain me. You would not have thought her such a fine lady did you hold her head over the pot."

"Nay, a true lady is at all times a lady." The sneer in his words, directed toward Amicia, was unmistakable.

Lyonene slept for a long while, waking once when the cabin was dark but sleeping immediately again. When she woke next, the cabin was bright and she felt much better; hungry, thirsty, weak, but alive, with a conviction that she was going to remain so.

It was not long until Amicia came into the cabin with a charger of food. "You look as if you might live now."

Lyonene drank deeply of the hot soup and ate a piece of bread.

"Morell will be glad to know you are soon to be recovered." She gave Lyonene a sly look.

The countess knew her meaning, and when she had eaten her fill—much less than she had thought she could— she lay back on the pillows, wearily. "I must sleep now," she muttered, aware of Amicia's scrutiny. At all costs, she must make them think she was still very ill. Then there would be a possibility that Sir Morell would leave her to herself.

The next day Lyonene felt much stronger, but she did not let it show to Amicia. Sir Morell came to visit her, and Lyonene mumbled something about the child she carried and clapped a hand over her mouth. She saw the knight's look of disgust before he fled. She was also very aware of Amicia's amusement and felt that the woman enjoyed the mummery and would not give her away.

Late in the day the ship stopped moving and shouts and orders were given as the vessel settled to a halt. Amicia came to her.

"We journey to . . . to your kin now. You are to ride

near me and keep from Sir Morell until you are well."

Lyonene thought she sensed a smirk in the pale woman's last words. She barely had time to snatch the lion belt from its hiding place beneath a cushioned seat. She did not know what instinct had caused her to hide it, but she had. The ivory box of Ranulf's was not to be found. She fastened the belt under the folds of the loose wool surcoat, above her stomach, pulling cloth forward to add bulk to her enlarging stomach.

Amicia noticed the increased width but said naught, and Lyonene was encouraged in the necessary deception.

There was no mummery involved when she was led down the side of the ship. The horrible rope ladder swayed and fled from her feet as she tried to find her way. Her weak arms began to tremble violently, both from the exertion and her growing feeling of danger.

A strong man took her waist, and she was pulled gently into the waiting rowboat.

"Careful you do not show yourself too fond of the lady," Sir Morell said, sneering at the big sailor who held her.

"I will not see her or the babe harmed. You swore they would not be injured."

"Nay, I'll not harm her. My plans for the lady bear little pain, but that is her decision. Amicia, can you not do something with her? She has no more life than a rag doll."

For an instant Amicia's pale eyes met Lyonene's green ones and an understanding passed between them. As Amicia ran her hand across Sir Morell's thigh, she and Lyonene gazed steadily at one another. They reached a silent agreement, now two women—no longer one with a courtly rank but a prisoner and one a captor, but only women, with the knowledge of all women. Amicia gave the briefest of nods, and Lyonene closed her eyes again, her body limp.

"She is still very ill, Morell. In truth, I fear for her life. The babe is farther along than I had thought and I think it pains her. You may of course take her as she is." Amicia gestured to Lyonene's pale, slumped body, a study in weakness.

"Nay, I prefer a woman and not a useless bundle of

228

rags. We will find a barber and see what he can do for her."

"I think we should go to the widow's straightaway. When a ship of the Black Lion's is found empty, it will cause much talk. We must go quickly and not be seen by others."

"Aye, you are right. I would not like to have Ranulf de Warbrooke find his wife before I have my ransom."

The climb down the rope was nothing compared to the hours astride a horse. It was all Lyonene could do to stay atop the animal. She tried to think of a way to escape, but they traveled always across barren land, the paths sometimes too rocky, steep, the struggles of her horse little helped by its rider's weakness.

Sir Morell often turned to look at her, and each time she managed to give some sign of great sickness. After the first day he stopped turning to her, and Amicia gave Lyonene a slight smile, which was neither acknowledged nor returned.

At night they camped, with only a small fire lit against the night's chill. Lyonene slipped a piece of charcoal under her surcoat and rubbed a blackened finger beneath her eyes. Then she created dark hollows below her cheekbones. Amicia looked at her oddly, but made no comment. When Sir Morell took her arm once, she leaned against him and gave him a wan smile. He pushed her away from him. She could not allow herself even the smallest smile of triumph.

On the third day, they arrived at an old stone donjon, the battlements crumbling about the top, the up and down squares of the crenellations indistinct. They were nearly at the wall of the castle before a warning was called.

"Sir Morell, late of Malvoisin," the knight shouted, and the rusty, uncared-for iron wheels began to move and the gates were drawn up. The drawbridge that lay across the shallow, garbage-filled moat was useless, its chains limp and broken, so only the iron-tipped portcullis was in use.

There was no more pretense that Lyonene was being taken to her relatives. The people around her talked freely of the ransom, either accepting that she knew of their plans or, she hoped, thinking her too ill to understand their words. Lyonene felt they were such fools. Only Amicia noticed the amount of food the prisoner consumed. The day before, Lyonene's horse had shied at a rabbit and Lyonene had used a great deal of strength in controlling the animal. She did not wish to land on the hard ground, even to prove her illness to the others. Her horse calm again, she looked up to see Amicia smiling at her, a smile showing that Lyonene did not deceive her and reaffirming their alliance.

They rode across the rickety drawbridge and under the old portcullis, each person casting upward glances, fearful of the heavy gate falling on them.

"Morell! You are as handsome as ever."

Lyonene watched from a bowed head as a tall, slim woman ran to Morell's outstretched arms. Her hair was completely covered, as was her neck, by the concealing veil and barbette.

"Come inside to the fire, I have much to tell you." Her words were ordinary enough, but Lyonene looked away as the woman's hands went inside Sir Morell's tabard. Lyonene was too aware of memories, of glad greetings, sad partings from her own beloved to even look at these two, so obviously lovers.

The sailor helped her from her horse. She took Amicia's arm, and they walked toward the crumbling castle. The outer wooden steps leading to the second floor looked hazardous.

"The widow sees to little besides her passion for men. Do not lean on me! I will not bear your weight longer. I am sure you know of the ransom."

"Aye, I do." Lyonene's voice was hard. "Such greed will see you dead."

Amicia smiled at her in the dim light of the cold hall. "You threaten me now, but I do not think you will easily forget that it was your greed for your child that brought you so quickly to my plan."

"Nay, it was not. I thought Ranulf loved you."

Amicia's strange laugh rasped from her throat. "You are more a fool than I thought. You should have stayed and fought for him, then."

"But . . . King Edward . . ."

"Be still! They will hear you. It is done and you will have long to brood on your foolishness."

"Aye," Lyonene whispered. "My foolishness."

"Amicia," Sir Morell called. "Bring our guest here to the light."

When Lyonene stood before the fire, she looked only briefly at the woman before her.

"What ails her? It is not something to be caught? I will bring no such disease to my house."

"Nay," Amicia answered. "It is but the sickness of the child. She will be well with rest and food."

"I hope this is worth my effort, Morell. Put her down somewhere . . . Amicia, is it? She wearies me just to look on her." Lyonene sank heavily onto the uncushioned bench, there being only one chair before the fire and that occupied by the widow.

"You are sure this husband of hers will not find her here? I have heard of the man and I do not desire to wage battle against him."

"Battle!" Morell sneered. "Lady Margaret, you could not win a battle against an unarmed troop of eels, less that of one such as the Earl of Malvoisin."

"Morell, I know my defenses are not as they were when my dear husband was alive, but they train most vigorously."

Sir Morell threw back his head and laughed. "Such training as you give your men does not prepare them for battle, but rather drains them of what little strength they have. Now tell me no more of your strengths. The very reason I chose this place was because no one would believe such a wreck of a castle held such a valuable captive as the Countess of Malvoisin."

Lady Margaret did not seem to be offended by Sir Morell's words. "You underestimate me, as you always have." She clapped her hands twice and four men appeared from the corners of the room. They were ugly men, scarred, their noses and cheeks distorted from many blows and wounds. Their hands clutched weapons, ugly weapons—the spiked mace, the chained flail, the sharp, hooked war hammer, the heavy battle ax. From their belts dangled other deadly weapons.

"I am pleased to see you so well protected, Lady Margaret, but do you think a mere four men, even these four men, could hold out against the Black Lion, were he to make an attack? He is followed always by those seven devils of his." His hands tightened in anger.

"Do not destroy the cup, Morell! I know your campaign to be one of his guard, but he saw you early for what you are. No man wishes to guard his back from his own man. Nay! I would not advise you try to strike me. My own little guard would not take so kindly to your love taps as I have born them in the past. You do not seem to understand my guard. They are not to protect me, but they are for her."

Lyonene looked up to see the woman pointing at her.

"My men will never leave her. Should one from Malvoisin attempt to take her, the men will kill her before they even look to the attacker."

Sir Morell grinned. "You are more than I thought. The man will attempt naught when her life is in danger. You could hold her in an open field, in the midst of his own castle, and he would do naught but hand us the ransom, wagonloads of it. Aye, you are clever."

"I thank you, fair knight." She rose and slid her arms about Morell's neck. "Now I will tell you that my men keep her from you also."

The knight pushed her from him. "Nay, I want the woman and will have her."

At a quick gesture from Lady Margaret, the four burly men surrounded Lyonene's slight form on the bench. She looked even more lost, more alone, when they clustered around her, towering above her.

"The woman will be held, but as befits her, not as a whore for your use. From what I hear of this Black Lion, such treatment would enrage him, cause him to forget his senses, and he might force an attack, out of anger. If the woman were killed, we would receive no ransom. If the earl were killed with no heir, Malvoisin would revert to the English king and there again we would lose our ransom."

"There is an heir, she carries him now!"

"You are a sorcerer and know the child's sex or even that it will live? The woman looks even now to be at death's door." Her voice was heavy with sarcasm. "Nay, she will be well-cared for while she stays here. Alice!" She turned to a large, heavy woman who emerged from the shadows. "This is Lady Lyonene. She is to be your charge. Take her to the tower room that has been prepared and care for her. Do you remember all I have told you?"

The woman nodded and walked toward Lyonene, taking her arm in hers, firmly but kindly.

"That woman is to be trusted?" Amicia asked as she watched the two leave the room. "Lyonene has a way of endearing herself to servants."

"I am sure you have no such problems." Lady Margaret's eyes raked Amicia's emaciated form. "Alice is a mute and so cannot tell our secret. She is also simpleminded. I have told her of the coming child and she will care well for the precious little countess." She sneered at the closed door through which Lyonene had gone. "The woman's life seems to have no hardship. Born a baron's daughter, married for love to a handsome, rich earl . . . there is naught she does not have."

"Aye," Amicia said, grinning. "It is time she shared some of her happiness with others."

Chapter Fifteen

"Alice?" Lyonene stretched in the cold air, the heavy wool blankets inadequate for the damp cold of the drafty donjon. "You are well this morn?" She looked at the heavy woman bending over the fire, slowly coaxing it to life.

Alice turned and grinned at Lyonene, nodding her head.

"Your mother's cough is better?"

Alice pantomimed someone drinking from a cup and then pointed at Lyonene.

"Ah, then the herbs I recommended helped her. I am glad. It is too cold to be ill." Lyonene tried to sit up and instantly Alice was there to help her. "It is enormous, is it not?" She smiled as she rubbed her extended stomach. "Ranulf would be . . ."

Alice gripped the slim shoulders, frowned and shook her head vigorously.

"Nay, I know I should not. The memories are too painful even yet. Do you think there is a chance the boy gave my belt to someone? When Sir Morell caught him, he no longer had it."

Alice turned away.

"I know what you would say. It has been so long and there is no word. Lady Margaret says Ranulf does not answer her demands. Think you he will not pay the ransom? I have ever been a trial to him."

Alice turned to her with a hard expression, eyes narrowed in threat.

Lyonene gave a weak laugh. "I will not begin anew. You have heard too much already. What shall we do this day? Don ourselves in cloth of gold and ride our stallions across the hills of Ireland?"

Alice smiled at her and then went to a plain wooden

chest set in the corner of the room. With reverence, she opened it and lifted the leather pouch which contained the precious book.

Lyonene smiled. "It is a good day for reading. Tell me, are my guards well? They have not forgotten me?"

Alice shivered as she cast a fearful look toward the heavy oak door.

"Alice, they could not be so horrible as you seem to think. I have been here for four months and they do but sit and watch."

Alice merely looked at her. They had discussed the four guards before and nothing had been solved. She helped her mistress from the narrow bed, the heavy pregnancy making the younger woman awkward and clumsy. Alice loosely fastened the woolen garments about her mistress and then combed her long hair neatly into place.

"Think you I should cut it? Brent told me some of the women at court seemed to think it too long. I have told you about Brent, have I not?" At Alice's indulgent smile, Lyonene caught the big, work-hardened hand and held it to her cheek. "Of course, I have told you all there is to tell about me. You must be greatly bored with my stories."

Alice stroked her mistress's cheek in answer.

"Lady Margaret thinks you simple-minded. She would not like to know she is far from the truth. I do not think she would have you as my guard 'twere she to know your cleverness. Now, come and sit by me and I will read to you a while and then I will teach you more of your letters. A while longer and you will read this book yourself. Did I tell you Ranulf owns six books?" She stopped and laughed. "Do not look at me so. You are a fierce critic. I will tell you no more of my Ranulf this hour, but beware of the next, for I may remember a thing I have not told you. I doubt it, but I may."

They both turned as the heavy door creaked open and Lady Margaret appeared. "Well, you do not seem to be the mistreated prisoner." She sat down on a stool before the fire. "We have had no word." She looked ominously at Lyonene. "I understood this husband of yours loved you overmuch, yet he does not seem anxious to have you returned. My messenger returned yester eve and says the Earl of Malvoisin makes merry at court with the ladies there. This does not seem to be the bereaved husband who misses and longs for his wife." She watched Lyonene. "Have you no answer to this riddle?"

Lyonene looked away. "Nay, I have not," she answered quietly. "It was not I who said he loved me, but Amicia. I am a baron's daughter and mayhaps . . . Ranulf"—the name caused her to blink back tears—"has found another."

"Bah!" Margaret rose to walk to the large window, the shutters poorly latched, the cool early morning air whistling under them. "Whatever he feels for you, I would not expect this. You are by law his wife and he must know the babe is near full-term now. If not you, then his child. Morell will return to England soon to see for himself why no ransom is being prepared. I should have guessed Amicia to be such a liar. Your precious husband's steward has said he hopes you never return." She laughed at the expression on Lyonene's face. "You thought yourself well loved by everyone. You are a vain creature. Has no one said so to you before?"

"Aye, they have," Lyonene whispered.

"I am pleased that there is at least a whisper of truth somewhere in this old castle. Your guards grow restless. They wish to meet this husband of yours, for they have ever heard of his strength. What think you of seeing him pitted against the four of them? Morell thinks he could take them. Ah, I see you are not so sure. If I did not chance losing the ransom, I would stage such a show, for the man angers me at his insolence in not answering my messages." She looked away to the fire.

"If I am worthless to you, will you not let me go? I must cost you much in food and soon there will be the babe to care for."

"Aye, you are worthless to me, but there must be some value in you. It is true you have cost me much and you will need to repay these monies. After you rid yourself of the babe, mayhaps I can find your body to be a means to repay my generosity. Sir Morell might, I think, pay much for the use of it." She laughed again. "I will wait only a while longer. Your husband might think differently when you deliver his child alive." She left the room.

Lyonene was unaware of the tears that ran down her cheeks and only gradually felt Alice's rather violent shaking of her. "Why do you do this?" she asked as she looked into the maid's stormy face. "You are angry with me. What have I done?"

Alice pointed toward the closed door, then frowned at her mistress, vigorously shaking her head. They had been together for four months and in that time they had developed their own communication.

"You wish to tell me I am a fool," Lyonene stated flatly.

Alice released her and stood above her, hands on wide hips, a disdainful look on her face as she glared down her nose.

"I believe everyone. First Amicia's lies about Ranulf and now Lady Margaret's false stories. But what of William de Bec? Why would Ranulf's steward hate me?"

Alice threw up her hands in disgust.

Lyonene laughed. "I know what you say. It is hard for me to not believe them. Their lies are so logical."

Alice dropped to her knees before her mistress, taking the little hands in her own, her eyes imploring. She tapped her head with one fingertip.

"Aye, I should think for myself. I am sure Ranulf . . . cares for me. He must, but there was so little time. He hated me for so long and it is not easy to believe he changed. Do not shake your head at me. I believe I know my own husband. Ha!" She frowned at Alice's gestures. "I am sure I am smarter than my unborn babe. Why then has Ranulf gone to court? King Edward will not give him money for my ransom. The king wishes Ranulf to marry a Castilian princess."

She watched Alice. "You are right. Mayhaps Lady Margaret lies and Ranulf is not at court." She smiled at Alice's sigh of exasperation. "I am a countess, you know. At home there are servants who treat me with respect."

Alice put her head on Lyonene's knee and the young woman stroked the coarse hair. "Whatever I say," she whispered, "you are more than maid to me. Had it not been for you, for your long hours, days even, of listening to my endless stories I might have thrown myself from yon window. Would you like to hear more of the Round Table?"

At Alice's nod, she began, for she knew the woman loved to hear of the pageantry, the games, the food, the clothes, the powerful knights who wrestled and jousted with one another. There was not one second of the three-day tourney that Lyonene had not related to Alice, but they both loved to hear it again and both knew it kept Lyonene from thinking too realistically of the stone walls enclosing her or hearing the lies that surrounded her.

Late in the afternoon, Lyonene slept and Alice went about her duties outside the castle. When she awoke, she lay still and thought of the time since she had been taken captive. Mostly her days were spent with Alice in the tower room. Ireland was warmer than England, but still the stones created their own dreary and oppressive atmosphere. She had never even been outside the castle walls since she had first entered them, and this lack of sun and exercise did not help her mood.

Only lately, since the child had grown big in her stomach, had she dared leave the cramped little room, for Sir Morell always lurked near her, touching her hair, her shoulder, smiling in a way that left little doubt of his thoughts. She recalled with a shudder a conversation with him when she had first come to the castle.

"Why? Why do you do this?" she had asked.

He had sneered insolently at her. "Is not the great wealth I will receive from your husband enough?" His eyes raked her soft form. "Is not the person of the lovely Lady Lyonene enough?"

She had raised her head and met his eyes steadily. "No, it is not. I have been a fool to not believe in my husband, but you I do not think are a fool. There is more behind this than gold."

He smiled slightly and looked into his empty chalice. "Such knowledge from one so young! Shall I tell you a story?"

She had not answered and he had continued.

"You did not know your husband as a young man. He has changed greatly since he has known you. I came to him as a squire, as one of several young men, soon after his wife's death." He did not notice Lyonene's pained look. "Young Lord Ranulf! So strong, so ungiving, so black!"

He refilled his cup. "It is a simple story really. I was a young man, eager to please, anxious to do the bidding of a lord no older than myself. It is strange how we hate the people who take and then discard our first innocence. I served him for four years, four years of life I gave to that man and then I was not chosen for his guard. Nay, he said all his men must have his devil's blackness. So, for a bit of fair hair I was used and then tossed aside like so much rubbish."

He threw his cup violently toward the fire, hitting a glancing blow on the shoulder of one of the hounds, which leaped, yelping, and ran away.

Lyonene sat quietly behind the shield of her four guards. "Could there have been another reason? Mayhaps he chose his men because he saw something in their character which he liked."

Morell stood and stared at her, unaware of the guards' hands moving to their weapons. "I gave him everything! I was not sunk to the character I am now."

She met his stare, feeling inside her that Ranulf had seen then the man Morell could have been. Her husband was not so vain as to turn aside a good knight for so little a flaw as the color of his hair. "Is a man today what he was not yesterday?"

Morell's face had turned red and he had taken a step toward her, and then he felt the heavy hand of a guard on his shoulder. He had shaken it off, his eyes still on Lyonene's. "He will pay for what he has done," he said hoarsely, "and neither will I forget your words." He turned and angrily strode from the hall.

Lyonene shook her head as if to clear away the ugly thoughts and looked down at her enormous stomach.

Alice ran firm hands over the mound each day to check the progress of the growing child. Lyonene was sure her skin would split, so tautly was it pulled, but Alice reassured her it would not and that the babe was already turned correctly for its birth. Lyonene was growing anxious to deliver the child and rid herself of the heavy burden. She closed her eyes and thought of the moment of joy when she'd hold a black-haired, black-eyed babe in her arms.

Alice touched her on the shoulder and she jumped.

"I did not hear you come in. Aye, I would like to go to the Great Hall. I get some pleasure in seeing Morell's disgust at my waddling. If I were not so tired of carrying my own stomach about, I would wish I could remain so for a long while. Think you he would tire of me if I remained so for several years?" She rubbed her stomach happily. "What think you of twins? Ranulf once said . . . Nay, I will not cry again." She laughed at Alice's quelling look.

"Well, I see our countess deigns to visit with us—two days together. We are indeed honored," Amicia said, greeting her. The Frankish woman smiled as Sir Morell looked away. "Morell, does she not look fit? I am sure she carries at least two children in that great belly of hers."

Morell gave Amicia a quick look of contempt and left the hall, and the woman smiled triumphantly.

Alice led her mistress to a stool by the fire. Lyonene smoothed her skirts as she looked about the hall. Lady Margaret knelt on the floor, the rushes swept back to make a place for her to roll dice with two of her men. Her laugh rang out across the hall. Occasionally, she ran her hand over the thigh of one of the men, and Lyonene looked away. Amicia was making her way to the gambling group. Some serfs—two men followed by another—carried firewood into the hall. The man behind was large, and something about him made her stare. Alice touched her shoulder and frowned; it was not seemly that Lyonene should stare at the serfs, especially not at men.

Lyonene looked away, but when she saw Alice return to her sewing, she could not help another quick glance. There was something about the man . . . Alice again caught her attention, and the maid left to fetch more thread. The four guards that were always near watched the people in the corner at their dice game.

The three serfs came to the fireplace before her. She looked away, fascinated by the weave of her woolen gown. She lectured herself for her stupidity. She had seen hundreds of serfs in her life and not one of them had interested her in even the slightest way, yet now she found she wanted to see this man's face. His hand took a poker and moved the logs in the fireplace. The action caught her eye, and as she stared at the dark hand covered in short, dark hairs, it stopped moving. She knew he stared at her, that all she had to do was lift her eyes and meet the owner of that familiar hand.

She looked up slowly, very, very slowly, fearful of what she would or would not see.

Ranulf's eyes met hers in an expressionless stare, the black irises pinpointed as they looked at the emerald-green gaze. His eyes swept the length of her, quickly, and then seemed to dismiss her altered form as he returned to her face.

She could but look at him in wonder that he should be standing before her, obviously unarmed. Should he be recognized, he would have little chance of defending himself against a man armed with a morgenstern. Yet underlying her fears was sheer joy that he should risk so much for her, that he had sought her out, that he did not lounge at court and forget her. She struggled to give him a word, a sign of her love, to tell him all her heart felt for him, to warn him of the danger he faced for her.

"They have set me to chopping wood," he said, his quiet voice conveying all the disgust he felt, the degradation of such a lowly task. Then he was gone; almost before she could blink, she sat alone again, his words hanging in the air.

She sat quietly for a few moments staring into the fire. She felt the laughter rising in her, rumbling and preparing for a sweet release. She struggled for control and the repressed laughter changed to tears, a mixture of joy and misery.

Four whole months she had not seen him and all the things that had occurred in those four months! She had been taken captive and held for ransom; not least, her body had greatly enlarged since she had last seen her husband. Now, as she sat amidst four fierce and horrible warriors, he calmly walked into the hall before everyone and what did he say to the wife he seeks? "They have set me to chopping wood." No words of endearment, no sweet words for her health or even for his child that swelled her belly before her, but only an indignant utterance that she would cause him to stoop so low to rescue her.

She buried her face in her hands, unable to still the emotions that shook her slight shoulders. He had come! Whatever he said, whatever he did was well, because he had come for her.

Alice touched her shoulder, a question creasing her brow.

Lyonene looked around quickly, but knew Ranulf was

gone. "Is it time for dinner yet, Alice? I vow I am famished." She smiled brightly up at her maid.

Alice grinned her approval at her mistress's hunger; too often she did not eat enough. But Alice also saw something else—a gaiety, a light in the green eyes—that had heretofore been missing.

Lyonene's feeling of anticipation buoyed her through the evening meal, yet more and more clearly was she aware of the danger that awaited her husband. She shivered as she thought of the audacity of him striding into the hall, so near people who could easily recognize him.

"You are cold?" Lady Margaret asked her and at Lyonene's negative answer, she continued. "I hope it is not the child. I am not prepared to be midwife yet."

"Nay, the child does not come. I am tired only from carrying the load. I will go to my room now." She rose and Alice followed.

In her chamber again, Lyonene gave way to her fears as she sat dejectedly before the fire. Alice was concerned for her and Lyonene unsuccessfully tried to allay the woman's fears. Lyonene did not tell Alice of Ranulf's appearance in the castle; Ranulf's life was too precious to entrust to anyone, even someone she knew to be her friend.

She went to bed earlier than usual, hoping that sleep would wash away some of her fears. Alice left her to go to her mother's cottage in the village, something Lyonene insisted on. It took her a long time to go to sleep.

The first thing she was aware of was a hand over her mouth, cutting off her breath. She thrashed about wildly, clawing at the hand.

"Be still, my Lioness. Do not take all the skin from my hand. Do you not still remember me?"

She recovered some of her senses and looked into Ranulf's eyes, soft and gentle, and so near her own. He moved his hand away.

"So you know me. It has been so long I thought mayhaps . . ." He stopped talking when he saw she began to cry. Quickly he pulled back the covers and lay beside her, gathering her in his arms.

She cried violently for a while, the deep sobs tearing at her body, then gradually beginning to lighten.

"I take it you are glad to see me again?" His light

words did not match his ragged voice or the catch in his throat. He ran his hand down her body, her shoulder, her arm and came to rest on the hard, enormous mound of her stomach, caressing, feeling the gentle movements of the babe. It was a quiet moment between them, a sharing of what they had created.

He grunted, his hand still but possessive on her belly. "You are grown so fat I hardly knew you."

"I am . . . not fat." She sniffed, controlling her tears. "It is only the babe who sticks out. The rest of me is the same," she said in her defense.

"Nay, you have not seen yourself from behind. You walk like a duck, swaying forward and back, from side to side. Even your feet turn out. Have they perchance turned orange?"

"Ranulf! You are horrible! You should say I am beautiful when I carry your babe, not tell me of my ugliness."

He lifted her face to his. "Aye, you are beautiful." He kissed her sweetly on her mouth, then on her damp eyelids. He saw that her tears began anew. "But you are still as a duck, a most beautiful duck, but a duck nonetheless."

She smiled, her tears ceasing and she snuggled again on his shoulder. "What think you of the duck you have made of me?" She covered his hand with her own and the child's sharp kick was felt by them both.

"Does the child move?"

"Aye." She felt him straighten in pride.

"He is strong then."

"I am sure he shall be born with a lance in one hand and a sword in another," she answered sarcastically.

"I would hope he'd have more consideration for his mother. You have not changed. You are as insolent as ever."

"Then you do remember me? You have not forgotten?"

"Forgotten? I could no more forget you than I could forget . . . to carry my right leg with me."

"Ah, so now I am compared to your leg. You are a most unromantic knight."

"You dare to call me unromantic! Look you at what I wear! I dress as a serf. This horrible wool has worn me raw as no chain mail ever could. I have even chopped wood so that I may be near you. And you say me to be unromantic. I have gone through hell to be here."

"Ranulf, my sweet. I am sorry to have caused you so much misery. It is all my fault."

"Here, do not cry again. The wetness makes the wool scratch worse and the smell blinds me. You will get no argument from me. It is all your fault and I demand to know why you left me. You constantly tell me I am ignorant, but never have I come near to equaling this stupid act of yours."

"I have not told you you are ignorant," she said.

"Do not evade me. Tell me why you left me."

"Ranulf, this is not the time. You must leave before those men find you are here. Alice tells me often of their treachery."

"Bah!" He waved his hand. "They are little more than an exercise before dinner. How can Alice tell you aught of them when she is a mute?"

"You know overmuch of me. Why do you not kiss me some more?"

"Nay." He pushed her back down to his shoulder. "I will not fight my son for you. One of us at a time will be in you."

"Ranulf!" She gasped at his crudity and then giggled.

"Now tell me why you left me."

"You are most persistent. I worry that my skin will never return to the way it was, that it will always be stretched and loose."

"It will always be filled with my daughters, Lyonene!"

She understood his command. "I thought you would marry Amicia. She said . . ."

"I know of this. Hodder has told me. I want to know why you believed the woman and why you did not trust me."

"I trusted you, but men always take other women."

"Do they? You know this for fact? And if they do, do they always marry them and forsake their wives?"

"Nay, but Amicia said King Edward . . ."

"Edward is my king, but he does not rule my life. He cannot force me to do what I would not."

"But what of Gilbert de Clare? He has left his wife to take a daughter of King Edward."

"You met Gilbert at court. You would compare him to me? He is a greedy man and Edward has been warned about him often. You will see problems with the man soon. He does not wish to please his king as much as equal him. Now what other puny reasons do you give for leaving me?"

"I do not know. They seemed so logical, Amicia's words. I saw letters from you. She had the ribbon. I saw you kiss her."

"Nay, you did not! You saw the woman wrap her ugly body about me. I had to restrain myself from tossing her to the ground."

"Ranulf, I have not seen you for a long while. Why must we speak of this unpleasantness? I have come to my senses. I know Amicia's words were false. I heard her tell Sir Morell how they plotted it all."

"We have all night, for I do not plan to take you from here until dawn and I wish to know what caused you to believe the woman's words. Had you more faith in me you would have seen a hundred letters and would not have believed them."

"It is as you say, but there were some things that I knew were certainly true."

"Name them."

Lyonene was silent for a moment, wishing Ranulf would not force her to speak of her doubts. "Amicia said that when she first looked at you . . . I know," she cried desperately, "I know her feelings. It was the same with me. Ranulf! You laugh at me! I tell you my innermost thoughts and you dare to laugh at me!"

He caught her hand as she swung to strike him. "You will not injure my babe by your headstrong movements. So, Amicia told you she could not resist me after even the first look at me."

"I do not understand it now, either. I vow I am a fool to want such as you. You are a vile creature."

He kissed her forehead. "You are a liar and I shall see your sins confessed when we are home. Lyonene, now, here in this dark place, I will tell you something, but I say it once and once only. Hereafter I will deny it was ever said."

She moved her head back on his arm to look at him. Ranulf's honor was so strong that for him to say he might ever even consider a lie made her look at him in astonishment.

He ignored her. "There are times when I boast to you

of my beauty, but it is only because you look at me so. I will tell you that you fair drool at the sight of me. Do not protest, for I know I look at you in a like manner. But what you see in me is not seen by other women. They think me too dark or ungraceful in my form."

"What you say is not true! What of the women at court? I had to fight them from you."

"Think you they would be so interested in me if I were not so rich? It is Dacre who is the ideal of beauty."

"Dacre! Why he is as the underbelly of a fish. His eyes and hair have no color, and he is so thin he casts little shadow, even."

"You seem to have spent overlong studying him."

She ignored him and ran the back of her fingers along the unshaved whiskers on his cheek. "And when he has three days' growth of a beard, from a distance he looks to be a girl; you can tell no difference. Know you that in certain lights your beard shows almost blue?"

He kissed her fingers and smiled at her. "It is good to know you feel so, but it does not change what I try to say to you. I wish, by this confession, to prevent what happened from occurring twice. Although you made a fool of yourself over me on the first day I saw you, other women do not."

"You lie again! I have never made a fool of myself over you."

"True, you have ever been calm near me, except mayhaps when you lusted after me when you bathed me, or threw yourself into my arms when I but showed you the longbow, or when . . ."

"I acted no differently than I had with a hundred men. There! I have repaid you. Nay, I do lie, so do not glare at me more. And what of you? Do you marry all the women you meet after one day?"

Ranulf pulled her back to his shoulder. "I see I accomplished little. You are stubborn and will not heed my words. But listen well and remember this: You need never fear another woman languishing about for me after a few brief meetings."

"Then you say she could after a few longer meetings?"

Ranulf shrugged. "It has been known to happen. I am a most skillful lover."

"You are . . ."

He kissed her and stopped her words.

"I will not argue with you. Try only to remember my words when another woman, cleverer than you, seeks my gold."

"I cannot remember that I am to believe anyone thinks you ugly. Know you that your eyes have flecks of gold in them?" She felt him laugh against her.

"I concede. I am the most handsome of men and shall never deny it again."

"Ranulf," she began timidly. "If you say you are not as I see you, am I also different from the way you see me? You have said you think me beautiful."

Ranulf laughed again. "Alas, it is not so. I fear I heard of your beauty for three years before I ventured to Lorancourt. I vow I was no little curious about this girl who caused grown men to speak in whispered tones."

"This is true?"

"Aye, but I will not say more or repeat it. You are too vain now, although I do not see how you can be when you are so fat you near push me from the bed."

"It is you who has made me fat. If you were slim and not such a great hulk of a man, I am sure I would not be burdened with a child half the size of that great horse of yours. So do not complain to me of discomfort, for it is my skin which is near to bursting with him."

Ranulf hugged her to him. "If I did not love you so well, you would be a bother to me with your sharp tongue." He felt her body stiffen against him. Puzzled, he asked, "What have I said that causes this?"

"You said that you loved me," she whispered.

"Certainly. I have said it often enough. Why should it cause you to pull away from me?"

"You have never said it."

He pulled her chin up. "Do you cry again? I understand this not at all. There has never been a day when I have not told you I love you."

"Nay, you have never done so. Amicia knew you had not and when I saw one of your letters that said you loved her . . ."

"Do not forget that I did not write those letters. But what you say cannot be true. If I have not said the words, then my actions have told you. Each time I make love to you I tell you I love you."

Lyonene sniffed. "But you have made love to many women. Did you love them also?"

"Nay, I did not, but it is different with you." He stopped, for he realized she could not know how he was different with her. "Have I not been kind?"

She worked to control the tears. "You are kind to all women."

"Mon Dieu! You will drive me mad. There! I have just told you I love you."

"You curse me and that is to be taken as a declaration of love? Forgive me if I do not see your logic."

"I have no logic near you. What other woman causes me to lose my temper or makes me laugh? What other woman do I chase across the water or do I dress as a serf to rescue?"

"Your wife? Isabel whom you loved so well, that drove you near mad with grief when she died?"

Ranulf was stunned for a moment and could not speak.

"I know how you loved her. It is in your eyes when I mention her or the child. I think I cannot replace her in your heart."

"Do not continue," he said, his voice cold. "You misread me sorely if you think I bore that woman any love. I will tell you what I have told no other person and then you may judge for yourself what caused my grief."

He told the story of a young boy and a faithless wife without feeling, as if it belonged to another. The room was quiet and Lyonene could imagine the feelings that had been stored so long, the emotions that had changed a happy boy into the brooding man who had earned the name of Black Lion.

They lay together quietly when he had finished.

"That is why you raged so on our wedding night," Lyonene said quietly.

"I have never raged. I am ever good and kind."

"You were such a brute I would have left you had I not said vows to you."

"You said you hated me, but I did not believe you."

"Aye, you believed all, all Giles said. I am sometimes glad for that Welsh arrow, although the scar it left is most ugly."

"I love you, Lioness. I do not know how you could have

doubted me. I love you more than myself or my yet to be son or . . . Tighe."

Lyonene shook with laughter. "Now I know your words are true."

"I shall keep a list of your insults and repay you properly when this great belly of yours does not prevent me from getting within a cloth-yard of you."

"I shall look forward eagerly to your instruction." Her eyes sparkled in the dim light and she moved her leg over his thigh. He was too aware of her skin under his hands, the way her hair caressed her cheek.

"You are a cruel woman. Now be still. There is only a short while before dawn and I must tell you our plan to remove you from this place." His hand was on her stomach, and a sharp kick from the baby made him frown. "It has been long since the Round Table. Is not the babe due soon? Will you be able to travel?"

"It is a full half-month before he will be born, I am sure."

"That is soon. Mayhaps we should wait until after his birth. Your Alice will see to you."

"And then Lady Margaret may decide to move me elsewhere, or other mishaps. I would not like to take a newborn babe into the cold air. Now he is warm and protected inside me. Alice says he lolls about upside down in a nest of liquid."

"We will go then, on the morrow. I wait for my men to come now."

"How did you find me?"

"It was not easy. We had to keep our secrecy, so it was spread about that I was at court, that I did not care about my lowly wife and would not pay the ransom. I am glad you did not hear that story or I am sure you would have believed it."

"Nay, I would not," she lied.

He gave her a suspicious look for her too-fierce disavowal. "Dacre's cousins and your father's have sent spies everywhere. No one thought to look here. This woman, this Lady Margaret, is known only for her lechery for young men. It was not thought she would dare to encourage my wrath."

Lyonene felt fear, as she always did when Ranulf became the knight who was feared by so many men.

"But what caused you to look here?"

"Sainneville saw your lion belt."

"But the boy that I gave it to—they found him and hung him."

"And rightly so. He sold it and gave no thought to helping you. He made a mistake in selling it to one of my men. From there it was not so hard to find you. A few mugs of poor ale and these guards boasted of the lady they held, of the four guards ordered to kill her should any attempt be made to rescue her."

"How did you get in this room?" she asked, suddenly surprised that she had not asked it before.

Ranulf inclined his head to the shuttered window. "I but threw a rope around a crenel and lowered myself."

"But what of the guards atop the tower?"

Ranulf gave a half-smile. "Did you not know the Lady Margaret has hired four new knights for her crumbling castle? They are strong, virile men, a little too dark for her taste, but she overlooks that flaw."

"Your guard!"

"Aye." He chuckled. "Gilbert says the woman is most inventive in bed."

She ignored him. "You have been here long then. Why have you not posed as her knight and not as a serf?"

"The woman is somewhat clever. She allows no one near you but those four men and two of her knights. We were not sure it was you she held captive, so one of us had to get inside the hall. My men are not so brave as to wear these stuffs." He plucked at the harsh wool. "Or to chop wood."

"I think I shall be forgiven all, but not that you had to lift an ax outside battle."

His look affirmed her opinion. "Now I must go, for it grows light soon and I do not wish to be seen so plainly against a stone wall. I came but to warn you and to tell you to make ready. There is no way to bar the door without someone outside hearing us. My men will come soon and then we will attack. Have clothes ready and whatever else you need."

"But, Ranulf," she cried, clinging to him. "What will you do? How will you take me from this place and not risk your life?"

"Do not do this. I have risked much already. Two of

my men will come to your room before light and you must obey them in all they say. Do not do aught that is foolish. Do you heed my words?"

She could but nod.

"They will protect you while the rest of us see to your four guards. Now do not cry more." He rose and held out his arms to her and they clung together, his hands running over her nude back.

"You are even bigger than I had thought. I can hardly reach around you."

"I fear my sweet days of being carried about are at an end."

He grinned at her and lifted her in his arms. She was embarrassed by her distorted form and sought to cover herself. He brushed her hands away. "Nay. You are a silly girl. It is my child who stretches you so. If you can carry him, I can at least look upon him." He smiled into her eyes. "You are beautiful fat and beautiful thin. I think I would love you had you three heads." He kissed her mouth but drew away when she began to return his kiss with ardor.

"I must go." He lowered her to the bed and put the covers about her. "You must miss Malvoisin much," he said, sneering at the crude covers.

"I miss the master more. Ranulf," she murmured, her arms holding his face close, "I love you."

He kissed her cheek and then stood up, tall, powerful above her. "I have known it always, of course, but it is good to hear."

She smiled, knowing that his words hid his true feelings. It seemed that he was gone instantly, and she saw only a foot as he pulled himself up on the rope.

Chapter Sixteen

She awoke slowly, groggily, unsure of her surroundings. She stretched one arm to reach for Ranulf, wanting his warmth close to her, the security of his nearness. Her eyes opened in bewilderment when her hand met only an empty coldness, and not her husband's warm flesh. Her situation came to her and she sat up, the cover clutched about her.

Alice looked up from her sewing to smile at her.

"It is late?" The maid's nod was affirmative. "You have let me sleep long." Alice merely smiled and looked down again at the patched woolen garment in her hands.

Lyonene stared at her thoughfully. "You know, do you not? I do not understand how, but you know."

Alice grinned at her, the shared secret obvious between them. The stout woman rose and brought clothing for her mistress.

All day they stayed in the room, glancing anxiously at the shuttered window. Late in the day Lady Margaret came.

"So, you do not wish to honor us this day with your presence? I am sure Sir Morell will miss seeing you."

"He does not often look at me, so I cannot know what you mean."

"He leaves this day to travel to England and see why this husband of your does not send your ransom."

Lyonene smiled up at the older woman, her hand on her stomach, pressing lightly against the kicking child. "I had thought you were sure he had no use for me since he long ago went to court."

Lady Margaret frowned. "You seem confident this day. Did I not know you to be so well guarded, I might think you held some secret."

Lyonene smiled at her blandly. "It is the child. I think

he comes soon. Surely you have known the placidity that comes to a woman just before she gives birth?"

"Nay, I have not been so cursed as you with a swollen belly. I prefer my pleasures without such punishment. Should your labor begin, have Alice fetch me and I will send someone from the village. Do you understand my words, Alice? You are to come for me if your mistress has an ache in her belly."

Alice looked at her blankly, a study in ignorance, and nodded vigorously at her, eyes shining, mouth slightly open.

"How you bear her presence each day and remain sane is not of my understanding," Margaret said with a sneer.

"Her intent is good and she attends to my needs most adequately."

"I must go now. I have hired new guards to see to your protection. Morell assures me that all is right, but I cannot help but be uneasy."

"Oh?" Lyonene looked at the fire. "Are these guards as fierce and ugly as my other four?"

Lady Margaret laughed, a quick snort of laughter, making her thoughts known. "Nay, they are in truth most handsome men, strong and vigorous. When you are no longer as you are now, I shall give you to one of them. You will like their looks, as I hear you favor dark men." She turned and left them.

Lyonene felt Alice's hand on her shoulder. Their eyes met. "Aye, I know 'twas wrong and I came too close, but she could not recognize them as Ranulf's men. I am pleased Sir Morell leaves. Ranulf says he will have no problem with my guards, but I am pleased there will be fewer men to fight."

Nightfall came and still she waited, a small bundle of clothes by her side. Her nervousness increased as she thought of Ranulf's danger, the danger her foolishness had caused. Before she went to bed, she spent hours on her knees in prayer. Only Alice's mute commands made her retire.

Surprisingly, she fell asleep quickly, awakened in the dark, again, by a large, warm hand over her mouth. She looked into Sainneville's dark eyes.

"My lady, it is good to see you again."

She took his hand for a moment, joyous to see a familiar face, a friend.

"He is not worthy of such attentions, I assure you. Can you believe I had to force him to climb down that rope? He said he feared the castle crumbling about his ears."

She smiled at Corbet, his jests and light words tearing at her, so glad was she to hear them again. "Nay, I cannot believe it. You are well, both of you?"

"Only now that the sun has come out again. Malvoisin is a dark place without its golden mistress."

She smiled and then laughed, joy filling her, tears clouding her eyes. "Sir Corbet, you have not changed and it is most pleasant to see you again. Sir Sainneville, do you work to keep him from mischief?"

Sainneville winked at her. "I see you know him well. But it is not he who has caused the problem of this journey."

She put her hand before her face. "Nay, do not lecture me. My husband has not lost a moment in recounting my misdeeds. Tell me true, has he actually chopped wood?"

The two dark guardsmen grinned. "Aye, he has," Corbet said. "It was an easy task for him, and we often gave him our encouragement from our posts atop the battlements."

"You did not!"

"We could not lose such a chance. How many men ever are put in charge of their lord?"

"It is Hugo who will need to fear for his life."

"What could Sir Hugo have done?" she asked. "He is a most quiet and peaceful man."

Corbet tried to keep his laughter quiet. "Lady Margaret put him in charge of the serfs. Lord Ranulf thought to escape his duties as serf, but Hugo had other ideas. He is a brave knight."

"My husband?"

"Nay," Sainneville said, laughing. "Sir Hugo had more courage than any of us. He leaned against a wall, ate an apple and then pointed at our lord. I can just hear him, 'You there. You look to be a sturdy fellow. You chop while these lesser men tote.' I wonder that Lord Ranulf's curses did not char the wood."

Lyonene covered her giggle. "It will not be Sir Hugo who suffers, but I for causing all these problems." She looked across the room and saw Alice sitting quietly on her pallet in the corner. "You know these men, Alice?"

Corbet smiled. "It was she who obtained our jobs."

Alice pointed to her eyes, then theirs and Lyonene laughed. "Alice must have realized you were of the Black Guard, for I often tell her of Malvoisin."

"We are honored to be mentioned by one so lovely. A damsel in distress is our most favorite mission. I wish only there were a fiery dragon to slay in your honor."

She leaned back against the stone wall and looked at them. They laughed, but their mission was indeed serious and could cost them their lives. Yet they acted as if 'twere no more than an afternoon's outing. She started to rise and Alice came to help her. She had slept in a woolen garment, ready for a quick escape.

The two guardsmen stared at her, her new shape unfamiliar to them. "I can see what has happened to the sun."

Lyonene looked at Corbet in puzzlement.

"You have swallowed it."

She laughed at the jest. Now was not the time to reprimand them for insolence. Now they were bound together by the ancient tie of friends amongst strangers. Later, at Malvoisin, they would return to the old formality, but now the circumstances were changed. Alice helped her into a heavy surcoat and mantle—warm, sturdy clothes.

"You will not change your thoughts and come with us, Alice?"

Alice smiled, touched Lyonene's hair and shook her head. Her family and her ways were Irish. She did not wish to leave her home.

Further talk was silenced by a cry outside the door. Lyonene was astonished at the speed with which Corbet and Sainneville moved. The two men put their backs to the door, keeping out the men who so violently tried to open it.

"Get her near the window!" Sainneville commanded to Alice. "If need be, lower her down the rope. Herne waits below."

They could hear the clash of steel outside and loud voices. The pounding on the door decreased by half and then ceased altogether as Ranulf and his men engaged the guards in battle. Lyonene sat on a stool near the window, her face white, her nerves taut, threatening to snap.

Ranulf's battle cry was heard through the oak door; indeed, it seemed to fill the very stones of the donjon. Lyonene could but wait and listen, listen to the horrible cries, the sounds of steel and iron as they struck wood, stone and human flesh.

Sainneville and Corbet watched her. They could do nothing to help their fellow guardsmen or their liege lord and the waiting was harder for them than the battle.

When she thought she might not live much longer, so great was her paralyzing fear, Ranulf's voice sounded outside the door.

"Open!"

Corbet and Sainneville threw back the heavy door to reveal a blood-encrusted Ranulf. His expression was wild—fierce and frightening.

Lyonene tried to stand and greet him, but her legs would not support her. Alice helped her.

Ranulf merely glanced in her direction, satisfied that she was unharmed. "Morell gathers men together, a few hundred. Gilbert has seen them riding hard toward us. He must have gotten word of our presence. I have sent a messenger to Dacre's cousins and they will meet us due north of here."

Ranulf took one great stride across the room and lifted Lyonene into his arms, hardly looking at her. "Herne holds the horses below. See you to my weapons," he instructed, nodding to Corbet.

Lyonene buried her face against Ranulf's mail-clad neck, the smell of blood overpowering. She did not know whether it was the smell or her terror, but her stomach tightened and pained her. There was time only for a brief farewell look to Alice.

Eight black horses awaited them outside the donjon, with Tighe at the head. Ranulf lifted her into the saddle, and she clutched the pommel as another pain gripped her.

"You are unhurt?" Ranulf demanded, his haste making his words harsh.

"Aye, I am well."

"Then I must see to my man."

She turned in the saddle to see Maularde being

helped to his horse. His left leg was bleeding profusely and his tabard showed a long, jagged cut.

Ranulf exchanged a few words with his knight and then returned to Lyonene, mounting behind her.

"He can travel?" she asked.

"Aye, for a while. He took an ax blade in his leg. He must have it attended soon or he may lose his leg, if not his life."

Lyonene looked ahead as Ranulf took the reins and spurred Tighe into a gallop. Another pain left her breathless, and she realized the babe had decided to meet his father. She gave a silent prayer for time, time enough to escape Sir Morell's army that followed them.

They rode fast and hard for near two hours when Ranulf called a halt. Lyonene clutched her stomach, grateful for the stillness, the relief from the jolting horse. Ranulf dismounted and walked to Maularde.

"I fear he has fainted, my lord." She heard Hugo's quiet voice.

Lyonene whirled to look at the guardsman. The strong, dark knight slumped forward over his horse's neck. Blood covered one whole side of rider and horse. The sight did nothing to relieve the pains she already felt.

"He can ride no further," Ranulf said, his voice serious. "My wife also grows weary. I will stay here with them, there is a shack beyond those trees. You must ride even harder than before, for if Morell's men see you and know I am not with you, they will return here and find us."

The six men nodded gravely, understanding the situation.

"Dacre's men await you. Give me any cloths you have for Maularde's leg. Go now and do not return until it is safe."

They nodded and several prayers for safety were said as they quickly removed extra clothing from the leather bags behind their saddles.

It seemed incredibly quiet when they were gone. Ranulf took the reins of both horses and led them into the woods to a little stone cottage with a pegged, half-missing thatched roof that offered some shelter. Ranulf left the horses and riders hidden under some trees as he drew his sword and thoroughly checked the property. Only when he was sure that it was empty did he return to the horses.

He lifted Lyonene from the horse and set her to her feet. She leaned back against a tree for support.

Removing Maularde from his horse with the gentleness that was needed was not an easy job, but Ranulf knew the man's life depended on his care. Ranulf's legs bent under the weight of carrying his guardsman into the dark hut. He carefully stretched him on the dirty floor rushes.

Lyonene clutched her stomach as another pain gripped her. They came closer together now, and each was stronger than the last. There was no time to be frightened as she thought of Maularde's life. She entered the little cottage.

"Here," she said as she knelt by Maularde. "I will tend him. You must lift him as we remove the chausses. Fetch the extra cloths. Can we not have a fire?"

"Nay, we cannot. I but hope Morell's men do not see this place. Morell! I should like to meet him myself."

"Do not waste the time thinking of him. Go and find water and a vessel to hold it. I must cleanse this wound and bind it."

Ranulf left her silently, before he saw her eyes close against the tightening of her stomach.

"It is the babe?" came Maularde's ragged whisper.

She smiled at him and smoothed back his sweat-dampened hair. "Do not speak now. We will care for you and you will be well, but you must rest also. And aye, it is the babe, but do not say so to Ranulf."

"I think he will know soon enough."

"I fear your words are true. Quiet now. I will hurt you more, for I need to remove some bits of iron from your leg."

Ranulf returned with a large pottery bowl of water. "It is broken, but it still will hold some water. Maularde speaks to you?"

"Aye." She looked at the guardsman fondly. "He worries for my safety."

Ranulf looked at her for the first time, saw the strain on her face. He touched her hair, caressing her cheek.

Lyonene bent forward against a pain. Ranulf pulled her to him.

"The babe kicks you again?"

"Aye, he kicks most vigorously. Now tear some linen and wet it so that I may help your man."

They worked together, silently, as Lyonene carefully removed the bits of iron with a green stick that had the bark stripped from it. She had to stop often to hold herself against the pains that were closer and closer together. Ranulf said little when she bowed her head against the pain, but supported her back and shoulders.

At last Maularde's leg was bound, and although they thought he slept, he opened his eyes and spoke to them.

"Now it is your turn, my lady."

"Aye," she agreed, smiling, "I fear you are right." The pains had little time between them now.

"What is this?" Ranulf demanded.

"Your babe comes, my lord," Maularde whispered.

"It cannot. There is no woman here to tend to the birth."

Lyonene managed a bit of a laugh as an even stronger pain gripped her.

"Lyonene, you cannot deliver now. You must wait until I fetch someone."

"Nay, Ranulf, do not leave me. Help me to lie down."

He pulled her to his arms gently and she felt his strong body begin to shake.

"I fear I add to the blood on you, for birthing is messy work. Ranulf! I but meant to make a jest. Do not take on so. It is easy work."

He laid her carefully on the rushes. "I will fetch moss to make a bed for you." His voice showed his strain. "There is time?"

"Aye, a few moments."

Ranulf hurried from the cottage.

Another pain gripped her, and as her hands clawed at the floor rushes, she felt a warm, solid hand in her own. Maularde's strength and nearness reassured her.

Ranulf returned quickly and spread the moss beneath her. He saw the hands held between his wife and his guardsman. He did not break the contact, but was glad for it. Lyonene drew her legs up, pushing downward at each pain.

Ranulf took charge of himself and used his estoc to cut her underclothing away. He wiped her forehead and murmured encouragement to her as the pains shook her. They were quiet as they heard the sounds of a hundred horses nearby, knowing it could be but moments before

Morell found them. They all sighed in relief when the riders passed.

There was not long for stillness, for Lyonene's water broke then and Ranulf, having helped with many foals, knew the babe was coming. Maularde dragged himself nearer her head and kept her from screaming as the baby's head appeared. Ranulf did little more than catch the babe as Lyonene gave one last push.

Quickly, he removed the cord from the child's neck and the mucus from its tiny mouth. The child let out a great wail of protest at its new, cold environment and Ranulf hurriedly tended to cutting the cord and discarding the afterbirth.

Maularde seemed to have been invigorated by the child's birth, and it was he who wiped the squalling child with a square from a velvet tabard. He wrapped the infant warmly, gently touching the thick crop of black hair that covered the wrinkled head.

He handed the child to the exhausted Lyonene, and she touched the little face, the tiny ears.

"I would see this child of mine," Ranulf said quietly and took it from her. It was night and they dared not strike a light, so Ranulf held the babe in the moonlit doorway and removed the swaddling cloths to study the small body.

Lyonene could see his profile, the glow of the black eyes as he held his child; it was a private moment for the two of them that no one else could share. The enormous hand of the Black Lion was gentle when it touched the tiny fingers, and Ranulf smiled when the babe curled its fingers around its father's dark, war-scarred finger.

Ranulf replaced the clothes and returned the babe to Lyonene's arm. He touched her cheek gently, his eyes liquid, showing the depth of his feelings. "I thank you for my son," he whispered before he stretched out beside her and slept.

The four slept peacefully, bound together by shared hardship and shared joy. The babe woke them, and they all joined in the pleasure of the child's nursing, in his new delight in that age-old bliss. In the early dawn hours there was no separation between lord and vassal or even father and friend, but instead a union caused and blessed by a new life, an innocent being, whose wondrous presence transcended earthly bonds. The three adults smiled at one another and were as one.

They slept some more, and the sun shone brightly on the new day when they awoke again. Ranulf helped his guardsman outside the cottage to relieve himself and then carried Lyonene outside, the baby left with Maularde.

They sat together, Lyonene in Ranulf's lap, for a few moments before returning. He kissed her mouth gently and sweetly.

"I take it then that the boy pleases you?" she teased.

"Aye, he is the most beautiful of babes. I am sure there has been no finer," Ranulf said in all seriousness.

"You do not think him ugly and red as most fathers do?"

"Nay, he is not red. He has my skin color and my hair. Have you seen the way it already begins to curl about his neck? And he shall have green eyes like his mother. Already he shows a strength befitting a knight, and he has a headstart on being a large man."

"Aye, that he does, I thought he might split me in twain with the size of him."

"Nay, you are wrong. He did all the work. He fair pushed himself into the world."

"Ranulf!" Then she laughed, for she saw his beginning smile. "You did not look so sure of yourself at the time."

Ranulf clutched her close to him. "I will say my fear now, but I did not know birthing was such hard work. You are so small and my son so large."

"I remember no pain now, so do not fear for me. It is enough that I have pleased you."

He leaned back against the tree. "Aye, Montgomery is perfect and I shall . . ."

"Montgomery! You have named him and not consulted me? What if I have chosen another name and do not like your name for him?"

Ranulf shrugged his shoulders. "It would not change me. My son's name is Montgomery de Warbrooke, Fourth Earl of Malvoisin. It was my grandfather's name and shall live again in my son. We shall return soon to my island and he shall be baptized. Dacre will come and be his godfather and Maularde shall be his other godfather."

"Maularde? Should you not ask Geoffrey, your brother?"

"Nay, Geoffrey would much rather have a girl to treasure and spoil. My man has earned this honor."

"He has. For godmother I shall ask Berengaria, if that suits your preconceived plans."

He ignored her snide remark and his eyes held a faraway look. "I would that my mother could see him. She longed so for a household of children."

Lyonene searched for some words of sympathy but could find none. "I am sure she must have been somewhat content to give the world such a handsome boy as you."

He looked at her and then grinned. "It is true, for she agreed with your opinion of me. Mayhaps it is good she never saw how worthless Geoffrey has grown."

"You have little opinion of your brother. I find him quite handsome and sweet-natured."

"You do not rile me this day. I am too pleased with my son."

"I but pray he only looks as you and does not possess your vanity or arrogance."

He kissed her neck. "Nay, he will be a sweet child with the honeyed words of his mother. Have I said I love you this day? That I love you more each day?"

"Nay," she whispered, "but had you done so, I would have welcomed your words."

He abruptly moved his lips from her skin. "You are a curse to me. You leave me alone for months and I can find no woman to my taste and when I do see you again, you rival my horse for size and now I must wait until you heal from my son. I do not think I will kiss you until I can finish the matter."

"You are a most considerate husband." She ran her lips along his neck.

"Lyonene! You will cease this behavior. Now tell me what gift you desire in reward for my son. I will fetch you a crown of stars if that is your want."

"Ah, my most gallant knight, you are most generous, but I will leave the stars for all to enjoy. There is naught I desire but to return home to Malvoisin, to the people I know and love, and I wish for the health of my son."

"There must be some small thing you wish, some jewel?"

She thought a moment. "I would like the return of my lion belt."

Ranulf flashed her a broad grin and fumbled beneath her to the pouch at his side. His eyes sparkled as he handed her the beautiful belt. "Your merest wish is my command."

"Oh," she cried as she clasped the gold belt to her cheek. "You do not know the agonies I have endured over this belt. All else was taken from me and I had naught else to use for a bribe. I have never owned aught that I love as well as this belt."

Ranulf continued to smile. "What of me, Lioness? Do I not share in some of that love as one of your possessions?"

She smiled up at him. "I do not own you, Ranulf. No one could own you."

His face was serious. "I fear you are wrong, little Lioness. If ever a man was owned by another, it is I."

Their eyes locked together in a moment of deep meaning and timeless love that went past a day-to-day existence or fleshly rapture. Their souls touched one another.

The baby's crying brought them back into the present, earthly time. "Montgomery cries for his mother."

Ranulf stood easily with his wife in his arms. "Then we shall bring him all that he desires. The son of the Black Lion will find the world is his if he but asks."

Lyonene laughed. "I can see I will be cursed with two of you, for you will certainly make the boy in your own image."

"Aye, and our Lioness will adore us both."

"I fear you know me too well."

This time, when Lyonene nursed her son, Maularde discreetly turned away.

"He is a fine boy, is he not?" Ranulf bragged.

"Aye, my lord. The strongest I have seen at his age. I wonder if it could be the great mop of hair?"

"What think you of being the boy's godfather?"

Maularde was speechless for a moment. "I would be honored," he said in his quiet voice. "In truth, I do not feel myself worthy of such honor."

Lyonene covered her breast and held the sleeping child against her, toying with a lock of black hair that was beginning to curl beneath his little ears. "I think you have earned the honor, since you helped bring the child to the world. Not many godfathers can claim such a deed."

The dark knight smiled. "I will love the boy as my own, you can be sure."

"I think you begin to already," Ranulf said and then was quiet as he listened. "Someone comes." Ranulf drew his sword and Maularde pulled himself to his feet, braced against the sharp stones of the cottage wall. He put himself between Lyonene and the door.

As Ranulf stood on the threshold, he looked in question to his guardsman. "While there is life in me," was the grim answer.

Lyonene sat quietly, protecting Montgomery from even a thought of harm. She looked quickly at the back of Maularde and saw his leg had begun to bleed again. Yet he stood firmly, disregarding the pain and the fresh tearing of the wound, faithful to his duty to protect his mistress and his new lord.

"Hail the Black Guard!" They heard Ranulf's voice from somewhere above the crude cottage, a hidden place where he watched and prepared for attack. He dropped to the ground before the narrow door and then disappeared as he ran to greet his men.

Maularde sat down again, heavily, keeping his leg straight before him. He allowed the pain to show on his face. He gave Lyonene a timid grin. " 'Twere I alone I fear I would set up a howl. It is good that I am in your presence."

She could not return his smile, knowing his light words did not cover his pain. They could hear the laughter of Ranulf and his men. How Ranulf had changed in the last year! Maularde seemed to read her thoughts and they shared a smile.

"We have a visitor," Ranulf said. "Nay, he is a most welcome visitor and I was well able to handle him alone. He is a strong warrior. Already his strength has frightened me."

The Guard were silent, not understanding their lord's words.

"Maularde," Corbet called. "Are you finished now with your shamming and ready to return to work? My lady, I did not see you at once . . ." He halted as he saw the babe.

Sainneville looked in puzzlement at Corbet, wondering

what could ever silence such a man. He also stared at the tiny black-haired infant, who slept in his mother's arms.

As each man of the Black Guard entered the room, he paused and then dropped to one knee, head bowed. It was a full moment and a great tribute to Ranulf as first one man and then another kissed the little hand and paid homage to their lord's heir. Lyonene blinked back the tears at this honor. She saw also that Ranulf's jaw seemed to be less securely held than usual; indeed, it seemed to tremble.

"Hail to the son of the Earl of Malvoisin," they shouted, the stones quivering with the resonance of their voices. Montgomery did not care for the noise and set up a howl that was easily heard above the men's voices.

Ranulf smiled at his son proudly. "I fear the boy does not like you as well as I, my men."

Corbet recovered his voice. "Well, it has taken almost a year exactly for this son, from the day of your marriage to now. You have won us a few wagers, my lord."

Ranulf frowned a moment in puzzlement and then grinned. "I will guess that Dacre has a hand in this. I shall be glad to see him pay. If he seems reluctant, I will gladly help you collect."

Lyonene looked away, pretending not to understand their words, but secretly vowing to someday repay Lord Dacre for his presumption.

Ranulf stepped forward and gently took the boy from her. He took him outside and his men followed. She went to the window and watched as her husband proudly unwrapped the boy and displayed him to his men. She could hear his boasts of the boy's strengths. It made her warm to see the tenderness, the protective way Ranulf held his son.

A fire was lit, and Gilbert and Herne went to seek a nearby village so they could have food and clean linens for the babe. Lyonene knew no bath had ever been as welcome as this one inside a crude Irish hut. For the first time she carefully bathed her new little son, admiring and marveling at his perfect features and at the eyes that, as Ranulf had said, grew more green each passing hour.

They stayed there in that little hut for two days, more to give Maularde's leg a chance to heal than anything else. Since the knight refused to ride in a wagon, Ranulf and his men rigged a sling for him on his horse so that his leg remained straight on the return journey to Malvoisin.

They traveled slowly, resting often, and Ranulf was especially attentive to Lyonene's needs, always ready to offer his help to her. She never asked what had happened to Sir Morell or Amicia, or even to Lady Margaret, but several times she saw Hugo and Ranulf in deep conversation and somehow sensed that they were forever safe from further treachery.

At Waterford they boarded a ship to return to England. Lyonene did not know if it was her happiness or the fact that she no longer carried a child, but on the three-day trip she was never ill and indeed enjoyed the soft air, the tangy smell of the sea.

It was a long five days' travel to Malvoisin, and never had she ached for such a journey to end. Even the ferry ride to the island seemed to take a day. By the time they saw the gray towers of the castle before them, Montgomery was seventeen days old and beginning to gain weight. He slept nearly always, often cradled against his father's strong arm, oblivious to the many people and events surrounding him.

Trumpets blared when they were in sight of the castle and the villagers and castlefolk ran to greet them. The word of the child had reached them and they crowded to see him, raising loud, joyous cheers when they saw the healthy crop of black hair.

"Ranulf!" Lyonene touched his arm. She looked ahead to several people seated on horseback, just leaving the castle walls. She spurred her horse forward, heedless of the guardsmen who immediately followed her. When she was close to the horses, she dismounted and began to run, her arms outstretched. Her mother met her, and their arms locked together and they cried in their gladness at seeing one another again.

"You are unharmed, my daughter?" Melite questioned. "They caused you no pain?"

"Nay, I am well and very happy to be home. Father is here also?"

Melite stepped back and Lyonene embraced her father, who hastily wiped away a tear.

"You look well, my daughter. You look as fit as the lioness I named you for."

She beamed at both of them.

"And she has produced a lion cub for your grand-child, a green-eyed, black-haired, iron-lunged cub at that." Ranulf threw one leg across Tighe's back and slid to the ground, not even jolting the child he so proudly held.

Melite took the baby and touched the sleeping face. Together they walked through the east barbican and into the inner bailey, where the castle servants waited to see the babe. When at last they entered the Black Hall, it was Lyonene who first saw Brent. He sat alone on a cushioned window seat, unsure of himself and his place among the strangers. Ranulf and Lyonene had been away for over four months, and to a child of six years, they seemed like strangers to him.

Lyonene went to sit by him while the others took Montgomery and admired him. "Brent, it is good to see you again."

"And you, my lady." He twisted his tabard hem in his hands.

"Would you like for me to tell you how Lord Ranulf saved me? How he came through my window on a rope, how he chopped wood?"

Brent's eyes lit. "The Black Lion chopped wood? I cannot believe you."

As she told the story, she saw him relax. Gradually he lost his nervousness and began to feel he had a place. Ranulf came to them, carrying Montgomery.

"Would you like to see my son, Brent?"

"I . . . yes," he said hesitantly.

Ranulf knelt to the boy, and while Brent studied the baby, Ranulf watched Brent. "Of course he is small and quite worthless."

Lyonene raised her eyebrows at Ranulf's statement.

"It will take some men such as you and I, and of course the Black Guard, to train him before he can become a knight. Do you think we could teach him?"

Brent's blue eyes glowed. "Aye, I do, my lord."

"And as my page, you will watch over him and protect him?"

"Aye, I will."

"Good. Now I must see to my castle. Has all been well since I was gone?"

"Oh, yes, my lord. Walter has let me have my own tiercel. He says . . . " The boy stopped at the door and waited impatiently for his master.

Ranulf gave his son to Lyonene, and as she held him, her husband put one hand behind her head and pulled her face to his to kiss her softly and lingeringly. "I cannot believe the child is mine, for I vow it had been more than a year since I last touched you." He kissed her again, a movement from the child keeping him from crushing her to him.

"Lyonene," Melite called.

Ranulf stepped away from her. "What think you they would say if I threw you across my horse and carried you away?"

She leaned near him, one hand on his chest. "I am willing to test their words, whether they be anger or joy."

Ranulf touched her hair, his thumb grazing her eyelash. "You are a wanton woman. Who would feed my son?"

"We could take him with us."

"You are a devil to tempt me so. Have you no honor?"

"My honor is you, and I would follow you wherever you led."

"Lady Melite, come and take this daughter of yours away. I find her still to have no manners before her guests."

Melite smiled from one to the other. "I fear I must defend her. She was ever a good and sweet child before she looked at your lordship."

Lyonene giggled.

His eyes sparkling, Ranulf shook his head as he looked from his mother-in-law to his wife. He paused at the door for one last glimpse of Lyonene as she cooed at the child, smiled peacefully as he harkened to Brent's demands and followed the boy.

Melite did not need to ask after her daughter's happiness, for it showed on her face—her contentment and joy with her husband, her son, her home. Melite was glad to see the peace and harmony that reigned.

Chapter Seventeen

The news of Lyonene's safe return spread quickly throughout the kingdom, and guests began arriving. She ran to Berengaria's arms as they clasped one another, joyous to see each other again. Travers was followed by his son, a seventeen-month-old boy who looked exactly like his mother and thus was a pretty child. It was a contrast to see the angelic boy near the ugliness of his father.

"I know what you think," Berengaria whispered, "and I am glad also he has the look of me. But come, I would see what that great black husband of yours has produced."

Berengaria exclaimed over the green-eyed child with pleasure, as everyone did, and Montgomery already seemed to preen under their affection. "He has the look of his father already," Berengaria said, laughing.

When Ranulf returned to the castle with Brent, he walked beside Dacre and the two men laughed at some jest together.

"What have you done to him?" Berengaria asked of Lyonene. "He is changed and is not the same man I have seen for years."

Lyonene shrugged. "He is always like that with Lord Dacre. They are no older than Brent when together."

"Nay, you are wrong. I have seen Lord Ranulf and Lord Dacre wrestling with one another since I was a child, but never was there such a light in your husband's eyes. You have tamed this Black Lion."

"Nay, I hope I have not. If I remember correctly, there are some fierce ways about him that I enjoy overmuch."

"Remember?" Berengaria questioned. "The boy is near a month old."

Lyonene told her friend briefly of the months in Ireland.

Berengaria shuddered. "I do not think I wish to hear more of your time in Ireland. I would not like to be away from my family for so long. But I think you most fortunate in your husband. Had I been so stupid as you, I think Travers might have left me to them."

Lyonene blinked a few times at the blunt words, but then agreed that the idea had plagued her a bit. Their words were halted by the entrance of Dacre and Ranulf.

"Here is that wife of yours and still as pretty as I remember. Do you draw a sword on me again if I touch her?" Dacre asked.

"If I challenged you, it would be the end of you," Ranulf said quietly.

"We shall have time to test your words." Dacre laughed and then turned and whirled Lyonene in his strong arms, tossing her into the air before pulling her close to lustily kiss her mouth. She cast one glance at Ranulf, and her suspicions were founded; her husband scowled blackly at them, his body held rigid in an attempt to control his emotions.

"You are a sweet little morsel, almost as fine as my Angharad."

Lyonene pushed at Dacre's shoulders; his hands were on her waist and her feet were high off the floor. "And how is your wife, Lord Dacre?" she said loudly. Then, in a quieter voice, she said, "Unhand me or I shall tell everyone something Lady Elizabeth told me of you."

Dacre stared at her a moment, then set her to the floor and began to laugh. "Were not Angharad the size of my horse, I would have brought her here and you would be a fitting match for my hellion. Did you hear this bit of a girl your wife threaten me? Look at her." Dacre stretched his arm above her head. "She dares much."

Ranulf smiled at his wife, then looked back at his friend. "I would rather know what Lady Elizabeth says of you."

Dacre's face lost its smile. "Hmmm. Well, I think I might not like that known just yet."

Ranulf threw back his head and laughed. "We will

see my son and then my men wait for you. I believe there is a matter of some gold to be exchanged."

Dacre thumped his friend's back. "This is one debt I am willing to pay most eagerly, for in truth I did not think you man enough to do it."

They left the solar in friendly argument and shortly the room was filled with women. Lucy, who had cried for hours at Lyonene's return, Kate, Melite, Berengaria and Lyonene. They spent happy hours as they prepared the baby's baptismal gown.

Lyonene still thrilled at the delight of nursing Montgomery and found a peaceful sharing between herself and the child. He grew bigger each day, his eyes searching faces and lights that loomed above him. Already he was beginning to distinguish his mother from all the other hands that held and touched him.

Malvoisin was overrun with guests and their retainers. Mattresses were brought from the cellars and aired and set up throughout the houses. The bedrooms of Black Hall were filled, and as was fitting, beds were set inside Ranulf and Lyonene's chamber. At night the curtains to their own bed were drawn, but they were much aware of the sleeping noises of those around them.

Lyonene snuggled her nude body next to Ranulf's, her breasts against his back, one leg across his thighs, her soft skin delighting in the hard, hair-covered surface. He turned to her quickly, pulling her close, her soft, round body in direct contrast to the steel-muscled Black Lion. His hand roughly caressed her, savoring the creamy skin, the fullness of each curve.

Lyonene moved her hips closer to him, feeling his ardent desire for her, and her excitement increased, her hunger for him, the pent-up yearning built up over the months of separation. She ran her hand down the long muscles of his back, her palm rubbing hard, her nails curled, unrestrained in her growing passion. She ran her mouth across the enormous roundness of his shoulder, touching the hot bronze skin with her lips, her teeth, her tongue. She nibbled the side of his neck, moving beside him, her breasts taut against the thick hair of his chest, the tickling softness sending shudders through her body.

She traveled to his earlobe and felt his breath against her hair, deep, quick breaths. She pushed him back against the sheets, rubbing her thigh between his legs, exalting in her power over him. Her hand trailed along his arms, feeling the restrained power, the strength that she alone could control, could use to her own advantage, for her own whims and fancies. Her breasts brushed against his chest, the pink peaks just grazing the skin, the soft hair. A low, deep, harsh sound came from her throat as she touched the tip of her tongue to his parted lips, and the sound changed to an animal laugh, guttural, as she felt him quiver beneath her. She bit his lower lip, twisting it, touching the fullness of it with her tongue, drawing it forward, purring, caressing him, her body moving ever nearer its goal.

"I am hungry, Melite. Fetch me some food or else send one of the maids to do it, but I cannot sleep in a strange place when I am hungry."

William's words reached them inside the curtained bed. Lyonene, through instinct, immediately rolled from atop her husband at the sound of her father's voice. Ranulf pulled her back to him, but a loud crash brought his eyes open, stilled his hand on her hip. He sighed and clenched his teeth together in an effort to calm himself.

"Sir William, may I be of assistance?" he called through the curtains.

"Nay, Lord Ranulf, I but meant to find the door and then the kitchen, but it is strange here and I cannot find my way." Another crash punctuated his words.

"I must go or your father may destroy my hall as well as my pleasure this night." He looked in accusation to his wife. "You should be glad he is your kin or else I might throw him out my window and be done with his clumsy ways. I will dress and join him in his meal. I think it takes me a long while to sleep this night." He leaned forward to kiss her cheek, but when her hand slipped to his stomach and caressed it, he drew away from her. "Nay, Lioness, I will not perform while your father thrashes about like a wounded boar."

He stepped away quickly and left her. Lyonene slammed her fist into the pillow and then began to pray forgiveness, for the oath she had thought had been directed against her own father. She was asleep when Ranulf returned, a heavy smell of wine on his breath, and only sighed peacefully when he drew her to him and also slept.

The household was awake early the next morn, and Lyonene felt herself drawn into a whirl of preparations for Montgomery's baptism. In the afternoon the solemn ceremony was held in the chapel of the Black Guard's hall, the sunlight filtering through the beautiful windows of colored and leaded glass. Berengaria gave the quiet babe to Father Watte, who immersed him in the blessed water. Montgomery set up a loud howl which made Dacre grin at the strength of the child's lungs.

Later, in the Black Hall, gifts were given, cups set with jewels and gold plates. Lord Dacre presented his godson with a saddle, small, made for a pony, with the leather embossed with the lion of Malvoisin. But of all the gifts, the favorite was Ranulf's gift to his wife. It was a tall, covered beaker, the top and bottom of gold filigree, set with emeralds, pearls and diamonds. The belly of the vessel was rock crystal, hollowed and etched with a scene of a lion and his lioness sitting quietly, surrounded by four romping cubs. The gold foot was inscribed with words of Ranulf's love for his beautiful young wife.

As Lyonene held the exquisite beaker and read the inscription, she raised cloudy eyes to Ranulf's. "So you will not forget again," he said, answering her unasked question. She put her hand behind his head and drew him down into a kiss that both showed her gratitude and told of feelings much stronger than gratitude.

A cheer filled the hall for both the birth of an heir and for the happiness of the day.

At night, Lyonene fell into bed exhausted, alone, while Ranulf sat and drank with Travers and Dacre. She felt his reluctance to join her in their bed was due to the previous night's happening and tried not to wish their guests gone.

On the third day, entertainments were planned. William caught his wife and daughter in the Great Hall. "I wish to see this son of mine at his work. He has promised to instruct me in the proper training of my men." He put an arm around Lyonene. "You have done more than well, my daughter. He is a fine man and does you proud."

"Aye, he does, father."

Lyonene spent the day with her mother and Berengaria, and she promised them both cuttings from King Edward's roses. It was after dinner, when the house was quietest, that a boy brought her a message.

"A man gave it to me and said it was from Lord Ranulf."

She smiled at him and sent him to the kitchen as she hastily removed the tablet from its pouch.

I wait for you at the spring north of Calbourne Church.

Ranulf

Her heart fluttered like a young girl's, not at all the heart of a respectable wife and mother. She tossed the pouch on the bench. She could see no one or she knew that she would not neglect her guests for a love tryst with her husband. Quickly she went to the stables and bid Russell saddle Loriage for her. She had not ridden the stallion since her return, and even the feel of the black horse's power further excited her as she hurried towards Ranulf and the joy she knew awaited her.

She laughed at herself as the hood fell away and the wind tore the sedate circlet and fillet from her head, tangling and tossing her hair in wild, abandoned disarray about her shoulders. It was wondrous to be free, free of demands and duties and responsibilities, and to be hurrying toward her lover, their meeting enhanced by its secrecy and forbidden air.

She kicked at Loriage's side and the animal leaped forward, as exhilarated as his pretty mistress, mane and tail flying in the cool wind. They seemed to fly together, floating across the gently rolling fields, near houses, trees and watching people.

At they drew nearer the spring, Lyonene pulled back on Loriage's reins. The last time she had seen Ranulf's writing had been when Morell had forged the letters to Amicia. She looked around her, seeing the bushes and trees as hiding places, and suddenly she was afraid. She had never really known what had happened to Morell or Amicia and now the fact that she didn't know haunted her.

Loriage felt his mistress's change and tossed his head, flaring his nostrils, lifting one hoof in nervousness. "Hush, Lori," she whispered, but she could not calm her own fears.

Neither the prancing horse nor the wary mistress saw the rabbit, and when the horse was aware of it, the little animal was beneath the slashing hoofs.

Loriage ducked his head and Lyonene, her thoughts turned elsewhere, went sailing over the animal's head.

Ranulf came riding toward the spring just in time to see his little wife flying through the air and landing with a loud wet smack in the icy-cold spring. Quickly, he dismounted and ran toward her, but already she was sitting up, wiping the water from her eyes and looking about her in a bewildered manner.

Ranulf stood on the bank and grinned down at her, his hands on his hips. "I had thought to have an obedient wife, but there are extremes. I am sure, madam, I said 'by' the spring and not 'in' the spring."

She looked up at him, startled, and then glared. "I should think you would be concerned for my welfare," she said haughtily.

He walked down the bank and offered her his hand, and she did her best to pull him in with her but could not. He smiled at her as her teeth began to chatter and then swung her into his arms to carry her to dry ground. "What were you thinking to allow that devil horse of yours to throw you? Mayhaps I should feed him to the pigs."

She moved closer to Ranulf, trying to get warm, but also thinking of how very long it had been since they had been truly alone. "It was not Loriage's fault, but mine alone. I was . . . thinking of else."

He moved her head from his shoulder and his black eyes were hard as he stared at her. "I have had enough of this. Am I so unworthy of your trust that you hide from me your thoughts?"

She stared back at him. They both had concealed their thoughts and feelings from each other too often, and the short time they'd had together had been fraught with difficulties because of their lack of trust. It was not easy to speak of the time in Ireland. "The letter you sent," she began. "I was not sure it was yours. The forgeries—from before, I mean."

He pulled her head back to his shoulder, relieved that her problems were so small and yet so sensible. He stroked her wet hair. "We have much to learn, do we not? I cannot blame you for what you did, thinking as you did. But we must learn to give, to trust. Here, what is this?" He could feel her hot tears even through the thick velvet of his tabard. "For once I am a good and chivalrous knight and my lady cries for it. That is not the way it should be."

She smiled at him. "For me, you are always good and chivalrous, and I have always loved you."

His eyes sparkled. "Always?" he teased.

She frowned slightly. "Except when you first made love to me and hurt me and when I saw Amicia in your arms and—"

He silenced her with his lips, moving quickly to her throat. "Do you not think we have had enough talk? Are you not very cold in those wet clothes? What say you we remove them?"

"Tell me again that you love me."

When he looked at her again, his eyes were very serious. "I love you completely and totally, more than my own life, and I beg your forgiveness for all the pain I have caused, for the weakness of my love that made you so mistrust me."

She put her fingers to his lips. "These are wondrous words, but I do grow colder each moment and soon my son—our son—will need me. Or have you forgotten what to do with a woman you carry about in your arms?"

"You are an insolent baggage. See you how I punish such insolence."

"I am a most willing and eager pupil," she whispered as he pulled her closer to him.